MUBA DREAM

AND 18 LEGENDS FROM THE LAND OF NOD

By

DR. JOHN (SATCHMO) MANNAN

INTRODUCED BY SONIA SANCHEZ

ILLUSTRATED BY JAMES BALKOVEK

Mubassa's Dream and 18 Legends From the Land of Nod

Illustrations by James Balkovek

Aladdin's Books International

Division of Lost Lamp Publications

M Mannan Esq

PO Box 20478

NEW YORK NEW YORK 10021

St Croix US VIRGIN ISLANDS 00820

aladdinbooks@yahoo.com

ISBN: 978-0-578-18308-4

PRINTED IN THE UNITED STATES OF AMERICA

Contents

An Introduction to Mubassa's Dream

By Sonia Sanchez

"Bedtime stories must soon grow up and go to college some-day but their infancy and early steps are composed of greatly treasured memories." These are the words of the author of this book as he relates the dreams and drama that accompanied his dual role as writer and fortunate father of story demanding children. Before we discuss the book itself, the story the author/father tells about how and why the book was written is a well wrought, fanciful and fantastic tale in itself.

Spun from the silkworm of his imagination, the tales in this book were spirited out from this father's mystical journeys to the land of NOD. Each night the father's spirit soared across the moon and passed guards assigned over dreams and imagination (by permission of The Most High). He was then allowed into the inner most chamber of the mind to glimpse the many treasures of the night hidden in "the land of Nod". The father quickly stuffed the pockets of his imagination with some of the inner mind's treasures.

Returning to the earth, the father (John "Satchmo" Mannan) dropped sachets of many magical and mystical stories on his children's pillows and tucked in the night! He often fell asleep in the midst of the story; his mind rolled up like a scroll.

In the morning, the stories were gone. Only the prayers and the good deeds of previous days greeted him like dew drops of joy. He could nowise remember the previous night's story. But one day, years after his children had reached maturity, the bedtime stories returned knocking at the door of the author's mind in the form of three strange creatures who appeared to him in dreams and daydreams and ordered him to write them down for all of humanity. They appeared to him as follows:

1. a poor old woman dressed in rags but wearing gold studded earrings, a gold necklace and a gold ring. She called herself "MS Parable" or "Ms Legend".

2. a vengeful gigantic black Nightingale who locked the author in a cage forcing him to write to gain his freedom (The nightingale himself had once been a caged pet.)

3. a troll called "A Tale Told by an Idiot "who escaped long ago from a volume of Shakespeare and calls himself nowadays by an alias to wit: William Sheik Sabir from The People's Republic of Harlem.

Well never ask a master fantasy story teller and doting father to give you the back story behind his fantasy book. You may get a huge smile, a wrinkle of the brow, a twinkle in the eye and an apple pie story that leaves both of you laughing!

One of the author's tales in this book that struck me was that of "LOOFMAN". Loofman the King ("The Magnificent", he called himself) hated music. He thought he could kill all music by having his soldiers break all of the flutes and instruments in his kingdom. He arrested all of the singers and forbade the very act of singing. He chased away all the singing birds and hunted them down. The ultimate penalty to any singing creature was death. One clever bird escaped–the royal blue Nightingale. Her song was so beautiful that a certain pitch could turn apples into gold.

The king's hunters and soldiers hunted the blue Nightingale night and day with orders not to kill her on sight. Loofman did not want her dead until she revealed her secret of turning apples into gold. Finally, Loofman was successful in learning the Nightingale's secret. Then...Sorry, you will have to read Dr. Mannan's <u>Mubassa's Dream and 18 Tales from the Land of Nod</u> to discover one of many magnificent and surprise endings.

Dr. John Mannan, as author of a treasure chest of tales, legends and riddles, has mastered the ancient art of writing the instructive parable. His are delicious parables wrapped in the stuff of legends hidden in the turquoise of exquisite allegory which capture mind, heart and soul.

In <u>The Mango Leaf Who Wanted to Fly</u>, a simple lesson is taught to a wayward adolescent mango leaf-along with geography, botany, herbal medicine, philosophy and other subjects. After a 50 year odyssey in a strange world, he returns to his home tree in Jamaica and finds an uncanny way to meet his family who have already "gone to heaven."

Layered with multidimensional symbols, The Legend of The Stoop-Sitters, The Legend of the Ox and the Tiger and The Mouse Who Went To Court find themselves placed in the mythical and magical People's Republic of Harlem. The first story is a mystical "tale from a nightingale". The others the author calls "tales told by an idiot", a brilliant bow to a soliloquy in Shakespeare's Macbeth.

Still, other stories link natural phenomena with metaphysical messages. <u>The Gift, The Tale of The Ocean The River and the Rain</u> is a yoga stretch for the mind that causes us to ponder and wonder what is the hidden story behind a simple act of rain.

Love unites and conquers all in <u>The Ruby and the Pearl</u> but it is also a child of choice, chance and destiny. Another interesting facet of Mannan's work is his uncanny ability to create worlds which embrace our inner Nirvana and his ability to marshal the reader to identify the great issues that touch and concern the human society, the human story and the politics of power. For example, in <u>The Great</u>

<u>Meeting of the Mind,</u> he discusses the disruptive role that husband and wife bandits Mr. Information and Miss Information play when they are deployed by an evil master mind who invades THE Great Hall of the Mind to gain control of society by interrupting a democratic debate among the seven council members of the mind.

The mischievous duo(acting like terrorists) fire bulletins all over the Great Hall, causing panic in the Hall of <u>The Great Meeting of the Mind</u>. This story is written in the style of a play and an odyssey from the vantage point of the janitor who works in the <u>Hall of the Mind</u>.

The stories of this book also teach civil, political and moral values. They discuss the opportunities and challenges associated with decision making, leadership of self and others. After one learns in Loofman that ideas cannot be destroyed with weapons, nor music with broken flutes, we discover the alchemy of the good idea displacing the bad idea when the good heart is fully engaged and one is persistent and patient.

Stylistically, the stories cover several genres of style in their presentation and can appeal to children as young as 8 and adults as old as 88, to fans of Harry Potter and Shakespeare.

<u>The Frog of the Ocean and the Fro g of the Well</u> has a tone as Elizabethan and serious as Hamlet, as satirical as <u>Gulliver's Travels</u> and fantastical as <u>Arabian Nights</u>.

The <u>Legend of the Hole</u> reads like a tribute to Edgar Allen Poe while <u>The King, the Donkey and the Pachyderm</u> reminds us of biting satirical stories of Aesop with a twist of modern day politics and good humor added for good measure.

Lastly, <u>The Power of A Drop</u> is sheer motivational inspiration. Read this one, drink a cup of green tea and go out and "remake the world" or at least the part that you think you control. Your one drop of optimism, joy, wisdom, etc. could make a huge difference in your life and the lives of others.

In conclusion, this book contains many wonderful and beautiful stories that serve as inspiration for the human struggle for dignity and distinction. They embrace the freedom to dream the beautiful dream and to make the world more wonderful for all.

Mubassa's Dream is at once a very entertaining, engaging and enlightening "THE CAT IN THE HAT COMES BACK" for adults and a playful Plato, Socrates and Imhotep for kids.

In the end, this book in time can be much more than a fantasy classic or classic fantasy. It is a poem of wisdom and a song of wonder.

Bedroom stories can indeed grow up!

Author's Dedication and Foreword

With the Name of G-d, the Merciful Benefactor, the Merciful Redeemer, this book is dedicated to children at heart everywhere meaning those adults who have never lost their natural sense of wonder and those pensive children who dare to seek the meaning of life in the stories recited to them by adults.

Parts of this book stem from some of the stories that I made up each night, i.e. stories that I made up and I related to my children as I reclined next to them and we fell asleep! However, I happily encouraged my children to make up stories on rare off nights or when I suffered from severe droughts of imagination.

Other stories were brain children of my contemplation on the meaning of life. They are written in the genre of fables, tales, legends and parables and designed to be conversant with the inner voice of human imagination.

The healthy feeling of human imagination is a prime and integral part of the development of the human soul. It is the mother of the great questions and the father of many of the great answers that dawned in the human experience. No doubt there are so many benefits that humanity enjoys from the stupendous technology that embraces the 21st century, but the pendulum has swung too far to the left side of the brain.

Our world spectacularly suffers too much from the deficits of artificial imagination, artificial intelligence.

Our internet spawned minds hunger to watch and consume the ready made meal of the videotape rather than chew over the steak, tofu or what have you of a written hand held text.

We want to see our music (even our love songs) acted out on screen instead of producing the movie in the studio of our emotional nature and watching on the screen of our creative imaginations, experiences and inner selves.

Videotapes can be good theatre. They unite and make uniform the visual perceptions of the viewers. The creativity of the producers, actors and directors are on full display. The imaginations of the viewers, on the other hand, are paused in a carefully contrived state of mind.

The diminution of our imaginative powers as 21st century people is a greater crisis than global warming. It rivals the threatened loss of our moral sensibilities as we grow further and further out of touch with the orbit of our human-touch experience and in touch with the abyss or black hole of virtual reality.

Civilizations have risen and fallen, but today unchained addictions to artificialism and virtual reality has placed humanity at war with itself ie. its own human potential. The triumphant fulfillment of the excellence of man as a social being installed on the throne of the natural order requires intelligent interaction and imagination. It requires harmonization with the natural order (the laws of the Creator.) and imaginative and technical ability to shape and mine the material world for its greatest and best possibilities of service.

So this book is dedicated to the survival of human imagination and contemplation and the ancient tradition of teaching by parable and simile. The Bear Stories, the Seagull Story, and the Palm Tree and the Cactus Story are all commentaries on the human predicament and the intimate relationship between the brain and the heart.

These are also about conflicts within the human community of the mind (various humans' versions of man's life on earth).

They are also about conflicts concerning various human perceptions of reality and the role of human individuals in human society (The Legend of the Leaf and the Mango Tree). Some believe all the waters in the world are in the little well that they control or perceive and others believe that all the waters of the world pour into a limitless ocean of human potential (the Frog of the Ocean and the Frog of The Well etc.).

I am an advocate of the dignity and distinction of man.. I believe (although there are rivers who never meet the sea) that all human life has a great destiny to wit:

A) The destiny of the better self over the selfish self

B) The destiny of the group picture of human excellence over the human domination of a few individuals over the many and

C) That the destiny of the good nature of man must be established over the myth of man's inherent evil inclinations.

The so called "heavenly religions" of the world and the great philosopher thinkers should be in accord on this issue.

The stories in this book are dedicated to the victory of the child of many questions in each of us.

Lastly I want to say "Thank you" to the children I have touched and who have demanded good from me. By being there and asking me for stories, they have inspired me. Xiomara, Yasmin and Rehan Mannan (my children), Jose Sevilla (my grandson) and various elementary school students. Thanks also you to the children of Sister Lois's Learning Tree in the Bronx and the children of the Sister Clara Mohammed Elementary School in Harlem.

Special thanks to Dr. Sonia Sanchez for her encouragement and introduction award winning artist James Balkovek for art which brought my words to life; to Yasuko Otake for her invaluable encouragement and support; Sis Ruwhiy Muammad, Acting Principal Sr.

Clara Mohammed Elementary School in Harlem for her use of certain portions of the text and critical feedback, Diogenes Rodriguez, my friend and critic, to Sangita Mishra for word processing and editing this book.

Finally, thanks is due to the late Imam Quasim Bakrideen who contributed financially to the project, Imam Izakel Pasha who allowed portions of this book to be used in the Sister Clara Mohammed Elementary School curriculum and many others. Most of all, praise and thanks to G-d for any good that comes from this labor of love,

May G-d, The Creator, be pleased.

Welcome to the Land of Nod
GREETINGS!

I John am your brother and partner in tribulation, illumination and jubilation. I have traversed the two hemispheres of the mind and the seven regions of the heart. The North and South poles of thought I have charted. I have never been downhearted. Indeed I have travelled on occasion to the very gates of the heavens in my dreams. I remember once in a dream. I knocked on one of those the gates until my hands were as red as lobsters. Finally they let a portion of my soul in through the side door (the security entrance) to a holding room called the Land of Nod. I was kept awake in this holding room for nights beyond forgetting. It was a place of peaceful turbulence and turbulent peace.

Welcome to the Land of Nod, a place most curious, most serious and most mysterious! Here in Nod—every heart finds its song. Here in Nod ideas come to life. Here Cain /Cane left his origins and found a wife named "Sugar" and young Joseph discovered a dozen dreams walking in their sleep day and night..

Here I drank a thousand tales of mystery, tears and laughter while I sipped successive cups of a golden tea called "Ba Bao Cha" or "Tea of Eight Treasures" Here while sipping in my thoughts I saw blue, red, orange, yellow, indigo, green and perplexed purple skies. Indeed shortly after, I met most curious and unusual creatures in strange and mysterious settings.

One was a Blue Nightingale, a songstress of a thousand tales who imprisoned me. Each day she insisted that I be her muse or that she could be mine. Her assistants were an inseparable sinister pair of birds.-a black crow and a black raven who sat guarding my window sill each night in winter and summer Acting like some strange somber security guards assigned to my dreams, they haunted my mind from places unseen. This was especially true when I was writing the epilogue part of The Stoop Sitters.

One night I received another visitor in my Dreams, a bald headed idiot named William Sheik Sabir. He claimed that I met him in high school and he claimed also that he is the ancestor of William Shakespeare. He claims Shakespeare wrote a play about him called Othello (The Moor). He's crazy. Indeed! I know. Thrice Crazy!

I also met a mysterious old homeless lady (elegantly dressed in blue) who lived in the trunk of an Oak tree. She was a rich repository of ancient mysterious tales.

Then there was this old conch shell on the beach that I pick up and placed to my ear. This ancient conch shell told tales beyond the reach of my imagination. One of them was The Frog of the Ocean and The Frog of the Well.

I have met so many wonderful creatures in the land of Nod. .:Fools and Kings, April and December, Winter and Summer, Fall and Spring "Neverary" and September ! I met the world skipping on a rainbow, powerful rain drops that glow, mysterious roses growing on the slopes of the Mountain of Love, and Peaks of Blue Reasons towering above the hue of poems and the music of all seasons.

In the Forest of Feelings, I met a majestic brown bear cub named Mubassa who wanted to become a man. He was my very first mysterious encounter.

Whether you are a man or a woman, a boy or a girl .a tree or a reed or even a mere seed, if you can read with your mind and think with your heart you can make it to The Land Of Nod.

It may put a smile on your face! You may never want to leave this place.

**"All Aboard ! All Aboard ! All Aboard the train of thought!! All Aboard the train of wonder!
By the stars By the dreams and by the silent thunder !
Welcome to the Land of Nod !**

Mubassa's Dream

Part one
The Bear Who Would Be A Man

Once upon a Rhyme in Masai land
there was a bear named Mubassa
He lived in the forest of Enchantment
between the mansions of the moon
and the splendor of the sun

To the north lay a farflung sea
To the East, the fiery desert of the day
To the West, the icy mountains of the night
To the South, a poem called Africa
A poem from a drum
A drum from a dream
where coconuts and happiness
are multiplied by two

Prince Mubassa was an only child-a lonely child. His father was always hunting fish and gathering honey. His mother did her best to teach Mubassa the ways of the bear clan.

He loved to do things that bears like to do, but he was a little different. He loved to play with ants and see them fight one another. He was always asking his mother questions, which was a very good thing to do. But Mubassa did not like playing with other bears or sharing his things, which was not very nice. He always thought he was better than other bears in the forest. So much did he think himself better than the other bears that he was often heard telling colleagues, "I am better than you."

One day, he asked his mother questions that would change his destiny. "Mother," he asked, "who are the wisest animals in the forests of the world?"

"Of wise animals, there are three, my son," replied his mother. "The old owl who sleeps in the mountains by day and guards the forest at night. For verily, it is he who sees in the night that which is unseen and both sides of the moon are not hidden from him. Then there's the raccoon. He is also very wise. He has rings around his eyes for he seldom sleeps and is a constant observer of life. And of course, the lowly earthworm, who is blind but understands the roots of things that stand on the back of the earth. Understanding, my son, is the highest form of knowledge."

Mubassa bear cub listened and then queried, "Oh mother, who is the strongest and most powerful of beings that walk or fly? Is it the eagle?"

"No, my son," said his mother.

"Is it the lion?"

"No," his mother replied again.

"The elephant?"

"No," his mother repeated again, "it is man. He stalks and protects, he saves and kills, he sows and reaps, he spends and keeps, he elevates a tree into a house, and grinds the mountain in dust. He is appointed ruler over us."

"Then I want to be man," Mubassa bear cub insisted.

"That you cannot be, my son," his mother responded, "G-d made you to be a bear and a rose to be a rose, so be the very best bear you can possibly be!"

Mubassa bear cub became angry at his mother and said, "I will leave you, my mother, and seek the counsel of the wisest animals."

So Mubassa bear cub set out that night until he came to the house of the old owl.

"Good evening Owl," said Mubassa bear cub.

"What can I do for you, young bear cub?" said the owl.

"I want to be a man," said the bear cub.

"Well!" exclaimed the owl, "that's an unusual request! Let me see…mmm, if you can answer these questions, you may be on your way to being a man indeed," the owl pondered. "Which is greater, the world that is seen or that which is unseen?"

"Why, the seen, of course," smirked the bear cub. "The unseen is nothingness!"

"Close your eyes," said the owl, "Is not love greater than the heart? Love is unseen. Is not truth greater than the tongue? Truth is unseen. Is not music greater than the flute? Forget it!" said the old owl. "You don't know what a flute is anyway! I'm going to bed. It's almost dawn. I must be gone to the mountain."

When dawn arrived, Mubassa bear cub spied the earthworm collecting the morning dew, the wisdom of the night.

"Earthworm! Earthworm!" cried Mubassa bear cub, "grant me a favor from thy wisdom."

"What do you seek of me?" the earthworm replied. "I am but the lowliest servant of 'The One Who is Greater.'"

"Earthworm, Earthworm," demanded Mubassa bear cub, "make me a man or I will crush you underfoot!"

"Errors, terrors and monstrosities! Oh my!" sighed the earthworm as he vigorously crawled into the nearest hole in the muddy morning.

Mubassa bear cub became even angrier and began tearing up the earth, overturning rocks and uprooting trees in search of the earthworm. But the lowly earthworm lingered not. The morning concealed him like the web of a spider curtaining the mouth of a cave.

So began Mubassa bear cub's second day journey away from home.

Soon after, Mubassa spied old raccoon sitting high up on an old portly pine tree. "Raccoon! Raccoon! Listen to me!" Mubasssa cried. "Wise animal of the forest, come down and help me!"

"Oh Mubassa bear cub," replied raccoon, "how are you and your family? Your father passed by here not too long ago. How is your mother?"

"I do not know," answered Mubassa bear cub, "but I do know that I want to become a man."

"Well, well, just what kind of a man do you want to be?" queried old raccoon. "You do not even know the way of your father, nor the condition of your mother. Your father is your brain and your mother is your heart."

"A powerful man," replied Mubassa bear cub. "One that stalks and protects, saves and kills, reaps and sows and all things men do."

"My goodness," pondered raccoon, "you can't be all those things at once. You can't be good and evil. Night and day do not sleep on the same bed. Besides, you are a bear cub. You should try to be the very best bear you can be. Learn who you are, learn what you can be, bear your path and reach the stars."

"I want to be a man!" insisted Mubassa bear cub.

"Alright, alright, alright," mused raccoon, "but first we must eat and you must agree to be honest with yourself."

"O.k., o.k., anything you say," Mubassa bear cub eagerly responded.

Raccoon went down to the river and pulled out three huge fish from the water, filleted them, added a few berries and spread out three dishes filled with these items on a picnic table.

Raccoon ate from one dish and Mubassa bear cub from another dish until they were both full. Raccoon went back down to the river to wash his hands as all raccoons are constantly doing. When he returned, he did not see the third dish.

"Who ate the last fish dish? It was not ready to be eaten!" wondered the raccoon out loud.

"It was not I," firmly replied Mubassa bear cub.

"Then follow me to your destiny," raccoon spoke in an urgent tone. He began to walk toward the river while Mubassa bear cub followed close behind.

When they reached the river, the raccoon stepped into the water and was soon walking on the water. Mubassa bear cub looked on in amazement.

"Come now, follow me," said old raccoon, "To be a man you must master your feelings."

Suddenly Mubassa found himself walking on the water too. When they reached the other side of the river, raccoon turned to Mubassa bear cub and said, "Who ate the dish of fish?"

"Certainly you don't suspect me, for I did not touch it," replied Mubassa bear cub.

Soon they found themselves on a flat land of ice, a frozen river high up in an angry mountain. They had started climbing down the mountainside when old raccoon suddenly jumped up and began flying through the air like an eagle.

"Come now," he shouted to Mubassa bear cub, "if you really want to reach the land of Man your spirit must soar, like an eagle."

Mubassa bear cub became so frightened that the hair on his neck and face stiffened like the quills of a porcupine. Nevertheless, he wanted to be a man so much that he jumped up and began flying too, just like old raccoon.

They flew through the veil of time, through the land of seasons-snow, spring and summer, and finally landed smack in the middle of

June in a land far away to the north. The veil of time tossed Mubassa gently from its hammock. Mubassa had fallen into a sleep deeper than a dream.

When Mubassa finally awakened, he found himself alone. He sighted what seemed like a small crystal clear lake shaped like a triangle. What a beautiful little lake, he thought to himself. But where was the raccoon? He was alone. He didn't like to be alone. He couldn't bear it.

"Raccoon! Raccoon! I need you," he cried. "Raccoon, raccoon! Where are you?"

Nothing answered, not even a bird. Not even a breeze. There was no one to talk to, not even the trees would talk to him and Mubassa indeed knew the language of the trees.

That night was one of the loneliest nights of Mubassa's life. Not even the lovely moon could console him. It seemed as if even she turned away from him, as cloud after cloud covered her face like "the dance of the seven veils". Mubassa knew he was a long way home and that the only friend he knew was sleep.

Then morning came. Morning came and sounds like clarion bells were ringing in the hills. There was a voice singing in the still of the morning.

"What's your name?" said a soft voice, gentle as the wind in the middle of June.

Mubassa opened his sleek-carved eyes. It was a little girl's voice. Somehow the bells were still ringing, or was it her hello? She was a beautiful bronze shock of a girl with wavy dreads that laughed in the wind.

"Oh, my name is Mubassa," he said.

"My name is Rose-Nuri," she replied. "You're going to be late for school, aren't you?"

School . . . ? thought Mubassa. "What . . . ?" Then he caught himself in mid-sentence. "I'm talking! I'm talking! Human talk," he shouted. "I'm a man! I'm a man! I can stalk and protect. Save and kill. Sow and reap. I'm a man! I am a MAN!!!"

"Of course, you're talking human talk. You're a boy, aren't you? I don't know about that other stuff you're talking about," Rose-Nuri responded as she shook her head in utter amazement.

"I mean, err . . .I mean, what does your name mean?" stammered Mubassa, his heart torn between excitement and embarrassment. He couldn't stop himself from stuttering as he spoke. Dare he tell her that he was a bear? No, she'd never believe him.

"My name means Rose of the Night and Rose of the Light. . . and what does your name mean?" she sauntered back.

"It means Strong Bear," Mubassa said proudly.

"That's funny," mused Rose-Nuri, "you don't look like a bear. Are you a Native American or something? Strong Bear sure sounds like an Indian warrior's name."

"I don't know," said Mubassa. "I'm like the old river. I don't know where I came from and I don't know where I'm going."

"Well, you must be an orphan," said the girl sadly.

"Let's go to school," Mubassa suggested, "I sure am hungry."

"You don't go to school to feed your body. You go to school to feed your mind. That's what mom and dad always say." Rose-Nuri commented.

"O.k.," said Mubassa, "what's the name of your school?"

"Good Hope School, of course," was her reply. "What other school is there to go to? You go in with good hope and you come out with good hope!"

So Mubassa went to school with Rose-Nuri. He sat in the classroom and wondered, what a strange experience! Science, reading and math. He ate food out of the garbage can when nobody was looking and during recess he would run to the lake to look at his face and laugh. He had come out bronze like Rose-Nuri. Maybe a little darker. His hair was curly like the wool of a lamb.

His muscles, though young, rippled like a stone thrown into a lake. His smile was soft as the sunrise, glowing with happiness. He was quite a handsome boy.

Each day his friend, Rose-Nuri, would go home to her parents and Mubassa would go and sleep in the forest at the foot of the triangular lake.

One day Rose-Nuri asked Mubassa where he lived. He explained that he lived in the forest and decided to tell her his secret. Rose-Nuri somehow believed him and promised to keep his secret and never tell anyone. Finally, Rose-Nuri convinced her parents that Mubassa was an orphan. By the time July came around, Mubassa was living with her parents, Peter and Janice Bunyan, Rose-Nuri and her older brother named Eric.

Soon Mubasssa became endeared to Eric and Rose-Nuri's father, Peter. They did a lot of things together. They played games like baseball and basketball. They built tree houses and went rock climbing and fishing. Mubassa taught them a few tricks about catching fish, and they were always amazed at how he easily caught fish with his bare hands.

Mubassa was happy. He even liked summer school and found reading to be a lot of fun. Once in a while he thought about his parents, but hey, they were living a bear's life. He was going to live a human life. All was peaceful, All was calm, All was bright like a shining lake deep in the turquoise of his soul.

Summer fell into the arms of autumn and the bright leaves turned red, gold and brown. The nights became cold as the winter's song was in the wind.

Soon the fireplace crackled with laughter. The fire ate wood chips and small logs as if they were popcorn. Mubassa ate fish, his favorite dish. All this, he thought, would never ever end.

One night in December, Mubassa was sitting by the fireplace and Peter, his adopted father, a tall John Henry of a man, was cleaning his gun. It was a high caliber Winchester rifle with a telescopic sight. Rose-Nuri was sitting next to Mubassa writing a poem.

"What is he doing?" whispered Mubassa to Rose-Nuri.

"He's cleaning the rifle to go hunting," whispered Rose. "In the winter, dad goes hunting. Once we went to Africa on a safari and dad shot a lion. See the lion's head on the wall?" pointed Rose-Nuri. "And look, there's a water buffalo's head that dad also shot that summer. Over there is one of the deer heads he shot in the forest of feelings last winter."

Mubassa stared at the wall. "Wow, that's awesome," he whispered to Rose-Nuri. "I would like to go hunting, but I was taught only to hunt for food when you are hungry."

"No, silly," explained Rose-Nuri, "dad does it for sport. Although we did eat the deer."

"Oh," sighed Mubassa, "I don't think that's right."

"I sort of agree with you," chimed Rose-Nuri, "but tomorrow dad is stalking for deer and hunting for rabbits, and we definitely eat rabbits and deer meat which are very delicious."

"Really?" wondered Mubassa out loud.

"Hey, Mubassa," said Eric, who was just walking into the room, "do you want to go hunting with me and dad tomorrow? We're going to get some rabbit and deer meat for the winter."

"O.k.," Mubassa said hesitatingly.

"Dad, can Mubassa go hunting with you and me tomorrow?" queried Eric.

Peter, who was still cleaning his rifle said, "Of course he can. Since Mubassa has a good nose for catching fish, maybe he can help us track down deer and rabbit as well."

Morning came, ringing like mission bells again, but this time they seemed to be tolling for someone's soul. Mubassa awakened. Rose-Nuri was not there.

"Let's go!" Eric shouted.

Soon they were all dressed and ready to go. The three had snow shoes on. The snow shoes felt so big that Mubassa thought he had his old bear feet on again.

Soon the three were covered in a tangled web of deciduous forest. Pine, oak, elm, birch and others vied for the precious sunlight. Imagine trees fighting over scraps of sunshine?

"There's a rabbit over there," said Mubassa, pointing in a northerly direction.

"Where? Where!" exclaimed Peter. Soon they had bagged a deer and three rabbits with Mubassa's help.

"Great gosh!" exclaimed Eric's father. "Mubassa, you see like an eagle and run fast like a deer. You're a natural born hunter."

Mubassa laughed to himself. Only Rose-Nuri knew his little secret.

They were about to turn homeward when suddenly an angry growl and ominous shadow startled the afternoon. There were several very loud snaps of branches. Something was rushing toward them. Something was about to attack them. Eric's dad raised his rifle in the direction of the sound and fired a shot that seemed to go a thousand miles into the future. The rushing sound got louder and closer, the growl angrier and angrier. Eric's father raised his rifle again. Mubassa knew something was terribly wrong. He felt very confused.

"Don't shoot! It's a bear!" Mubassa yelled.

"You're crazy kid," shouted Eric's father. "I need a bear's head for my wall collection. Now, out of my way!"

The bear suddenly appeared in the clearing and stood up on its hind legs. It growled and shook the earth with a terrible quaking.

"Don't shoot!" yelled Mubassa again, as he tried to knock the gun out of Peter's hands. Peter pushed Mubassa away.

"Crazy kid!" he shouted. "I need this bear!"

The bear did not attack. It stood growling as if guarding its sacred place. Peter aimed the gun again, this time at the bear's head.

Mubassa kicked him in the ankles and said, "Don't shoot, that's my father! That's my father!"

The gun went off anyway, but missed the bear's head. Instead, it hit the bear's leg.

"That's my father!" Mubassa cried desperately.

At that moment, the bear turned and ran off into the bush. Mubassa followed, seemingly with his heart in both his legs. Both his legs felt strangely heavy and out of place. The bear ran. Mubassa ran. With the strength of a panther, he bolted and soon caught up to the bear.

Suddenly the bear turned and swiped at Mubassa with such a powerful paw that the blow would surely have killed Mubassa if it had been more accurate.

"Father, it's me!" shouted Mubassa. "It's me, Mubassa, your son!"

The bear stood and continued growling. Mubassa could see its right hind leg was bleeding profusely from the rifle wound. Suddenly the language of the bear clan came back to him, and Mubassa spoke bear talk. *Bearcanese* it's called.

"Baba duey ayabana cumoney!" Meaning, "Dad I can help you!" The bear stopped growling and there were tears in its eyes. Mubassa had gotten through.

"Baba duey ayabana cumoney!" Mubassa cried again.

Mubassa's dad responded, "Ibn baba ayabanu min falakuna!" Meaning, "Son help me please!"

Mubassa took off his hunting scarf which was white and tied it around his father's leg as tight as he could above the wound and the bleeding soon stopped. Suddenly his father grew frantic. He pleaded with Mubassa.

"Ibn Mubassa, yalan fil beitun, ummaya habibula kaitir khalifa-nan safiritanan." Meaning, "Son, come home. Your mother misses you. It sounds like many people are coming this way. Mubassa, you must decide!"

Mubassa replied with tears in his eyes, "Baba duey anna khalifanan anna aklaat khalifanan yalan baba duey yalan anna ayabana." Meaning, "I cannot go. I am a man. I've eaten human food. Run my father, run. I will help you!"

Mubassa's father responded, "Ibn Mubassa, la me ayubana las shadu am fofama ruh fil beit." Meaning, "My son I do not need your help. I believe your destiny will bring you home."

And so Mubassa's father left with storms of tears in his eyes and a rainbow in his heart.

Soon there was a vigorous rustling in the woods. One thing Mubassa knew was that it was neither Eric nor his father. Mubassa was standing in a clearing surrounded by trees. He looked up and discovered the source of the rustling sound. It was the trees that surrounded the clearing. They were moving their limbs and leaves as if stirred by a mystic wind. Now their trunks were moving too, marching in place to some unseen drummer.

Mubassa knew something was terribly wrong. Perhaps something had upset them. He tried talking to the trees in the language his mother had taught him long before he had become a man.

"Aw wa woorr aw worr, ruh, ruh, ruh, groah, groah, aw wa worr," Mubassa growled at the trees as he stood in a clearing. "Oh trees, oh trees, what do you see oh trees."

The trees answered not. The breeze too had knotted his lips, it was so difficult to speak. The shivering of his soul against the battering blast of wintrer thundered in Mubassa's heart. Mubassa was lonely. Mubassa was lost. He was like a person who could no longer bear the tempest of two minds, one gloomy, one glad. His father had been shot and his human stepdad had done it. "Did it feel like this to be a man?" he wondered. "Did it feel so confused?"

Mubassa tried talking to the trembling trees again, using the best bear language he could remember. This time several more trees who had been sleeping stirred, peeling off the slumber of

December's wintry song. They shook the snow from their sleepy branches and stretched their limbs as trees often do, though men perceive it not.

Seeing that these new trees had stirred, Mubassa implored the trees a third time. "Aw wa woorr aw worr, ruh, ruh, ruh, groah, groah, aw wa worr," he growled.

Seven gnarled Dutch elm trees lifted their limbs toward the quiet before the setting sun. They appeared to be sisters. They spoke not but moved forward together inch by inch toward the clearing, their seven huge limbs casting one huge shadow as they moved together toward Mubassa. Soon they were moving quickly, as if part of an army of marching trees. Trees marching into battle or else hunters closing in on trapped quarry. Their stumps pounded the ground in place like gigantic marching feet.

Mubassa began to stutter in amazement. "Aw woorah, aw woorah, graah, graah. Oh trees, oh trees, what do you want?" He gasped as the seven Dutch elms approached him.

The trees stopped. They had surrounded Mubassa. Suddenly, their humongous trunks shrunk from pillars to six foot saplings. The saplings then became human torsos. The limbs became human arms taking on human likeness. All the while, loud shrieking screams came from inside the trunks of the seven trees as they twisted and turned, giving birth to newborn forms. Mubassa felt trapped, caged by a strange new feeling that surrounded him for the first time. Fear, Fear! Fear!! He fought this feeling of fear with his very soul and wrestled it to the ground. He was exhausted. He looked up and stared into the death-like faces of seven of the ugliest witches you ever did see. Their bodies had six arms each. They wore large bark hats that partially covered their faces.

As they moved closer still, Mubassa saw that they had the faces of ferocious white timber wolves. The witches began growling, snarling and roaring, bearing their sharp silvery fangs as they shattered the beauty of winter's sunset. Their cold blue marble eyes were locked on Mubassa like radar. The other trees were trembling in the bitter breeze.

"Ah, what a lovely little brown jelly bean of a boy we have here," smirked one of the witches.

"We shall have him for dinner tonight," snarled the second witch.

"Yeh, we shall cook him over a fire," snickered a third witch.

"Just like a little marshmallow that he is," laughed the fourth witch.

"Why do you want to eat me? I have done nothing wrong!" Mubasssa declared.

"Because you don't look like us," snarled the fifth witch. "And we have power over you."

"Well it shouldn't be that way," Mubassa replied. "There should be peace, justice and freedom for all creatures."

"In your dreams! Our way is the way of the world, sonny boy," laughed the sixth wicked witch.

"Besides, we've been waiting four hundred years for a little marshmallow like you to trespass on our holy ground," said the seventh witch. "How dare you hunt in our forest!"

"Who are you?" asked Mubassa. "I too am part of this forest. I will change things when I become king of it."

"We are the wicked witches of Candor," said the leader of the group. "More we cannot tell you, except that we need your mind, your heart and your strength for our secret recipe. You will never become king if we can help it, so say your prayers sonny boy!"

Mubassa wanted to run but he could not move. Had the witches cast a spell on him? Maybe. But all he could do was blink his eyes and try to ease his bewildered mind.

The wolf-faced witches began pulling off their arms. Each witch pulled off four arms and placed them on a pile in the clearing. As the arms hit the ground, each became a tree branch.

Mubassa saw the witches set the branches on fire. The fire roared and crackled like a quiet thunder in a bottle.

Mubassa tried again to move his arms, but he found them bound by some invisible cord. In the meantime, the seven witches of Candor, looking more and more like wolves each passing moment, began dancing in a circle around the flame, shrieking loudly and chanting a maddening rhyme.

"Dance witches dance, till you pick a number. We get a century older but not a century dumber. Ring around the rosie, we'll always tell a lie. Four and twenty brownies, we cook them and they die. When we go to eat them, our limbs get young and strong. We are the witches of Candor, and all we do is wrong! We understand, we 'under man', we under hearts to feed our little clan."

Mubassa was getting weaker and weaker as they sang. All he could do was sleep. All he could do was pray. Prayer was his friend and sleep his pal again. He felt alone. He felt alone as never before, but he believed that the G-d of bears and men would somehow rescue him. But for now, he sat tied up, bound by the cords of a miserable dream. Suddenly the lowly earthworm appeared to him as he was falling asleep.

"Oh Mubassa," shouted the earthworm, "did you find your dream? Did you become a man? Did you stalk and protect, save and kill, sow and reap?"

"Oh earthworm," cried Mubassa, "would that I could be a bear again! I would be the best bear I could be. For surely, some among men are good, but some are evil. But I need to be the best bear I can be. Give me your wise counsel earthworm, and your best advice."

"You are in big trouble," said the earthworm, "but perhaps it is not too late. A being must change his life before the great sleep descends upon him. Knowledge of self is better than a kingdom. Faith is the unbreakable light that never fades. Truth is the path toward happiness. So tell us please, Mubassa, who ate raccoon's fish?"

"I did," Mubassa slowly replied. "I made a mistake when I lied. I can forgive myself but will Raccoon forgive me? Will the Great One forgive me?"

"You have opened the door," said the earthworm, "but we will help you by the power of the Great Spirit. The One Who Is The Creator of worms, bears and men. He shares His throne with no one, and we are all His servants."

Mubassa cried tears and rainbows as he listened to the earthworm. Then suddenly a lot of earthworms emerged from the earth and they began tearing away at Mubassa's invisible cords. The cords that bound his body and soul.

Then Mubassa saw an army of at least 100 raccoons emerge from the forest on all sides. The raccoons ran toward the dancing witches and started biting their legs and feet. The evil hags were running and screaming in a circle as the raccoons bit their toes. They became so desperate that they soon jumped into the fire. When they had done so, the fire went out and all that was left when the smoke cleared were six white stones covered with mud.

The night passed, enjoying a restful sleep.

When dawn arrived, Mubassa looked down at himself. He was once again a strong bear. He felt so proud. He soon found himself in familiar surroundings. He saw a whole tribe of raccoons standing by the roadside. Grinning from ear to ear, he greeted them warmly.

"Good morning Racoons," he waved to them.

"Good morning Prince Mubassa," they shouted.

"Thank you. It is you who are royalty," Mubassa replied.

Then Mubassa passed by a coil of earthworms, chilling in the mud on the side of the road.

"Good morning Earthworms," Mubassa exclaimed. "I shall never forget you. No longer shall men use your bodies to catch fish if I have anything to do with it."

"Good morning, Prince Mubassa," the earthworms murmured.

Soon Mubassa arrived at his house. "Mom! Dad! I'm home! I'm home and I just want to be the best bear and the good son that I can be."

His mother ran up to him and kissed him. His father gave him a great big bear hug.

"Son, you are home. You have saved your life and mine. You are now Prince Mubassa and soon to be King of Bears."

"But dad, you are the king," said Mubassa.

"Yes I am. But one day the Great Spirit will call me to visit the great forest. His book is in the hearts of bears and in the hearts of men. So submit to His will and ask for His forgiveness."

And so Mubassa became King of Bears. He was kind to all. He remembered the earthworm especially. He remembered his promises and his Lord the Creator.

However, there would come a time when he would be tempted as no bear had ever been tempted before.

One day, years later, a most beautiful woman was walking in the forest, practicing her lyrics to a song. Her voice was so beautiful that flowers opened their petals to hear her better. Mubassa recognized her face. It was Rose-Nuri. She screamed when she saw him, but then he spoke to her in plain English, calling her by name.

"Mubassa," she cried, "is that you?"

"Yes it is me," Mubassa replied joyfully.

Rose-Nuri wept with joy. She hugged him.

"Oh Mubassa, now you are yourself," she said "I have kept your secret all those years. But I always wish you were back home with us. Dad and Eric are okay. Mom and Dad want me to be married. Somehow, I had hoped to marry you if you were still around."

"Oh Rose-Nuri," sighed Mubassa, "I am King of Bears. I could never be a man again. But I will always remember you and the good times we shared. In fact, I will carve your name and my name in the bark of the Sequoia tree, for I did love you and love never dies. Even if I am a bear."

Rose-Nuri gently replied, "Mubassa, I shall teach men to respect the forest and its animals as long as I live."

So the names of Mubassa and Rose-Nuri were carved in the heart of the Sequoia tree which became petrified and lasted for over ten thousand years in a petrified forest of love, a place where the past, present and future meet for lunch.

In the forest of feelings, any who entered the forest with evil intentions were met by an army of raccoons, worms and bears trained by the great Mansa Mubassa, King of Bears.

So, my children, by the token of the moon and her many mansions, by the splendor of the sun and his expansions, By the hurricane that will surely come, By the One who is the only One, be your best self, be all that you can. Seek good for yourself and good for the land.

This is Mansa Mubassa bear cub's story, about the bear who would be man. The quest for empty pride and glory or things that will not stand. Knowledge, truth and honesty are things worth pursuing. Peace, justice and love, if you know what you are doing. So go to sleep, oh ye sons and daughters. The sleeping sun too must reach its destiny. Beware the evil in murky waters and rivers that never meet the sea! Peace be with you and with your mothers and fathers, and all people good and true and Peace to Mubassa Too Wherever You Are!!

"Mubassa's Dream"

Part two
Sun Bear Learns a Lesson

This is part two of a glorious story
a song wrung from the poem of time
when the moon was young
and the sun in his glory
and words were roses still in their prime

When the far flung sea
was still married to a breeze
but the balance
between the lands of the deserts
and the lands of the trees
were first threatened by the revolt
of the storm people

When the forests of the world
were still one
but the travesty of treason
had begun to cause the species
to disappear
and birds to vanish from the air

"Oh Fie!" you say,
"This happened so long ago,
who indeed wants to know?"
but come wind, come rain,
come shine, or come snow,
or sundry clime
stories must have the rhyme of reason
and the reason of rhyme
for history is one
and a lesson once begun
is a lesson for all time

Mansa Mubassa, King of Bears
was ruler of the enchanted forest of feelings
His throne thrived for 40 years
during which time he was dealing
with saving the lives of nature's heirs
the animals, the trees,
the bees, and the bears

Seven were the wars he did wage
against the greed of the trappers
the Storm people and kidnappers
who would put peace in a cage
and make mischief destiny's rage

And so this story takes place
in the 30th year of winter
of King Mubassa's reign
a story of treason without good reason

And it came to pass that Mubassa, King of Bears, ruled the forest of feelings for thirty years. During that time the forest grew greener. Trees were planted everywhere by birds on the wing. Over thirty thousand hectares were planted every year. No hunting of animals for sport or for fun would occur. Armies of raccoons, fleets of piranhas, squadrons of wild geese and divisions of driver ants stood ready to defend the peace and justice to the end.

Mubassa, King of Bears, was king and friend of animals as had been his father. He only hoped that one day the Righteous Ruler would appear and ascend the throne. He was the man who would protect the animals from men, stop the unkind killing of trees and be the caretaker of the Earth. A man who if he took a blessing from nature would give it back. Such had been the first man and his family, but now men were governed by greed and not respecters of need.

Mubassa's once brown fur was turning grey. He knew that one day he would have to go to the Land of Nod, but Mubassa had young children. He had married a young wife Sophia, from the island of Philo ("The heart of the Earth" as it was called in those days). He would miss her and her children would be sad. So he asked the Lone One to renew his strength and grant him respite until his children reached the age of reason and had seen the summer and winter of at least a dozen seasons.

The Lone One must have heard his prayer. All of the animals respected Mubassa, and still none could defeat the "Artful One," not even Cassius, the wily and strong mountain lion.

One day when the sun had risen, but not too high in the sky, Mubassa heard a terrible howling bear cry tearing away the idyllic peace of a magnificent morning. It was his son's voice "Sun Bear." He would know that voice even if it was obscured by the whisper of a thousand winds. His son, Sun Bear, was in trouble. Sun Bear appeared in the clearing. He was supported by the powerful arms of his two sisters Iman and Ahdlan. "Father!" shouted Iman, "come quick, Sun Bear has been wounded!" Mubassa ran in the direction of the voices.

"My son, my son!" he cried, "bring me some honey, quick!" shouted Mubassa, "And fetch Sophia," he ordered his daughters.

Mubassa quickly covered the wounds with clean clay to stop the bleeding. Meanwhile, he picked up Sun Bear in his arms and carried him over to the palace. For two days and two nights Mubassa wept and prayed while his wife Sophia and his daughters looked after Sun Bear with shining kindness, herbs of accacia, and with words of comfort and love.

Finally it became apparent that Sun Bear would survive and on the third day Sun Bear could finally speak.

"Where did this happen?" asked Mubassa, "Who did this to you?"

Sun Bear related how he had traveled to the edge of the forest. He had heard strange voices and the sound of many running human feet. He followed the sound of the running feet and when he came to the clearing he saw a man screaming at a woman. The man had a large club in his hand and it seemed that he was about to hit the woman. "I knew this was wrong," related Sun Bear, "so I tried to stop him. You've always said, father, when you see evil stop it with your paw. If you are unable to do this, stop it with a roar; and if you are unable to do that, stop it by opposing it in your heart."

"Yes son," said Mubassa, "go ahead."

"The next thing I knew they both pulled out knives and stabbed me from the front. The next thing I knew I was hit from behind. I felt my flesh being torn from my back."

"Let's see his back," demanded Mubassa. There were large tear marks on Sun Bear's back as if it had been ripped by a powerful force.

"Cassius! Cassius! Cassius!" said Mubassa, "I will punish you. This is the work of Cassius, the mountain lion. He has joined the Evil humans. Guards! Guards! Guards!" shouted Mubassa, "Guards! Guards!"

The chief of the driver ants, the general of the geese and the captain of the raccoons appeared before Mubassa.

"Why did you not protect my son?" inquired Mubassa angrily, "Am I not your leader? Are you ungrateful?"

"We are extremely sorry, King Mubassa," sighed the general of the geese. "Very Sorry."

"Of course we were not there," chimed in the chief of the driver ants.

"Nonsense!" said Mubassa, "Ants are everywhere!"

"Sire," challenged the Captain Raccoon, "we cannot always protect the young from their ignorance and you told Sun Bear never to go to the edge of the forest. He is not prepared to deal with people."

"You are right," sighed Mubassa, "all of you get out of here. You are dismissed! Dismissed!" shouted Mubassa, "And find out where those humans live that did this to my son."

"Yes oh King," they chanted in unison.

"God be with you," said King Mubassa, as he realized he (had) lost his temper.

Then Mubassa turned to his son. "Sun Bear, I thank the Lone One that you have survived this ordeal."

"What did I do wrong, my father?"

"You did nothing wrong my son, but sometimes with wisdom you can achieve a good result without a bad side effect. For example, if a fly annoys you, you can shoo it away with a wave of your paw instead of swinging at it with a rock, and thereby taking the chance of hurting yourself or someone else."

"What do you mean?" asked Sun Bear.

"I mean," said Mubassa, "in the instant case, if you had just roared the man and woman would probably have run away. Since most people are afraid of bears your roar would have been enough to stop the violence. Know yourself my son, and how others think of you, and in a thousand conflicts you may emerge victorious. It was a trap, and of course if you had just roared you could have defended yourself better. Certainly by traveling to the edge of the forest you put yourself in danger. Man is a hunter, a killer, a shedder of blood. Stay out of his way and perchance his way will not find you. There are only a few men who are righteous Sun Bear, but you do not know their marks or the signs of them. You do not know the marks of men."

"What are the marks of men?" inquired Sun Bear.

"My son and my daughters," exclaimed Mubassa, going to his daughters Iman and Adhlan, "the marks of men are seven." explained Mubassa.

"First there are the Sun People. The Sun People are very gracious and generous. They share without stint their talents and possessions. They are creative, compassionate, helpful, and shine their light equally on the good and the vile."

"They are however individualistic and tribalistic, utterly ununited. Soon, therefore, night must overtake them. However, they are resilient people and will rise again whenever they unify and achieve balance in the sharing of their gifts."

"The Rain People, are very sober minded. They will never waste their talents or time on a desert. They will go where things are green, i.e. already promising, and deposit their investments. They usually prosper wherever they go. Unless they are taken off course by a wayward wind. Their lives are quite short unless they find a residence in a home of a lake or a river."

"The Wind People are full of will and have a strong sense of purpose. They are gatherers of knowledge and tales which they carry on their backs from one place to another. They are great communicators, but they also cannot be trusted, for they have been known to change direction and loyalties without notice."

"The cloud People are confused. They store or hold a lot of information indeed but the information belongs to others. They go wherever the wind blows. They are not leaders but followers.

Sometimes they confuse others by blocking out the sun of truth."

"The Storm People are angry at life. They want to do it harm. They will attack anything established until they capture it. If they capture it, they will destroy it. If they destroy something, they will never replace it . They move on, always seeking new conquests, whether it be hearts or a city, it does not matter."

"The Snow People are smart, cold hearted, calculating. They seek to covet and cover whatever they say they discover, and yet call it their own. They imitate life. They are (steal) workers. They appear to be friendly at first. However, later they will deceive you by a most wise stratagem. Then they will move into your house."

"The Rainbow People. They are wise, balanced, generous, fair-minded people. They are strong when they are united. When they are united, you see the rainbow in the sky and all will admire it from afar and seek their council. When they are united and have faith in themselves, they become benign rulers. These are ways of men's thought and men are what they think, not how they look."

"Wow!" exclaimed Sun Bear, "how do I know how to deal with these people."

"Which people are not harmful to bears?" chimed in Iman.

"And from which people will come the 'Just Ruler'?" added Adhlan.

"Ah!" said Mubassa, "All men were created to be 'Just Rulers' (care-takers of nature), but they have reshaped themselves by their own self-ish desires. Verily, I say to you, trust no man until his brain has married his heart and his heart has submitted to the Lone One and seeks harm to no creature. Such a person can be identified by long observation of his conduct and then you must check to see that it doesn't change. Such a man is 'Just Ruler'. It will be easier, my children, to find the footprint of an ant on a black rock in the stillness of night, than to find such a man. But whenever you find such a man, your heart and your mind will agree, and doubt will not be your companion."

"What shall we do if we find such a man?" asked Sun Bear.

"Obey Him!" said Mubassa. "such a man is a friend of the forest, do you understand?"

"Yes my father," explained Iman.

"Yes," added Sun Bear.

"Of course," said Adhlan.

"What if such a man were to change, overnight?" asked Sun Bear.

"Then oppose him with all your might, with all that you have in your power, for he is an Evil One. Fight him until oppression is no more, and wait for a true believer to appear, as we are doing now."

Mubassa counseled his children into the night and into the next morning, and sleep overtook his children.

The dawn awakened quietly in the forest, washed her face with dew and they set out for her father's mansion in the zenith of the turquoise in the sky. Then came the chief of the driver ants to the second palace of Mubassa, King of the Bears. A Luxurious den in the stone faced mountains.

"Oh sire," inquired the chief of the ants, "we have found the humans who did this evil thing to Sun Bear. They are in the Northwestern part of the land and dwell in a town called Antioch-Barnum, and they run a prison for animals called a circus."

"Good! Keep them under observation," ordered Mubassa, "and publish throughout the land that Sun Bear my son will have a funeral. The funeral will be be Sabtu and all will be required to attend."

When Sabtu arrived, Mubassa Bear staged a magnificent funeral. Sun Bear's body was supposedly secreted in a pine log coffin, carved and carried by six bears. The mourners, including, Cassius the mountain lion, eulogized Sun Bear and all saw the coffin lowered into the ground. Night descended on the mourners and the burial site was then guarded by a squadron of raccoons. That very night, Mubassa called in the chief of the Driver Ants.

"Keep Cassius the mountain lion under observation," he ordered. "See who he speaks to and report to me. Take no action against him."

"Yes sire," answered the chief of the Ants, "We are already undercover."

"Yes you are," smiled Mubassa, "Now keep it that way."

That very night at mid-night, Cassius the mountain lion stole outside the forest and headed toward Antioch-Barnum. He went to the house of Mr. and Mrs. Woodcutter, the same people who had stabbed Sun Bear two days before.

"Come in Cassius," said Mrs. Woodcutter, "Congratulations, you did a lion of a job!"

"Yes I did, I delivered Sun Bear to your people," reminded Cassius. "He fell into the trap and now you will reward me as you promised."

"Of course we will reward you," reminded Mrs. Woodcutter. "Now you said you want one lamb every day for 7 days and a wife from the Barnum Circus, is that what you want?"

"That's what was promised," said Cassius the mountain lion.

"You may take the lamb now," said Mrs. Woodcutter. "My husband shall negotiate obtaining a young lioness from Barnum Circus, so be patient."

"I am patient, but hurry up." Cassius added, "I have no wife since Leona died five years ago in that war against hunters, called by that idiot King Mubassa."

"You don't like him, I see," laughed Mrs. Woodcutter.

"No I don't" roared Cassius the lion. "Death to him and death to the forest. I hope you cut it down. I don't care. I live in the mountain-side now. And the forest I use sometimes for hunting."

"Yes, we will cut it down. And sell all of the wood. And when Mubassa is out of the way there will be no successors and nothing shall oppose us. In fact, if we get enough money, we'll burn the forest down and sell it to developers for a theme park. We'll be millionaires.

We'll take the money to Manhattan and buy a condominium over-looking Central park. Anyway, trees belong in parks and on streets, and perhaps someday in museums." They all laughed.

"Well, don't forget to get me a wife" reminded Cassius.

"I remind you however, Mr. mountain lion, those lionesses in the circus are mighty huge."

"I don't care," said Cassius, "I can handle any woman lion any-time." They all laughed again and Mrs. Woodcutter presented the mountain lion with a fat lamb, which he promptly killed and ate.

"See you tomorrow," reminded Cassius as he slinked back to the mountains.

The chief of the Driver Ants got news from his scouts and relayed the news to Mubassa, even before the mountain lion reached his lair.

Mubassa's fur curled in anger when he heard this story.

"We shall catch that lion Cassius 'the liar' in his own trap," Mubassa commanded. "Gather a squadron of raccoons. Set all of the lions free in the Antioch-Barnum circus. I want that done this very night before dawn. Lead them to the door of the woodcutters. Gather 100 spiders and have them spin a hunter's net. Or else dig up that old hunter's net we buried in the war against hunters five years ago. On second thought," Mubassa said, "we'll use spiders. A spider's net will be invisible."

And what do you want us to do with the net when we complete it?" queried Captain Raccoon.

"I want you to capture Cassius the lying one on his way to the woodcutters house, but wait until he gets very close to the house before you do so."

"Shall we bring him back?" queried Captain Raccoon.

"No leave him in the net. His fate shall be arranged."

So while the night had not yet become hoary with age, Raccoon led a squadron to the circus Antioch-Barnum and opened the cage of the lions. There were seven lions in the circus.

"Come with me," beckoned Captain Raccoon, "and I will show you lions a place where you can have tender lamb for dinner." The lions were eager to follow the Raccoon who led them to the house of the woodcutter. "Shh," whispered the Raccoon. "Now all you have to do is knock on the door of the woodcutter at dawn and you will be shown the lambs which she keeps in the barn."

And so the seven lions slept in front of the door of the woodcutter until dawn, and then their leader knocked on the door. When Mrs. Woodcutter opened the door, she almost fainted.

"Frank!" Frank!" Frank!" she screamed, "Cassius's family is out here and he has double crossed us, and they mean us harm."

The seven lions demanded that lambs be provided for them at once, but there were only six lambs left, since Cassius ate one the night before. The seventh lion, a lioness of great strength and size, became very angry. "Who is this Cassius?" she inquired as she roared at the woodcutter. "Well," the seventh lioness continued, "If you don't provide a lamb by tonight, that is, this Cassius guy does not return with the lamb that you spoke of, I will eat you myself."

The woodcutter and his wife shivered and shook, and shame and fear descended upon them.

That night, Cassius headed for the woodcutter's cabin. He was shadowed by the driver ants and a squadron of bats flew overhead with a hunters net woven from invisible spiders thread.

When Cassius reached the edge of the forest, just outside of the woodcutter's cabin, the bats dropped the spiders net over him. He struggled and strained and shook and shivered, but he was trapped in a web of his own guilt.

"What is it that you have put over me?" Cassius called to the bats. "I am a follower of King Mubassa."

"It is your royal robes, you traitor!" claimed the bats.

Meanwhile, the seventh lioness became impatient and she killed and ate the woodcutter and his wife. They begged for mercy and forgiveness for all that they had done.

Meanwhile, the keeper of the Antioch-Barnum circus was desperate and he sent out a posse to recapture the lions. The posse searched and searched until they came upon a screaming mountain lion, Cassius, trapped in a net.

"Back to the circus with you pal," shouted one of the animal catchers as he seized Cassius's net with the help of two others.

"I don't belong in the circus," explained Cassius, "I am a mountain lion."

"Aw shut up pal," responded the animal catcher, "You're lion. You're Lion."

"No, I'm telling you the truth!" pleaded Cassius.

So Cassius was hauled off to the circus, where he joined the other seven lions that were captured, and returned to the circus also.

Life in the circus was no bowl of strawberries for lions. Cassius was only a mountain lion and not as large as ordinary lions.

Moreover, Cassius was bullied everyday by the lion tamer, who thought he had forgotten the lion's tricks which everybody liked to see in the circus. He was also forced by the other lions to marry the lioness that had eaten the woodcutter and his wife. This added to Cassius's agony, since the lioness was stronger than him and pushed him around all the time.

Three risings and settings of the moon passed. The day came when Sun Bear led a raid on the Antioch circus, together with the Driver Ants and the Raccoons. They freed all the animals out from their prisons except the lions. Sun Bear did not free the lions partly because they killed the lambs out of greed and not out of need. When he saw the face of Cassius the mountain lion, he started to go over to Cassius to taunt him and to show him that he, Sun Bear, was still alive. Suddenly, however, he changed his mind; he remembered his father's words "Son, never gloat over the misfortune of others even if you think they deserve it."

Sun Bear turned his back on the temptation and headed home. But poor Cassius, the mountain lion, saw him as he peered out of his cage. "Hey! Sun Bear, you're supposed to be dead!" shouted Cassius in despair, "You're supposed to be dead! Hey Sun Bear, come back here!" Sun Bear turned and said, "Cassius, may peace be upon you and the mercy of the Lone One."

Sun Bear had learned his lesson. He felt that one day he might be a wise king like his father. Needless to say, Mubassa and his wife Sophia were very proud of him. They were also very proud of Iman and Adhlan who took care of the freed animals and helped introduce them to the ways of the forest. Thus ends the story that never ends. And, of course, there is more but it's time to go to sleep! Stories before sleep. Thinking before action. The mind is the father. The heart is the mother. Unite them in good and give birth to your most beautiful self.

Epilogue

And so you daughters of my heart
and sons of my soul
resist the storm that tears apart
and renders compassion cold

A kind word and good deeds
are among the richest treasures
in a world of manufactured needs
and overrated pleasures

Keep ever the Even Way, the path that is plain
for there are blessings in the sun
and there are blessings in the rain

and if death makes all things one
remember the rose of life will bloom again

Seek always the ways of knowledge
for experience is the most expensive college
besides, wisdom has it's season
faith overcomes fear,
and then favor follows reason

History an endless tunnel of mirrors
teaches us it's most valuable lesson
nothing is at first what it seems
nevertheless take a swing at your dreams
no runs! no hits! No errors!

You must overcome those fears
that make life a delicatessen
selling both men and some bears!

I'll see you soon where the past, present and future meet for lunch. By that time, you will be awake.

The Legend of the Leaf and the Mango Tree
(The Little Leaf who wanted to fly)

There once was a handsome mango leaf who lived on a Mango Tree in St. Andrews, Jamaica. His name was Joshua Hikmah Evergreen III, or Joshua Hikmah for short. Joshua was always dreaming about flying, about leaving the custody of his parent, his tree and his roots.

His parents, on the other hands, (two twigs merged together) were quite conservative and strict. He also had two older sisters, growing on either side of him, who were quite bossy busy bodies (Janilla and Khamila).

Joshua's parents always talked about how they came from good seed and a royal blessed family stock of trees, going back to India and Africa. They urged Joshua that one day, he would be great, if he stayed put.

They even promised that he might grow up to become Prime Minister of a beautiful Mango blossom like his uncle Stanley, and perhaps after, the standard bearer of King Mango Fruit himself, like his uncle Wilfred.

Joshua Hikmah Evergreen III was quite a proud and stubborn little mango leaf. And so, when a very strong wind came along, he jumped off the twig, or "off the vine". He saw, at last, his chance to fly.

His sisters and parents cried out, but Joshua was gone! gone!! gone!!! He was flying, flying, flying, or so he thought.

The tempest wind blew Joshua everywhere. First the wind blew him east across the Atlantic Ocean, to Africa. Then the wind blew him north to India and China. Then the wind blew him across the Pacific to California, and finally east to New York City. There, he finally came to rest in Central Park. He was far away, so far, far away from home. He finally realized he had no power to fly at all.

On a rainy day in New York, in early September, a botanist named Livingston discovered Joshua.

"What is this little mango leaf doing here in Central Park?" Livingston wondered.

Livingston sighed and placed Joshua in a Botany Collection Scrap Book. Identified with a name, date and serial number, an inscription that read "rare mango leaf found in Central Park." This was inscribed right above the head of Joshua. It was like a jail tag.

Joshua Mango Leaf even felt like he was a prisoner doing time in a prison of cruel circumstances. Here he was a mango leaf imprisoned between two sheets of cold plastic far, far away from warm Jamaica. Moreover, poor Joshua was stuck in the scrapbook tucked away on a cold metal shelf for 50 years. The botanist Livingston would die.

Amazingly. the only thing that kept Joshua green all this time was faith and hope. He held on to tremendous hope and optimum. He also slept for long periods of time, and dreamt of his two sisters and his parents. Miraculously, he even grew.

Finally, one day, the grandson of Livingston, the Botanist, took out the scrap book. He wanted to show his girlfriend his grandfather's leaf collection. And add some leaves from the park of his own.

He took the scrapbook to Central Park, and as they both sat on the bench behind the Metropolitan Museum of Art, they perused the pages. Finally when they came to the page, on which the mango leaf was imprisoned, his girlfriend remarked about how handsome the leaf was and insisted she touch it. She couldn't believe a leaf could be green for fifty years.

Well, they opened the plastic sheets that had imprisoned Joshua for so long.

Joshua stretched his arms and yawned, as the fresh air kissed his face. Just then, a strong gust of wind named Gale, the daughter of a strong storm mom named Mama Storm (Mrs. Storm to You), came along. She liked Joshua too. So she snatched poor Joshua out of the girl's hands.

Gale took Joshua home to her mother, Mrs. Storm. Mrs. Storm showed the mango leaf to her husband, Mr. Squall.

Mr. Squall met with his family and spoke to Joshua privately and decided "I'm making sure this little Mango Leaf gets home."

Mr. Squall picked up Joshua and carried him down the East coast lane to Nature's Post Office. There, an express male hurricane named Patrick, the post master general of the day, blew poor Joshua all the way back to Jamaica. He blew Joshua Hikmah Ellington III right back to a place called Mango Walk in Dallas Castle, St. Andrew, Jamaica.

There, poor Joshua was deposited like an Express Mail package right in front of his family tree. He looked up high and low for his parents. The tree had doubled in size in 50 years. He looked up but he could not find a way to attach himself to the tree again.

He soon found out, that some other twigs and leaves had replaced his parents and sisters on the branch long ago. He asked the mango tree, "What happened to my parents and sisters?"

The wise Mango tree responded "Your parents and family have gone to heaven." The mango tree further explained.

"They were taken to heaven by an herbalist named Madagascar."

"Madagascar, who's that?" shouted Joshua the Mango Leaf.

"Stay low on the ground, and soon you will meet him" explained the wise mango tree.

So, not much time elapsed, when at dawn, Madagascar came. He reached down and saw Joshua lying on the ground.

"What a rare mango leaf for my tea!" explained Madagascar to himself. "This will indeed cure my patient who is going blind from diabetes."

So soon, Joshua found himself immersed in a jug of hot water. His strength being drained by a school teacher that was going blind from diabetes. The popular school teacher sipped tea from the essence of Joshua that sat in his cup as he read his students' essays.

After the man finished sipping all of the tea, Joshua found himself attached to a mango tree.

It was not a mango tree he had ever seen on earth before. It was so beautiful that it was in the highest of the seven heavens!! It was so tall that it would take an earthbound man seven days to climb its highest branches! (A balanced enlightened man could climb it in seven minutes.)

Nevertheless, it was the sweetest mango tree in paradise! It was the best mango tree in paradise!!

Joshua Hikmah Evergreen found himself merged on the same branch as his parents and sisters. They had arrived in paradise also, because they too had been used to save the lives of sick and injured people.

Joshua had been used as a cure for a good man, and even though he learned that he could not fly, he learned that he could soar if he became part of a good deed.

"A LEAF SEPARATED FROM ITS TREE CAN BE BLOWN ANYWHERE. BUT HE WHO ATTACHES HIMSELF TO THE TREE OF GOOD DEEDS WILL BE PLANTED IN HEAVEN"

25 OCT 2015 JSM

Bah-Humbug!
A Recession for The Birds

Flying north past interstate I95, somewhere between the Bronx and Westchester County, you could easily miss it if you blink. That is, unless you are a child.

Surrounded by "Chuckee Cheese (children's play paradise on one side), Dunkin Donuts on another side, a "Going out of business sale" at Circuit City, electronic store and a Chinese buffet food bar, sits the <u>New York Convention Center for Sea gulls</u>. It consists of 100,000 square feet of almost deserted blacktopped parking space left waiting at the altar for a mall.

This Camelot (parking lot) for seagulls is a huge gaze gathering, sprawling Mecca for hordes of sea gulls each winter. Seven days, between 5am and 11am in the morning, hundreds of seagulls hold court. You see them begging for scraps of donuts and bagels from <u>Dunkin Donut</u> patrons walking like zombies to their cars. You see them waiting patiently until the Dunkin Donut's girl dumps crumbs from the breakfast leftovers into the stiff Bronx wind.

They fight violently for those crumbs offered by passer bys and they kick quite a few brave pigeons to the curb in the process. At least 4 days a week just before 8am, an old man, a former merchant marine and his son bring a shopping bag full of crusted bread (bits of Italian, French pita bread, tacos and such fare) to offer to the sea gulls.

Then there is the pigeon lady with the 3 cornered hat and red neck scarf who comes daily without fail. She's not a seagull lover, but a pigeon lover. But the seagulls respect and expect her because there's no contest when seagulls and pigeons vie for the same crumbs.

But then Monday, the week of December 2008 was different. Fourteen days had already passed and the Dunkin Donuts girl never came out once to toss these donut crumbs and her dreams to the wind. The old man and his young son never showed up. The woman with the 3 cornered hats was A.W.O.L. (absent without leave) and the ice storm clouds of a winter blizzard were convening both in the southern and northern skies.

Bernie, the Chief of the Sea Gulls, was worried. He feared that his people would starve if no one came to give them crumbs from human tables.

Things were getting out of hand. Crumbs were not in people's hands. Instead, some people with handfuls of crumbs and bird traps were stalking pigeons and roaming around the parking lot like drunken wolves on the hunt. How ominous!

The pigeons went for the bread crumbs, but the seagulls were too smart. What, humans eating pigeons?? Could seagulls be far behind?? What was the world coming to??

"I wish Old Owl were around. He'd know what to do." Bernie mused from his telephone cable high above the parking lot.

Winter solstice was coming. He could hear Old Owl's voice at last year's annual Seagulls' Convention.

"Birds get the word…Do something for self before it's too late. December 23rd, The Day of Darkness for birds, is fast approaching. Do something for self before you can do nothing at all!"

Bernie observed how everyday seagulls were giving up. Some were just laying down in the parking lot and dying of starvation. Others wandered, flying in deep circles of depression. It was a bread crumb famine!

It was recession for birds. The great famine that the great grand-father seagulls had warned about. Bernie wondered. Were the old man and his son eating the bread crumbs themselves? Were those Dunkin Donut patrons eating all of the donuts? All of them?

Bernie sent away for "old sage", a 75 year old bird named Albert Ross Dean, who flew across oceans to give great inspirational speeches to birds.

When he arrived, Albert Ross Dean ascended to the top of the stage high wire telephone cable high above the parking lot. "My fellow birds of the sea," he started, "we have been blind for the past 33 years even though – our leader the owl taught us well. The seas and lakes are full of fish yet we beg for crumbs from the human monsters' tables. Have ye no pride in yourselves."

Bernie: "Hold up! Hold up!" interrupted Bernie "you 'cats' can't just come in here and bring that doom and gloom!"

Dean: "Don't curse…Bernie you used the 'C' word. We got kids here!"

Bernie: "I meant you can't just come in here and just 'ax' us to leave and hunt in the ocean. We've got rights, plenty of rights.

Rights from the state and federal government, rights from the city. Rights and privileges that seagulls took hundreds of years to earn.

We are not dirty pigeons! We are not puny sparrow! The Fed-all, Steak, and Loco government have got to bail us out! There must be more bread crumbs in Washington and in city hall than you can shake a feather at. Why can't Grace Mansion, that Mayor's dining hall and the white house throw out more food so that seagulls could eat?

They might bail us out! They owe us. Human beings have even taken and used our names to make money. You know Jonathan Livingstone Seagull, don't you?"

Dean: "Bernie, the bread crumb days are over. It's a recession.

People are eating bread crumb themselves now. People are even eating birdseeds. So, as I was saying:

The Creator gave us bird's beaks, brains, wings and balance so that we could hunt for ourselves.

You must leave this accursed parking lot and head out to sea with me.

There the Creator has provided sustenance for all the sea birds. We must become producers instead of Consumers.

The recession is for the lazy birds. The earth has not shrunk, nor the sea dried up. The sea and earth fed our ancestors who hunted here. Now all you want to do is hang around parking lots. Soon the humans will Be eating us and keeping us in cages."

Sister Seagull: "That's right! That right, Mr. Dean, that's right!

"Praised G-d" (shouts sister Marie Seagull) "We fought for the right to access this parking lot, to perch on building without being poisoned and trapped like pigeons."

Dean: "Throughout all of our demonstrations among humans, we have been deceived and bamboozled. We believed that once we occupied the roof tops of government buildings without being harassed, poisoned, etc., Scare crowed, Jim Crowed or killed, then we could brake down the barrier of prejudice against and amongst birds.

So I say, my fellow sea birds, don't be a jive turkey waiting to be stuffed with artificial feed only later to decorate some human tables. I say let's take to the sea, I say let us fly to liberty, to liberty or death. Who will follow me on the path that flies steep into the wind?!"

Shouts: "Glory, Glory, Glory," shouted others, "Glory, Glory, Glory!"

Whereupon a host of seagulls flew upwind toward the ocean in the east. The golden sun seemed to warm the wind gently. The wind was at their backs and they flew into high noon. They would become a great nation.

As for those who remained behind, they faced an increased

threat of starvation. Others were too weak to fly. Most were killed and stuffed by humans for the holiday.

Bernie: OMG James it's a recession for birds too! Or is it a recession in our thinking? Or is it a sign of the times?

There were signs all over the Bronx which read "Seagull served today". (Roasted Seagulls were on Bronx menus.) Their feathers were used for pillows sold on "THYPILLOW.COM". Their voices are stored in capsules of brutal history.

Trickle, Trickle, Trickle crumbs falling from a table do not an economy make; only the ready, the willing and the able can knead the dough to make a cake.

"They will never make a seagull sandwich out of me!"

These were all the last words beak-carved on a wall by Hurricane Seagulliga (a jet black seagull from Africa) before he escaped from his prison cage in a rundown Harlem slaughterhouse near 127th st. and Amsterdam Ave.

He is a fugitive now. There is a $10,000 Smart Bird Award for his capture. Some believe he fled to Cuba. Some believe that he is somewhere off the coast of Costa Rica. Others say he is hiding somewhere in the People's Republic of Harlemia and that he roosts 3 nights a week on the roof of the National Action Bureau (NAB) just to listen to the jazz that's played every Thursday, Friday and Saturday night next door at the Pelican Club. His favorite blues is *Bah Hum Bug Baby Recession is for the Birds Bah Hum Bug Baby Recession is for the Birds.*

So, my feathered friends, it's easy to tell a human being's parking lot is a seagull bird's hell. What would you do if you were a seagull?

Tale of the Shell

(The Frog of the Ocean and the Frog of the Well)

Once upon a time in the East of Nod there was a frog named John Solomon who lived in the sea and by the sea. There were seven oceans at that time but frogs lived in only five of them. Two were left for future use and for very special or rare visitors.

Now John Solomon was a gentle frog, a wise frog and a curious frog. In fact, he was King of all of the Frogs of the Ocean and of all of the frogs who lived by the seas. John Solomon was always reading and exploring and he always wondered about the worlds beyond the sea, beyond the worlds in the sky and the wonders of the land.

For example, there were frogs in the sky called rain frogs but none of them ever lived long enough after they fell into the ocean for King John Solomon or his court to examine them. Rain frogs act just like giant sweet blue rain drops . They melt just like raindrops falling in the sea. They bounce just like raindrops falling on your head. Five seconds to fifteen seconds are as long as they last. Some falling "rain frogs" turn into sea frogs. Others do not. This was one of the mysteries of East Nod.

One day, one of those rain frogs was trapped in an air bubble .He survived seven minutes, long enough to explain that the rain frogs

DR. JOHN "SATCHMO" MANNAN

come from one of the seven heavens and that there were other frogs in the universe, even in Nod itself.

Hearing this, King John Solomon, whom we shall often hereafter call "the Frog of the Ocean", became more interested in discovering whether there were any frogs who lived in other parts of the Land of Nod. For him, everything in Nod was "inner space". Everything out side of Nod was "outer space".

Finally on the ides of May, the Frog of the Ocean set out with an ambitious expedition to find out if there was frog life in the great and magic Land of Nod. He packed his ideas in the suitcase of imagination, said his prayers and assembled five of his most trusted servants: I Frog the Knight of the Eye, Hear Frog the Knight of the Ear, Touch Frog the Knight of Feelings, Taste Frog the Knight of Judgment, and Smell Frog the Knight of the Nose that Knows Good from Evil and Right from Wrong.

To travel, the Frog of the Ocean and his five trusted servants, called the Council of Common Sense, all took their positions in the Royal Dream Pods (made of seaweed and moon beams).

They pushed off gently toward the west, where each night the sky meets the lonely Sea of Darkness. Due west with all deliberate speed and cautious heed they sailed. Soon they were out of sight, when they passed gently on the right the island of Musat, an island where all music goes to rest after it is played.

Nearby, thereafter, lay the island of Tora Denka where curtains of the day descending meet turquoise nights of dreams unending. Here dreams are bundled, wrapped in small photons of light and sent to billions of dreamers each night by Star Dust Express and Serenade Satellite.

Our adventurers passed these two islands and five other smaller islands on the right. Seven in all. All outposts of the night that disappeared in the mystic mist. Tora Bora, Tora Yama, Tora Mora, Tora Qalam, and Tora Zora (where hails The Mystic Kiss of the Sea Maiden).

Deeper they sailed. Oh so deeply they sailed into an unknown abyss-into the silence of the rhythm of the bleakness of the sea. Steadily, they sailed into the silence of the rhythm of the bleakness of the sea. Madly, they sailed into the dashing and dancing rhythms of the bleakness of the Sea of Darkness.

Mightily, they prayed that they would be safe from harm. But nothing could they do to avoid the storm that would suddenly appear like a monster of treachery hiding in the lair on the lee side of history.

The sea was upset! The Royal Dream Pods were spectacularly in danger of immediately capsizing. Sea owls and sea wolves, who usually feed on small fish called "Slims", were circling round the Royal Dream Pods, looking to make a meal of our peaceful friends.

The cruel unkempt winds did not conceal their contempt as they descended from above to stir the sea like a giant spoon. It was a spoon-stirring wind that seemed bent on dissolving the Royal Dream Pods as if they were 6 simple lumps of sugar being stirred in a giant hellish drink, or else 6 precious diamonds washing aimlessly down the sink.

Round and round, the water churned as if the sea were a bottomless black coffee urn percolating a rancid smell that seemed to ascend from some sea born hell. Round and Round the wind spoon-stirred and stared and stirred and stared.

Then the spoon of the wind suddenly reversed its direction and the ocean swelling from below defied gravity's eyes and rose up high. High it rose up to a place where the sea actually meets the sky. And the voice of many waters ascended to the heavens to stand like columns, 5 columns holding up the atmosphere or 5 watery sentinels posted by an unseen command.

"Do not fear!" yelled the Frog of the Ocean over the swelling sounds that swallowed them. "We must be very near where we should be. For surely at the borders of worlds, the edges collide and so we must be on another side of NOD."

"We fear not, your Majesty!" the five servants sighed-those Knights of the Ear, Touch, Nose, Taste and Eye!

Their journeys and missions were just beyond these giant watery columns which, acting like 5 fingers of a hand, tossed the Frog of the Ocean and his 5 knights upon dry land. Yes, they were still alive, but they had landed on the Beach of Forgetfulness.

After they had awakened on the Beach of Forgetfulness, they actually forgot to anchor their Royal Dream Pods to the ropes of reality, and their Dream Pods drifted far away into the deep purple of night.

"How would they get home again?" they thought.

But the King, the Frog of the Ocean, did not worry. He was a frog of science and a frog of great imagination. And when science and imagination get together, many problems can be solved and many new things are possible.

So they traveled a short time together on the <u>Plain of Dreams</u> until they came to the Lake of Good Fortune, and there they ate a final meal of fish together. Whereupon the Frog of the Ocean assembled his five knights and sent them out to see what they could see, and find what they could find and report back. Each of the 5 knights bravely scattered in 5 different directions, promising soon to return and reply. Their duty was not to flinch or sigh. Their duty was to search or die; to advise and devise a way forward when the mind meets a challenge.

Good Common Sense, the illustrious five knights, can only serve the alive mind, which thrives on good advice and counsel in all its affairs. They protect and provide for a king if the king does only one thing: Call them and send them out and about to scout ahead of all important decisions. The Frog of the Ocean was wise to deploy his knights ahead of his face in that wild and restless place called Nod!!

Now, let me explain that the Land of Nod was partly desert and partly oasis. It was a land of lakes, a "Plain of Dreams", a "Forest of

Feelings", all topped by 7 Blue Mountains called the "Mountains of Reason" or "The Mountain of Reasons", choose your pick.

The land of Nod is a fully occupied nation of the mind. Rural and Municipal, Cosmopolitan and Mundane, Sophisticated and Original, Urban and Urbane ideas are types of citizens who live next door to random odd thoughts. Some ideas live in mansions. Others occupy crowded cerebral apartments where information is stored.

Facts that you learn in school may live next door to rules that you learn from your parents. One lives in a crowded apartment, the other in a palace type mansion.

Yes, Nod is a nation state, a notion state of the mind, which is at once fully awake and partially asleep or reclined. Nod has its rush hours and traffic jams. It dwells between night and day and calls neither its master.

Keep in mind that the universe is mental and all things that we see once were ideas; just as grownups were once upon a time children. In Nod, mind is over matter and the mind sits on the thrones of imagination and contemplation of real life situations.

In this unexplored part of this world of Nod that John Solomon, the Frog of the Ocean had never known, sallied forth the brave knights of THE COUNCIL OF COMMON SENSE from the throne. They sallied forth to discover something new, as knights of common senses often do. Were there other frogs in Nod's inner space or were they alone the only race?

After wandering a day and night from the throne of his master, the Knight of the Eye was the first servant to come back to his master.

"Dear Master," he exclaimed "I have seen a town of talking plants armed with sharp spikes and short thin swords. Master, I have an eye, but only you and your mind have insight or understanding of what indeed I have seen."

"What is your report, whether they be near, far or at the edge of the universe, were there any frogs?" ordered the Frog of the Ocean.

"No master, no frogs did I find. Yesterday I arrived at a town of talking cacti (the plural of cactus)-some of them red, yellow, orange, indigo. Some of them violet, blue and green in hue. They were apparently involved in a town hall meeting where they were trying to elect a new king. I asked whether any frogs could be found. The cacti began to shout and frown and were getting ready to throw their spines at me. 'Gruff Gruff Gruff of frogs we had enough!' they shouted at me."

"Why were they so angry?" asked the Frog of the Ocean.

"These cacti were once frogs," explained the Knight of the Eye.

"But they lost their golden manners long ago and grew non sharing hearts. Fate turned them from frogs into lonely grouchy Cacti. No other plants can survive among them for they drink and hoard all the water, just like they had when they were frogs. Cacti are a selfish breed. They often hoard what others need."

"Job well done, O Knight of Eye. Get rest. We will travel soon."

The next day, the Knight of the Ear returned.

"Master! Master! Master!" he shouted "I heard music, beautiful Music but found no frogs. Master, yesterday I came upon a place only accessible by flute. I could only get there by playing my flute. You see, Master, yesterday when you sent me out, I stopped to play my flute. I was playing my flute when suddenly, I heard the music from a very strange place. So I followed along with the melody, and the song led me to a place called The Town of The Palm Trees. It was a windy Town of Palm Trees, who all were singing and playing instruments, as if they were part of some great jubilee orchestra."

"All the palm trees were lined up in rows, and when the wind blew east they all bowed west and when the wind blew west they all bowed east. I inquired Master whether anyone had seen other frogs anywhere. After listening to their beautiful music, laughing, weeping, dancing and crying, The Royal Palm Tree stopped the music and led the orchestra into a rousing rendition of 'GRUF GRUF GRUF of frogs we had enough!!!' I played my way out of there on my battle flute and now I am back again with you."

"Well done, O Knight of the Ear," exclaimed the Frog of the Ocean "I wish that I had two knights like you. Then I would hear the stars falling before they entered the sea."

Three days passed by like three gentle but swift winds of time, whereupon the third knight, The Knight of Touch/The Frog of Feelings, returned to the Frog of the Ocean.

"Master, Master, Master!!" he cried "I have spent the past 3 days lost in the Forest of Feelings, and there I came upon 3 towns joined together by a triangle road. The first town was a town of dogs who were sitting on memories, the tombstones of their old dead masters, all of whom were dead poets. The dogs were looking for new masters who were scientists, but still they were dogs of poetry. In a prior time, they were 'the dogs of war'. When I pet the dogs, they responded gently but when I asked whether they had seen frogs, the dogs roughly barked 'Gruff Gruff Gruff of Frogs we had enough.'"

"Next, oh Master, I spied a fourth town of strange human like beings that resembled the brown mandrake plant. I saw them all sitting on long stools of solid gold, holding tin cups and pointing to their plant like mouths (as if they were begging for food)."

"I felt badly, not knowing what I could .My eyes flowed like rivers of compassion and they filled their cups. But when I inquired of these beings whether they had seen any frogs, they all pointed listlessly back to the desert chanting: 'Gruff Gruff Gruff of frogs we have had enough.'"

"The third path that I took on the Triangle Road in the Forest of Feelings," continued the Knight of Feelings "led to the Kingdom of Ego-ica. This kingdom had many small towns called 'Turfs'. There are, your majesty, many beautiful human maidens from every direction, north, south, east, west. They were all bowing before and talking to magnificent, 'perfect 10' foot mirrors. Well, the mirrors really couldn't talk back all that much. They could only say two words and a phrase. The words were: 'Yes dear' and the phrase is 'You are the most beautiful!'."

"Additionally, the mirrors seemed to listen intently but only speak after the maidens had bowed before them. None of the maidens had ever seen frogs and they all ran from me after I appeared to them in my frog shape."

"Don't they read books or have any idea that frogs could really be princes or kings in disguise? I told them Frogs look like me. They all shouted 'Gruf Gruf Gruf of frogs we have enough' as if it were some magic potion. And they were about to hurt my feelings, so I left. There was nothing to gain but hurt feelings."

"Well have you served me, Oh Knight of Feelings. Take a rest. We will travel soon." remarked The Frog of the Ocean.

On the next day, Taste Frog, the Knight of Judgment, came back with his report.

"Master, oh your Majesty, you will never believe what delicious scrolls I have eaten in a place called the Kingdom of Dod (pronounced 'Dad' in their language.) They call their place 'the home of the brave and the land of the free' even though there were no frogs to be seen anywhere. I met the king of the Kingdom of Dod but he was a machine! A machine called The Happiness Machine. Everywhere I looked, men were seated in one of two rows which stretched as far as the eye could see. They all sat in a lotus position. They were chanting something as coins spilled out of the hands of the giant Happiness Machine, which itself was shaped like a giant metal man, a giant robot with electronic flashing eyes. One row of stern looking men all dressed in red on the right, were receiving gold coins from the Happiness Machine with their left hands and counting with their right hands. Then they poured the counted gold coins into holes in the grounds called 'Investibules'."

"When the Happiness Machine made its second pouring, they

were eating the gold coins which you could hear chin-a-ling in their bellies."

"The other row of men on the left was dressed in blue. They were receiving coins from the Happiness Machine with their right hands, counting the money with their right hands and giving it away to invisible shadowy beings called 'Compassionites'. These 'Compassionites' transformed the shape of the coins into bricks in a hidden room. They then returned with trays of gold bricks, which they dutifully fed into the belly of the Happiness Machine. These men in Blue were also eating coins on the second run of the Happiness Machine, but you could hear the coins settling in their feet. The belly of the Happiness Machine was like an oven of blazing fire. It greedily consumed the gold bars and left none of it alone."

"I wondered, your Majesty, what the row of blue men did with their left hands which they held behind their backs or hid from sight, but no one would speak nor could I get any information. The hum of the Happiness Machine drowned out so many voices. But when I asked the Happiness Machine itself whether it had seen any frogs it belched: 'Gruff Gruf Gruf of frogs we've had enough!'."

"I was all prepared to leave, your Majesty, but I found a place to eat at the Happiness Museum. There, while being served a delicious dinner of 5 scrolls (baked rolls seasoned by the secret letter "S"), I discovered that the King Happiness Machine had a twin brother in a land far away! This twin brother has only one arm and rules his subjects with unfulfilled iron clad promises. He feeds his unruly subjects a porridge of Words seasoned with the secret letter "s" These sweet words, after being chewed over, are never digested. They are 'words' while in the mouth, but they become 'swords' in the stomach."

"Oh what a cruel, cruel king is he."

"He is not wise like you, O great Frog of the Ocean. But maybe in that land of the One Armed Happiness Machine, there are frogs just like us. But that is speculation. 'Maybe' is not proof! Perhaps is just poof."

"Spoken well, my faithful servant" commented the Frog of the Ocean "rest ye well, we shall travel soon."

On the next day, Smell Frog the Knight of the Nose that Knows reappeared to give his report. "Master! Master!! Master!!!" he shouted three times, "We have won. I have sniffed out the information that we need to guide our sacred journey!"

"Speak, O Knight of the Nose" ordered the King. "What did you find? Where forth did you inhale knowledge? Where forth do you exhale wisdom?"

"I visited the Kingdom of Mum (they pronounced it 'Mom'). It is also called the Kingdom of the Conscience. There, I found 3 Queens; one seated on a globe round like the earth itself, another seemed to be holding up the sky with 2 tent poles, and the third Queen was reading a book called 'The Mother of Books' to 5 school children seated at her feet."

"The Kingdom of Mum, or Conscience, was a most beautifully pleasant and clean place. All of its citizens, who are called Moms, were eager to help you, oh great Frog of the Ocean, and answer all of your questions, including helping you seek out other frogs in the land of Nod. 'However,' the Queen, who seemed to hold up the heaven, said 'you will only find what you are looking for if we leave the East of Nod entirely and cross the Mountains of Reason which divide East from West, Divide Feelings from Thinking and unite both worlds in a higher plane/plane after we cross the Mountain of Reason. That is my report, your Majesty!"

"You have spoken well, O Knight of the Nose." said the King "Let us all prepare to climb this so called Mountain of Reason. Ford we will every stream between us and our dream until the answer surrenders."

Thereafter, the King of Oceans led his entourage over the Blue Capped Mountains of Reason following a steep road called "Faith

Road." The mountain was so high that air seemed to freeze at the summit. It was slippery, even more dangerous than when Hannibal of Carthage crossed the Alps with elephants in 218 BC.

At the top of the Mountains of Reason, there was a King who lived in a magnificent ice blue palace surrounded by glaciers that looked like frozen rivers of diamonds. His name was Will-Fred. He was the King of Will or "Will dom." He had two crazy brothers, Wiki Will and Wacko Will, and a little sister named Princess Goodwill-Jones. After the usual courtesies and inspection, King Will-Fred issued passports to the Frog of the Ocean to pass over into West Nod and what he described as the Kingdom of the Well, a world walled off from other worlds.

"Beware, beware!" warned King Will-Fred. "There is a Queen in West Nod, an Empress who will cut of the heads of strangers. Many have travelled, none have returned."

"Thank you, Your Majesty" bowed The Frog of the Ocean "My Council of Common Sense and I have taken every precaution. We have taken good planning, good deeds and prayer with us as guides and wisdom, diplomacy and patience as invisible ministers."

After 7 days travel and 7 nights travel, the Frog of the Ocean finally arrived in the Kingdom of the Well. Thereupon, he saw a great well in a very expansive desert. As they approached the well in the desert, the Frog of the Well appeared on the lips of the well and spoke. She too was a ruler. She was the Queen of the Well, The Frog of the Well. Her name was Josephine The Priscilla. Sometimes called Empress Josephine. She was quite beautiful but wore an eye patch like a pirate because she only had one eye that could see.

Her entourage of frog servants all wore the dark glasses that you see blind people wear. These frogs had blind eyes, not blind minds. The Queen alone had an eye that could withstand raw natural light. No surprise, for it is written that in the land of the blind, the King or Queen is the one with one seeing eye.

"Royal Butler, indeed these are intruders!" the Queen Frog of the Well bellowed. "They have disturbed my beauty rest."

Thereupon, her helpers surrounded the Frog of the Ocean and his servants like blankets preparing to cover the night, "We come in peace! We come in peace!!" insisted the Frog of the Ocean.

"We only wanted to know if you guys existed…We are simply from two different worlds!"

"Of course I exist!" bellowed Queen Josephine "and I am most beautiful and most wise among the creatures of the Lone One… Why do you seek to invade our peaceful little well?"

"Death to Invaders!" shouted the Queen of Well's army of frogs.

"We come in peace," insisted the Frog of the Ocean again. "We could only enhance your beautiful well."

"Where then are your gifts and your tribute?" insisted the Queen.

The Frog of the Ocean responded: "I have nothing to share, your Majesty, but what your eyes have never seen! What your ears have never heard! Wonders you have never touched or tasted!" insisted the Frog of the Ocean. "The perfume of wisdom is sweeter than a water rose." he continued.

"Listen, intruder! The whole world is in this well, or come to it to drink of my sweet waters…Surely you dare not speak of ghosts, spirits and unverified invisible beings not proven by science. I only respect what I can see, hear, taste, smell or touch," she countered "so show us something of great wonder, for I believe all the important treasures of life are already in my well. My well is this world! Not certainly whatever alien homelessness you came from. I think you will surely die!!"

"Seize them!" bellowed the Queen the Frog of the Well.

Whereupon her 3 armies, led by the Duke of Confusion, Lord Vassal from the State of Confusion, the Duke of Illusion, Lord Vassal from the State of Illusion, and the Duke of Conclusion, The Lord Vassal of Desirable Endings, surrounded The Frog of the Ocean and his Brave 5 Knights. They were greatly outnumbered. All the 5 Knights of Frog of the Ocean drew their weapons in the twinkling of an eye, so prepared they were to die for their king.

The Ear drew its Battle Flute. The Eye its Laser Beam. The Nose its Stink Bomb. Taste its Gut wrenching Spray. Feelings it's Laugh to Death Ray or several assorted weapons, including the Tears-Minator whose victims cried themselves to sleep or into helplessness.

"Sheath your weapons," commanded the Frog of the Ocean.

"We come in peace-No green blood will be shed here today."

Whereupon the 5 knights sheathed their weapons with the same speed they had drawn them. They wanted to fight but theirs is not to reason why. Senses must obey their king or die!!

"Butler, take their weapons" re-bellowed the Frog of the Well.

"Yes, your Majesty" bowed the Butler-a big red bull of a frog was he! The five knights looked at their master for directions. The Frog of the Ocean nodded in assent and away went the weapons of the 5 knights.

"We are your guests" explained the Frog of the Ocean. "In this land of the well you are Queen but in my world and ocean, I am King. Kings and Queens should serve their subjects well." counseled the Frog of the Ocean.

"I own this well," countered the Queen "it is enough I have provided this for my subjects."

The Frog of the Ocean snapped "I can fit, Mademoiselle, 70 million of your wells into one of my seven oceans!!"

"Prove it or die!!" shouted the Queen. "And if I am right," responded the Frog of the Ocean "then your face shall bow to the east and your throne shall bow to the west."

"You will see that I am right when I say the world is in my well. We have all things of value here." the Queen persisted. "My rightness will surely lead to your beheading. We have not beheaded a king in a longtime."

"What if you are wrong?" queried the Frog of the Ocean. "What if the world that one lives in is not the entire world? What if the world of oceans that I live in is only the well of an even bigger world or universe? What if we are all only ideas that once lived in a giant brain? What happens if the sun melts or turns into rain?" wondered the Frog of the Ocean out loud.

"You dare to instruct us?" snarled the Frog of the Well. "We know all the mysteries of the dark. The Rivers of Now, the Rivers of the Future, the Rivers of the Past, all we have explored. We have traversed all with both sail and mast."

"Well, Mademoiselle, may I and my Council of Common Sense explore the wonders of your world?" pleaded the Frog of the Ocean.

"Please, Sir, but I insist you not bring all of your 5 knights with you," the Queen smiled. "You will soon submit willingly to my power."

"Why?" insisted the Frog of the Ocean. "My servants have been disarmed and they pose no threat to you!"

"A lady has to have security!" the Queen of the Well retorted.

"If you must," replied The Frog of the Ocean. "It's your world, as you say."

"I volunteer to remain behind, your Majesty." insisted Touch Frog The Knight of Feelings.

"O my faithful servant!" The Frog of the Ocean replied. "I trust in the Lone One that only good will come from all of this."

Whereupon Touch Frog-the Knight of Feelings was bound and dragged away by the Queen's guards from the State of Confusion. The Frog of the Ocean knew that feelings had not left him for good. Without his feelings, however, the Frog of the Ocean was beginning to feel cold. What would you do if your feelings left you? Without feeling, without compassion, without love, the universe would freeze over. But life must go on despite how we feel.

So the Queen of the Well escorted the Frog of the Ocean to all the rivers that ran in the well and beneath her well. There were seven rivers. Seven rivers in all. There were rivers who never met the sea. These rivers were the fathers of tremendously steep waterfalls. All of the waterfalls were created from these rivers who never meet the sea. The rivers themselves were dammed by strong wooded structures and the calcified hearts of dead well frogs.

Each river also had several cataracts in its stream, and so the river ran blindly, seemingly without direction, in search of a final ocean. Nevertheless, the trip was quite a pleasant excursion (even if it was a little dark). Throughout it all, the Queen of the Well bragged generously that there were no worlds better than hers. She had stored in her Queen-dome many objects that had flowed into the well from rivers of the past (swords, carts, and ancient merchandise) and from the rivers of the future (coding mechanisms, electronic mind pencils, transporter machines, dishwashing robots.)

The Frog of the Well was very proud of all these things. "Now show us your world if you dare." She challenged.

"Your Majesty," bowed the Frog of the Ocean "Please uncork or undam one of your rivers and I will take us to the Oceans of Eternity."

"As you wish" ordered the Queen, for now she was very curious.

Curiosity is the beginning of the journey of the mind. And so, her helpers undammed one of the rivers that flowed from east to west, from the past to the future. The King and Queen and their entourage then boarded boats, made of moon shade and bamboo that floated through the world of wells, through the land of Nod and into one of the greatest of the seven seas in East Nod.

Upon seeing just one of the seven seas, the Queen fainted and was overwhelmed.

"We are all frogs but our addresses are different? I have searched for your well, but you have never opened your mind to search for mine. Open your mind and you will find precious treasures buried in the mine of the heart. Certainly circumstances and time have kept us apart."

Then the Frog of the Ocean showed the Frog of the Well the seven seas.

"What did you mean," inquired the Frog of the Well "when you said my face would bow to the East but my throne to the West?"

"I meant that your heart and mind would be torn between two desires. Your heart would be drawn to my ocean but your mind could not forget the world of your wells that you left behind."

"How do I join two winds blowing in opposite directions?" asked the Queen Frog of the Well.

"Will you then join your throne with mind (mine), Madame Queen," pleaded the Frog of the Ocean "Keep your Well and I will grant you besides ruler ship over 2 of the new oceans that are soon to be occupied. So then our worlds will be completely joined and our two winds will blow in the same direction."

When she awakened from her fainting spells, she was quite surprised to find Touch Frog the Knight of Feelings standing with his brothers I Frog the Knight of Eye, Hear Frog the Knight of Ear, Taste Frog the Knight of Judgment and Nose Frog the Knight of the Nose bowing to the King Frog of the Ocean. And behind them, bowing to the Frog of the Ocean, were her own armies led by the Lord Vassal of Conclusion, and behind him the Lord Vassal of Confusion (except now he was clearly thinking) and the Lord Vassal of Illusion, except now he embraced a greater reality. In addition, the Knight of Feelings aka The Knight Of The Heart had recovered the weapons of his fellow knights, including the prized Battle Flute of the Knight of the Ear.

"How did your Knight of Feelings get free?" queried the Queen "Why are my armies bowing to your throne?"

"By my Majesty's leave I, Knight of Feelings, cannot be separated from my master by chains" responded Knight of Feelings, bowing to the Frog of the Ocean. "Nor can compassion be separated from its object, nor true love from the house of its heart…I converted your armies while I was your prisoner. For if the heart is conquered the city surrenders. I am the Knight of Feelings"

"Enough!" ordered the Frog of the Ocean "I have asked her Majesty the Queen of the Well, Empress Josephine, to unite her kingdom with mind/mine and you, Knight of Feelings, are spoiling the mood." Wherein the Knight of Feelings bowed 3 times to his Lord and took his gentle leave.

The Queen of the Well cried "Certainly, Frog of the Ocean, with all my heart, I will rule only as your partner and not as your servant."

"So be it," ordered the Frog of the Ocean enthusiastically.

"So Be It," exclaimed the entourage of both parties.

So the two kingdoms became the <u>United Kingdoms of Oceans and Wells (UKOAW)</u> aka The United Kingdom Nation of Oceans and Wells (UKNOW).

For her exclusive travel on the high seas of life, the King gave her majesty, the Queen, seven ships: FRIENDSHIP, SCHOLARSHIP, RELATIONSHIP, KINSHIP, FELLOWSHIP, SPORTSMAN-SHIP AND HARDSHIP.

The Queen found HARDSHIP unseaworthy and gave it back to the King for repair. Well, Kings will be Kings and Queens will be Queens UKNOW!!!

And so the Queen Frog of the Well and the King Frog of the Ocean lived happily ever after. Both her eyes became opened and all of her citizens could soon see without sunglasses.

Once in a while, Queen of the Well and King of the Sea would sit on the "Veranda of Spring", on the Isles of History, and watch those strange rain frogs pour down from heaven. They may even have figured out where they came from, but that is another story in itself.

Epilogue

I would be remiss, dear reader, if I didn't tell you about the latest bulletin from Nod. Nineteen golden years later, many things came.to pass. The Royal couple had two children Prince and Princess Frogs, named John Solomon II {Ocean - Meritas} and Josephine {the Magnificent} of Wales.

The Knights of The Council of Common Sense each also found wives and became wealthy. The Knight of the Eye wore glasses but he became The Knight of Insight. The Knight of the Ear wore a hearing aid but he became The Knight of Understanding. The Knight of Feelings became the Knight of Love and Compassion. The Knight of Taste also became Chief Justice of the Supreme Court of UKNOW. The Knight of the Nose became Lord of Intuition and Chief Interpreter of Dreams.

The Lord Vassals of Empress Josephine also advanced quite well. They became the Ministers of The Two Oceans that were once vacant but now teaming with cities of frogs.

After years of SEA-Urban migration and Gentri-frog–cation, middle class frogs were rushing to get back to the city. And of course, those ministers changed their names from Illusion, Confusion, and Conclusion to Clarity, Parity and Charity.

All was peaceful and uneventful until one day, as the Frog of the Ocean and the Frog of the Well sat on the <u>Veranda of July</u>, in the Year of the Frog +7176, when an Ambassador for some foreign star-spangled frog nation led a huge entourage of refugee frogs who were seeking the safety, freedom and prosperity of the <u>United Kingdom of Oceans and Wells</u>. These very ,very tired, very weary, very hungry and somewhat depressed star spangled frogs pleaded that The Frog of the Ocean and The Frog of the Well let them enter into and stay in the <u>United Kingdom of Oceans and Wells</u> without passports.

They claimed that they should be helped because they were indeed victims fleeing injustice, hunger and extreme sadness-called "The Down on Your Own Home Blues."

The Ambassador (His name was Monsieur Seuss) explained that all of those with him lived in a "Dreamocracy" far away, where it was absolutely guaranteed that every frog could engage in "the pursuit of happiness" without being afraid of the frog government.

In fact, it was written in the Constitution of the "Democracy" in the Juneteenth Amendment that even shadows did not have to follow their frog master anymore, or carry the baggage of dancing with a frog's every movement.

Shadows, in fact, were free in this so-called "democracy". They could own their own lily pads, croak after midnight, even read books or escape into the night without reporting for duty the next day.

"There are no other places under the sun where the shadows of things are free from their masters," the Ambassador bragged.

"Why do you come to us?" asked the Queen of the Well. "Shadows are not free in our kingdom and I do not know how to free them, even if I wanted to."

"Well," continued Ambassador Seuss "In a dreamocracy there are 1% 'dream makers' and 99% citizens called 'dreamocrats.' The 'dream makers' make the dreams and the 'dreamocrats' believe in them, but somehow all of us have become servants now to the one armed Happiness Machine and his ministers who live in The Great Log Mansion while we live in frog houses and roofless lily pads. Each of our frog houses by law has a statue or replica of the Happiness Machine in it. We must feed our little Happiness Machine everyday with coins from a fish's mouth. Of course, we had to catch fish from the Huckleberry River to get this coin."

"If we put this coin in our little happiness machine every day, we are able to pay those mean tax collectors. Then we are allowed to keep one fish per household every day. We also earned a chance to win a Jackfish Pot for 1 million coins at the Blue Moon drawing, called the 'Mega Dream Stakes' or a 'Dream Steaks', depending on your spelling."

"Then there is the 'Mega, Mega, Mega Dream Stakes for Life'. You get an artificial log cabin and all the fish you can eat in a lifetime. Naturally, all of us 'Dreamocrats' looked forward to the Mega Mega Mega drawing every Blue Moon day."

"What happens next?" the Queen of the Well inquired.

"The Dream Makers insist now that we each put 10 coins from the mouths of fishes into the Happiness Machine each day to get the same meal, or as an alternative, a tooth from the mouth of the ferocious sea wolf. A tooth from the mouth of the sea wolf is called 'A Wolf ticket'. 'Wolf tickets' are highly desired by the government. They are used to pay the army of the Dreamocracy."

"Not being able to pay the Happiness Machine quotas, we 'Dreamocrats' can no longer believe in our country's anthem: 'A Holler and a Dream'. So we left and told that king of tyranny 'Liberty or death! Gruff! Gruff!! Gruff!!! We frogs have had enough!!!' So please help us SOS (save our frog skins)," the Ambassador pleaded. "We need to move to the United Kingdom of Oceans and Wells."

"How many of you guys want to move into our kingdom?" asked Queen Josephine.

"12 X 12,000 legions of frogs from the order of Anura." replied the ambassador.

Josephine the Queen of the UKOAW (UNITED KINGDOM OF OCEANS AND WELLS) was deeply moved by all of this. Her vassals (army leaders) the former Lords of Confusion, Illusion and Conclusion were also very moved.

However, John the King Frog, who called upon his Common Sense Council of 5 Knights, is still thinking about the ambassador's proposal. Four Knights are against one Knight. Touch Frog The Knight of Feelings is in favor of allowing the Dreamocrats to resettle in UKOAW. The King, for his part, leaned over and whispered to the queen, "My Darling Josephine, there is so much to explore in the inner space of Nod, Gruff Gruff Gruff. Dear Queen of Frogs, I think we have enough frogs here, don't you?!!!"

What would you do, dear reader, if you were King John Solomon or Queen Josephine Pricilla too and Ambassador Seuss asked you?

"And would you, by golly, really free your own shadow too?"

MY GOODNESS! Goodnight dear reader!!!

History & Introduction
to the Ruby and the Pearl

This story comes at last from the Land of Nod after a deep hypnotic sleep. It began in the Land of Lute 35 years ago. Lute is a place that I visited hearing a flute and listening to the voice of Inca singer and Peruvian princess Yma Sumac about 1979.

The world of poets and revolutions underwent changes and so did I I spent an Arabian Night (longer than 1,000 nights) searching for myself, the true voice of my pen and to find the door or gateway that exists between music and the written word.

While in law school, my poetry went into exile until I wrote <u>Tales of The Nightingale</u>. Still, the Ruby and the Pearl (which preceded the nightingale in my heart) slept in me, it seems, for centuries.. Now it stirs from its slumber in the land of Nod, awakened magically and only by the touch of love!

The First Touch we feel in this world coming in and the same touch that we hope to feel going out.

The Legend of the Ruby
and the Pearl

There was once a Ruby
In the Mountain of Love
That desired a Pearl
In the sea
For she was the Pearl of his soul
From all eternity.

It appears he knew her one time
When they were both a speck of dust
Blowing in the cosmic storms of rhyme
That became the world and us.

Then once, once then
They spoke so briefly
Ever so briefly
But so endearingly, tenderly.

And as creation grew
They became separated
One became a ruby in the mountain
And the other a pearl in the sea.

And they never saw each other
Though they had been
The best of friends
And the best of lovers.

And so timelessness begot time, begot time
And they grew further apart
The Ruby dwelling in a mountain
That grew taller
And the Pearl in a sea
That got deeper
With each passing glance of the rain.

But he never gave up hope
And whenever the winds from the ocean
Came to visit the caves of the mountain
The Ruby would ask:
"How is Pearl my beloved, the envy of the sea?"
And the wind would whisper:
"She's locked in an oyster, so far away from thee."

But still the Ruby clung to hope
And never a word doubting spoke
Not even to himself
As he lay there on that rocky shelf.

And the Ruby's love was well known in the sea
Such was the tale of the rivers
That flowed from the face of the mountains
Bringing down the rocks and debris
Of legends built up by time
And hackneyed poetry.
And so the centuries passed on.

And then one day,
One magic day
A young boy "Aziz" and little girl "Aviva" whom he called
    "Bint"
Came to play
Near the cave where the ruby lay.

And the young man was throwing
The little girl's doll in the air
Taunting and teasing her
Almost to tears.
And when the doll rolled into the dim lit cave
She said, "Retrieve it now, you rascally knave."

And right beside the dolly's hair
He saw the Ruby lying there.

"A ruby! a great ruby!" he cried.
And rubbing it on his shirt with pride
He put it inside his pocket
And ran straight home as fast as he could hock it,
Leaving that poor little girl standing there
Alone in the cool sea mountain air.

And that was the end of a beautiful friendship.

Anyway, when the little boy, "Aziz"
Showed his father the great stone
And how the brightness of the ruby shone
The old man scratched his head awhile
And said,
"Allah has given us a precious thing

For this would make a precious ring.
Come, let us put it away
It'll be yours to wear one day."

And time begot time, begot timeliness.
And twenty years passed
And the Ruby lay buried alas
In a wooden chest
Beneath that house
On a knolly crest.

And all the while in that darkened place
The Ruby never gave up faith
Till the day he was struck by a blinding light
That broke the long and sleepless night.

And a voice said,
"I am going to make you a wondrous thing
For tomorrow they shall crown me King
And I shall wear you on my royal ring."

And that little boy had become quite a man
In fact the wisest warrior throughout the land
In that African kingdom of Tetuan.

And in the twinkling of a mystic night
The time finally came
When the Ruby and the man grew great in fame
And from Europe, Asia and Samarkand came
The sick, the whole and the lame
To hear the wisdom of the King
And spy the Ruby's flame.

And so a year passed this way
When came the (feast) of Shamal Nassim Bey
A fabulous springtime holiday
Celebrated on the Ides of May.

It was a custom handed down by hand
That gifted singers throughout the land
Would compete
Displaying some unusual feat
That spoke in part
Of the prowess of their art.

There was a visiting woman from Khartoum
Whose voice could make flowers bloom,
A man from Juba whose voice could tame a lion
And melt a sword of iron.

But the highlight of the evening
Was a young woman of great beauty
Who signed her name:
"The Believing Servant of Allah
Owner of Rubies and the Flame."

And when she sang her song
All the trees bowed their heads
To what sounded like the music of paradise
It's been said.
And all the guests sat like ice
Being melted in the sun
As they beheld the wondrous voice
Of this warm and gracious one.
And her voice wove a web

Over their eyes
So that sleep took some by surprise.

And as she sang, it was not long
Before it seemed that all the birds from Tetuan
Had joined her song,
Or so some say who dreamed
As they listened to the melody
Of that strange, delightful rhapsody
That spoke of heaven and earth
And of God Who bestows dignity and worth.

And the King was moved to tears
And asked,
"What woman is this?
That moves so near my heart
Without my consent?
Certainly this woman is an enchantment
Some illusion of sight
Or either an angel from heaven sent."

And when she had done
He sent for her.
"Woman," he asked,
"Pleasure to see
Who is thy father
I ask of thee?"

And the woman replied
"I am Aviva an orphan who my father denied
I am the servant of G-d, on Him have I relied."

"Then," said the King,
"I will ask thy heavenly Father for thy hand
And make you Queen of half my land…
Tell me who maintains thee?"

"The birds," she replied.

And no sooner had she sighed
When a brilliant blue bird
Four feet in span
Dropped a pomegranate
In her hand.

"You see," she said, "I have no need for thee."

And the crowd gasped at her reply
For anyone who disrespected a King
Could surely die.
This was indeed a serious thing.

"Woman," said the King, "Do you know to whom you
    speak?"

And she replied,
"G-d's pleasure alone do I seek,
And as for thee, it's my belief
That I speak with but a common thief."

"For I knew you once when you were a boy
We were friends before you stole my toy
When you found that Ruby you turned
And carelessly our friendship spurned.

Believe me, my heart was shattered
It's just the principle that mattered."

"Ah," said the King, "I remember well
The story of which you tell.
What would compensate for my part?"

And she replied, "Return the doll for a start."

"This is nonsense, I can't give you the doll
It would be impossible to find it after all."
Said the King.

"Well," she said, shaking her pretty head
"Neither have I my presence to give
I should never forgive you
Long as I live."

"And what, fair maiden,
Would substitute for the doll instead?"
He asked.

"Only a pearl as big as your head
Or one perfect as your ruby." was her reply
As fire flashed forth from her eyes.

"Impossible!" he shouted,
"Be ye gone woman from my sight
Lest I jail you in prison
This very night!"

And as she left
His heart was bereft
His soul was in despair
And even the ruby seemed to lose its flair.

And it stayed that way
Until one day
One magic day
The King said to his vizier,
"Vizier General, drag the sea
And do not fail
Or I'll land you all in jail
Find me a pearl perfect
Large as my ruby without defect.

"By the power of Allah
In the name of Allah
Inshallah (G-d willing)
It shall be done," said the vizier,
As his staff all answered as one.

Two days later the vizier returned
With a basket full of pearls his work had earned,
"My King," he said, "I report to thee
These are the best pearls in the sea."

"Rubbish," said the King, "You have failed
Certainly now you'll taste the jail."
And he tossed the pearls outside.
"Give these to the forbidden swine
Who roam about and on refuse dine
Out! Out!" he shouted.

"But my King," said the vizier
"You should come along with me
For you are an appointed King of land and sea
Perhaps the waters of the world
Will respond to thee
And yield up the mystery
In recognition of thy majesty."

"If Allah pleases," said the King
"Tomorrow morning, I shall do this very thing."

And so in the dusk of the third morning
After he had risen to pray
In that old religious way
The King set out
Just when the sun was dawning about
Before the sea gulls had climbed
To the awning of the heavens.

"Today," he said, "we shall drag the sea
Until she yields up her mystery."

And they'd been rowing seven hours
Along the coastal seas
When they came to a rubied mountain
That towered in the lees,
And the face of the mountain
Was the color of the King's ring
And the King said to himself,
"This is indeed a mysterious thing."

"O Ruby," said the King,
"This must be the place where I found you."

And the Ruby responded
By shining forth its brightest light.
And the King commanded the vizier,
"Lower the net.
Let's see what we shall get."

"Dive!" said the King, "dive!"
Shouting to his five Royal divers
"And don't come back alive
Until you have filled the net with pearls."

And very soon they tugged the line to hoister
To the surface a giant oyster
Whose shell was red in tone
And like the brightness of the Ruby shone.

And when the King opened the oyster shell
He found sitting in the oyster's swell
A pearl perfect of priceless price.

He fell to his knees in prayer
And bowed his head and hair thrice
To his Lord in praise
His face toward Mount Arafat
In Mecca where the Kaaba lays.

Later he laughed like Aziz the boy
"This is the pearl," he cried
As if it was some toy

"This will turn her head."
He was overcome with joy.

And so it came to pass
That the King married the little lass
Of his youth
Aviva Bint Solomon the wise the beautiful the pure of heart
    and eyes

And for her dowry he gave that girl
A truly splendid thing,
A gemstone from that queen of pearl
Carved into a ring.

And this she wore with such great pride
As she walked along by his side
And when they would kiss,
They would hold hands,
And the Ruby would touch the Pearl
And say something like this:
"O Pearl, you are lovely as ever
I never once wondered whether
You were worth 10,000 suns of waiting for."

And the Pearl would sigh like the sea
And say, "Ruby of my heart whom I adore
Please don't say any more."

Epilogue To Legend of the Ruby and the Pearl

The Ruby and The Pearl are Together-Forever
Good deeds and dreams
Should NEVER surrender
Love and patience
Soon will live in splendor

This is true for boys and girls
For young and old
For shy and bold
For rubies and pearls

Like the Pearl
Forsooth, Love is inseparable
From Beauty and Truth

Like the Ruby
Love is inseparable
From Truth and Beauty
Passion and duty

For indeed the brain
Is the husband of the heart
And the heart is the wife of the brain
And in the Divine Kingdom of the Mind
Inseparable Twain they live and thrive

We Poets and Pens
Are mere citizens
Of a quiet mystic place

Floating on a speck of dust
In starlit outer space

Enough! Enough is said!!
Of rubies and of pearls
Say the Creator is most compassionate
"The Lord of All The Worlds"!!!

The Legend of the Palm Tree
and the Cactus

With the name of My Lord, Who created!
The Compassionate, The Merciful
By the moon in her courses
By the highways in the sea
By the ant in the road
By the poem of the tree
This is the story of friends
Who fought adversity, and
About a love that never ends

The wings of the pen often travel from afar.
The butterfly of now is the cocoon of then,
When the sun rode the back of a cow
And the moon the wings of a wren.

Once upon a time, my daughters, when the world was still a whisper and the earth but a little girl, skipping between sunshines and rainbows, there were two friends, the cactus and the palm tree.

They lived in the garden of the world, north of the mountain, and south of the sea. They were the oddest couple you ever did see.

He was thirty feet short, dumpy and bald, without any bristles or spines
at all, except five thin metallic spines. These spines, in addition to being
his senses, were indeed endowed with fine powers of "tel-leaf-pathy."
TEL-leaf-pathos power (sometimes called "tea leaf pathy) is the ability
to transmit and receive messages from one plant mind to another plant
mind within the same species i.e. in this case one cactus to another.
His roots were sound running some ninety nine feet
Below the ground. He was optimistic and never wore a frown

A cactus, he was, of superb intelligence, gracious and kind.
Many a maiden tree found him quite a find.

The Queen of Palms was elegant, demur and fifty feet tall.
Her bark was brown with no defect at all.
She was as slim as summer with a samba waist.
Cluster of dates embroidered her face.
Her African weave, her slender fronds, her resourceful mind,
Her words both gentle and benign,
made the Queen of Date Palms quite a find.
"What do they have in common?" other trees would wonder, in
whispers that at times seemed louder than thunder.
Yes, trees could talk in those days, and still can,
and if the world wasn't oh so terribly loud!
The trees could hear each other above the crowd, above the drone of
planes, the din of mundane. Things, sacred and profane.
I'm also informed they could, it seems, communicate by many other
means, by message birds, by wind-grams, by root cable
and casting shadows, in the sheen of the moon, when they're able.
The cactus and the palm tree did indeed have much they could barter.
They both shared a love of Sophia and water, "Hikma and Maat"
Whatever the name, wisdom and water, it's all the same.
Yes, wisdom and water my daughters.

Wisdom from the birds of paradise, who traveled from afar, and shared
stories from far-off lands, like Asia, Maya and Sudan.
Owls, who held nightly classes in philosophy with other birds,
would find the cactus tree a willing host, an avid student and provost.
As for the Queen of Date Palms, the Osprey and the Albatross
often visited her court by the sea, where they lunched in her shade
and shared their knowledge of history and geography
with parrots who were professors in the Queen of Date Palm's

University of the Trees.

The University of the Trees boasted a five hundred foot courtyard,
flanked by colonnades of Royal Palms. Birds from all over the world
came to "The Court" to exchange ideas.

It was well guarded by soldiers of the Queen. The Papaya Bats, fierce
fighters of the night, were hidden away.
The honey bees patrolled the day, the driver ants protected the road,
with porcupines for sappers.

As for water, the Cactus, King of plants, was the greatest collector and
connoisseur. He drained rains and mined rivers beneath earthen
plains. He could compress three quarts of water into four inches of
space. His favorite downpour was rain number 2,004.

He kept it in the cellar. It was semi sweet, had body, and a stellar flavor
that one could sip and savor, as the setting of the sun reached the
earthen floor.

Rain number 2,004 was also a special time, you see, because during
that rain the roots of the Cactus met the roots of the Date Palm tree,

near a river beneath the earth that runs to the sea.

That was the beginning of a beautiful friendship.

For once the roots of the Palm Tree and the Cactus became established underground, they could set up a "root cable" network to communicate with each other. They did not have to rely on wind grams and message birds to communicate like others. They understood each other. In time too, the Queen of Date Palms also became a great collector and connoisseur of water.

Her dates became sweeter and sweeter, sweeter and sweeter. As this summer of sweetness went by, and the golden dates of the Queen Date Palm ripened and fell, they were found by a colony of harvester ants, who used the ripened pulp for food. The harvester ants discovered that upon eating the ripened dates, their old ants became young again; their Queen became fertile again; and their young ants could fly.

The University of the Trees researched this matter and discovered that the sweetness of the golden dates contained a substance which caused the reverse revolution of molecules, and of the electrons that revolve around the nucleus of atoms in the molecules, thereby reversing the direction of the march of time, and reversing the ancient process of aging for as long as access to these dates could be had.

The sweeter the dates, the more potent they became. Until the Queen of dates ordered 11,000 of her date palms to be planted. These palms became date palm trees. They were called her daughters or "The Virgins of Paradise."

The golden dates became sweeter and more potent. Sweet, so sweet, potent, so potent that she became the envy of the East, the pride of her subjects, and her neighbors whom she ruled by love and respect.

There was, however, another part of this world.
A part where a cruel royalty
reigned by fear and terror,
trickery, deceit and error. And so
West of the Sun, North of the
sea, there dwelt a family
of mighty oak trees where Old
Father Oak was King of the Forests.

He was six hundred years old,
six hundred feet tall and his
mighty branches spanned six hundred feet.
His trunk was sixty feet in girth.
He claimed to be the strongest
tree on earth. He supported
thousands of birds who did his
bidding. Some of the higher rank
lived in palatial Nests,
framed with blossoms and petals
others not so fortunate, made of nests of thatched straw

Some birds were fearsome
bark eaters and wood peckers
whom the King secretly
dispatched against his enemies.

However the King's official
army was composed of
Red Wood Sequoia trees. Trees
so tall that their branches were creepers standing outside

the gates of the first
of the Seven Heavens

Hawks, Falcons and
eagles of war nested
in the lower branches of the
Red Sequoia, All under fealty
To Old Father Oak Tree.

The Vizier of King Oak Tree was an Ever Green
Tree who was stationed some
six hundred yards from
King Oak, Its roots linked with the King's
underground so that old King Oak
was in constant contact with his vizier.

King Oak had been married
twice. His present wife was a
bad tempered but beautiful mango
tree, four hundred years his junior:
whose seed a tern had flown over
from far India as a gift and
tribute to the King. The Oak tree did not
devour the seed but planted it
near himself in the summer of rain
(number 6003).

You see, O reader, the King
simply demanded that tribute be paid
to him by all conquered enemies and subjects
ie. the trees and birds in his kingdom
Tribute took the form of seeds, nuts

and first fruits. The seeds, nuts and fruits were
collected by toucans and
terns, often called tax collector birds,
and were constantly placed as if on an altar in front
of King Oak. Thereupon Oak's giant pincer
roots surfaced and eagerly
devoured the prey.

Failure to pay the King tribute
would be reason enough for the bark
eating birds to be dispatched to
punish the offending trees.
It is written that King Oak's wrath often touch those closest to him.
For example, King Oak tree's former
wife was an elegant Dutch Elm tree
who was dying of a dreaded disease,
When King Oak tree divorced her,
he ordered her to be uprooted
and planted out his sight. It took
sixty eagles and all their might
to move her on a starless night
Lady Dutch Elm was moved to a place
called "The Rings". A place
of dead, deserted things named after
The round circular "Age Lines" in the stumps of trees that can be
read after they are dead,

One can tell the history of every tree this way. Some even believe
that the destiny of tree is inscribed in the rings and in parchment
of dead leaves. Who will the tree marry in the case of a male and
female tree??(like the papaya) How many blossoms and fruits will a
tree bear? How will it fare? How will it die? With whom will it share

its shade? Will it be victim of the blade or the teeth of a beaver? It is most certainly true that such destinies are kept in the Book of Heaven. (The destiny of both the ant and the plant is not unknown.) Indeed all things alive. But this was a world into which men had not arrived. Only plants and ants and birds and such things thrived in this place called NOD.

My Lord shapes and is shaping all things, summer, winter, fall and spring. Man was only a plan in the making. Trees and gardens were first-and so I am permitted to tell this tale-a parable for the wise, a laugh for the young, a twinkle in the eye of those who ponder and thirst for the great wonders of history and of the mind.

Oh the Dutch Elm was so upset with King Oak for his betrayal and so jealous of his New Mango Tree wife that she began to chew her own bark.

"I'll have my revenge!!" she raged and raged and raged... "No matter what the age or the season I will see the Mango Tree burned alive for treason. I will skin her bark alive and also The Great King Oak will regret what he has done to me. Listen to me, Oh you Leaves of the Forest, Mark my Word You Birds of the Trees. The Mango Tree will die and King Oak will flee and I shall be Queen of Everything! Everything!! Everything!! Everything!!" Dutch Elm Tree cackled and cried herself to sleep every night in the <u>Forest of the Rings</u>. The stumps of the trees in the tree cemetery became her friends and every night and every morning she talked to them like this:

"Rings, Rings, Rings of Dead Trees, what future do you see for me?" she would chant. And the rings answered back in reply "Oh Queen Dutch Elm Tree, fairest in the land, King Oak's treachery shall not indeed stand-beware a bright word from heaven and you shall be part of a palace with servants whose job it will be to maintain your great beauty."

"When shall this be?" asked the Dutch Elm of the Rings.

"Behold, one day a visitor shall bring news that renews but beware the bright word from heaven." the Rings replied.

This type of exchange went on every day at sunrise, noon, five, and sunset, and midnight besides. The Dutch Elm Tree was never satiated. Her anger was not ever to be abated. Jealousy, dear reader, is like a green lizard that eats his own scales and anger is a fire blizzard that burns its own maker and makes a slave of those who do not master their own rage.

The time has come. The time has come and I was awakened to continue to write this story, a tale that wags my head, with visions of brightness and dread. There is a sunbird in Nod. There is a moonbird in Nod. The sunbird heard about the famous dates of the Island of Virgins. So he undertook a journey to visit the Queen of Date Palms and her court of virgin palm trees. Now the sunbird is a bird of paradise, a sign of the happiness of life-wherever he visits, brightness brings smiles and optimism to All hearts. Yes, even the hearts of trees. Yes, trees are alive. They can smile or be sad. They can be happy or mad.

So when the sunbird heard about the Queen of Palms and her dates of youth and her wisdom and love of truth, He wanted to see for himself. He traveled over 20,000 miles over sea and land to meet the Queen of Date Palms. He left the rising sun in Japan, China, India, East, traveled over Russia and south to Arabia Felix, went to Ethiopia, Mali and Dakar, far west to Brazil and traveled North still without rest until he reached the Island of Eleven Hundred Virgins, the Virgin Island where the Royal Queen of Date Palms held her court.

The sunbird never got lost. This GPS was the select rays of the sun. Each day he followed the trajectory of one ray that guided him for the day on his way until the sun went down. That's when the sunbird slept and set aside his crown. Now he stood before the crown of the renowned Queen of Date Palms.

"Your Majesty," the sunbird sang "I have traveled far to see if it is true what they, the birds of life, say about you."

"What do they say about me?" the Queen of Date Palms demanded.

"I am only a Tree…The Creator made me and I exist for His pleasure until I return to Him I share all that He has given me, wisdom, pleasure, and poetry. I give fruit. I give shade. I give healing, and I give a poem to those I inspire for I am only a sign to those who read my ways! Peace upon me the day I was born and peace upon me the day I shall die. Sunbird, my palace is your home for as long as you'll stay. Partake of my fruits. Make your nest in any palm of your choosing. My daughter will sing you to sleep and no harm shall come to thee…Just Beware whatever you use leave it here."

"Thank you…" said the sunbird.
"No wonder the winds
speak of your great nation."

"Fruit, O sunbird, I was born to share
When the student is ready the
teacher appears. Take what
you need in dates from
my daughters" said the Queen
pointing to 11,000 smaller date
palms surrounding her.
"Then drink of water from my
Friend, the cactus, and
you will be renewed."
"But take care," she added
"that you take no dates
with you, lest envy and
greed be spread and

mount up on the wings of war."

The sunbird ate his fill of dates
and drank water from the cactus.
Soon, the sunbird had fallen asleep in
a pile of dates.

As the sun slipped down beneath the blanket
of the horizon, the moon bird
appeared. The Moon Bird, empowered
by night and the lamps of the
night, made a noiseless appearance.

The moon bird had heard about
the sunbird's visit to the court
of the Queen of Date Palms
and he was anxious that the sun bird
have no advantage over him.
So as the sunbird slept, the
moon bird stole by the guards
of the court. Using moon rays
as canards for the image of his flight.
He slipped through the cracks
of the night.

The sun bird could not be awakened at night,
so the moon bird could take what
he wanted of the forbidden dates.
The moon bird ate as much as he
could, wrapped some in banana
leaves and flew off to find the
cactus and his famous water.

"O Cactus, Kings of plants,
In the name of the Queen I demand
that you provide me with some of that
vintage water stored down in your
cellar" demanded the moon bird with a
sonorous bellow.

But the cactus was
immediately suspicious when
he saw the moon bird with
a package wrapped in banana
leaves hanging beneath his breast.
The cactus also knew that the
Queen of Date Palms would
be sleeping at such hour of the night.
"What are you carrying in that package?"
queried the cactus.
"Why that is not your concern!"
the moon bird puffed.
But the cactus, who had
developed a keen sense of smell
for water, recognized the scent
of the date water in the dates
and surmised that it was from
the orchard of the Queen of Date
Palms. He started to give the
alarm but waited. He waited until
he was able to cable the Queen
through their underground root work.
Then he discovered that the
moon bird was an intruder.

Guards! Guards! the cactus boomed.
Out of the seams of the Night
seeped huge flocks of Giant Papaya Bats.

As they approached the moon-bird,
the moon bird flew backward like a humming bird but as fast as a tern.
The Bats meanwhile fixed
their radar screen on the moon bird.
But the moon bird evaded them
When he saw an infrared beam
in the glow of the moon, he followed
it like a thread through the night.

North he went, faster than
the sound of a pebble rippling
in a brook faster than thunder
on the back of lightning,
Or a roar on the wave of the ocean.

The Bats were in close pursuit until
the moon bird, feeling the magical power
of the Dates, pulled away. Away across
the border, west of the sun,
North of sea into the Kingdom
of the mighty Oak Tree.

The bats turned back in formation
They dared not to invade another nation.

As soon as the moon bird entered the
Oak Tree's Kingdom he was intercepted
by a flock of Night Hawks and

Night Falcons. But being King of the
Night Fliers the moon bird out maneuvered
his speedy pursuers, leading them through
a desperate chase through the forest,
bogs and sewers until he came to the
Land of the Rings. There, he was
approached by a squadron of
ravens who offered him safe conduct and haven to the abode of the
Dutch Elm Tree
"You are safe in my branches,
O bird of the Moon" assured
the Dutch Elm Tree.

"King Oak's minions cannot reach
you here, from whom do you flee and
who did you fear?"

"I flee from myself sometimes
the moon bird replied and I fear
offending your highness who has
been wrongfully put away by your
that uncaring oaf of an oak."

"Stay awhile" insisted the Dutch
Elm Tree with a smile.

"You are too kind" replied the
Moon bird "Here's a tribute to
your greatness" The moon bird placed
some dates on the ground
in front of the Dutch Elm Tree.
"This fruit" he continued

"is sweeter than any fruit on
earth. It will fertilize your soul
and renew you with its sweetness,"

The Dutch Elm tree tasted the fruit
and gave some to her ravens.

"Indeed" she said after tasting
it "this date is the sweetest
fruit ever born by a tree."

Immediately she felt renewed,
the boils on her trunk became
healed; the breaches in her bark
disappeared, her leaves became full
"Oak shall soon be mine and this mango tree
firewood" laughed the Dutch Elm.

"You forever have my gratitude, O Lady
Dutch Elm tree" exclaimed the moon bird
"The bounteous shade of your generosity is
eclipsed only by the penumbra of your beauty.
As for the dates, they are guarded by the
best fortification. They may only be taken
in the same manner that the night steals the day.
If not, there will be a great loss of limbs
leaves and wings."

"Leave these things to me," smiled the
Dutch Elm Tree, "Tomorrow I will consult The
Rings, The Rings of History that hold
the mystery of all things that have a beginning."

"That I will do Lady Elm" yawned the
moon bird, "the dawn is now parting the
curtains of the night; weariness surrenders
to none but slumber"

"Sleep on, moon bird" Whispered the Dutch
Elm Tree, "soon the moon and sun shall be
yours and I will have my King Oak and my revenge."

Part II The Plot

The Night gives birth to a thousand plots of the heart every minute. Some are sweet contemplations or good thoughts. But so many
others are brainchildren of treachery and secret arts. And so on the
night of the moon bird's visit to the Dutch Elm Tree, the Night
wore a frown and a million ears embroidered on her gown. Slipping
in the corners of the dark, with ears attached to his heart, was Old
Sleepless Owl. He had sworn allegiance to Dutch Elm Tree and was
one of her advisors. Old Sleepless Owl was also one of the secret
spies working for Old King Oak Tree. Since he was a witness to all
that transpired on that fateful night, he decided to betray his mis-
tress to gain the favor of King Oak Tree.

No one had ever seen Old Sleepless Owl sleep at Night and during day, he was most often awake for 12 hours. Old Sleepless Owl
could not contain his glee when he overheard the Moon Bird's and
Dutch Elm's treasured conversation. He immediately cloaked his
saucer-like eyes, like shades drawn over a window, and stole his way
North, carrying the daggers of a vital secret on his tongue. Secrets
that he meant for King Oak Tree's ears to hear. As a face well recognized in the Kingdom of Oak and as King Oak's special servant,
Old Sleepless Owl was saluted by all the guards as he made his way

to King Oak's palace. There, after being searched, he alighted directly on a listening branch of Old King Oak Tree. Yes all trees have a listening branch just like you have ears.

"Your Majesty," the Owl trembled "forgive my intrusion at this bewitching hour of the night, but my ears have been to and fro and have compassed what you would never know!"

"Speak, bird, Speak!" ordered King Oak Tree in a gruff voice.

Whereupon related the Old Sleepless Owl the transactions of the evening.

"So you hate your boss and you don't want her to be beautiful... Is that right?" probed King Oak.

"No sire," responded Old Sleepless Owl "You are my boss!"

"You are a bird with 2 hearts." observed King Oak "Who can trust you...and where is your proof of the power of these dates?"

Whereupon, the sly Old Sleepless Owl produced a stolen sample of the dates and after pretending to eat one himself, he gave the second one to the King. Immediately, it strengthened King Oak's bark and made him appear as a young tree again-moments later, the effect began wearing off.

After tasting the Dates of Heaven the second time, King Oak Tree's bark became young and supple. He felt the sap of youth flowing freely within his limbs and branches. His yellow leaves became green again and acorn blossoms emerged from his renewed branches.

"Wow!!" he shouted. He immediately had the Vizier tree summon his Council of Six-The Bushido Warrior Tree, The Promising Evergreen Tree, The Gingko Tree, ETZHACHAYIM(the Old Emperor or Kabbalah Tree), The Northern Fig Tree and The Tall Maple Tree.

Each tree intertwined their roots with King Oak and the Conference of the Six Wise Ones began. Wherein the Old Sleepy Owl related the same story he had told the King and when the

Council of Six beheld the youth and vigor of their King, they were truly amazed and flabbergasted.

"Who can bring the throne of the Queen of Date Palms into submission to mine (mind)?" queried the King Oak of his esteemed Council.

"I can" replied the Bushido Warrior Tree "The birds in my branches are the bark strippers who have the strongest beaks. They are strong, fast and well suited for the job of making your enemies submit, my Lord."

"No, No, No" said the King Oak "destruction of the Queen and her retinue may lead to destruction of the miraculous quality of the dates. I want control of the quality."

"I will have her uprooted and planted next to you, your Majesty" proffered The Promising Evergreen.

"Same Difference!" mused King Oak.

Then, the "Old Emperor Tree" spoke up, "Your Majesty" he said "it would be prudent to send Queen of Palm's delegates request tribute from her throne Five Hundred Tales of these dates each month."

"I imagine that might work." chimed in the Fig Tree.

"No!" cautioned the Maple Tree "There must be reward or harm. Threat and promise must never be separated-because they are twins born from the same mind...and they have served me well all this time."

"Remember," added the Gingko Tree "this can only work when the threat is very near and the promised reward is not too far off."

"Hmm" mused the King Oak Tree "I will send a brigade of falcons to deliver my messages. Then I will have built by the Robins and Bluebirds a Royal Ark that can be used to collect the date palm offerings. This Ark will be used to collect the tribute every month... and dates must be put in this Royal Ark or vehement war will ensue and we will have them carried off into our captivity. What think you Emperor Tree and Vizier?"

"Ah" said the Old Emperor Tree "Why use lightning when Thunder is just as effective!"

"Agree" chimed in the Vizier.

"Agree," said all the other members.

"As for you Owl, you will get your reward." laughed the King Oak whereupon King Oak Tree had Old Sleepy Owls eyes sewed shut by his terrible falcon surgeons and one ear of Owl's stuffed with beeswax.

"Why me??" shouted /the Old Sleepy Owl "Why me??"

"You cannot be trusted with secrets." explained the King Oak, "One day I will have your eyes restored by our surgeons and your one ear unplugged but until then you will be my guest at the palace."

Whereupon, the falcons tied down the wings of Old Sleepy Owl with strong spider web ropes and tied him to a pillar in Forest Palace-a palace made of the tree bodies of his enemies.

"You Dope"" laughed King Oak Tree "you still have hope!!"

"Ha Ha Ha," King Oak Tree laughed insanely until the whole sky and forest seemed to shake with his laughter.

Old Sleepy Owl just wept with regret while being tied like a stalk to the pillar of time in the heat of the day and the chill of night devoted to insidious crime and plots.

Very soon, the crafty Lady Dutch Elm Tree came to know that her esteemed citizen, Old Sleepy Owl, had betrayed her. He was missing from both his secluded night perch and the day cage to which he never returned in the morning. However, Lady Dutch Elm's Blue Scent Tracking Birds trailed Old Sleepy Owl's scent to the border of the King Oak's Forbidden Circle, the so-called "Tree-A-Gon" sector.

The "Tree-A-Gon" is the official neighborhood where all of King Oak Tree's advisors and ministers were planted. They were ranked in concentric circles, according to status/value and their nearness to King Oak Tree's confidence and trust. The most trusted were planted closest to him. Sometimes, those trees gifted with wisdom who might be traitors or poplar (popular) in the forest were planted in the "Tree-A-Gon", so that he could watch their movements closely, especially the kind of birds who might visit them.

For in the world of trees, birds and their loyalties could make the difference between maintaining a foliage fulfilling life and the stump status of death.

The forensic evidence culled by the Blue Scent Tracking Birds showed that Old Sleepy Owl had even traversed the <u>Inner Circle of the Council of Six,</u> and that he had probably spoken directly to King Oak Tree himself.

When Lady Dutch Elm Tree got the shocking report, she got so angry that her bark boils returned. Horrid, red patchy spots the size of golf balls of anger popped out of her skin all over her bark.

"I have to get to those blessed dates before King Oak!" she screamed. She consulted the tree rings immediately:

"Rings! Rings! Tree Rings of Fortune" Dutch Elm pleaded among the tree stumps that were at once her oracles and deliverers of constant advice. "Speak to me, O Tree Rings! Do you see Blue Skies for me in light of Old Sleepy Owl's wretched Treachery?

The rings answered "Oh Queen, Queen Dutch Elm Tree, fairest of the Trees among the wooden throng. Alliances, Alliances, Alliances!!! can make even spider's webs strong. And does not the spider among have the flimsiest kingdom. Send Thy BA (spirit) south quickly, O Lady Dutch Elm, let it flee to Queen Date Palm Country, and the dates that you seek will indeed be brought near to thy power."

Now, dear reader, the BA is one of five parts of the soul, according to ancient scientists, among the trees and later, among men who studied in the valley of the Nile. The BA part is the impression that you make on the world. You as the world sees you, not you as you see yourself. It can be partially captured in a picture or a hologram and sent to faraway places if there is a way of transmitting it.

Lady Dutch Elm Tree, being from the royal line of the Dutch Elm Dynasty before her failed marriage to King Oak, knew how to make BA transmitters.

Once Lady Dutch Elm understood the oracle of the rings, she weaved a "BA" vessel from 3,000 of her own leaves. This took her 3 days, and it made her look bare like a winter tree in early Spring.

Next, she ordered that the moon bird be jailed for "his own protection". Actually, she did not want to be betrayed twice. So the moon bird was literally put on ice (dragged by Falcons to the snow chamber of a cave deep in the forest of feelings). She planned to de-ice him later. Actually, he could survive 5 years in frozen suspended animation. Unless he was imprisoned in a glacier. Then he could be preserved thousands of years.

The race was on. The Dutch Elm sent delegates of 18 Ravens to the Virgin Islands who flew her BA vessel, or transmitter, so that she could hologram her image through the vessel to the court of the Queen of Date Palms. Of course, this is a very ancient tree technology. Trees today have lost the art of the organic hologram.

Shame, Shame, Shame what civilizations have done to Trees nowadays. Nowadays, trees are imprisoned like criminals on tree lined streets! Surrounded by vile concrete walls called sidewalks they are shackled and tortured by the urine of dogs or else deprived of freedom of association on plantations called botanical gardens where they are forced to parade their beauty for donations. Please forgive the rantings of this admirer of trees. Down with arbor–cide!! Men and trees need a tree-ty (treaty).

"What brings you to our beautiful island?" the Queen of Date Palms asked of Lady Dutch Elm Tree. Appearing via her "BA" before the throne of the Queen Date Palm Tree, Lady Dutch Elm screamed "Treachery! I warn of Treachery!! Treachery! A treason! against decency, your majesty, that stirs a lady tree's soul," bowed the Dutch Elm Tree in her hologram.

"Continue, Lady Dutch Elm, my council and I are listening." responded the <u>Queen of Date Palms.</u>

` "Old King Oak is planning to make vehement war against your esteemed domain and steal the legacy of the golden dates for his selfish aims. He will first demand your tribute or your death but the conditions of his tribute make death look most attractive." advised <u>Lady Dutch Elm Tree.</u>

"What then do you propose?" asked the Queen Date Palm.

"If you please, your Majesty, that I seek to form an Alliance with you and that I put my <u>War Ravens</u> at your command, I have 15,000 fierce ravens and crows in my defense force."

"What do you want in return-15,000 tales of golden date palms?" sneered the Queen of Date Palms with a frown. "And I suppose that the golden dates that you sampled were stolen by that criminal, the moon bird, from my realm. He violated international law by taking stolen goods across the line of international waters.

"It would be nice if your most generous majesty could assist me, considering that I am sick. Your Majesty, and only you can treat the Dutch Elm Tree Disease that King Oak thrust upon me...Look upon my boils, your Majesty. Only your date palms heal them. We lady trees must stick together. "continued Lady Dutch Elm Tree.

"I know that you are a woman tree scorned by the one she loves." added the Queen of Date Palms.

"You are well informed" sighed Lady Dutch Elm. "I confess that I hate King Oak for his meanness and his Lady Mango consort makes me sick!"

Then, Queen of Date Palm turned to the Cactus and the other Minister Trees that were cabled into her roots.

"What say you, Cactus, to this strange offer?"

Cactus replied "Oh, my Queen, it is a dangerous offer. However, when Kings enter a small country such as ours, they seek to utterly destroy it! So we must bide our time so as to prepare a good defense. Accept this ladies offer of assistance temporarily. Give her some dates, but watch her carefully! I will also begin to build my origami decoys-of 20,000 paper birds that we will fly as false kites drawing an attack upon them by King Oak's war birds. We need 3 weeks to make these decoys, for verily war is deception. When King Oak's warriors engage these kites, they will find themselves forever stuck to the bird attractive sticky tar that I'm placing on each and every of those kite-birds. I need 3 weeks to train the mongoose warriors how to make and fly these kite-birds."

"What do you say, Hoopoe bird?" asked the Queen.

The Hoopoe bird was one of Queen Date Palm's favorite counselors. She deeply loved the Cactus and the Cactus loved her also, but in matters of decisions she tried to keep a cool head (called "Coco Noggin" in the tree Caribbean).

"Your Majesty," said the Hoopoe "I have travelled to and fro and so have my spies. We have seen and assessed King Oak's military might. King Oak has under his command 30,000 bark strippers, 10,000 root eating birds, or sappers, 15,000 scout birds, 5,000 leaf eaters and 10,000 Engineering Birds or Math Birds plus an army of brown tree eating moth We cannot match such numbers in battles unless war is fought on battlefields most advantageous to us and that, your majesty, is not here."

"And where would that be?" injected the Cactus "I suppose the Bermuda triangle, or one of 12 magnetic vortexes of the world."

"Not a bad guess," said the Hoopoe "for over a vortex all things not radar guided will be swallowed by the earth's magnetic field and disappear."

"I'm thinking of a vortex called the Sun Dagger that stands between here and the North" continued the Hoopoe "some 20 degrees west and north of this location .So if we send our radar guide day bats north as decoys we can force the enemy to fight us over the Sun

Dagger vortex. Our day bats will escape the magnetic maelstrom by use of their unique radar."

"Wow," said the Queen of Date Palm "You guys must figure this out. I have this crazy, tricky Lady Dutch to deal with."

"Agree" the Hooper and the Cactus chimed. "Leave it to us, your Majesty!"

"Now Lady Dutch Elm…your wish is granted. Please deliver your 15,000 Ravens and Crows within three days. We will house them on the island of St. John until their services are needed, if and whenever King Oak attacks."

"Done" said Lady Dutch Elm through her BA.

Meanwhile, the King of Oak Tree finished the Royal Ark and sent a delegation with the letter of surrender and allegiance that he wanted the Queen of Date Palm to sign with sap from her own bark. The agreement called for her to deliver 500 tales of golden date per month as tribute and to accept King Oak as her one and only King forever.

The Queen of Date Palms sent back a request for mercy and 100 tales of date palms to King Oak as a gift. Attached, the Queen wrote a note saying that she had to consult The Judge Tree and her lawyer birds before she signed any international treaty.

Upon learning the Queen of Date Palms had not immediately submitted to his power , King Oak Tree began to prepare his army, an invasion force containing 20,000 Bark Strippers, 10,000 Fire Generating Falcons to drop fire on the enemy, 10,000 root eating birds or sappers, 10,000 scout birds, 5,000 Math Birds who could rebuild any garden-state that was conquered. King Oak decided to give Queen Date Palm 10 days to change her mind.

It was May (originally called "Come What May" on the Tree Calendar) and King Oak wanted to conquer Queen Date Palms kingdom before the Atlantic hurricane season arrived. The Atlantic Hurricane Season, for thousands of years has lasted from June 1 until November 30th.

Meanwhile, the sunbird, also called "The Seeker", found out the truth about the stolen dates and decided to take the case to the moon bird and the evil plan of the King Oak Tree to the <u>G7 Council of Winds</u> for judgment.

The Council of Winds would soon convene at the <u>Annual Conference of Storms, Tempests, Typhoons, Hurricanes and Monsoons</u>. It met in the North of Africa once a year. At the conference, all the winds of the world were registered and met as members of the Justice Assembly. The heavy storms were members of <u>Security Council</u>. There, heavy winds were also members of the G7 or the <u>Council of Seven</u>.

Over them was an appointed master and over the master, of course, was the Lord of Worlds-the Creator, who is Lord over all beings and knows what is open and what is hidden. His truth, which is Truth, sits on the throne of the true reality, which no creature can comprehend.

In those days before men, the heavy winds or storms dispatched smaller winds to hunt down fugitive and criminal beings. Yes, back then the winds of the world were more united. The sun bird carefully presented his case to the G7 and accused the Moon Bird and King Oak of attempting to destroy the peace of the earth by their actions and their contemplated actions. The Council of Seven sat in deliberation thinking about sunbirds evidence. They dismissed the sunbird without ceremony and assured him that he would soon see clear and convincing evidence of their decision.

Through intelligence provided by the Cactus via his 5 needle/spine communications with Cactus relatives in the North, the Queen of Date Palms soon learned the King Oak was about to mobilize a 50,000 bird invasion force and send them against her domain in seven to ten days.

Cactus was worried because he only had seven days to construct 5,000 of a 20,000 kite decoy bird order and to them attach the sticky tar-baby mud that would ensnare attacking birds.

Following their plan, he and the Hoopoe Bird decided to send 5,000 giant day bats north toward the Kingdom of Oak Tree with orders to engage King Oak's forces over the vortex of the Sun Dagger. North east of Florida, and north of Georgia.

King Oak learned through intelligence that the Queen of Date Palms was about to launch a preemptive strike, so he was determined to strike first. He added another 10,000 birds to his strike force as reinforcement.

The day bats had flown as far as Port of Savannah and when they saw the air force of King Oak Tree. Immediately, the day bats feigned fleeing South. King Oak Tree's forces gave chase. The 5,000-day bats split into 2 forces-one fled over the Bermuda Triangle vortex and one over the Sun Dagger vortex.

They were pursued vigorously by King Oak's army of bird monsters and killers. The bats flew toward the two designated vortexes with all their speed. They were a mite slow. Hundreds of them were torn to shreds in flight by the beaks of falcons and fell from the sky into the arms of Mother Earth. Six Hundred were lost, and then another six hundred, until there were only 3,800 left.

Six Hundred made it to the Bermuda Triangle and Six Hundred to the Sun Dagger vortex. The others were lost casualties. Soon after they arrived over the vortices, the pursuing bird monsters began to get dizzy and fly in circles descending lower and lower until they were eaten up by the swirling sea. The day bats escaped easily using their radar. They headed back to the Virgin Islands. But King Oak's whole invasion force was lost in the sea!!

King Oak's entire invading army was destroyed, but King Oak would not be denied and soon cobbled together a second army. It would take weeks to prepare a second invasion.

Meanwhile, Lady Dutch Elm, sensing opportunity, launched an attack from St. John, not against King Oak but against the Queen of Date Palms, her own supposed ally. Oh what treachery lived in this alliance! Cactus's worst fear was coming true. Queen Date Palm's small army of body guards were not enough to defend her and her daughters. Lady Dutch Elm's forces would take one hour to fly from St Johns to St Croix. and reach the royal palace of the Queen of Date Palms

The Cactus, hearing news of the surprise attack from a Cactus relative on St John island, sent his personal guard of 5,000 Yellow Birds to protect Queen Date Palm.

The Yellow Birds were the originators of Calypso, and when they sing even their enemies would find themselves dancing mon dancing!! And for a while after they finished singing, the calypso music would keep the enemy on mellow mood lock-down.

After he dispatched his personal Yellow Birds body guard (which left him defenseless), he sent TELEAVEPATHIC messages to all Cacti in his family on the islands of St Croix and St Thomas to send their security birds to defend the Queen. Next, he ordered the mongoose to fly the kite birds over the palace surrounding Queen Date Palm, 1,000 kites at a time, upon first seeing a wave of an attack.

Lady Dutch Elm Tree's forces, seeing the kite birds, believed they were being counterattacked, and she had lost the element of surprise. However, much of Lady Dutch Elm's forces were being sucked in by the kites and falling from the sky. The rest started to fall into the ocean over Shoy Point and Buccaneer Beach.

Then the Yellow Birds began to sing and the Falcon enemy and the Lady Dutch Elm army began "dancing", not dancing, but "DANCIN".

All day, All night, they danced until the Dutch Elm Army of birds fell asleep. Then the Sleepy night species of mongoose cut their throats.

Now, all this did not protect poor Cactus. There was no music being sung by Yellow Birds in his neighborhood where he was planted. So Lady Dutch Elm's Army scouting division tore the body of the unprotected cactus into 13 different pieces and scattered his body throughout the entire Virgin Islands.

The Queen of Date Palms was devastated when she realized that she had won the war, but she lost the love of her life-poor old Cactus. She had the Yellow Birds find and gather the 13 pieces of his body that had been scattered and prepared for his funeral.

At the funeral the sky began to darken. Leaves and debris were circling over the horizon like shadows.

It was a hurricane!

A terrible hurricane, coming out of the sea!!!

The winds soon reached 110 miles per hour. The wind rain turned coconuts and mangoes into bullets of mighty power. The winds blew and blew and blew. A second hurricane was on its heels. The palm trees and tropical trees knew what to do. They would just bend their knees and bow their heads to the King, or the Creator. The 2 hurricanes were headed North toward New York. Soon they would arrive upon the gate of the Kingdom of the Oak Tree and they gathered off the coast of Long Island and challenged him to reverse his evil ways.

But King Oak replied arrogantly "I am what I am. I am King of Trees, I never apologize" His wife, Lady Mango, was just as arrogant and told the hurricanes "Go back to Africa!"

Then the two hurricanes joined forces and destroyed many trees in King Oak's "neck of the woods". Suddenly, King Oak and his Mango Tree wife were picked up and smashed into so many pieces that they looked like a children's jig-saw puzzle.

Treacherous Lady Dutch Elm was not spared. She was picked up and smashed, however, into 4 neat pieces. Here, tree rings or stumps were blown out of the ground and she lay dead among them.

The moon bird was never discovered

Ole Sleepy Owl was de feathered and seen flying around in circles talking like an idiot. He and his family were confined to The

Bird Brain Mental Hospital, which in those days was called The Bird View Rehabilitation Facility.

Then, there was a solar eclipse. The sky was black for 3 days, until there came from outer space a great light. A great light coming from a capsule. It landed in the Forest of Feelings and then the sun rose like an infant in the east. Out of the capsule stepped 2 human beings.

"This must be earth." said the man.

"No kidding, Adam" said the woman. "This sure ain't like the garden we once lived in. This is a mess!!"

"Give it rest, Eve" said the man. "We have to start a new life here."

"I guess so, darling, it's your fault" she replied.

"No it's our fault" said the man "The Lord of the Worlds said He would help us and we will have a great destiny in this place that He called earth."

"No kidding, Adam" the woman answered "Well, I'm cold. Start a fire and build me a house and find something to eat... then I'll cook."

Adam then spied the body of the Lady Dutch Elm broken in 4 smooth pieces and in three days he had completed a rough house. It was too rough for the woman, who got splinters from the wood.

"Adam" she cried "these walls are hurting. Please make them smooth."

Whereupon Adam found 5 smooth stones and began polishing and smoothing the walls.

Thus the prophecy of the Rings to Lady Dutch Elm came true. One day, servants would shine her face and make her more beautiful.

As for Queen of Date Palms, her scientists found that the roots of Old Cactus Tree, which ran 99 ft beneath the ground, were still alive. They, with help from surgeon birds, reconstructed the pieces of old cactus's body and after 7 days of stem cell grafting, Old Cactus began to yawn and stretch. The Cactus was alive again and as soon as the Queen of Date Palms heard the good news, they both decided to get married so that they would never be separated again.

And so, their roots were connected permanently and they lived happily ever after and so did their children. So ends the story of the Palm tree and the Cactus.

Epilogue

If you ever visit the island of St. Croix of the U.S. Virgin Islands, you would see many instances of the Palm Tree and the Cactus together. They seem inseparable. This is especially true at Point Udall (17 degrees 45'20 N64 degrees 33'55W), the Eastern most part of the United States and the Azimuth of its first sunrise.

Yes, there was love before people entered the world and there was jealousy, hate and competition among plants. But plants always talked to each other. www.bbc.com/.../20141171 (Plants Talk to Each other) See also Dr. David Johnson's work at the University of Aberdeen; see also Krulwic Wonders plants-talk-plants-listen-here-5-how www.Npr.org/sections/Krulwich/2014/04/29/3079811803.

By talking, the trees did not destroy each other as they competed to take nourishment from mother earth. The coming of men meant that many trees would be cut down to build human houses.

On the island of Staten Island in New York, Native Americans found a house built by early humans.

Legend has it that after it was built, the first woman occupant began to loudly complain that the house (the Dutch Elm Wood house) was too small. So a man named Adam expanded it by shaving sheets of wood from the strange ring marked tree stumps that he had seen near by the broken Dutch Elm Tree.

He expanded the walls using these stumps and also made chairs out of them.

Still, the woman loudly complained that the house did not have enough windows. So that family moved and the house was occupied by owls until the Lenape people (Native Americans) acquired the house in 1000 BC. But the Lenape people, after 5 generations, soon abandoned the house. The inhabitants kept on hearing wailing walls that cried in a shrill female voice. This wailing and crying happened every night from midnight until dawn. The owls moved back in.

Next the Dutchman, Pierre Bilou, acquired the house in 1662. He recognized the rare red quality of Dutch Elm Wood with which it had been made and he restored the wood to its optimum beauty. He called it the "Dutch Elm House".

But the voices finally drove the Dutch inhabitants of the house crazy and descendants of the English Duke of York moved in.

The house was passed to Stillwell and then Perine. No one could endure the crying and wailing.

So today the house has come to be called Billou-Stillwell-Perine House. It is located at 1476 Richmond Rd, Staten Island, NY. It is listed today as a haunted museum!

No one has been able to live there recently.

One day, a boy visiting from Holland, named Adam, recorded the following conversation or dialogue heard coming from the walls of "haunted" house. Here is the English translation of what was recorded...

"Oh humans! I am Lady Dutch Elm Tree, Queen of Trees-I ask Why, Oh Why, have 'The Rings' deceived me? Do you think I am beautiful?"

This is the voice recorded coming from the East Wall of the house.

The answer coming from the Western part of walls and the chairs made of tree stumps was as follows:

"O Queen, we are the Masters of the Ring. Did not New York City restore your walls and varnish you not long ago? You, Lady

Dutch Elm, are still the fairest among those who sit on the wooden throne."

"Really?" replied the Dutch Elm East Wall. "I am, I am, I am Beautiful, I am so beautiful, beautiful, and beautiful!!!" and it was repeated again and again like a broken record.

The bodies of other great trees from the era of The Great War between Trees and the arrival of man have long been turned and rendered into saw dust, fossils and star dust.

Whether among plaster or ants or among men, few things change. The play of life at different times has a different name and indeed different actors, but the plot and the parts have not changed in eons. Among men, there are three types of actors times three types. (3X3)

The good, the bad and the confused. The believers, the nonbelievers and the hypocrites. Then there are "the seekers", "the sleepers" and "keepers" of the flame of truth and justice. These are the actors. The world is the stage. On one edge of the stage is excellence. On the other side is pestilence. Excellence is on the right stage. Pestilence is on the left stage.

In the tea leaves of time, The Legend of the Cactus and the Palm Tree will always be remembered as a wonderful story. It is designed to be told around the fire place and it's embers-or at bedtime, or anytime the mind packs its bags to go on a journey. But one thing is certain. Love triumphs as long as trees are blowing in the wind and love sings most wonderfully, riding the back of the wings of spring!

"Author exits stage right!"

The Gift: The Story of the River, The Ocean and The Rain

Part 1: The Setting Sun

If someone gave you a beautiful gift wrapped in a wonderfully attractive wrapping, what would be the consequences of not opening it?

Well firstly, as you might imagine, you would fail to get any benefit at all from the gift, at all. Secondly, others who could have benefitted from the gift would also not receive its blessings. Lastly, "The Gift Giver" might be insulted, maybe angry, about the gift not being opened, used and appreciated. He might scold or reprimand you when he sees you in person.

This is a story about the gift within and the gift without. There is a gift within each person. There is a gift in each human being. A gift that no one else could ever have. It is planted in you like a seed. It's as unique as each snowflake indeed and just as delicate. Did you find your gift?

Did you find it sitting on the couch of your heart? You had not arrived home in the presence of your own mind when Giver gave it to you. So He left it in the living room right there on the love seat of your heart so you'd find it when you arrived.

Search the streets of yourself if you are the restless type. Travel the alleyways and side streets of your dreams. You'll find your gift standing there...standing, it seems, off the corner of change and boulevard of quiet blue moments of the midnight air. People may even see your gift standing next to you and say "Oh my gosh-you have a gift for that."

More likely, however, you'll find your dream sitting silently in the living room of yourself. Alone in the quiet of the dawn, you will see her sitting there on the couch of your heart. Find it! Open it! Share it!! And say "thanks" before the home of the earth. Life is a gift to be shared while there is time.

Part II The Rising Moon

Once upon a time, the heart was a gift placed high on the top of a tall red mountain. For it is written in the scrolls that only the heart can knock at heaven's door. It was placed close to heaven. And so it is written that where the heart goes, the brain cannot always follow. So the heart was placed high in the mountain, immersed in an unblemished and pure lake of chrystaline water.

The waters of the great lake gushed up from a source hidden deep in the soul of the earth. The heart had two servants at her beck and call. In the heart lives the moral sense of the human being about what is "good" or "bad" and secondly, the very compassion center of the human being that is able to show and receive true love. True love, a commodity most hard to find, dwells in the soul of the heart. Now, at the foot of the mountain was placed another great gift. It was a gift carried by a giant who had once towered over the mountain and over the heart. He was called "The Rational brain", and He once thought of himself as absolute King over the emotion, the drives, the senses and all seven provinces of the mind. Some say that till this very day, the brain is still placed above heart but only as a look out, a body guard, a guide, a defender, a knight doing battle for the way of the heart.

As soon as soul learned to walk, the brain towered above the heart. But that was long ago before the brain giant was temporarily turned into a tower of salt in The Epic Battle of the Evil Assault by a master enemy of tricks and illusion. The Master Trickster caused the brain to fall from its high place above the heart. And so the giant brain crashed, temporarily fell down like a Tower of Salt. No one could revive him, it was written, until one day when he would be touched by the kiss of true wisdom and love...Then the brain could regain his balance and the human story could find its way on the straight path.

Meanwhile, there was another great gift that was placed at foot of mountain. It dwelt in the roar of the voice and the voice of the roar of the shining sea. Knowledge was placed on the face of the sea and on the floor of the sea. Knowledge was dispersed in the form of the salt of wisdom and the salt of common sense. These two salts gave the ocean its identity and sense of self and wellbeing. Knowledge and wisdom symbolized by the two salts gave the ocean the roar in its voice and pride in its spirt. The gift of the heart as it looked down from the lake upon the ocean knew that something was missing in her life. The gift in the ocean felt the same way as it looked up at the mountain. The heart was in constant prayer for its peace and satisfaction. The ocean lowered his head every day in a Kowtow position, touching his head and nose to the lowest place of the earth...The lowest part was hidden in the deep ocean, deep in the water, of his thinking. One day, in a storm of desperation, the ocean stood up tall as a 200 ft wave and called to the mountain in a loud and desperate voice. He could wait no longer. "Why do you not come to me, Oh Mountain? I am lonely to talk to someone to share my knowledge and wisdom and receive whatever thing of good that the Lone One has placed in Thee."

The mountain responded "Oh Dear Ocean I know that you are a deep thinker but I cannot move. I am stuck holding my place less the earth slide into your space. But I will send you a gift of sweet water from The Lake of Goodness and Compassion, which is called the heart, the heartland, the land of the heart. You will find her most pleasing to thee."

So the mountain shook and shook and shook and the water of the Lake of Goodness and Compassion began to roll down the face of mountain like blue tears running down a copper checked face. The blue tears stream converged and became a single river that ran down the face of the mountain. It was River of Goodness and Compassion. It was a sweet, sweet, sweet, thrice sweet water. The river met the sea. The two waters mixed and the sea water was heavier than the sweet water. Thus the sea carried the river. He carried her in waves of his arms. The sweet water of the river and salt water of the ocean soon got married. The salt water was the husband, the sweet water was the wife. But sweet water, being sentimental, missed her mother (the lake) and her sweet water family scattered throughout the heartland. She wanted to visit the heartland in the mountain to see them again. So the light of understanding-the servant of G-d visited the sweet water, which floated on the surface of the ocean and took a portion of the sweet water up from the ocean into the sky.

In marriage, the sweet water had become educated and wise. The ocean became calm and loving, like a gentle tropical island sea. Although sometimes, the husband had a temper and caused a tempest or storm. The sweet water of heart was lifted up into the heavens by the sung understanding, travelled over the mountain in a cloud and came back down at night as rain from heaven. It rained and rained in the sight of the moon, the revealer of the unknown things hidden in the dark. Rain benefited to all creatures wherever she visited.

All the creatures of the earth saw sweet water coming from the sky and shouted "Oh sweet water, how beautiful you are and my, my, how you have changed." The sweet water, as rain, was called "revelation". Revelation and rain makes things grow in the 3 places-the land, the mind and the spirit. The seed of destiny that is hidden in the dark drinks the elixir of trust, which will make it flower. Yes, the rain makes things grow-even the mind that ponders, you know. Surely the heart, like rain, is elevated higher than the mountain and ocean where it first began. Rain has been to heaven and back. Rain. She made it to the heavens and her husband, the mind, is waiting for her to come home. Rain is the coming home of the spirit. At night, it often rains in the sea and the river still flows there. Don't worry-she has not gone anywhere.

And so the sweet water and the ocean are in love forever, and the brain and the heart dwell always together. Most times, they live in peace. But sometimes, sometimes, there is an occasional storm. What can one say, even the rose has thorns. Even the lonely, beautiful one growing on the side of the mountain.

Part III Before The Rise of Dawn: The Epilogue and The Reflection

In time (in due time) after a long drought, rain of revelation-the secrets of sky and the earth and of things unknown came down from the seven heavens like the rain of 1,000 months in one inspired night. It fell upon the face of the fallen brain that had turned to salt. The rain was the kiss of true love and the brain began to regain its balance.

"Where is my heart?" the newly awakened brain asked.

"I am here, my husband!" answered the heart. "I am closer to you than your thoughts than light is to the sun and wet is to rain. Where have you been?"

"I was asleep. I was assaulted-attacked by an idea that was not right. I fell and I turned into salt and I could not reach you…Thank G-d for the rain."

"Yes, dear" said the heart, "the rain is a sign of true love. Let's dance in it. Let's sing in it. Our love and balance will only grow in it."

"Now you're thinking," laughed the brain.

"Who, me? I always thought" laughed the heart "I told you what was fair and unfair, what was right and wrong by my feeling." replied the heart.

"But you, dear husband, invited our enemy to dinner-and so he attacked you and we were separated."

"Yes you were right, dear" said the brain "I should have listened to you."

"Yes we should listen and respect each other." chimed in the heart.

And so the two held hands and walked in the rain, singing, dancing, thinking and enhancing their beautiful relationship. And that balance was the place, the setting, of a great, great gift!!

Look around, don't you see the river and the sea dancing in the rain. United forever, the heart and brain! Oh, what a wonderful world. And so, the ocean and the river received a gift from the Giver. They embrace each other enthusiastically.

Rivers can talk, but Rivers do not crawl. Rivers do not walk, River run. Rivers run. Rivers run to meet the sea. The ocean is such a gracious and selfless host of destiny. They are lifted up together to visit heaven and return. Don't you see? Life is one fine sign of love for its creatures by The Divine Mind.

Oh my child what a wonderful night!

What a WONDERFUL DAWN!!

WHAT A WONDERFUL WORLD!!!

Part IV Just After Dawn

Run like the river-sit like the sage/
So look to the
Heaven, as time turns the page
Look to the earth
Look inside to discover
Your worth.
Do not sit in
The wrong crowds
Laugh heartily in life but not
Too loud
Stand up for justice
Extend your arms in love
For the sea stood up
And discovered its heart
In the mountain above
Love and Truth conquered all
Balance and obeying the good
Prevents the salty fall
Of the brain
And be not sad
For there are blessings in
The clouds and
Blessings in the rain

Hamburger Dust Up
Old McDonald vs. New McDonald

Once upon a time, Ole McDonald had a farm in the country in the state of <u>Cownecktocut</u>. Back then, Cownecktocut was called the Hamburger State because it supplied the rest of the nation with cows for restaurants, school cafeterias, diners, etc. Cows were from various species. Some were fat. Some were athletic. Some could even jump over the moon. Some said cows used to be the state bird in prehistoric times, when cows had wings and were called Steertasaurus Rex. Ole McDonald grew up on the farm and knew everything about farm animals, especially cows. On the farm he had lots of cows and cow dogs who watched over the cows.

New McDonalds had a fast food McDonalds Restaurant in the city of Newburgh, in the state of <u>Mass-Food-Chew-It</u>. It was called Mass-Food-Chew It or Mass-Food Chew Bits because everybody knew how to chew and nobody knew how to cook.

Yes of course restaurant owners, that elite class who had graduated from M.I.T. (Mass-Food Institute of Technology), were expert fast food handlers, so called cooks. They were called burghers and ran the City of Newburgh, the courts and even the police department. Ordinary people, however, only knew how to eat in restaurants like McDonalds, Burger King, and Wendy's. And nobody had a stove in their kitchen. It was felony crime for citizens to own a stove in this fast paced town!

The state of Mass-Food-Chew- It, of course, was flat like a desert because most of the people were fat and over time had mashed down most of the hills, trees and grass in the state. New McDonald grew up in Newburgh city and was an animal doctor/veterinarian and a fast food restauranteur who had graduated from M.I.T.

Ole McDonald entered into a written contract with New McDonalds to supply McDonalds "Golden Arches/Hamburger Heaven" Restaurant with fresh cows for 2 years so that New McDonald could make and sell his Quarter pounder Hamburgers. Mr. New McDonalds sold just about 1,200 hamburgers a week. All he did not sell, he ate himself. (Yeah, he was fat!!)

Anyway, a normal steer weighs 1,200 pounds and will yield 350 pounds of meat in steaks, roasts, etc. You could make ground beef out of all of that, but it might taste greasy because of all the fat, gristle, etc. ground up.

If you used only the soft lean trimmings of the cow, you get 75 pounds of pure nonfat ground beef. If each burger weighs 4 ounces (1/4 pound), you would be able to get 300 burgers. However, if you ground up the whole cow (except bones), you would get 1,200 burgers. Well, 1,200 burgers a week is exactly what New McDonald sold in his McDonalds Restaurant.

Consequently, the written contract called for Old McDonalds to sell New McDonalds one 1,200 pound cow each week for 104 weeks. Each cow was supposed to weigh 1,200 pound- no more, no less.

Every week, the contract was executed smoothly. Old McDonald always gave New McDonald his cow, which weighed exactly 1,200 pounds.

Sometimes, Old McDonald would put his cows on an up diet or a down diet. He put his fat cows in a cow gym to make each of them make the mean and lean weight of 1,200 pounds. Sometimes, he would fatten his skinny cows by giving them wheat grass milk shakes from the Dairy Queen Animal Dream Shop.

Anyway, everything went smoothly until Never-worry the 14th 2030, when Old McDonalds sold New McDonald a cow named Jessie that he had imported from the <u>State of Confusion</u> (they used to call that state "AR-Texas" because it followed AR- Kansas in trying to establish an independent billion dollar barbecue sauce economy.)

Anyway, Jessie the cow weighed 1,200 pounds, and New McDonald paid the normal $1,200.

However, when New McDonalds put his newly purchased cow in the <u>Hamburger Holding Pen,</u> Jessie the 1,200 pound cow gave birth to a cute baby calf who weighed just 200 pounds. New McDonald cruelly turned the mother into hamburger meat, kept the birth of the calf a secret and raised it in his cruel Hamburger Holding Pen. He just kept going to the Dairy Queen every day to buy formula to feed the calf organic wheatgrass milk shakes. This went on for 11 months until the cow weighed 1,200 pounds by December.

Well, New McDonalds decided not to buy a cow from Old McDonald that December-because he already had one, the calf whom he called Bint Jessie. Old McDonald was upset and suspicious about the possible reasons why New McDonald might have broken their contract.

Well, the Dairy Queen spilled the secret and told Old McDonald what had happened. Old McDonald was hopping mad because he believed that New McDonald had played a dirty trick on him and mistreated one of his cows, "Jessie", by killing her for hamburger meat and not allowing her to raise her daughter/calf poor ole Bint Jessie.

Also, the contract said Mr. Old McDonald would buy 1 cow every month, every month without fail. Also, as Old McDonalds saw it, New McDonalds had bought 2 cows when he bought Jessie…and that he should pay for the second cow-if not $1,200 then 1/6 the price-the price for 200 pounds i.e. $200.

Old McDonalds also thought that New McDonalds should have returned the calf, or the mother and the calf, after the calf was born. He claimed that Jessie and her calf would have been exchanged for another cow. Old McDonald called New McDonalds a thief, a liar and a cruel man. And challenged him to a duel.

Calmer minds prevailed. The matter went to the County Court of Common Sense Second Circuit in Cownecktocut Old McDonald vs New McDonald Docket 784 Jan 2031. Old McDonald sued for breach of promise to buy a 1,200 lb. cow each month and unjust enrichment, because New McDonald got a 200 lb. calf for free. New McDonald replied that if the cow was pregnant, the calf belonged to him because he bought the mother-and therefore everything inside the mother.

If he had bought land, and the land had gold, he argued that the gold was lawfully his. Old McDonald fought back and claimed that New McDonald was unjustly enriched-that he was able to get 1,200 free hamburgers because he hid the calf and did not disclose the truth.

The Supreme Court Judge of this Old McDonald versus the New McDonald case #789, Honorable Felecia Darling Clementine, has asked you to write an Amicus Brief ("Friend of the Court" brief) to help the court decide who is right and who is wrong. You must give your reasons for your opinion. You must help the court do substantial justice and follow the rules of law in making its decision and determination

1. Who is right and who is wrong, Old McDonald or New McDonald?

What should we order Old McDonald or New McDonald to do so that this never happens again?

The following findings of fact are also given in this time.

XL

Finding of Facts

1. Neither Old McDonald nor New McDonald knew Jessie the Cow was pregnant.

Jessie weighed 1,200 lbs. when she was sold.

The Bill of Sale stated it was Bargain and Sale transactions and Jessie the cow was sold "As Is".

You must consider these laws of business in making your decision.

Law #1

The consumer is usually right in that the seller must disclose what he is selling, including any hidden ingredients in the merchandise.

Law #2

A seller or merchant is responsible for knowing what he sells.

Law #3

No man shall become rich by underhanded tricks or dishonesty and should repay the victim any amount the victim has lost.

Epilogue

Old McDonald and New McDonalds were also not happy with the decision, because their lawyers charged too much money-more than what Jessie and all the hamburgers in heaven are worth! They were also angry at each other for another reason. It seems that somebody called "Mack the Knife", an infamous killer and hired gun, entered McDonald's "Golden Arches/Hamburger Heaven" at 3 O'clock in the morning and set loose a pack of voraciously hungry cow dogs inside of the restaurant.

Well all of a week's supply of hamburgers "went to the dogs"!!

New McDonalds accused Ole McDonald of setting up this atrocity. But Ole McDonald claims that all of his cow dogs were at home sleeping in their beds at 3 AM. (No exception).

So when the two finally met each other accidently one day outside the Dairy Queen, they got into a Milk Shake fight. A Huge Milkshake Fight!! OMG, there was enough milkshake thrown around to make a small milkshake lake in Newburgh town.

Both Old McDonald and New McDonald were arrested for disturbing the peace and other charges. They were both sentenced to 48 hours community service in the city's cow pens.

Well, the cows finally got their revenge on both McDonalds. They ceremoniously kicked Old McDonald and New McDonald to the dark side of the moon.

On the dark side of the moon, is a place where cows rule, yep, and people are their butlers. The people butlers serve the cows grass soup and wheatgrass burgers while wearing grass skirts or pants. The humans are forced to wear T-shirts that read "I am a Coward". Here, the cows eat with special long handle silver spoons and people graze in granola fields. Wow!!

As for the Dairy Queen, she hit her head on an ice cream machine and can't gossip anymore. Her husband the Burger King is still very upset.

I am out of the office so I don't know if she's died or not, but Popeye said the funeral will be at Church's in San Antonio Texas. It's probably just gossip.

Go figure. Ron McDonald wrote about it in his Book "Have it your way-Burger King is a Tyrant" published Fast Food Press New York, New York 2036.

Meanwhile (on earth), cows around the nation are marching on Washington to protest the opening of a new national fast food restaurant chain called "BURGERS R US"!

Melody and the King
of the Ravens

"Heaven raves when it spies a generous soul."

JSM 2016

Once upon a time, there was a very poor girl named Melody who lived on the border of the kingdom of the Ruby City. The Ruby City is a very ancient city known for its gold castles and government buildings with Ruby studded domes. The Ruby City was on the atomic timeline border with another city-a very poor city, but one known for its great and magnificent music and magnanimous culture to wit-The People's Republic of Harlemia.

Melody lived in an old Cold War bomb shelter in a deep cold benighted basement beneath a Harlemia sidewalk grate. She was only 15 years old and she was so poor that she had only one simple cotton dress, a smart looking polyester school frock, a pair of homemade shoes made of thick glossy magazine covers sewn together and a ragged overcoat passed down to her from her big sister. Her big sister had long ago ran away-in an effort to cross the border into Ruby City.

This was, of course, very difficult to do. Most people (thousands who attempted the journey) never made it. Often, they became victims of the emerald toothed alligators who guarded the blood red waters that surrounded the Ruby City or they were torn to pieces by the black falcons or olive owls that guarded city's Great Ruby Gate day and night. Some became victims of the "eating wall" that surrounds the Ruby City. It swallowed anyone who touched it, anyone who reached it, anyone who tried to breach it unless the applicant recited "the magic ruby passwords of the day."

Melody's father had fought to tear down the walls that wa lled out opportunities for the poor to advance out of poverty. He was dead (killed in the Wall Street Wars between the mercenary armies hired by the rich "Rubyites" and the ragtag armies of the poor political revolutionaries). Her mother was blind and disabled.

It seems that "Lady Misfortune" herself had personally set up Melody's table. Of course, there is no such person as "Lady Misfortune". There are only three things that a life must confront-challenges, opportunities and decisions. Those were the words of her father that she always carried with her and, of course, there were other words too numerous to mention.

Melody had two sterling gifts or skills besides her very sharp mind. One was her ability to sing and the second was her ability to bake. Her father had told her before his death, "Melody, always keep two of your skills polished and ready to go. Ready to feed and defend your life. To know only one thing in this world is not enough. Master all that you are gifted for."

Melody's blind mother had taught Melody how to bake and Melody could bake! bake! bake! She could even bake blind folded. Everything that she baked came out superbly delicious. Her mother's indefatigable determination to survive inspired Melody tremendously.

All that she needed now was a chance and she believed that she could bake their way out of poverty. Besides, she had so many creative pie recipes that any boss might gladly pay her way.

Finally, in the struggle to survive and help her mother, Melody was given an opportunity to work for a young businessman, Raymond Shabazz Solomon, owner of the Raymond Shabazz Super Bakery in Harlem. She was assigned to work with the owner's son, Raymond Shabazz Solomon Jr., age 16. She shared her recipes and specialized in baking special dessert pies. These pies were a product line bearing her name (A right that she bargained for):

1) Melody Honey Bean Pie Supreme
2) Melody Supreme Carrot Pie
3) Melody Irish Dublin Custard (White Potato) Pie
4) Melody Harlem Mango Cheese Cake
5) Melody Squash Pie
6) Melody Pumpkin Seed/Cinnamon Cake
7) Melody Fig Nut Bread
8) Melody Peanut Punch Cake
9) Melody Ginger-Sorrel Pie
10) Melody Eight Treasures Fruit Pie
11) Melody Ginger Meringue Pie
12) Melody Mandarin Orange Meringue Pie
13) Melody Mango Peach Meringue Pie
14) Melody Three Berry (Black, Blue, Boysenberry) Pie

She was very proud of her work and she became good friends with Raymond Shabazz Jr., who was also attending high school.

Working 30 hours a week and going to school as an A student was, nevertheless, a challenge. Melody made just enough money to buy food for her and her mother. The money also helped to pay her mom's medical bills. Melody never complained. She was very grateful to have a job and to be able to test out her own pie recipes. As part of her pay, Melody was allowed to take home 5 loaves of bread 2 times a week.

Five loaves was too much bread to eat, so Melody thought that she might trade it for other stuff that was needed such as: coal or wood chips for the old coal burning furnace that was in the shelter space, or fresh drinking water and toiletries such as toothpaste, etc.

One winter afternoon, Melody was walking on her way home from the bakery. She was walking in the midst of a very windy, wet and temperamental snow storm. A very wet snow was spilling out of the sky like a spilled pitcher of curdled milk that messily covered everything. Trying to navigate those sloshy and slippery streets, Melody lost her footing slightly and fell forward. As she fell, a large brown (once warm) loaf of hero bread tumbled out of her bag onto the cold white December sidewalk…A gaggle of crows (seven to be exact) descended upon the brown (once warm) bread and snatched it from the cold embrace of the snow. The crows quickly kidnapped the loaf and carried it off to a deserted alley not far from Melody's destination. Her soon to be warm hole beneath a grate on the snow covered streets of Harlemia.

"Well, those birds must have been very hungry." Melody surmised with a wistful smile.

She continued walking, until she reached the <u>Harlemia General Store</u> and traded in the remaining four loaves of bread for coal, wood chips and other items. The next time she got 5 loaves and headed to the <u>Harlemia General Store</u> to get supplies, she stopped at the same spot, waited and left one loaf of bead on the ground for the hungry crows.

Crows in the city always patrolled the urban byways and highways of human sympathy, seeking assistance. Their natural habitat had been destroyed by intrusive human industry.

So each time Melody received her 5 loaves of bread, she faithfully left a loaf or half loaf in the same spot where she had seen the gaggle of crows. Each time, the seven crows seemed to be waiting. They descended to the earth and carried away "the bread of life" to members of their waiting families.

This pattern went on twice a week, through 90 days of winter into the ides of March (March 15th)-the predawn of spring and thereafter once a week until the ides of April.

A funny thing happened one day after the ides of April. The seven crows descended, but there was an 8th bird with them. He was obviously a Black King Raven with a unique ruby red breasted coat of feathers. He appeared to be the leader of the crows. He was much larger than any crow and the seven crows treated him with such great respect.

Ravens are indeed rare in the city and she knew of none with a ruby red breast. The Raven flew over to Melody and dropped out of his mouth right in front of her a large gold nugget. Melody, seeing that it was intended for her, was quite surprised and thankful. She didn't know what to do.

"Thank you, Mr. Bird." she smiled. The Raven cawed in Raven speak but Melody did not understand bird language.

She ran home as fast as she could and hid the gold nuggets in an auxiliary storage bin for coal underneath the bomb shelter furnace. This bin had never been used. It was a small emergency wall bin-long ago deserted.

Nevertheless, coal is coal and gold is gold and it's not often that the two minerals ever meet in this life. The gold nugget immediately confronted the coal nugget who called himself "King Coal":

"I don't know why that stupid girl put me in here with you guys. I am gold. I am an aristocrat, royalty and the eminent crown of minerals. So I am better than you. I belong with my own class and kind. You coal nugget guys are losers; Otherwise, you would have been chosen to become diamonds a long time ago!"

"Not so," replied King Coal. "We belong to the auxiliary division of the Knights of Coal. We coal nuggets have been deployed by heaven to keep humans warm by being fuel for a master furnace. Or a furnace which is our designated master!"

"Ha Ha Ha," laughed the gold nugget "you fools will soon be condemned to die in the fire, but I will be treasured forever!"

"You are an arrogant fellow indeed," replied King Coal "The fire takes us to heaven because we are serving the Creator by whom we were given existence to keep humans warm!"

"When more of my gold family comes," sneered the Gold Nugget "you will be cast out of this bin of existence."

"Don't brag, Gold Nugget!" cried King Coal "You have become a reason, or excuse, for humans to kill each other-so do not be arrogant, but be among the humble, grateful and wise Everything on this earth has dignity: the little leaf, the mere seed and the mighty tree cannot claim superiority one over the other. So you debase yourself with arrogance, my brother mineral!"

The coal nugget (a King Coal soul) extended his hand in friendship to the gold nugget.

"Don't touch me with your dirty hands!" yelled the Gold Nugget. "I am not your brother mineral."

"I will not touch you brother," replied King Coal "but destiny surely will."

The meeting of lumps of coal and nuggets of gold is quite another story. There are a million stories, love, hate and fate going on all around us, but we mostly focus on our own existence in our sliver of time.

Naturally, Melody was puzzled about the origin of the gold nugget, but she counted it as a blessing from G-d. The next day, after trading her loaves of bread for coal and leaving a loaf for the crows, Melody encountered the King Raven and the seven crows again. They brought her another gold nugget, slightly larger than the first gold nugget. This pattern went on for 25 days until Melody had accumulated 25 gold nuggets. All of them she hid in the auxiliary coal bin beneath the old bomb shelter furnace in the hole where she lived.

Spring finally came with her entourage of warm days. Finally, the birds began to rebuild their nests and Melody gathered up the 25 nuggets and brought them to a gold smith/pawn broker named Sal. Sal owned a pawn shop on 125th street. Melody wanted to have the nuggets assayed or evaluated as to how much they were worth.

"Two Hundred Four Thousand." barked Sal the goldsmith as he examined the 25 nuggets. "That's all they are worth."

"Dollars?" asked Melody.

"No madam, pennies!" the goldsmith screeched back sarcastically.

"Let me keep them for safe keeping." the goldsmith insisted. "I will give you a receipt for them…that will be safer for you rather than these nuggets traveling around with you."

"Ok," sighed Melody reluctantly after examining the receipt thoroughly.

The next day, the goldsmith (who knew the 25 nuggets of gold was worth over two million dollars) hatched an evil plot to take Melody's gold to his bank, turn it into cash and escape his business and residence in the city. The bank was suspicious and refused. Sal was so angry. But he was more greedy than angry.

He placed one gold nugget-the oldest one-in his safe deposit box in the bank as an emergency reserve. It was the first nugget Melody had been given.

He intended then to call a taxi or Uber car and go to the airport. He could fly to Pirate City, Panama and hide Melody's gold there. So he stuffed 24 of Melody's nuggets back in the bag.

He closed and padlocked his pawn shop and was on his cell, calling a car. Fortunately he did not get very far.

He came under attack from 24 angry crows directed by the King Raven, and was forced to drop the nuggets and run blindly into the street. His eyes and face were smarting from the bird bites.

"I've been robbed!" he shouted "I've been robbed!! I've been robbed by crazy black birds."

He ran into the police station. However, the police thought that he was blindly insane and dropped him off at the Harlemia Hospital Psychiatric Center. There, he was chained to a bed in a room with a renown madman named <u>William Sheik Sabir.</u>

On Friday afternoon, Melody stopped by to feed her raven/crow friends as usual. She was shocked when her bird friends returned a sack full of 24 nuggets to her (only one was missing). The red breasted Raven gave her a note which looked exactly like the same receipt that she still had in her pocket from Sal the evil goldsmith. It read: "This is from Heaven, by the way, Be Grateful, Be wise. And the melody of your life shall be sung by heaven"

In the ensuing months that followed her new stroke of fortune, Melody purchased a home for her mother and the best healthcare money could buy. She located her lost sister. She helped to build a new library at her school; a soup kitchen for the poor and an urban bird sanctuary.

She even discovered how to make waterproof shoes from glossy magazine covers.

Lastly Melody opened her own bakery.

When she finished college, she got married to Raymond Shabazz's Solomon Jr. She and Raymond Shabazz Solomon Jr. started a pie factory based on Melody's unique recipes. Eventually, there were 24 pie factories and hundreds of employees.

The pies became so famous that they were even exported to <u>The Ruby City,</u> The Turquoise City, The Sapphire City and other bejeweled cities located on Great Ring Finger Island. Thousands of pies were delivered each week by teams of 24 Black birds or "4 and 20 Blackbirds" in British speak. {Actually, they were crow delivery crews, not Black birds.)

These entrepreneurial birds had even established their own corporation by hiring a mouse lawyer named "SOLOMON BROWN" Their business was called "UPS or "UPPS"" (United Pie (Parcel) Service).

So many others were inspired by Melody's story that new family businesses sprouted up like roses all over Harlemia.

These new Harlemia businesses produced exotic food products, newly designed clothing, music products robots and many other things that the citizens of the Ruby City sought to buy by any means necessary.

Soon, the gates of the Great Ruby Wall were opened to trade between the two people: the Rubyites and the Harlemites.

Trade is a builder of bridges and the matchmaker between the groom of peace and bride of prosperity.

Epilogue

Now, that first arrogant gold nugget did not fare so well in life. He ended up in a cold lonely safe deposit box in a bank vault. Sal, the owner of the safe deposit, died in jail and the gold nugget in the safe deposit box was forlorn and long forgotten. Locked away, this gold nugget was not able to shine for 1,000 years.

One day, however, a very poor bur brilliant orphan boy named Warith Green was playing among the old walls and ruins of a once towering bank building. A crumbling wall almost fell upon him as he discovered a bright shiny box buried beneath all the rubble and detritus of a ruined civilization. When the poor boy opened the box, he ran home as fast as he could.

"Aunt Malady, Aunt Malady, I found gold! I found gold!" he yelled at the top of his lungs. Aunt Malady (his guardian) was poor and unable to speak, due to a birth defect which rendered her speechless, but she was a gifted composer and collector of songs. When she saw the gold nugget, she wept with joy. She sold the precious gold nugget, bought a house for her and Warith to live in and she scheduled special therapy for her throat.

After the throat surgery, Aunt Malady could speak eloquently and she pursued a career as a singer. Oh, she sang the most beautiful songs. One of them was a ballad about a generous girl named Melody who lived a long time ago.

The gold nugget was purchased by a merchant and ended up in the crown of the King of Blue Landia–a Kingdom where the sky meets the bright blue sea.

Certainly, the Creator is most forgiving. The gold nugget was thankful for after being in the dark for a thousand years and not being able to shine. He had learned a valuable lesson!

As for the king of the Ravens, one of his great great great great great grandsons became an inspiration for a great late 31st century Harlem poet named Edgar Allen Leroy Poe XIV. The poem called "THE HOLE TRUTH" in this book was an ancestor of his inspiration.

Time moves on; circumstances engage in repetition, and men are left with only challenges, opportunities and decisions to meet with their prayers and deeds.

By the token of time, crows, men and ravens share one creation. What affects one affects all. Challenges, opportunities and decisions meet and greet every life. Decisions lead to destiny. Unselfishness leads to happiness and freedom. Value lies in purity of intention. Virtue lies in the remembrance of G-d and resides in the fearless and generous heart.

So it was in the case of Melody, gold nuggets coal and the Raven.
So it was.
And so it is.
And so it may be again!

A Tale Told By An Idiot: The King The Donkey & The Pachyderm

Once upon a time, in merry ole England in 1215 AD, the archbishop of Canterbury made peace between a greatly unpopular king (King John) and a group of 29 rebel barons who demanded a voice in government and limitation of the king's "My word is law" power. They signed a document called the Magna Carta (The Great Charter or Letter of Liberties) which gave lords, dukes, earls and other such august persons the power to advise and check the King's power. This was at "Runnymede", a water meadow in Surrey ole England, right by the Thames River.

This was the putative beginning of Parliament (House of Lords and The House of Commons) "men who parlay" or speak. Parlay means to speak in French, as in "Parlez vous Francais", translated to "Do you speak French".

French had been the official language of the English courts since 1066 when William of Normandy France conquered England. English was still spoken by the masses (the common people) although nearly 80,000 French words came to dwell in the apartments that once belonged to the English language. Words like joy and partisanship were a passionate French couple living in England. Check your dictionaries of etymology please!

As time passed, there was crisis in succession. Twins (two boys) named Andrew I and Andrew II were born to Sophia, the merry old Queen of England.

They were born at a place and palace called "Runny Nose", across from original Runnymede. This is where our tale of fiction begins. Now only one of these twins (Andrew I or Andrew II) could become king. Andrew the First had a cleft lip, an ugly nose and a most punkish un-kingly gait. So the King and Queen shipped Andrew I, the uglier of the two boys, off to America in the 1790's and gave him an American identity. He was lodged with the Jackson family, a renowned Scottish/ Irish family living in South Carolina, who had once supplied generations of butlers to the throne before that dreadful "Revolutionary War".

Andrew II stayed in the royal palace and grew up to be very fond of hunting. He hunted foxes, partridges, pheasants and boars every day. He was a "huntin man". There was one thing that Prince Andrew hated. He hated rain, because rain spoiled his hunting possibilities. He hired a sorceress, a witch and a Native American to make it stop raining. They all failed. So when Andrew became King, he continued to hunt and hunt and hunt, but he hired a <u>Royal Weatherman</u> to predict whether or not it would rain or snow.

They all made mistakes, and he had them all beheaded or locked in the Tower of London until they rotted. Finally, he put out a call for the job of <u>Royal Weatherman</u> and offered 10,000 pounds sterling of gold a year to anyone who could get the weather right. One man emerged who predicted the weather right 18 days in a row. His name was Atrocious Pomp, son of an infamous farmer who the people called "Atrocious Rump". For his part, the farmer was called Atrocious Pomp, because of his 2 foot high hair do and the cheap perfume he wore from Paris to disguise his most ambitious barnyard body aroma.

Nevertheless, the King hired this farmer, "Atrocious Pomp", to be the <u>Royal Weatherman</u> and ordered him to move into the Royal Palace at Runny Nose at once. The king warned the farmer that on the day he made a mistake or messed up the King's hunt-he would be beheaded. The frightened farmer, "Atrocious Pomp", insisted on bringing his donkeys (two of them) to live with him in the palace.

"Why must two crude stupid animals live in my palace?" shouted the King to the famer when he learned about the unusual circumstance.

"Well," said the farmer "I rely on my donkey and his family to predict the weather. When it's going to rain, my donkey's tale/tail stands straight up. When it's going to snow, he farts like a tuba player."

"Well," said the King "I will hire your ass to be the Royal Weather Man, and he will be of those brought near to me. What is your ass 's name?" continued the King.

"His name is 'Jack' and his wife's name is 'Dumb'." replied the farmer. "The two are inseparable." he added.

"Do they all have the same gifts?" queried the King.

"Yes, your Majesty" replied the farmer. "Yes sire, the whole family-their tails go up when it's going to rain and they fart like a tuba player when it's going to snow."

"Move all these asses into the Parliament at once." ordered the King "I will not tolerate asses in my palace!"

Now, dear reader, this is how so many jack asses and dumb asses got their start in government. They came to be members of Parliament, and in the U.S. the same sacred order of nitwits became popular under a man named Andrew Jackson, who famously chose the symbol of the donkey in his campaign literature for president.

Andrew I and Andrew II?

Who in the world said ESP doesn't work?

Andrew Jackson used the symbol of the jackass after he beat the British at the Battle of New Orleans in 1816.

I remember too that a long time ago, Samson killed 1,000 Philistines with the jawbone of an ass. (Judges 15:16) I guess they didn't call "jawboning" filibustering in those days!

Jack asses and Dumb asses in government certainly made people angry but jack asses and dumb asses got only <u>one</u> thing right. They can read the political weather which today is called "the polls." So their place in history and government is firmly assured.

Well, the tale doesn't stop here, because as King Andrew got older he became embroiled in a lot of wars. He desperately needed money to pay his soldiers, feed them and buy arms and ammunition. So he created the post of Royal Exchequer, AKA Gold Digger, also known euphemistically as the Royal Minister of Mines. Professionals were hired to go out in the field and find places where gold was buried. Many men who claimed they could find gold were beheaded by King Andrew, because they failed. The old King put out an announcement offering, 10,000 pound sterling of gold a year and the post of Royal Exchequer/Gold Digger to anyone who had the skill of consistently finding buried gold. Well our friend, Atrocious Pomp the farmer, showed up again.

The farmer was a rich man by now and had moved to India-the Eastern part of the British Empire with the money the king had given him for his asses.

"Your Majesty," demurred the farmer "I have just the trick for you to find all the buried gold you want. My friend's nose knows the gold."

"Proceed" said the king.

The farmer clapped his hands and in walked a Royal Elephant named "Ralph". "Ralph" was put to the test for 3 days, during which he found buried treasure from the Roman Empire, the Greek Empire, the Vikings and the Cavemen. Even gold on sunken Spanish galleons (ships which had sunk in the English Channel long ago), Ralph was able to sniff out.

"Your elephant certainly has a nose for money." surmised the king with a broad smile. "I will make this Elephant and his family the Family of the Royal Exchequer Gold Digger of Mines and give you 10,000 pound sterling of gold a year." The king said to the farmer.

"One request" asked the farmer. "I need permission to take one of the elephant's family to the United States of America. I need you to sign the export license."

"Granted" said the king "you are indeed a strange fellow."

Well, the rest is history. The Elephant (Ralph's brother in law) and the farmer came to America and established a party called the G.O.P. that means "Gold is Our Priority". They believe in "hosing the people" and building wealth (gold). Today you have Elephants on one side of the aisle of history and Jack asses on the other side of the aisle of history.

They all meet together at the Washington and London watering holes or political pubs called "gridlocks". But that is another story. It's called "Gridlock and the Three Barons (Candidates)" or "Gridlock and Thread Bare Economics".

By the way, "Atrocious Pomp" the farmer never went back to merry ole England. One of his descendants ran for president in 2016. He is a famous descendent whose last name is very similar to Pomp's, and he is very rich, a magnificently rich man. He wears a pompous hairdo, lifts and 9 1/2 pounds of cologne. He is admired by millions but his enemies say that he needs a haircut and a horse whipping, but not in that order. He has a penchant for pretentiousness and not to be outdone by his showmanship. Some call him "the Devil's Apprentice"; others call him "The Angel's Banker" but at a manifestly fierce debate, or at a GOP shindig, he always "trumps."

Well, it seems dear reader, that farmer "Atrocious Pomp's" gamble paid off. He could have lost his head, but gained the world. Your writer is not a gambling man. I am not selling any donkeys or elephants. I just know Elephants and Donkeys are here to stay in the politics of culture and the culture of politics, in war in peace, piece and war, from the Champs-Elysees to the "Great White Way".

Never underestimate a donkey. They are not as stupid as people say. Elephants are elegant and cunning, no matter how much they weigh. They too have political agility and can dance a fancy ballet!

The Second Tale of an Idiot:
The Legend of the Ox and the Tiger

Baa, baa, black sheep,
Have you any wool?
Yes sir, yes sir,
Three bags full;
One for the master,
And one for the dame,
And one for the little boy
Who lives down the lane

Once on the Upper East Side of the jungle, lived a Tiger whose beauty and fierceness was world renown. She belonged to a tribe of Tigers called the "emerald tigers" or "the Metal Tiger" family, whose eyes gleamed green as emerald stones.

Originally in the mountains of Japan this tiger roamed, but now the entire earth had become their home. They were great hunters, but with the dispersion of man they became the hunted. For decades, Hunters came from all over the world to hunt this Metal Tiger to showcase their heads on elite palace and hunting lodge walls.

The eyes of these Tigers were crystallized and worn as jewelry and charms. At one point, there was only one tiger left of the entire Metal Tiger tribe. Her grace, her symmetry, her pride, her intelligence inside, did not allow her to be caught by traps set by villagers. Ordinary bullets could not pierce her skin, for these Metal Tigers were said to be born from higher souls sent down from heaven. Only diamond gold or silver bullets mined from human greed, and not need, had a chance of killing her. Arrows or spears whose tips were made of these substances might work also. She was swift, strong and wise. She seemed always two steps ahead of death.

One full moon night, a party of seven villagers caught Metal Tiger napping in the moonlight. They crept upon her with diamond tipped spears lifted high. Then, all at once, she opened her eyes and sprung toward the moon in the sky, eclipsing its fullness like a window shade pulled over the brightness of a street light. The jungle became dark for a few seconds, dark as a purple night. The hunters ran frantically, frozen frigid in fright.

"What tiger is this?" they cried "whose shadow blocks out the moon at full tide."

They ran. They ran as fast as possible for their village, holding their hearts like wicker baskets in frozen hands. The tiger ran too. She knew they would be back in the morning with more hunters. She ran and ran, until she came upon a pastoral land full of sheep and ox. She ran till she came to a wretched barn-old and worn as winter's rhyme. Its wood was dangled and tangled like a weaver's yarn, woven on the loom of time.

She ran inside and almost cried herself to sleep. She was so tired of running and just wanted to rest. Suddenly, she heard a loud thumping on the wall and from a wooden stall emerged a barrel like voice.

"Who goes there at this ungodly time of night?"

"It is I, the Queen of Tigers." The Tiger answered in a roar.

"Queen of Tigers" yelled the stalled walled creature. "It is I! The King of the Ox." the voice replied. "I've always wanted to meet you… I read so much about you."

"Me?" said the Tiger.

"Yes you," answered the Ox. "You are quite a celebrity!"

"I didn't know an Ox could read," sighed the Tiger. "Aren't you afraid I will eat you?" she continued.

"Ha, Ha, Ha" laughed the Ox. "Me, afraid of Tigers? My ancestors drank with lions at watering holes in Africa...No problem... besides, you are too intelligent to attack someone who can help you."

Just then, the two heard loud voices in the night. Trackers' banter. Bright was the flicker of distant torches carried by the villagers, fluttering and flickering in the turquoise winds of the ether of the night.

"Quickly," whispered the Ox. "Hide in this big bundle of hay and do not make a sound."

The Tiger buried herself in the hay as the torches made their way toward the barn.

"No tiger here" concluded the leader "just a stupid old ox."

The Ox had astutely wiped clean the tiger tracks.

"I agree." said one of the leaders of the village.

"She can't be here!" yelled another one from the party of seven village hunters.

"She would have killed this poor old ox."

"That doesn't mean anything." said one of the men. "Maybe she is hiding here somewhere."

With that, the hunter picked up a pitchfork and began to stab the hay. The Ox made his move and coughed up sticky gooey phlegm onto the hunter's face. The angry hunter threw down the pitchfork and yelled at the Ox.

"You stupid old ox. I'm going to come back and make ox stew of you-and you are going to be my last meal before we behead the Tiger and pluck out her emerald eyes!"

"Don't be stupid!" pleaded one of the village men

"Let's go. That Tiger got to be miles from here...How could tiger and ox coexist in the same room?"

The men abruptly left (the leader of the seven villagers still cursing and wiping his face profusely). "Yuck, Yuck, Yuck!" he cursed. "Stupid stupid Ox…One day I'll kill you and make ox tail stew as sure as I live!!"

The footsteps slightly subsided.

"You can come out now!" yelled the Ox.

"Thanks," purred the Tiger. "You have saved me. I've got to leave the Upper East Side of the jungle. Where do you think I can go?"

"Harlemia" whispered the Ox.

"Harlemia, Harlemia, The People's Republic of Harlemia! We can apply for a job at the Circus Soleil. I read they have auditions at Randall's Island, in a place called the Bronx."

"Hey, how come you can read like humans?" asked the Tiger.

"Easy," said the Ox "My master, the boss's son, left newspapers and magazines all over this doggone barn. He used to read out loud and I soon picked up the words…After two years I could read any newspaper that he left behind on my own, and of course I would eat the newspaper-otherwise he'd be in trouble with his father for messing up this barn…So I read and eat newspapers and I digest their contents."

"So what are these newspapers doing all over your stall?" asked the tiger. "Mess! Mess! Mess!!" yelled the Tiger. "This is a most unnatural annoying mess. Even the jungle is more orderly!!"

"I have an idea," continued the Tiger. "I will ride on your back and they will think we're some sort of act. Nobody will ever believe that a Tiger will ride on the back of an Ox."

"Good idea." sighed the Ox. "But I may get tired of carrying you," he laughed "and throw you off!"

"Not funny." replied the Tiger.

"I got a better idea." responded the Ox "you can ride in the back of an old Ox cart."

"An Ox cart, what is that?" asked the Tiger.

"No time for civilization lessons." yawned the Ox…

"We must get out of here." he warned "Those men might come back."

"I agree." demurred the Tiger.

"How about that old wagon over there?" pointed the Tiger with her paw.

"Precisely," agreed the Ox "Now that's an ox cart. Hook it up to my back-fill it with hay and you hide under the hay and I'll pull the wagon down the road until we find a way to get to Harlemia."

"By the way, you are silly and annoying. You don't know how we even get to the heights of Harlemia?" cried the Tiger.

"The only way to Harlemia-the heights of Harlemia," answered the Ox "is to hitch our wagon to a star, or take a river boat up the crazy river of dreams or we can find a guide in the road that can take us via an overland trail. It's called 'The Ox-Bow' Tail."

"Stop bragging and let's find a guide in the road." suggested the Tiger. "I don't like swimming and stars are too far away."

"Maybe stars are really our dreams." said the Ox.

"Maybe, maybe, maybe…you just jump in the wagon, Tiger, and off we go. I'm pullin and you're riding. I am Ox. I am strong."

"Yeah Right! "sneered the Tiger.

So the two new friends meandered down the road. The Ox pulling the Tiger, who had her face hidden under bales of hay/under the veils of hay.

"How did you get into this world, Tiger?" asked the Ox.

"Well, I once had a twin sister," started the Tiger "and we lived inside of this little girl. She was called Little Girl Yellow."

"I was the good tiger living inside the Little Girl Yellow, but my sister was a tiger of evil inclinations or evil thoughts. I fought my sister tiger inside that yellow girl for food every day! Every day!! After a while, that Little Girl Yellow that I lived in only fed the evil Tiger's appetite for evil thoughts. I was starving; I lost tremendous weight.

Not a morsel of good thoughts was being fed to me and surely I would have died if I didn't escape."

"They tell me I am the last of the Metal Tigers who came to the world in this way. I am good tiger thought without a true home. They hunt my kind for my green eyes, my noble status and my balanced vision."

"So, one morning, I left that little girl. I came out into the forest. I ran into the forest and I have been hunted and running ever since from men with diamond spears, gold, silver and bullets."

"Wow, wow, wow!" cried the Ox "I too once had a twin brother, and I lived inside of this boy (young man if you will) called Little Boy Blue. Inside Little Boy Blue, I fought my brother for food. Hey, my twin brother was evil too. That Little Boy Blue that I lived in kept feeding his greedy evil thoughts and fattening my evil Ox of Thought twin brother that lived inside of him."

"Soon, I began to die. So I jumped out that boy and came to live in the world and become stuck in that old barn in that old stall. People always said I was different. My whole life was stalled and I was not allowed to hang out among the other oxen of the field. The family that took me in made me a companion for their son. Of course, being intelligent, I learned how to read. Through reading, I travelled through the world and universe, imagined and real."

"So I am a good tiger and you're a good ox." smiled the Tiger.

"Now let's look for that guide."

Soon, the two new friends came upon an old man in the road dressed in farmer's blue jeans and they asked the old man if he could guide them to Harlemia.

"Harlemia, the city of Refuge," he cried "That's a difficult place to find." sputtered the old man.

"My name is Master Brain, and I've been trying to find my way to Harlemia all of my life…but I'll give it that old college try once more."

So the old man walked with them 3 miles and became so tired that he gave up.

"I'm just an old man." he said "I may go back to my old ways… and as long as I do I will never find Harlemia…so good luck. Don't worry about me!"

"Try hard," said the tiger "not to go back to your old ways, old man, and soon we will meet you in Harlemia!"

Next, the Ox and Tiger and their Ox Cart came upon a young woman crying in the road. She had a yellow ribbon in her hair.

"Why are you crying, Madame?" wondered the Tiger.

"My name is Dame Heart…I am weeping for my soul because of my regrets…I made some bad choices and I'm trying to get to Harlemia-to the Temple of Refuge where my soul can find peace. I'm struggling with myself."

"Don't worry." soothed the Ox "Just show us how to get to Harlemia and we'll try to take you there."

"Thanks." curtsied Dame Heart as she climbed in the wagon. Dame Heart directed the wagon for 3 miles and then she jumped out.

"I am going no further." she cried. "My tears won't dry. I have to learn to forgive myself. Otherwise Harlemia will not open its gates to me. Harlemia is straight ahead. Keep going till you see a river. I can't go any further, but you can! My heart is stirred too heavy with feelings and worries. I have to put my feelings in my pocket and I haven't made any pockets in my dress yet."

"Good luck" soothed the Tiger "we hope you will join us in Harlemia soon."

Next, Tiger and Ox came upon a boy and girl by a stream, which led to a river.

The Ox and Tiger did not know whether the river was upstream or downstream. The boy and girl were skipping 5 smooth stones back and forth to each other on either side of the stream. "This is faith, you greedy sister." said the boy dressed in blue as he flung one stone over the water.

"This is charity, you selfish boy" said the girl dressed in yellow as she flung the stone back.

"Take that. This is judgment." said the boy. "Taste that and get some."

"This is intuition," replied the girl, throwing the stone back to the boy "use your nose, it knows."

"This is understanding," said the boy "hear that." as he flung one of the large smooth stones back across the water.

"Good afternoon," smiled the Tiger "could you two stop just a moment, just a movement? And could you please help us get to the heights of Harlemia (The People's Republic of Harlemia)??"

"Oh, certainly we are the boy and girl who live down the lane. Blue is our sky, yellow is our rain." said the boy.

"Yes, we are the innocence once in every man." replied the little girl. "Our evil ones have left us. Now we are for good. All men are born good and worlds and words remake them."

"Of course we know where Harlemia is. We'd have to cross the river and we too would like to cross over but we can't afford to pay the ferryman."

"Well, lead us." cried the Tiger and Ox together. "Perhaps we can pay the ferryman."

And so the boy and girl escorted the Tiger and Ox three more miles, the 9th mile until they came to the river where the ferry steam boat goes back and forth to the heights in Harlemia.

"All Aboard, All aboard. All aboard the 'A' boat, the Sky Boat .... next stopping at the heights in Harlemia...Paradise, Nirvana, A-hirah... Pay six pence a pair or a song of sixpence for a pair of seats. We are only taking couples today. Only Pairs. Find your partner, find your destiny."

"Sir, we don't have any money!" cried the Ox "Can we sell you this Ox Cart for 24 pence? You can use it to carry your passenger's baggage or hire it out to move people."

"Good idea" replied the Ferry Boatman. "There is profit in helping others."

"Get on Board! Get on Board! Little children" yelled the ferryman "Next stop the heights in the People's Republic of Harlemia!"

So the Ox and Tiger travelled Animal First Class, and the Boy Blue and Girl Yellow sat in Coach taking their 5 smooth stones with them. Soon they all arrived in Harlemia and were then escorted to a place called

"THE IMMIGRATION DISTRICT-OFFICE OF THE WALL His Majesty, The Grand Wizard of Immigration."

"Where did you two good animals come from?" inquired the Immigration Wizard's clerk "and what is your citizenship...I am the Clerk of the Grand Wizard of Immigration. See I have his ALL POWERFUL WHITE WAND OF ACCEPTANCE HIS BLACK WAND OF NO RETURN!!!

"We are citizens of the world!" shouted the Tiger boldly with a roar.

"Really?" shouted the Clerk of Wizards "Well, in that case, go back where you came from!"

"Wait, Please" interjected the Ox.

"Weight broke the wagon!" yelled the Immigration Wizard's clerk.

And the Wizard took out his BLACK WAND and chanted "RETURN TO PLACE OF ORIGIN!"

Immediately, the Ox and the Tiger soon found themselves inside the yellow girl and blue boy with whom they had been travelling.

"Welcome home." said the boy to the Ox. "I'm the house of the soul that gave your birth."

"Welcome home." said the girl to the Tiger. "I am the house of the soul where you were born."

"Our journey is over." said the boy.

"Our journey's over." said the girl.

Soon, the boy's and girl's bodies were transformed. Ox had entered the soul of the boy. His sibling was not home. Tiger entered the body of the girl. Her sister was not home. The boy became an older man, about 40, and the girl became a young maiden, but a woman none the less, about 25.

"My name is Master Brain." said the man. "I was once a boy but now I am a man."

"My name is Dame Heart." said the woman. "I was once a girl. Now I am a woman. The brain is my soul mate. He's best when he listens to me." She laughed.

"We made it to Harlemia!!" they both shouted.

"We made it Harlemia too." said the Ox.

"We made it Harlemia too." smiled the Tiger. "Thanks to Ox not being so bull headed."

The little boy and girl had grown up and reached the final development of their souls at the gate of Harlemia. The Tiger and Ox had returned to their places of origin as types in the human soul. The greedy evil twins who had evicted them from the souls of the boy and girl had been vanquished and exiled from the characters of the boy and girl. Soon, they were all dancing and rejoicing in the heights in the Republic of Harlemia to the joyous music of the soul, drinking Harlemia Shakes and eating Bean Pies and Harlemia Style Steak at Amor Cubano for the Tiger's appetite.

The Master Brain and Dame Heart, the Ox and the Tiger lived happily ever after. Once in a while they had food fights, usually bean pie versus Philly style steak fights. They hardly agreed on what to eat for dinner. What type of food for thought? Every day, however, they shouted from the Heights.

"Praise G-d!

Praise G-d for making goodness and life one happy family."

Epilogue

Man is good and inclined toward good. But there is part of man that seeks to deviate from the path to investigate the harmful and to the test the forbidden.

So this for every good Tiger, he or she is challenged by the evil tiger of wayward thinking.

And if there is a good Ox in Man, for every good Ox there is an evil Ox that challenges the Master of the house to follow him into a greenless pasture. The owner of the soul must evict the dangerous versions of the tiger and the ox from his life so that the good tiger and good ox can return.

In this case, the Wizard of Immigration only sent the good inclination of the soul here in form of the ox and the tiger back to its place of origin in the life of men and women. This is so that society can benefit from the sojourn of the human soul from ignorance to wisdom, from confusion to clarity, from blind faith to informed facts, from mediocrity to the divine spirit of human excellence. So today in lives of that man and that woman of this story, the Ox and Tiger live in happiness because their souls have joined.

Visit the People's Republic of Harlemia someday and you will see Ox and Tiger as the faces of a friendly couple, or a husband and wife holding the hands of a child, or just the magic of a happy face in a magic place.

The Third Tale From An Idiot:
Loofman The Magnificent and The War Against Music

King Insaan was a wise young man,
a wise balanced man was he
12 did he sire by Queen Reza-kia
The 13th was full of villainy!

Once upon a time, King Insaan was appointed the ruler of Land of Wake and the Land of Nod and all in between in the land of Ardustan. His job was to oversee the cultivation and proper utilization of all of the creatures in the land, sky and seas. He was a mighty, just and fair ruler, but most of all, he was compassionate and kind. His throne and palace was established in "The Ruby City" and they were indeed a magnificent pair to see.

The citadel of the throne was called the Ruby Luminescent City, because the palace's brilliant red lit dome lit up the sky like a lighthouse in the sea of the night. Some say that the sheer redness of the dome rivaled the planet Mars ("the red planet") when it made its heralded appearance in the springtime sky.

Each morning, King Insaan led the nation in prayer and then he visited the House of Mercy-a grand hall where he heard the complaints and grievances of any poor and aggrieved persons or creatures in Ardustan. He tried to find answers to all problems. He oversaw the giving away of food and clothing and the building of homes for the needy. Indeed, any of the creatures in the kingdom, even a mouse, could petition the court for mercy.

Each evening, King Insaan visited the House of Justice.

There, he heard the cases against detainees (those who were accused criminals) and any persons who were accused of breaking the peace or laws of Ardustan. If the evidence warranted it, King Insaan punished the guilty, but if there were extenuating circumstances, he showed restraint and allowed healing and restitution and reconciliation wherever possible.

Inscribed in the face, or façade, of the House of Justice was this adage: "After Mercy comes Justice."

By Queen Reza, King Insaan had 7 sons (Adamach, Yaya-Mosiach, Yusufan, Idrisi, Arun Musamu-deen and Ibrahim) and 5 daughters (Eyesha, Earisha, Felicia, Nosita and Tastiana.) By the royal consort Haga Hadiah (his first wife), Insaan sired his oldest son Loofman.

Loofman was strange. A short limp of a man, he was short in stature and a spectacularly short tempered individual. With respect to his miniature stature, his brothers teased him incessantly, calling him "Loofman the Midget".

Of course, this made Loofman very angry and unhappy. In fact, he hated three things in this world: his brothers, nightmares about his height and music He especially disliked the songs of Musea, the blue Nightingale, who sang each morning and night outside the window of the King's parlor

On a clear day, Musea's beautiful voice. could be heard throughout the kingdom. No wonder Loofman chose to avoid the ruby domed palace and decided to stay with his mother, Haga Hadiah instead.

Haga Hadiah lived in a magnificent enchanted castle that she designed herself. It was a castle made of gingerbread and generously surrounded by gardens of giant flesh eating plants. These plants were actually well trained guards that Haga used to keep people away from her gardens and the gates of the castle.

Haga Hadiah was a gifted enchantress who intensely hated King Insaan and his lovely wife, Queen Reza. Haga only lived hoping that King Insaan would die soon, so that her only son, Loofman, could ascend the throne as Master of the Lands of Wake and Nod; Lord of the Ruby City and Emperor of Ardustan.

Haga gnashed her teeth in hatred of Insaan and kept looking for the spell that could lay him low. But King Insaan was a very good man of deeds and prayers, whom G-d, the King of All, protected from Hadiah's spells and her blowing of smoke upon knots and pouring of potions over fire.

Soon, it came to pass that one day, King Insaan and Queen Reza announced that they would be visiting the Land of The Full Moon People far away, in the Land of Nod. It seems that the spirits of The Full Moon People were particularly low at that time.

Strange dreams shared the beds of their leaders night after night after night and haunted the minds of the people. It seemed that many people who slept in their houses in the land of The Full Moon People of Ardustan were dreaming the same dream. Every night, the fields of bamboo shoots turned into large wooden flutes, growing up high out of the earth.

Then, according to the dream, an armored madman dressed in red robes and galloping on a headless white horse, rode by each night and cut down all the bamboo flutes with a silver tipped samurai or flaming scimitar. The flutes bled profusely and covered the earth red in blood.

After the dream, many of the dreamers woke up to discover that the bamboo fields were empty and covered in blood. Just as mysteriously, however, new bamboo shoots would reappear right after the dawn prayer.

In a second dream, many of the birds of the land had disappeared (even cultivated chickens). The voices of birds had disappeared and a chicken was absent from every pot. In the morning, scores of birds were found dead.

All of the people in The Land of the Full Moon were depressed by these haunting dreams and the strange conditions that travelled with them…So King Insaan and Queen Reza (after preparation and prayers) set sail on a journey to visit the Full Moon People. It would be a perilous journey from the Sea of Light to the Sea of Darkness. The Land of the Valley of The Full Moon People lay far away in the North West corner of Nod. The journey would take a full 2 months by sea. During the anticipated short term absence, the Vizier Jafir was placed in charge of the Ruby City, The House of Mercy and the House of Justice.

Time begot time and soon 3 months, and 4 months, had passed. No word was heard from the King Insaan or Queen Reza as to when they had arrived. Then 6 months, and a year, passed and still no word had returned.

Royal Consort Haga Hadiah invoked the Law of Elder Succession, insisting that her son, whom she called Loofman the Magnificent, must be installed on the "Ruby Throne of the Trust". The Law of Elder Succession required the eldest son of the King to be placed on the throne after one year or more of the King's absence.

The Vizier Jafir agreed and so it was ordered and so it was done.

On the day of The Coronation, sad news alighted like a raven. King Insaan and his wise Queen Reza had been shipwrecked and drowned off the coast of the Rainbow Islands in the Sea of Light. They were victims of a violent pairing of sunspot storms and hurricanes who had visited the Sea of Light. The blue Nightingale, Musea, immediately fled the window of the Royal Palace as soon as she heard the sad news. Funerals were held in the absence of King Insaan's and Reza's bodies. Loofman the Magnificent was anointed

King of the Lands of Wake and Nod, Emperor of Ardustan and Lord of the Ruby City. So it was ordered, so it was done.

The first thing that Loofman ordered was that his 7 brothers and Vizier Jafir be locked up and chained in the Caves of Silence.

Loofman's mother Haga, (now called Queen Regent Mother Hadiah) had Loofman's 5 sisters sold into slavery to the wicked Lord Baltimoriani, King of the Nation of Merryland (Land of Crab-Fritters and Pleasure). They were sold for a paltry price of 60 tales of gold each (totaling 300 tales of gold).

The next thing Loofman did was to have his name and image sculpted on the face of every government building, landmark and palace and emblazoned and inscribed on every tale of gold issued by the Ruby treasury. "King Loofman the Magnificent" all of the objects would read. So it was ordered. So it was done!!

King Loofman next closed the House of Mercy and the House of Justice. He also closed the official palace once used by King Insaan in the Ruby City, and he moved the government headquarters to the Gingerbread Castle of his mother. Next, he declared war against all music in all forms in Ardustan. He ordered his soldiers, under the command of Captain Shabazz, to go from house to house and destroy all flutes and all instruments and to cut down all those who played them and who refused to obey orders. Captain Shabazz, himself, was one of the greatest musicians in the Ruby City. He cried when he destroyed his own instruments. But so he thought: his was not to reason why. His was to do or die. So it was ordered. So it was done.

King Loofman was still not satisfied because when he rode with his entourage through the kingdom, he could hear people singing. So Loofman ordered that all people had to stop singing or have their tongues tied or amputated, or else entirely face the dreaded jail of horrors. People became afraid to sing and stopped. So it was ordered. So it was done.

Next, those individuals who had called the masses to prayers were persecuted. The prayer callers were arrested for "Disorderly Conduct" and locked down deep in the Caves of Silence.

King Loofman was not finished yet. He soon ordered that all birds and singing creatures, especially hummingbirds, sun birds and creepers cease singing in 72 hours or face being shot by arrows or confined to cages deep in the salt mines of Ardustan.

Bravely, Shabazz, the captain of the soldiers, refused to carry out these orders.

"This is too much evil, your Majesty.!" Shabazz protested.

Loofman had Captain Shabazz immediately arrested for treason. However, when Queen Regent Mother Hadiah heard of Shabazz's intransigence, she had poor Shabazz turned into stone and displayed in the city square so all could see what would be the fate of anyone who disobeyed her son!

Next, King Loofman issued a decree offering a reward for the capture, dead or alive, of the old palace nightingale who had fled… Yes Musea was wanted for "Treason."

The reward offering gave an idea to The Ruby Throated Hummingbird, who sought and obtained an audience with King Loofman.

"Your Majesty, your Magnificent One!!!" ventured the Ruby Throated Hummingbird. "I can deliver to thee all of the traitors in the land among us, whether they be men or birds, who sing. I am well equipped for this job and I only seek thy permission to continue my life as a beneficiary of your generosity…Just feed me, your Majesty and give me a golden cage and make me of those brought near to thee."

"Granted," agreed the King. "You are now our unofficial spy, so act accordingly. I will have a large golden cage made for you under my gaze and you shall be fed the golden grain of the Ardustan harvest. And be of those brought near to my power but you must never fail me, even once! For the day that you fail, I will surely have you boiled in oil."

"Agreed!" replied the Ruby Throated One. So it came to pass that the Ruby Throated Hummingbird travelled to and fro and discovered many who violated King Loofman's edict against music. Because of his work, many were tortured, jailed and even beheaded for singing until at last, there was silence in the land. Not even the prayers were chanted for fear that a chanted prayer might be considered music by King Loofman.

Meanwhile, the Ruby Throated Hummingbird got fat as a pigeon and demanded that huge mirrors be put in his cage so "he could see his beautiful self", as he described it.

One day, as he flew to and fro, he heard an old cinnamon faced woman singing in an apple orchard. As she sang, all the little green apples on trees turned into red delicious ones, and then into golden delicious ones.

Then she pulled out a large golden flute from a green sash which she carried tied to her back. As she played the huge golden bass flute, a dozen apples turned to solid gold and dropped on the green grass. As she played the golden flute, a dozen more apples turned to gold and dropped on the soft green grass. Her face turned into that of a young beautiful woman. She put the golden apples into a burlap sack and returned to a little green wooden house in the west of the orchard. Her beautiful face shone brightly, as if lit by a heavenly light.

"What power is this?" wondered the Ruby Throated One and flew away to tell the King.

When the Ruby Throated Hummingbird arrived at the castle, he saw throngs of people protesting outside the Gingerbread Castle.

"We are starving." the signs read. "Feed us You need us!!" said another. It seems that with all of the hummingbirds, sunbirds and creepers being confined, food and plants were not being pollinated and so nothing was growing in the field. There was no harvest of food that people could eat. People tried to get close to the castle because it was made of Gingerbread, but the flesh eating plants began attacking them and they were forced to retreat and move farther outside the Gingerbread Castle.

"Let them eat Gingerbread." the wicked Haga laughed, as she sent plates of magic gingerbread to the hungry people. It only made the people sick and many of them died.

The army, under its new commander, Captain Booker Thomas, dispersed the crowd with ruby tipped swords which burned the skin on contact. Finally, when the Ruby Throated Hummingbird met King Loofman, the King ordered "Bring me that woman alive and her so called magic at once!!"

"Yes sir," replied the Captain Thomas "At all costs, Your Majesty."

"Do not fail me." ordered Loofman. "I want to see if our Hummingbird friend lies or is telling the truth."

So the King's soldiers approached the green apple orchard and found the old woman humming. She looked up and started chanting. As the soldiers approached, the apple tree limbs became arms and the twigs became hands. Then the apple arms and hands began furiously throwing apples at the soldiers. As soon as the apples were thrown, new ones appeared in the hands of the apple throwing trees. The soldiers screamed! The soldiers ran, bloodied and wounded. They ran, ran and ran all the way back to the Gingerbread Castle.

King Loofman was furious. "What kind of army are you? You can't even defeat a simple old woman!!!…You idiots capture her while she is sleeping and bring that blasted woman here alive with that golden flute or I will behead you all on sight."

"Yes, Your Majesty." bowed Captain Thomas. So they found the woman asleep at night in the little green orchard house and bound her with strong chains. They carefully grabbed the golden flute. So it was ordered. So it was done.

Chains clanking and bells attached to the chains, the little old cinnamon faced woman was dragged before Loofman the Magnificent, who wore his red royal robes that morning.

"Woman, I am Loofman the Magnificent...did you not know of my war against music?"

"You are a tyrant and a fool!!" screamed the old woman.

"Silence! Or I will have your tongue pulled out of your head!" barked Loofman.

"Then you will never know the secret of this flute." the woman replied bravely.

"I order you to teach it to me." he replied. "I heard it can turn apples into gold and other things."

"Yes it does!" replied the old woman.

"Bring an apple." requested the old woman.

"Bring the apples!" the King ordered his Vizier.

So it was ordered. So it was done.

The old woman sang with a most beautiful voice and with the blade of Captain Thomas behind her neck. The apples turned from green to red and then to gold, and then turned back into little green apples again.

"What Tomfoolery is this!" yelled the King. "I want the apples to remain gold!"

"I need the flute." said the old woman.

"Wait a minute." said the King. "If I play notes on the flute, I can turn apples into gold?"

"Yes, you can," answered the old woman. "but I must instruct you that while you play you must think of magnificence."

"Bring the flute," the King ordered. "and keep your blade on this woman's neck in case of treachery."

Then, finally, the King placed the magnificent golden flute to his lips. He blew hard at first but NO sound.

"Softly," said the old woman. At last, tones came out of the flute.

"Fix your lips like a bird." instructed the woman. "Look in the mirror so you can see the position of your lips."

So the King stood in front of the large mirrors that had been placed inside and outside the Ruby Throated Hummingbird's cage and pursed his lips like a sparrow, and at last a beautiful sound came out.

"Think of Magnificence and look into the mirror at the positions of your lips."

The King complied. Of course, he thought of himself as being "magnificent"!!

He was now beginning to play the golden flute. As he played and thought of himself as being magnificent, his legs started to feel stiff. Then, his arms stiffened and then his shoulders. He stopped because of the pain. Now only his eyes could move. They were the only thing that could still move. King Loofman had turned himself into solid gold!!!

Also, his spy, Ruby Throated Hummingbird, had turned into solid gold.

The old woman's chains snapped and before all stood the most beautiful woman with the most beautiful voice in the world. All of the palace soldiers and staff fell to their knees.

"Let us escape this place." said the young woman and the Captain of the Guard Thomas and all the soldiers followed her.

"Find Loofman's mother." ordered the old woman. The soldiers entered the Queen Regent Mother's parlor and bound her in strong chains. Haga had no time to cast a spell, as she was chained to her bed.

"To the palace." shouted the young flute carrying woman, who was now slowly aging again. The palace was reopened and the young woman ascended the throne. She reopened the House of Mercy and the House of Justice.

Next, she ordered that the treasury be opened and that the freedom of the 5 daughters of King Insaan be purchased from Lord Baltimoriani of Merryland. She freed the seven sons of King Insaan and Vizier Jafir from the Cave of Silence, and she freed all the birds locked up in the saltmines.

The grain hoarded by King Loofman was distributed. The people rejoiced and rejoiced and rejoiced! Finally, in front of the People's Square, the Woman of the Flute played a most beautiful song on the flute, while standing in front of the statue of Shabazz the Warrior in the Square of the Ruby City. As she played, the stones that had imprisoned Captain Shabazz began to break up. Out of the broken stones stepped Captain Shabazz, now alive in flesh and bones.

Next, the Woman of the Flute went to the castle of Haga Hadiah and played the flute in front of the enchanted Gingerbread Castle. The whole exterior wall of the Gingerbread Castle turned into solid gold on the outside, but remained gingerbread on the inside. The furious Queen Regented-Mother had just broken her chains but could not find a way to escape.

Haga Hadiah, using her teeth and hands like a pick and shovel, even tried to eat her way out of the Gingerbread Castle. As she tried to eat her way out of the gingerbread castle, she would encounter the solid gold wall that the mysterious old woman had erected. Haga was trapped!!

"Woe is me!" wailed Haga Hadiah, like a lone wolf as she sat day after day, locked away inside her own enchanted Gingerbread Castle.

Meanwhile, the old woman of the flute announced that Ibrahim, the oldest son of King Insaan, would ascend The Throne of the Trust. This until one day another yet unborn, a man named Nami Abu Naml, would replace him. "I must go away." said the Old Woman of the Flute.

"I am Musea. My father was mathematics and my mother was a poem. I am the Blue Nightingale who sat in the window of the Palace of King Insaan. I have answered the call of heaven and now I assume my true form." Just then, the Old Woman of the Flute changed back into a blue nightingale. She flew away and sat on the palace window and began to sing the most exquisite of beautiful songs.

As King Ibrahim ascended the throne, justice and peace spread throughout the Kingdom of Wake and Nod, the Land of Ardustan and the Ruby City. The birds returned. The hidden grain houses were opened and the people feasted.

The people chanted the prayers to the One G-d openly again. The bad dreams in the Land of the Full Moon People stopped and all people worked together to make the world of the human life a better place. At least for now.

Shabazz, the musician (the former captain of the guard), wrote a new genre of music that delighted the ears and minds of listeners and reminded everyone of the wonderful world that had been given to the human life.

And it came to pass, at last, that there was Peace, Peace, Peace in the Ruby City and throughout the entire Land of Ardustan.

Epilogue

A short time later, Captain Shabazz the musician died and so did Musea the Nightingale who had assigned herself once again to the palace windows. But their music gave encouragement, by the permission of G-d, to a new species of rose that only grows on the side of the highest mountains, like the Andes and the Himalayas. Snow cannot reduce its passion. Winds cannot unseat its roots. It is a rose called "The Rose of Love."

One day, a brave young man gave the Rose of Love, with its roots intact, to a girl named Maryam.

Maryam showed the rose to her parents, and it was so beautiful that the parents and Maryam planted that rose in The Garden of Man. Soon, that Rose from the mountain began to sing in The Garden of Man.

All who heard its song fell in love. The young couples got married and the old couples renewed their vows. Soon, the Ruby City was bursting with new people. From these new people came a great nation, a band of people enjoining what is right, forbidding what is wrong. This came under the new leadership of a king named Nami Abu Naml, a compassionate descendant of King Ibrahim-and of King Insaan.

The days of Loofman the Magnificent were long forgotten.

Visiting the Ruby City recently, I saw three statues in the Grand Museum of History: A golden one of Loofman-frozen in time and frozen in gold, a Blue Statue of Musea the Nightingale and one of Shabazz, with a poem inscribed in a pillar of marble and alabaster called The Death of a Musician.

I copied the poem. It is archived somewhere in the People's Republic of Harlemia, along with a stranded troop of idiotic tales that I have yet to tell.

But remember this, dear reader. Ideas are immune to the sword. Music can not be killed by breaking flutes. Minds are not killed by beheading.

Word and sword are separated by the letter "S".

"S" must indeed stand for sanity!! Just as "H" stands for humanity!!

The Fourth Tale Told By An Idiot

Snaz aka "All That Jazz" vs. Shabazz &
The Bean Pie Palace

Once upon a time, in the Republic of Harlemia, there was a "black tie" restaurant on the corner of 135th st. and Adam Clayton Powell Blvd (formerly Seventh Ave). It was called <u>The Grand Shabazz Bean Pie Palace.</u> It was run by a master of "chef-o-nomics" named Chef Raymond. Now, Chef Raymond was a genius of new recipes and he invented meals that could almost make you full just by smelling it. Of course he had his regular menu, which was boasted to be the best in the Big Apple.

On Saturday nights, Raymond ran a $35 special "All the food you can eat plus an evening of great Harlemia Jazz".

Now, most people could not eat much more than 20 forkfuls of food because the delicious smell of the food was just so filling. Many ended up taking home the Bean Pie dessert.

One day, an old sharp jazz hipster named Snaz, who suffered from acute reverse anosmia got hooked on the smell of Raymond's food. Acute reverse anosmia meant that he could just stand near the restaurant door and get full from just a few whiffs of the soulful cooking aroma coming from Raymond's kitchen.

For most people, there is some sense of fullness from smelling good smelling food because of the anatomic connection of the olfactory bulb in the nose to the ventromedial nucleus in the hypothalamus of the brain. This ancient connection linking nose, mouth and brain tells a person he is getting full and should stop eating.

People who lose this connection have acute anosmia and often gain a lot of weight because they can't tell themselves through smell that they are full or satisfied. So they over eat and eat! and eat!

Snaz (aka All That Jazz), of course, was just the opposite. So every Saturday night, Snaz put on his best black tuxedo and red bowtie and stood in front the Shabazz Bean Palace door. He smelled the food and listened to the great jazz that could be heard just outside the Bean Pie Palace.

He also gave a lecture about some tidbit of jazz or blues to all who would listen. For example, "Did you know" he would ask "that the Mississippi Field Hollers which were precursors of blues came from prayer calls of the Wolof people of Africa who were deposited in Mississippi over 160 years ago?"

People would tip old Snaz when he shared his rare knowledge of the music and Snaz would use the money to buy 2 chickens, a 5 pound bag of rice and dry beans and dog food for his dog "Faithful". Snaz was trying to make it week to week from Saturday to Saturday. He even asked Raymond of job as tour guide or emcee.

Raymond spectacularly refused and kept firmly asking Snaz to move away from the door or come inside and pay the event charge.

Snaz refused and become so much part of the Saturday scene that people began to look for him. When Snaz first started coming around the front of The Grand Bean Pie Palace, he was a whopping 400 pounds but after 26 weekends, he had reduced to a slim 220.

Raymond got so mad one day that he took Snaz to court and charged him with

1. Theft of service (Food and/ or music charges)

2. Unjust enrichment (Failure to pay for a defacto weight loss program)

3. A theft of intellectual property (Listening to original jazz without paying for it)

4. Obstruction of a means of ingress and egress (Blocking the door of the restaurant)

5. Tortious interference with a Contract between the business and the public(patrons)

6. Diversion of a corporate opportunity (making money from BP Palace customers)

The judge (Judge Rathbone Foot–Heart) was so mad that he started to throw THE BOOK at Snaz, but THE BOOK was too heavy and the judge too weak. So he gave Snaz thirty days to make restitution by paying for the music that he heard outside the restaurant, the food he didn't eat but smelled outside of the restaurant and for interference with BP customers.

With "judgement in favor of plaintiff Shabazz and being found guilty for theft of service", Snaz had to pay Shabazz $400 in US currency within 30 days or spend 40 days in jail.

Snaz thought that this was unjust, because he thought that he was rendering a service to the jazz listening public by giving information to customers. But being a hustler, Snaz somehow borrowed money from Jimmy, a childhood friend. He next changed $100 into quarters, or 400 quarters, and placed them in a black burlap bag along with 3 one hundred dollar bills. But after he put the money in the bag, Snaz bought some bean pie flavored/scented body oil from the Malcolm Shabazz Harlemia Market called "Here is my Heart" and sprinkled it liberally on the money.

He called Raymond outside the restaurant and said he wanted to pay him. When Raymond came outside the restaurant, he took the burlap bag and shook the 400 quarters and 3 paper bills in

Raymond's ear. The shaking sounded like the playing of an African percussion instrument called " Shekere."

"What are you doing?" screamed Raymond. "Are you crazy?"

"I'm paying you." Snaz replied. "Do you want to see and smell the money?" Snaz continued, opening the bag and inviting Raymond to stick his nose in the bag. Raymond acted instinctively and placed his nose near the mouth of the bag.

Raymond got so mad at his own reaction that he chased Snaz all the way to the 28th police precinct on 123rd and Frederick Douglas Blvd in Harlem. The parties all landed back in court and Snaz represented his own defense.

"Your honor, may it please the court, I heard the music outside the restaurant and so the owner heard the money outside the restaurant. This is equal to fair restitution. I heard the music outside. He heard the money outside. Your honor, I smelled the food outside of the restaurant. I didn't eat anything…so I offered the complainant the opportunity to smell the money outside the restaurant, and he did."

"If he smelled the money inside the restaurant, he would be unjustly enriched and owe me restitution. Because I never got that close to his food."

Judge Foot–Heart finally got so mad at Snaz that he picked up "THE BOOK" to throw at Snaz but dropped it on his own foot instead. This caused the judge to put his foot in his mouth to soothe the shooting pain in his big toe. The judge unfortunately choked on his own foot after catching a contorting charley horse

Today there is still a court named after this judge in the People's Republic of Harlemia, at 178 E. 121st Street NY, NY, 10031.

The old timers call it Judge Foot-Heart's Folly or The Harlemia Foot-Heart's Justice Center. It's well known for handling small claims and summary proceedings.

Snaz ended up doing 40 days and 40 nights in jail at Randall's

Rock for his inability to pay Shabazz damages and fine. However, while working in the kitchen as a cook, he became very popular for a dish he concocted called "Nubian Fried Chicken/NFC .The secret was the dipping sauce which he called "gobber's secret (a peanut punch under sauce with a sweet kiss of spicy jalapeno & jerk).

There was one English prisoner (rather wealthy) who was in jail because he could not be identified. The judge thought him therefore to be a flight risk and did not set bail after he was arrested at the scene of an auto accident.

He was fascinated by Snaz and loved his Gobber Chicken (Nubian Fried Chicken). He promised to help Snaz open his own restaurant when they both got out of jail.

He claimed that he was William Sheik Sabir, a writer and a descendent of William Shakespeare (THE WILLIAM SHAKESPEARE that is!!). He said Shakespeare's biological father was a Moorish man passing for British, whose nickname was Othello.

Ergo, Shakespeare was writing that play about his father!

All that William Sheik Sabir wanted to do was to move to The People's Republic of Harlemia, live a quiet life and finish his play: "IN THE LAND OF THE BLIND: THE MAN WITH ONE EYED IS KING".

It turned out that William Sheik Sabir was rich. He received money from a blind trust set up by William Shakespeare and William Shakespeare East Indies Company 1614 for all WS descendants.

Well, with Sheik Sabir's money, Snaz opened up a fabulous restaurant across the street from the Bean Pie Palace. Snaz's "Gobber Chicken" and his "Meet Me In Harlemia Jazz Showcase" produced long lines of patrons who wrapped around the corner of 135th street like a warm scarf around the neck of winter.

Well, so much for free enterprise. That situation put The Grand Shabazz Bean Pie Palace out of business. Raymond went bankrupt and became homeless. Soon he was hanging out in front of "The

Goober Chicken Palace" (the restaurant that had put him out of business). Holding the door for patrons of the restaurant and the jazz shows, he collected tips in a black burlap bag.

Snaz, who kept his own identity under cover, sent out his manager to offer Raymond a job. Raymond refused help, out of an abundance of pride. The second time, he refused out of an abundance of hopelessness The third time, he accepted out of an abundance of the fear.

Shabazz went on to eventually become the baking contractor for Snaz's "GOBBER CHICKENS R US", producing Shabazz Bean Pies, Honey Carrot Raison Pie, Irish Dublin Custard Pie, Royal Persian Peach Pie, etc. etc. etc. for the restaurant chain.

Shabazz never learned the identity of his benefactor. Snaz had a lot of class and never revealed it...Never limit a man to the small real estate of his hustle. As long he has inner integrity, he will win a bigger dream.

Greed, like the Cyclops, is indeed a one eyed monster...Ignorance is a beggar blind in both eyes.

Kindness opens the heart. The life of the rose will overcome winter and bloom again.

Bloom it must even among bitter shards of the shattered glass of lives who haunt the sidewalks of The People's Republic of Harlemia!

William Sheik Sabir finally finished his book.

Harlem became green, and there was dancing in the streets and in cafes on Frederick Douglas Blvd. Tales were told by idiots "full of sound and fury" to an abundance of Harlemia smiles!!

The Fifth Tale Told By An Idiot:

The Mouse Who Went to Court
(The Legend of Solomon Brown)

Introduction

Who can squeeze through a hole the size of a dime? Leap 4 ft in the air from standing on a square, any time? Drop down 5 storeys without harming a hair? Ride the A train for free without care of getting arrested for a crime.

Live like a millionaire without owning a dime. Eat steel, concrete or grime for breakfast. Withstand hot and cold, any season, any clime! I'm sure you have a clue of whom I speak or do you really?

According to the 2014 census, mice are now 2.1 million citizens strong. They comprise 25% of the population of the Big Apple. In some of the more affluent neighborhoods (affluent meaning food availability wise), mice are genetically out producing their human counterparts. In the final analysis, there are two nations in New York and The People's Republic of Harlemia. One run by a cabal of people, and the other run by a cabal of mice.

Yessiree Bob!! Both sides even have campaigns and elections.

This is not an unusual arrangement. Just ask the Shogun of Yorkville, the Sultan of Murray Hill or the Emperor of Brooklyn.

Rats have the run of the night and neither NYPD nor Homeland Security can do anything about it. It is just an admitted fact that people rule the day and that mice rule the night. Neither ruler ship is, however, mutually exclusive because regarding mice and men and men and mice, the struggle is the same. We share the same space, the same apartments, the same food .We down the same rib sticking pizzas by the slice. We scarf down, New York style, the same dirty water hot dogs. We are all New Yorkers! All of us!!!

There is also an unseemly outright clash between mice and human civilizations-A mutual mistrust and unreasonable fear one of the other. Grown up men have been known to run pell-mell when they see a rat or a mouse scurrying in the corner and a mouse can fight like a man when they are hemmed in or cornered. Go Figure!! Men often tout their own intellectual superiority over the lowly mouse by claiming that men are the first to have gone to the moon, for example.

Mice counter and claim that they were inside Neil Armstrong's space jumpsuit when he took that "one step for man" on the moon and "the other for mankind" (mice claim "mankind" is code word for the ubiquitous mouse).

Like UFOs and Lord Voldemort, no one talks about these things. Mice professors ask who is the most intelligent, the space shuttle chauffeurs or the passenger mice cooling it first class in the back seat of the rocket ship. If a passenger were seated in the back seat of a limousine or in the back of an Uber car, nobody would be confused about who is the mere driver and who is the boss, the celebrity the controlling entity. Well, that's the argument of mice regarding their preeminence over humans.

Within the civilizations of mice and men, there are deep divisions between rich and poor, the "haves" and "have nots", between the brown field mouse and his spotted cousin, the "mansion mouse". This story is about a well-groomed brown mouse whose tale made the headlines in the daily power press, on internet interludes and on blogger's columns worldwide. "Mouse Goes to Court Against Humans" some of them read. At the time the story broke, I was fortunate (and young) enough to be working for The Amsterdam News, centered in Harlemia.

The Amsterdam News, since 1909, has been touted as the largest African American newspaper in the country. Working on a story about Harlemia gentrification, I bumped into Thomas (Tow-mouse) Fortune, my counterpart reporter at The Hamster-dam News ("printing all the news fit for a mouse").

I was talking to Thomas about the gentrification of Harlemia, and he was talking about how "the fat rats" from downtown were taking over Harlemia. I was sitting on the corner of 125th street and 7th Ave, in front of the statue of Adam Clayton Powell. There, I met Solomon Brown, the phenomenal mouse lawyer who was being interviewed by the Hamster-dam News about his recent exploits and victory in the Supreme Court of the State of New York against Lord Drenched Cabbage.

"I always bring home the cheese" I overheard him bragging..

I tried to engage Mr. Brown, but Mr. Brown never spoke with the human press and pretty much kept to himself. Solomon Brown struck me, however, as a rather elegant "cat" (excuse me, I mean mouse). Dressed immaculately in a black 2 piece Armani suit, a red woolen vest and sporting a Black French Tam on his crown, he was quite the mouse around the town. His large rimless glasses were a bit too large, however. Light reflected off those spectacles like deflected lasers. We all moved to the front of the Lemuj mansion for lunch to discuss the case we had read about

As I was sitting in front of Lemuj mansion (a 20,000 square foot palace between 143rd and 145th st. between St. Nicholas and Convent), I saw ten Brinks Armored Trucks pull up to the mansion and men unload bulky sacks of pennies clearly marked "US Treasury (A Penny For Your Thoughts)".

I also saw another truck with a sign affixed which read "Jelly Beans R Us". 2,000 packs of jelly beans were being delivered in clear 100 lb clearly marked glassine plastic bags. Bald shiny headed mice, sharply dressed in blue and black double breasted suits and red bow ties, oversaw the unloading of the trucks and were taking inventory of the delivered jelly beans.

As the story goes, the Lemuj Mansion used to belong to a very rich lawyer named Joseph Dream-maker, AKA Lord Dream-maker. Now it belonged to Solomon Brown and his mouse friends. Joseph Dream-maker died January 15, 2016 (Martin Luther King's birthday), 2 weeks prior to my writing this story and to those trucks of money and jelly beans being delivered to the mansion.

Joseph Dream-maker (also called Lord Dream-maker) was a criminal defense lawyer and a real estate transaction lawyer who was once worth nearly 20 million dollars (net worth). He had loved this 66 room mansion, which was well over 100 years old, and which he shared with a friendly family of mice. The mice had once lived in one quarter of the mansion since the time of Alexander Hamilton.

Well, Dream-maker had expensive tastes and the mice who lived with him (members of the Royal Order Mice Americus ROMA) all ate caviar, truffles and pheasant under glass. They were all teetotalers and all savored bottled triple distilled water from the Harlemia river, (which ran under the mansion itself and much of Harlemia). Some of the mice who lived in the Lemuj Mansion were quite educated. For years, three of them had studied Dream-maker's Law Books, a book called "CPA Accounting for Dummies" and a journal called "Techies Are Us". Finally, after a summer of shade and lemonade, the leaves of autumn began to fall. The 2015 winter wove a quilt thick icy blanket that covered all in The Republic of Harlemia.

One fateful night, December 31, 2015, Joseph Dream-maker sat quietly in his study. At 12 midnight, on New Year's Eve, suddenly the East, West and South panels of glass shattered and three ruffians entered Dreamaker's parlor. They entered-to an accompaniment of neighborhood shouts of "Happy New Year!", firecracker cheers, guns firing in the air and otherwise normal New Year hullabaloo It was the perfect moment to commit a murder, or any noisy crime, because no one could hear Joseph Dream-maker scream.

The villains were three ruffians wearing tee-shirts which read respectively: Jubelo, Jubela and Jubelum (for a long time the people and the police thought the ruffians in question were the owners of the oldest Harlemia pawn shop "Master Juba's Pawn shop").

The 3 ruffians placed a large black bag over Joseph Dream-maker's head. They struck Joseph Dream-maker three times on the neck, heart and head, and they tied him up. They kept asking him for the combination of his Double Steel Safe, which contained over a million dollars USC and People's Republic of Harlemia dollars which were called "splib hops" or "splib-bop".

Joseph Dream-maker, despite the beating and torture that he received, refused to budge. "I will not give pearls to swine." he muttered. But within ten minutes, the mice of the mansion heard the commotion and charged the ruffians, biting their ears, eyes, nose, even severely biting the toes and soles of the ruffians' feet as they fled.

The 3 ruffians ran for their lives. They even jumped out of the same windows by which each of them had entered. The mice, in sum, had saved Joseph Dream-maker's life.

Joseph Dream-maker (or Lord Dream-maker if you prefer) was extremely grateful and gravely injured.

"You are my friends and you've been in this mansion before me-and I want to make sure that you guys are OK when I'm gone or if something happens to me." he related as the mice of the mansion gathered around him in the parlor with tears in their eyes. This is when the leaders of the mice began to speak up.

There were 3 leaders-Solomon Brown the lawyer and jurist, the sublime Common Law expert, Ivan "Mind Strong" the Master

Mathematician emeritus and CPA and Dr. Florence Higglebotham, Director of Mouse Health and Mental Services in The Peoples Republic of Harlemia.

"Well," said Solomon. "Why don't you give us a million dollars US currency and a million jelly beans (our currency) and we"ll take care of our needs and build a school in your honor."

"I can't do that all at once" replied Dream-maker. "That would ruin me and my reputation."

"How about if you give us one penny and double that one penny each day for 31 days?" offered Ivan "Mind Strong" (Mouse, emeritus CPA/ Mathematician) "That is a simple solution." he continued. "Give us one penny today, two pennies tomorrow, four pennies on the third day, eight pennies the fourth day and so forth for 31 days. We are suggesting a 31 day time period for payment into trust fund designated by us."

"Well, I can easily do that." smiled Dream-maker. "Write it up, Solomon, and I will sign it." Dream-maker continued.

Solomon responded "Lord Dream-maker, if you are the party to be charged with the responsibility for paying, then your language should be used preferentially and not mine. In a case where you draft the document in question, there should be no misinterpretation about what you intended to give. And no confusion."

"OK, Solomon Mouse," laughed Dream-Maler "I'll draft it so it can be executed (signed forthwith)."

"Please draft it in plain English, Lord Dream-Maker, so that even a high school mouse can understand." insisted Mouse Mind Strong

"I believe I can do that, Mouse Mind-Strong." replied Dream-maker with a weak wry smile.

"Yes, most certainly, you can sir." affirmed Mind-Strong.

"First, let's call the police." reminded Solomon. "After all, a crime has been committed and we are custodians of a crime scene until the police arrive."

Whereupon, Solomon called 911 and reported the robbery and assaults to NYPD. At least a half dozen experienced police officers promptly responded to the scene including detectives, forensic lab experts and the daily press, including CNN and ABC.

Lord Dream-maker stubbornly refused any medical attention and insisted instead on drafting a legal letter to safeguard his mouse friends in case of his untimely demise. The final agreement crafted jointly by Joseph Dream-maker and Solomon Brown read as follows:

"Agreement made this 1st Day of January 2016 between Joseph Dream-maker AKA Lord Dream-maker of 1765 St. Nicholas Ave. party of the first part and the Royal Order of Mice d.b.a. as Mouse, Mouse and Mouse LLC of 1765 St. Nicholas Ave. party of the 2nd part. Witnesseth In consideration of Ten Black Jelly Beans (Mouse Currency), Ten Dollars, U.S. Currency paid in hand other valuable consideration (including mutual respect and friendship) the sufficiency of which is unquestioned, it is hereby agreed as follows:

1. Joseph Dream-maker agrees and promises to pay to Mouse, Mouse and Mouse LLC (their assigned or succession if any) the sum of one penny upon the execution (signing) of this contract and to make double payment of the pennies accumulated each day until 31 days thereafter or until February 3, 2015 final payments is to be made.

2. Mouse, Mouse and Mouse LLC agrees to provide unique security services and caregiving services while Dream-maker is recuperating and getting better at the Lemuj Mansion and thereafter for the rest of his life.

3. Mouse, Mouse and Mouse LLC may not assign, or give away its duties re Dream-maker to anyone else because their services are unique and their knowledge of Dream-maker is special.

4. Neither Man nor Mouse may change or modify this contract unless in a jointly signed writing signed Joseph Dream-maker, Solomon Brown, Ivan Mind-Strong, Florence Higglebotham
5. In case of dispute, the aggrieved party can refer the dispute to the American Argument Association, Harlem Law shall apply.
6. This writing is the entire agreement between Dream-maker and Mouse, Mouse and Mouse LLC.
7. Done This January 2, 2016, in the People's Republic of Harlemia.

Sadly, as it turned out, Joseph Dream-maker perished suddenly on January 13, 2016. He died in his sleep that night after not returning to earth from one of his many dream journeys.

Hundreds of sad souls attended the funeral at Benton's Funeral Home on 141st and St. Nicholas Ave. Anyone who was famous in the People's Republic of Harlemia made it there.

Lord Dream-maker had no relatives, only 3 rather rotund sisters who sang in the church choir, the inhabitants of a fish tank and of course his beloved mice friends. After the funeral was completed, the real trouble began. No one could find a will that Dream-maker had ever made.

The sisters claimed that he had one with their names on it. They were his only immediate relatives.

It was unbelievable. A lawyer without a will is like a shoemaker with holes in his shoes, a blues without tears or a clown without polka dot underwear.

Fear and panic began to spread. Joseph Dream-maker was indeed dead. He was worth $20,000,000. He had accumulated $18,000,000 in debt. He owned publishing rights to some precious music, and lots of IOU's that people owed him reflected his generosity to others.

Dream-maker's three sisters were particularly stressed because they were in court trying to claim the Lemuj Mansion, all of his money inter alia. The three sisters had the locks changed on the Lemuj Mansion doors and called in Pedro DDP Inc. Exterminators to kill and get rid of our esteemed mansion friends-the mice of Lemuj Mansion. That's when Mouse Florence Higglebotham went into action and concocted a powerful potion of garlic, rat tails and vinegar from the mansion storage basement. The smell of this concoction placed in the ventilation system drove the sisters out of the mansion entirely.

The three sisters did not give up. The three sisters then engineered the appointment of Lord Drenched Cabbage ESQ as the administrator of the Dream-maker (lifetime and holding) Estate so that they could get control of the fortune. They had plans that included selling the entire mansion. Naturally, mice are upset when you talk about selling their home to KATZ Delicatessen and Pastrami.

As far as Drenched Cabbage is concerned, he was a rather aristocratic, obnoxious and arrogant hunched backed lawyer, having a rather infamous reputation for a ruthless court room manner and eternally picking his nose hairs. He had 3 gold teeth in the front of his mouth, wore red suspenders and high water pants. Drenched Cabbage took the case of the 3 sister's claim to the brink of victory.

The case was almost finished and the house and finances of Lord Dream-maker were about to be totally awarded to the three sisters when Solomon Brown (armed with an order to show cause) walked into Judge Pickles Rathbone's courtroom. On seeing the large brown mouse, Solomon Brown (with huge spectacles) enter the courtroom, the three sisters and their lawyer "Drenched Cabbage" fled from the courtroom and rain into a closet in Judge Rathbone's chambers.

Judge Rathbone pounded his gavel like he was hammering a large nail. "Order! Order! Order! Order!!!" he yelled.

Then, upon himself seeing the large brown mouse, Judge Rathbone turned red like a New Jersey tomato and stood up on top of the bench, waving his gavel in the air.

Judge Rathbone: Bailiff Bailey, what is a mouse doing in the courtroom? Kill him, Kill him, Kill him!!!

Whereupon Billy the Bailiff started firing 41 shots from his 380 automatic pistol, causing bullets to ricochet all over the courtroom.

Judge Rathbone: Stop you fool! Bailiff stop! You are going to kill someone.

Solomon Brown took advantage of the lull in the firing to pull out his Police Benevolent Association (PBA) badge. The bailiff stopped in his tracks and saluted the mouse. "Your honor, I can't shoot this here mouse. He has a PBA card. He's a PBA member. He's a member of the NYPD Police Benevolent Association. He is also carrying a diplomatic pouch. He is showing immunity letters from the Emperor of Brooklyn, the Shogun of Harlemia and the Great Mansa Musa of Parkchester/Castlehill in the Bronx."

Judge Rathbone: But, but bailiff what can we do? I can not have a mouse in official capacity in this courtroom!

Bailiff: Judge you know the law. This mouse has diplomatic immunity and it can only be revoked by the Steak Department.

Solomon Brown: May it please the court, my name is Solomon Brown, I am the managing member of Mouse, Mouse and Mouse LLC (Limited Liability Company). I represent the LLC for all purposes in this order to show cause INDEX #0072468. I have a power of attorney and an assignment of interest from the LLC. The order to show cause is duly signed by the Judge in Part 5 and duly served and placed on the calendar, your honor, therefore I demand to be heard!!!

Judge Rathbone: But my dear mouse, you are not a person with standing before this honorable court. A mouse has no rights that human must respect!

Solomon Brown: I am standing, your honor. You, sir, are the one sitting. You're doing a bad job of imitating the words of Justice Taney — in the Dred Scott vs. Sandford case 1857 when he said "A black man has no rights that a white man must respect. Taney's words are an insult to all creatures, including the human judiciary. You see, your honor, Mouse, Mouse and Mouse LLC is a corporate citizen of New York State and therefore a corporate citizen, or person, under the law. All corporations and LLC's are fictitious people chartered by the state and empowered with a legitimate right to sue and be sued. Mouse, Mouse and Mouse LLC, a person, signatory and beneficiary under the contract with the late deceased Lord Dream-maker, has a right to sue his estate for the benefits which the contract contemplates and that Lord Dream-maker himself intended to confer upon Mouse Mouse and Mouse LLC.

Judge Rathbone: Can you show me that an LLC formed by mice is a person, Mr. Mouse?

Solomon Brown: Solomon Brown, if you please.

Judge Rathbone: Whatever!

Brown: A corporation and/or LLC, your honor, has legal existence, or personhood, because it is given life by the breath of state sovereignty for the consideration of money. A corporate being can enter into contracts, sue and be sued from the time of the British West Indies Company and even the Virginia Company, which found Jamestown because the organizers paid the fees to the King. No fees, no Company. So it's the money that the state takes.

Judge Rathbone: You may be historically right but an LLC can not be founded or represented by mice.

Solomon Brown: We were founded and registered by the state of New York. We mice PAID the price, the registration fees, the taxes and the state of New York only wanted our money and sent us the papers. The state of NY never asked us whether we were mice or men. Where does it say in NY Law that a LLC or corporation can only be set up by humans? It can only be set up by paying the fee. You send the fee you get the flower. No fee. No power.

Lord Drenched Cabbage: Your honor I find that these proceedings preposterous. Why are you arguing with a mouse?

Judge Rathbone: I see, Mr. Cabbage, that you crawled back into this court room almost too late to address the record as usual?

Lord Cabbage: It's "Cabbage", French short "a" sound, your honor, like in massage, garage, not cabbage as in sausage or disparage or savage

Judge Rathbone: Whatever…As for you, Mr. Mouse

Solomon Brown: Solomon Brown, if you please!

Judge Rathbone: Whatever! I find that you are not a member of the bar, even if the LLC has standing (the right) to file the Order to Show Cause before the court asking that the Lemuj Mansion be given to Mouse, Mouse and Mouse LLC. You, sir mouse, do not have standing.

Solomon Brown: I do have "understanding", your honor. I passed a lot of bars on the way to court this morning, your honor, many of them full of drunk barristers. I have a power of attorney and nothing in the law saying a person can't appoint a mouse as his attorney in fact by power of attorney. Additionally, because I'm managing member of the LLC, I have a right to represent the LLC so long as I have a resolution or contractual power granting me the power to sue the estate of the late Dream-maker. Here, your honor, is the resolution. I hereby tender/give to you the resolutions. Bailiff, please place the documents into Judge Rathbone's hands.

Judge Rathbone: I have reservations, Solomon Brown, but based upon these documents I'll allow you to argue your order to show cause, "subject to the scrutiny of the appellate division". I do find nothing in our laws that restrict LLC to humans.

Lord Drenched Cabbage: Judge, granted an LLC has right to sue in court of law just like any other person. But a LLC operated by mice is a farce and a promise to pay mice for anything is a double farce!! So I object, as a matter of public policy.

Solomon Brown: Your Honor, several years ago (2009 to be exact), in this very city, the appellant division upheld the lower court's decision to allow billionaire so called "QUEEN OF MEAN" Leona Helmsley to leave $12,000,000 in her estate to a maltese dog named "Trouble". Two million of it was immediately expendable on the upkeep of the dog itself and $100,000 for the dog's body guards per month must have seemed surprising. But the dog was a beneficiary and a distributee of Leona Helmsley's estate and dog's right to that rights were protected by the judiciary of every relevant court in this state.

Under the Equal Protection Clause of the Constitution, the Fourteenth Amendment which provides for equal protection of the law to all citizens (beloved mice should have the same right to receive money as beloved dog.)

In fact under the Matter of Helmsley case, the beloved dog had the same rights to receive money as any human. This is settled law. So if a mouse has the same rights as a dog, and the dog has the same rights as human to receive money or property (its equivalent), then mice have the same rights as humans under the law. And that means mice, dogs and men have a right to sue upon a contract whether they are organized as a LLC or simply want to sue as individuals.

Judge Rathbone: What say you Lord Cabbage?

Drenched Cabbage: It's Cabbage, sir, as in massage, not cabbage as in savage, your honor.

Judge Rathbone: Whatever! Cabbage! Savage! Garbage! Baggage! What is your rebuttal counselor?!

Solomon: Well, your honor, we do not have a case where a mouse has NOT been allowed to try a case before the court in assertion of his civil rights.

Lord Drenched Cabbage: This whole affair is as ridiculous as it is unprecedented. The Leona Helmsley dog case was a terribly troubled case.

Judge Rathbone: "Ridiculous" is not an argument, counselor!! I find that Mouse Solomon Brown may proceed with his case. Call the case Bridgeman, Call it! Call it! Call the case!!!

(The three sisters of Dream-maker dressed in black began to cry.)

Judge Rathbone: Order in the court! Order in the court!!!

Bridgeman: Matter of Mouse, Mouse and Mouse LLC vs. The Estate of Joseph Dream-maker AKA Lord Dream-maker 2nd call Appearances please

Judge Rathbone: Call your first witness Mr. Solomon. I mean Mouse Brown...whatever!

When the trial began, Solomon Brown called Mouse Ivan Mindstrong as his first witness. He qualified Mindstrong a CPA as math teacher expert in finance and math. Through Mindstrong, Solomon introduced the Dream-maker agreement and promise to pay Mouse, Mouse and Mouse LLC into evidence. Mindstrong also testified as a witness to the agreement. And to the clause which called for Dream-maker or his estate to pay 1 penny upon signing and double those pennies everyday until 31 days had passed. That amount owed came to $10,000,000 plus dollars, according to Mindstrong's math.

Cabbage, the Real Estate lawyer and the lawyer for Dream-maker's 3 sisters challenged Mindstrong, claiming it was Mouse Mathematics and not human mathematics.

When Solomon proved that the math calculations used to reach that amount was human mathematics, Lord Drenched Cabbage fainted on the spot.

The Judge called a recess until 2pm in the afternoon.

Solomon Brown then called Mouse Florence Higglebotham, who testified that the mice of the mansion, under her supervision, had fulfilled their health care and other duties under the Dream-maker agreement until his untimely death.

She also testified as a witness to the assault and robbery upon Dream-maker. She testified about the chaos, her sounding of the alarm and about strange muddy foot prints left behind by three ruffians wearing tee shirts that read Jubela, Jubelo and Jubelum.

Lord Cabbage, taking an "empire strikes back" attitude, questioned the ability of mice to care for human beings. Cabbage got belligerent with the judge and the judge threatened him with contempt, and threw a volume of Shakespeare's Macbeth at the lawyer. The judge also threw his right shoe, but Cabbage ducked as it hit the bailiff.

After an emergency recess, Solomon then called Detective Henry "Iron Jaw" Harper from the NYPD 30th Pct (a foreman detective) to testify about what he found at the crime scene, including some unusual sets of shoe prints that contained sun, moon and star imprints on the soles.

Cabbage challenged the testimony as being irrelevant to the matter before the court which was, after all, the authenticity of Dream-maker's agreement with the mice.

Solomon offered the testimony and shoe prints subject to connection re the weight of the evidence being considered who had the best claim the proceeds to wit: The Mice or The Sisters.

Judge Rathbone allowed the testimony as long as Solomon could make it relevant to the issue of their legitimate claim to Dream-maker's money.

Harper was Solomon's last witness. He wanted to call the 3 sisters of Dream-maker as hostile witnesses (witnesses with competing or opposite interests) or (people who hated mice getting anything).

Solomon knew, however, that Cabbage had to call the 3 sisters to the stand or they would have no chance of getting Dream Maker's money No chance of getting anything. Solomon remembered his father's word. "Mice have to use Akido against humans." ie use your opponent's strength against him. So Solomon rested his case and waited for Cabbage to make his.

Cabbage called the three sisters to authenticate their birth certificates and to establish their loving relationship as sisters with the deceased Lord Dream-maker. Cabbage also inquired of each of them re the last time they had seen their brother, Dream-maker, alive and whether Dream-maker had shown them his will with their names on it. Also, how they had made an effort to find the will. All of the sisters testified that they had last seen their brother at a family reunion July 4, 2015.

Solomon saw his chance. Cabbage had opened the door that might allow him to place the sisters at the scene of the robbery and assault. He cross examined each sister and asked each sister to remove her right shoe after each sister could not remember what shoes they were wearing December 31, 2015, or the last time that they wore their shoes after the family reunion July 4, 2015.

Then Solomon called back Detective Harper to the stand .... Who appeared to match the shoe molds with distinctive sun, moon and star shapes to the shoes of the three sisters. All of the sister's shoes had the sun, moon and star shapes on their soles.

Detective Harper concluded that the sisters were now suspects in the murder of Lord Dream-maker.

Needless to say, there was pandemonium in the court room but Solomon was not finished. He also elected that the sun, moon and star insignia on the shoes were part of a gang of murderers called the MORON (Masonic Order of Royal Of Ninjas.) who killed and stole money from rich citizens of Harlemia and NY City.

As a result of the evidenced adduced in court, the Judge ordered the 3 sisters to be arrested for suspicion of murder.

Cabbage, after his summation, was hospitalized for heart failure. Solomon his invoked "the slayer law", which said no one can benefit the fruits of their wrongdoing.

The mice had the only legitimate claim. The court's decision was handed down in Solomon the Mouse. The mice had won!!

The estate of Dream-maker had to pay them …$10,500,000.00 and 2,000 lbs of jelly beans (mouse money) and interest of…0%… from February 3, 2015 to March 30, 2015, the victory of mice over men was heard around the globe. On Adam Clayton Powell Blvd in the People's Republic of Harlemia, the mice held a tickertape type parade from 110st to 145st and Frederick Douglas Blvd.

The downtown mice also had a parade up 5th Ave from 42nd st to 50th st on the Upper Crust East Side. The Mayor De Blasio declared it Mouse Appreciation Day.

When the Upper Crust East Side residents saw thousands of well-dressed mice in bright colors marching up Fifth Ave with police protection and 3 mayors in tow (Guliani Bloomberg and De Blasio), many of the women fainted and the men ran pell mell into the old war bomb shelter in the basement of the silk stocking district. Solomon was the hero of the year and made Time Magazine Person of the Year 2016 front page. But the story does not end here.

Epilogue

Needless to say, Solomon Brown became a very famous celebrity after the Dream-maker case. Lord Cabbage, on the other hand, was ridiculed everywhere he went. He was a louse who lost to a mouse. He went on welfare and lost most of his clients.

On the ides of 15 March 2016, Lord Cabbage challenged Solomon Mouse to a duel. He wanted Solomon dead. That would restore his honor.

Solomon refused, but Lord Cabbage persisted and went on a mouse killing spree using the best exterminators in the city. This, he felt, might convince Solomon to fight. Finally, Solomon — on the condition that he be allowed to choose the weapon.

Solomon wanted to stop Lord Cabbage's "mousetricide" and save the lives of innocent mice.

Lord Cabbage asked for this duel…Solomon planned to end it.

Solomon chose the 45 ARK(Assault Rat Killer) caliber Jelly Bean gun loaded with exploding Jelly Bean bullets. Don't laugh because if jelly beans ever pierce your skin and get into your blood stream you will die of a sweet tooth or acute type 2 diabetes. Lord Cabbage's second was Lord Cucumber. Solomon's second was Ivan Mindstrong CPA, who was also a sharp shooter.

The duel took place on Randall's Island at sunrise on April 15, 2016.

Lord Drenched Cabbage shot first…The first shot missed Solomon by inches. The next two shots hit him on the upper arm and on his spectacles respectively., Solomon however was wearing his jelly bean proof sunglasses that had been tested by MIT (Mouse Institute of Technology). Solomon Brown then fired his ARK jelly bean gun three times, knocking down Lord Cabbage's knocking out all three gold teeth. All with one bullet .Two other Jelly Bean Bullets struck him twice in the posterior as he ran from the field of battle.

After getting shot with 3 jelly beans, Lord Cabbage growled—like a bear and yelped like a puppy. He gave out and collapsed.

Poor Lord Cabbage was dragged to Mouse Memorial Hospital on Randall's Island.by the some–friendly-Island mice. He was bleeding a lot of green blood from his posterior. He was given a….mouse blood transfusion and the first mouse heart transplant into a human. Lord Cabbage survived, but within 3 days he had grown whiskers of a mouse. Every time he shaved or cut them off, the mouse whiskers grew back double the size. This really had a bad effect on his legal practice and he ended up being counsel-for Barnum Bailey Circus.

Solomon Brown eventually retired ad went to live on a small

Caribbean island, a place only known to two of his friends, Ivan Mindstrong and Florence Higglebotham. This was, however, the case that is why Solomon Brown came out of retirement.

The case of Mouse Worker of America vs. International Shoe-Works...

It would involve mice being paid one jelly bean a day to string shoe laces into sneakers such as Nike, Adidas and Jordan in the South so the brands could carry the label "made in America". In this land mark case, the Supreme Court ruled mice to be paid the same rate as humans, or 15 Jelly Beans an hour.

Somewhere in the Republic of Harlemia, there is a bronze Memorial to Solomon Brown the mouse.....who defeated humans in their own Court.

November 15, 2016...Lord Dream-maker's mansion became a Jelly Bean factory. Kids would want to work there after school and learn X amount for college. Scholarships are regularly given by Mouse Mouse and Mouse LLC and the Royal Order of Mice. The Jelly Bean factory of Harlemia is now a $50,000,000 dollar industry, and restaurants all over Harlemia sell jelly bean recipes such as jelly bean fritters, jelly bean eggroll, jelly bean cheese cake, jelly bean steak, General Tso's Chicken in jelly bean sauce, jelly yams, curry jelly vindaloo, jelly chutney, hot cakes in jelly bean sauce and the Harlemia Jelly Cake.

Solomon Brown's mysterious disappearance and his retreat to the Caribbean was a cause for concern. Nevertheless his statue looms in front of the Harlemia Court House. It towers over the Court House and the inscription on it reads "In loving memory of Solomon Brown, The Mouse Lawyer who went to court and won using Faith and DiligentPreparation."

The transcript of this'trial (his most famous and lengthy trial) is available by request by contacting your author (see Author's page) by email.

The Last Tale Told By An Idiot:
"Why the Fly Became a Fugitive"

(A Mystery Wrapped in a Puzzle Wrapped in an Enigma)

I NVOCATION

By the Bee in the mountain
By the ant in the road
By the majesty of the sun in his humble abode
By the stolen kiss of the moon
Upon the face of the night
By the eyes of the stars
And the sight of insight
Surely my Lord, the Creator, the All Mighty
Is most Gracious and Kind
He it is Who sends imagination
To enlarge the mind
Inspiration to expand the soul
Love to nourish the heart
Fire to warm the cold
And kindle the lonely candle that lingers in the dark

To lightning He has joined the voice of thunder
And opened skies to the eyes of our wonder
By his kindness, I am permitted to write
And by His mercy I walk aright in luminescent light! Amin

I. The Mystery: The Walk and Chance Encounter With Mysterious Old Woman

"There was an old lady who swallowed a fly
I don't know why she swallowed a fly-perhaps she'll die!
There was an old lady who swallowed a spider,
That wriggled and wiggled and jiggled inside her;
She swallowed the spider to catch the fly;
I don't know why she swallowed a fly-Perhaps she'll die!
There was an old lady who swallowed a bird;
How absurd to swallow a bird.
She swallowed the bird to catch the spider,
She swallowed the spider to catch the fly;
I don't know why she swallowed a fly-Perhaps she'll die!"
American Nursery Folk Song

Woman thou hast had
Five husbands and he
Whom you have now is
Not your true husband
John 4:18

I rarely venture beyond the walls of the People's Republic of Harlemia anymore except for an occasional exercise of mental excursion to avoid the perversion of sitting too long in one place.

Harlemia has everything a man needs, materially and spiritually. It's a sophisticated satisfying place. The beauty of all nations is reflected in her exotic face and her spiritual graces are enshrined in myriad steeples, domes and minarets of song and praise. There are dining spots of amazing elegance and enduring exuberance.

I wasn't always so isolationist, sedentary or deprived of wander-lust. When I was younger, I was an adventure driven man-world traveler, believe it or not (and my name is not 'Ripley' or Indiana Jones or Matthew Henson). Once, at 25, I took the "A train" to Africa (only a few of us knew about that route-It's now part of the 21ˢᵗ century 'underwater railroad'). We used to take the Upper Gulf Stream to the North Atlantic Drift, transfer to the Canary Islands Current and then ride on the back of the Guinea Current all of the way down the West Coast of Africa.

What a wonderful adventurous journey at 25 years of age. The A train was part of the molecular express line 700 leagues under the sea. Look it up-those currents on google. They have flowed for thousands of years between Africa and the Americas like a network of roads or highways under the sea.

We also used to take the "C train" along the eastern sea coast to Canada. Then we would take an overland route by train to meet and live among the Inuit peoples.

Those guys have almost 100 different words for "ice". (The three most important words for ice are "ice that has good fishing", "ice that a man can stand on" and "ice that can only bear the weight of a single sled dog". Knowing the difference can mean life or death!

Finally, of course, (by myself) I took the "D train" to Denmark-a remarkable place that appreciates the music of Harlemia. It was a great happy place with a winning attitude. I never found anything rotten there. The Nordic form of beauty is quite fascinating

All of the above happened when I was a member of the NHREC-the *New Harlemia Renaissance Explorers Club*.

Located on 135ᵗʰ Street and Barack Obama Way, two blocks west of Adam Clayton Powell Blvd, formerly 7ᵗʰ Ave, you'll find a sidewalk vault for deliveries to the <u>Harlemia House of Hotcakes</u>. Once inside to your left, you will find a door leading to the office of NHREC.

Yes, I was indeed once a "Traveling Man".

Nowadays, I'm just a walking man. I walk from north to the tip of Manhattan, which is all now a part of the People's Republic of Harlemia. Occasionally, I walk south, through what was once Central Park, to 59th Street. It's all wilderness now, inhabited by wild raccoons, liberated feral dogs, woodpeckers, sparrows, pigeons, seagulls called "livingstons" and an occasional owl.

Long ago, Central Park fell into disrepair. After the great migration from the Upper East Side, Chelsea, Murray Hill, Lincoln Center West, from 1990-2020 things got bad.

Time after time, jeep covered station wagons filled with down town settler's furniture took the trail north, just as Harlemia was again in vogue. Central Park became a dangerous trail where irresponsible settlers abandoned their pets because landlords in Harlemia did not want dogs or cats or pet snakes in their apartments. After the pets got loose, bandits took over the park.

So my walks in Central Park were a foolish adventure of the heart. I would talk to the trees, the squirrels, the birds and the breeze. Usually, I would just mind my own business but all my life I experienced that something mysteriously hidden or unusually exotic would cross my path whenever I least expected it.

It was a warm early Sunday morning-8:00 a.m. The Ides of July (July 15th to be exact) when something unusual happened. I started out from Fort Schaumberg Plaza Point, on the border of 110th Street and 5th Avenue. I headed south towards an outpost at the Bethesda Fountain, or the Bethesda Watering Hole, (as we writers now call it). It's still there on 72nd Street (mid Central Park), not far from the ruins of the old "Shakespeare in the Park" Delacorte Theatre.

The Bethesda Watering Hole sat like a temple jewel in an

overgrown wilderness, an oasis in the desert of a deserted and abandoned dreams. Seven were the stone water fountains that surrounded
this watering hole. They were sequenced like planets that occupied set
orbits around the sun. Each was spaced equally apart from the other.

In those hot and halcyon days of the 20th century, poets, musicians and artists surrounded the fountains showing off their talents
and crafts.

But on the Ides of July, in the 21st century, it was virtually deserted.

As I lifted my head up from drinking at the fifth of the seven
fountains, I saw an old woman standing over my right shoulder.
Dressed in a long flowing navy blue frock, sporting a too warm for
the season navy blue shawl, and carrying two large brown Macy's
shopping bags, she was a most unsettling sight. The bags were stuffed
with clothing and other accessories, evidencing all of the signs of
homelessness.

"Excuse me sonny," she whined. "My name is Samaria, Samaria
Parable Jane. Could you please help me fill up this water bottle? My
hands are not steady anymore."

"Why sure Ma'am," I replied, "it will be my pleasure. Samaria
Parable Jane you say?"

"You better believe it, from Parable, a Phantom City in the State
of New York! Sonny, I at one time had a palace, a house with so
many rooms you couldn't' count them all. I once had a thousand
suitors who would beg and beg to take me to the ball."

"A Phantom City! Wow!" I exclaimed, "And where is that?"

"Oh East of Somewhere and West of Nowhere, Sonny." she
calmly explained.

"You were married?" I continued, with some surprise as I noticed, at that moment, that the old woman was wearing a stunning
gold necklace, two gold studded earrings, a gold bracelet on her left
wrist and what seemed to look like a five diamond studded wedding
ring on her left hand.

"Yes, I was married five times. I've had five husbands, I've lived in 5 magnificent palaces, but the sixth person that I gave my heart to promised me wealth but made me homeless. I lost my common sense, I guess."

"Five husbands?" I wondered out loud. "What were their names, may I ask?"

"Eye-sack was my first husband. He was a man of vision-an optimist, an optometrist and an ophthalmologist. 'Early' was my second husband and he was a local musician with large ears who became a traveling troubadour. 'Smiley' was my third husband – he was a chef at one of those large hotels downtown. One whiff of his cooking and you would fall in love. My fourth husband was 'Felix', who was loved by many for his depth of compassion and his deep feeling soul. Yes he was a very compassionate and deep feeling person."

"My fifth husband 'Taj' was a tailor of fine taste and social graces. He was a teacher in the New York City public school called Fashion Institute…what a man for fine judgment and taste."

"So you've really had five husbands? Are they all still alive?" I asked, digging deeper than I really wanted to go. But sometimes when you dig deep, you find golden artifacts.

"Yep," replied the old lady. "They are all still alive, and all of them love me even though I have separated myself from common sense logic long ago."

"What is the name of your sixth significant other or husband?" I asked.

"His name is 'Grady', Adam Smith Grady, 'Greedy Deed' for short, that's his nickname." replied the old woman. "He is the one who caused me to fall into homelessness and lose all my possessions. I've been homeless six years now, living in this park. At night, I sleep inside that old oak tree over there. My pet owl, Max, stands guard all night. Daytime, I wander the streets, seeking a heart that will free or deliver me from the dangers of greed."

"I don't see any villain holding you captive, Madame." I proffered "Do you?"

"Oh sonny boy," she exclaimed, "some people hoard gold and never share their wealth with those less fortunate-so they are imprisoned by their greed for material things. Other people who are emotionally greedy hoard their love and never share their hearts with anyone. They are imprisoned by their own hearts. The third group is knowers of information and gatherers of understanding that can help humanity, but they keep their understanding to themselves. This latter group is imprisoned by the wealth of their knowledge and by the poverty of their intentions. With their thinking, they will never travel to the seven heavens, maybe not in the first heaven. They will wander on the earth and be at the mercy of strangers. The benefits of their knowledge will soon be out of their reach."

"And this latter description must be your case," I surmised boldly "because I see you wearing five very expensive pieces of jewelry and I would think you could sell them and even buy a house with the money if you wanted to."

"Precisely," smiled the old woman "I, myself, have been robbed 70 times and even the thieves cannot remove my jewelry. I was a gemologist and I cannot remove them until someone conveys the tale given me to share with all humanity. The curse of selfishness binds me to the earth. Only a selfless teller of tales can free me if he or she accepts the job."

"What tale is that which will set you free?" I wondered, "I will tell it for you!"

"I have a pen that talks to me and begs me for stories night and day, day and night."

"It is the tale of How or Why the Fly Became a Fugitive. Will you relate it to the little ones and the big ones and the happy ones and the sad ones and set my soul free from the poverty of the spirit and the greed of the mind that hoards what it should not hoard?"

"I will tell the people your story with all my heart," I promised the old lady, "and if my pen likes it, she will assist me."

"Very good" said the old woman. "If you agree, I will send my owl to you this very day and he will lead you to the story of 'Why the Fly Became a Fugitive.' The story may not come from his lips but he is a servant like unto my conscience and speaks for me. He will lead you only to a path which knows no crookedness."

"Oh woman," I said, "You have 5 husbands, but the sixth one does not love you, it seems. But I am a 'Son of Words' and what I write will be written on the scroll of the hearts...The five (5) common senses are the husbands of our thoughts. They go forth ahead of our knowledge, enriching, providing and protecting our way. They give our eyes 'insight', our ears 'understanding', our feelings 'sensitivity', our taste 'discernment' and our nose 'intuition'. If you lost these 5, you have lost your way and a stranger is misleading you...but I will tell our story."

"Oh sonny, I can't thank you enough," cried the woman with blue tears falling onto her blue shawl. "Thank you for your kindness for until you release me, I am a woman of the blues. Blue is my dress, blue is my shawl, my shoes, blue is the color of my heart. The blues are in my soles. Blue is my life. I ain't got nothing to lose but the blues." she smiled. "As for yourself, you will find that which you are missing."

"Just one childish question, please, before you go" I pleaded "Are you the old lady who swallowed a fly hundreds of years ago? Is that why you want this story told? And what am I missing?"

"Sonny I swallowed The Fly 'Beelzebub', The Lord of the Flies but I did not die!!" The old woman snapped, "Aint no fly can undo me Sonny, even if he can whistle dixie!...I just want to be free! Free from the lower self the selfish self...as for what you are missing, I can't say." Then the old woman hurriedly walked away, and I saw her walking straight into the trunk of a very large, gnarled oak tree.

The old woman disappeared right into the oak tree, as if she were walking into a virtual trap door in the 5th dimension, or into an invisible seamless holographic door! Even the shopping bags were swallowed in by the oak tree's trunk. The only thing that did not enter the tree were those blue suede shoes that she had been wearing. Inside the shoes was a note which read, "Thank you Sonny."

I left the shoes in front of the tree, but when I got home, strangely I saw those same blue shoes again, sitting on the floor of my closet. I did not know what to do! I was so tired, so tired. Just so very tired!!

The last thing I remember is staring up at the large blue pendulum clock opposite my bed-as the pendulum swung from left to right, left to right, back and forth, back and forth.

Then the clock grew larger and larger as I nodded from side by side, until it covered the whole wall opposite my bed. I stared transfixed, like a large, frozen unblinking blue eye.

Meanwhile, the pendulum was swinging, swinging, swinging, like a sideways sword of Damocles, searching to behead my very consciousness. Then the pendulum stopped and the door of the clock opened. Out of the door came a giant blue owl who stared at me and shouted "Who? Who? Who??" three times. I replied "John, John, John". He handed me some blue shoes which I put on, and I instantly found myself in the Land of Nod-a land beyond the reckoning of earthly time.

II The Puzzle: Journey To The Land of Nod

I had been walking through the park in the day, but now I was walking through the Land of Nod, searching for that tale that the old woman had told me about. Searching, searching! Searching!! Searching deeply the depths of my own soul.

There are many roads in the land of Nod, but I kept walking upon the straight path that is steep. It can ascend to heights of 50,000 years in one day. So its inhabitants say.

Walking and searching for The Old Woman's Tale, I became so weary that I almost went astray. The blue owl flew ahead of me, marking the way.

Finally, I came to a magnificent garden, a garden in the sky, wherein I met a Fig Tree named "Salem" (at least that is what was carved on his trunk) and an Olive Tree named "Becca", who were sitting in each other's shade, sharing gentle sips from the invisible glass of a summer breeze.

I sat between this elegant couple and enjoyed their treelike conversations, which they were most eager to share without hesitation.

In the clearing to the North, I thought that I noticed the large Blue Owl hovering over the face of a well. I was thirsty and curious, so I moved closer and closer. As I got closer, I saw that the large blue owl was no longer there. Instead, I saw a young woman dressed in white gossamer veils, which appeared blue from a distance because they reflected the color of the sky.

Perched upon the lips of the well, I saw that she was most beautiful woman that I had ever seen anywhere on earth or in my dreams. The brightness of her smile and the allure of her eyes imprisoned me and freed me at the same time. My soul had become a poem; my spirit a song beyond the quaint abilities of bamboo flutes. I had to draw near to her. I felt compelled to be as close to her as light is to the skin of the sun, or softness is to the skin of a sweet ripened peach. Suddenly, I had fallen under the spell of love.

"Oh woman," I exclaimed "I wish that I were a fish so that I could swim in the deep waters of our love. I wish I were a song so that I could be sung by your lips."

"Silly man," the woman exclaimed "Of course you love me, because I am your own heart. One day you will recognize me. Your brain has got you this far and in the <u>Land of Wake</u> you have led me wisely, my husband. For the brain is the husband of the heart. In the land Nod you cannot lead me. I am the heart and I can lead you to places that brains never go. So husband, follow my footsteps. Did you not teach me that every man has 5 eyes:

1. Physical Eye governed by light

    The eyes of insight and hindsight governed by experience and knowledge

    The Eye of Logic that sees the point, or pattern or organization of things

    The Astral Eye or the eye of imagination

    and Faith The Eye of the Heart

You do not yet have the eye of heart, my husband. I, the heart, can travel back 30,000 years to the story that you seek. So now in this world of Nod, you must follow me faithfully as I have followed in the Land of Wake." she concluded.

"I will follow you in my thoughts," I replied. "So lead me through the veil of time, my love."

So I followed this lovely creature in the garden that I believed and hoped was my very own heart until I came to a golden door marked "DNA", A Door that suddenly opened straight away.

I really didn't know if DNA meant "Do not access", or whether it was the biological door of the human past that my Heart had led me to. But it was too late to hesitate. A strong tornado gust of a wind pushed me into the abyss behind the door, and I fell through the glass of history and all that I could hear was that sweet, sweet voice which said "Come my husband, follow me…follow me…."

And follow and fall I did. I must have crashed through several veils of heavens for over 1,000 generations. I kept seeing numbers and pictures flashing in reverse order, like a number counter in my head (1975 1875 1775 1675, 1575 10,750).

"FOLLOW ME, FOLLOW ME!!!" shouted the voice of my Heart.

"I cannot fly!" I shouted back. Her voice yelling "Follow me…follow me…Trust me…trust me…" became fainter and fainter.…I just kept falling until I could hear "follow me" and "trust me" no more.

Each number that I past as I fell was tied to a picture of a civilization. Rome, Persia, Greece, Nubia, Egypt, Atlantis, Axum, Azteca & Mu. All of this I saw while falling, falling back through time. 20,776 BC 25,776 BC until I came to the number 27,000 BC and there I saw nothing but untamed wilderness. I opened the door in front me. My wife, my heart, whoever she was, had disappeared, it seems. I could only find half of myself. One useful eye, one useful hand, one useful leg etc.

I still had my silver gilded pen with which to write. My mind seemed intact. All of my dreams had followed me to this new place like silent obedient children. All 70,000 of them sat like attentive children in a well behaved kindergarten classroom. I was in the kindergarten of life and the sky was a like a gray chalk board and on it was written:

"Kind Hearts are the Gardens
Kind thoughts are the roots
Kind words are the blossoms
Kind deeds are the fruits
Write Oh Scribe what you are given
Things not said should not be scriven"

So descended upon me a voice reciting
My mind suspended my pen hand writing
Could writing such a tale
Put my soul in mystic jail?
Was I part of a devious plan
Conjured to defeat half a man

Part III: The Puzzle's Wife: The Tale of the Fly

"In the early days of man, nearly 30,000 or more years ago, the earth was divided into 4 regions. Forest, glades and jungles, deserts and plateaus, a land of gardens and a fourth composed of frost, ice and snow.

The garden was most beautiful, high in the mountains like the mountain rose. It sloped gently down in valleys that led to the sea. It was a different world. There were no uncaring candy wrappers or plastic bags blowing in the wind. No empty bottle or aerosol cans of flowered scents on the ground or un-cola cans on the virgin sands. Pollution had not frightened the rain forests or the trees. Animals never knew about the word "zoo" and trees were not planted in concrete museums called sidewalks.

As for the garden in the mountain, it seemed as broad as the sky domed by turquoise rainbows. It was a wonder to the eye. The garden was called Harmony. The village of man laid down by the sea in a warm and verdant valley.

The zebra, the elephant and the giraffe all shared the garden's grass. The spider, the ant and the bee were footloose and fancy free. The lion, the buzzard and the crow didn't mind that the going was slow. The loose mongoose and the monkey were number one pranksters, you see. And the fly—well the fly was a fly who was very, very sly.

There was Peace! Peace! Peace! Except for a squabble or two about who was king, who was the wisest, the prettiest, and who was the "who" of who.

The only thing that brought fear or a tear to the eye were rumors that the ice hunters from the north were coming. Men of cyclopean mentality they were; myopic hunters of animals and kidnappers of men.

No one knows just where they were from or where they would go, only that their kingdoms and hearts were made of snow. Their sudden raids made everyone afraid. They loved not the ways of the gardens. They were the "ice men".

Some say that they were consorts of an evil Warden, a Whisperer hidden in leaves. A Whisperer between snowflakes who deceives.

But back in the garden, it had long been settled that the Elephant was the King of the Garden. The Elephant had thrown the lion out of the ring in a fair fight, eons ago. You might say the lion was "over-throned".

The ants thought they were smarter than the bees because they had built cities in the garden, while the bees seemed content to flit from flower to flower and then to make honey in the safety of mountain towers or numerous tree colonies. They thought they were cultured and not materialistic.

The giraffe looked down her nose on the zebra and bragged about her elegant neck and high society. She often called the zebra a poor excuse for a horse. The zebra protested, perhaps too loudly, and told the giraffe to get her head out of the clouds.

The monkey and mongoose argued about who could pull the biggest pranks on people, who was the bravest, the most cunning or most knavish.

The monkey said he once put on a hat and a disguise to cover his eyes. Then he went to the Village of the Man and got a gig guarding banana stands. Well, you know what happens when you have a dog as a security guard for a frankfurter wagon. Need we say more?

The mongoose would listen with a yarn. He claimed his dining room was in man's barn and that no one was looser than Mr. Mongooser, for he said he could snatch the "sunrise crow" from a rooster at dawn.

The crow and the buzzard were sort of funeral directors. They fussed and argued and cried over scraps of animals who died.

The fly, the crafty old fruit fly, was a loner and very, very sly. He didn't work. He got by on whom he got by. The fly had only one friend, the spider, Ms. Sylvia Snyder. Lady Snyder was also a loner. She was in poor health, a widower with wealth and plenty of capital to spend.

The fly and his spider lady friend played dominoes together, slapping the domino web until the wee hours of the morning.

The fly talked a lot of trash while living off human stashes of bananas, cashews and calabash. The fly would often brag that he could be King because neither the elephant nor the lion could beat a fly in the ring. He said, "If I buzz, buzz, buzz around in their ears, they'll leave the ring in the saddest of tears."

He bragged that he was more beautiful than the giraffe or the zebra because he had these gossamer wings that could flutter three hundred times per second and reflect the rhapsody of the rainbow.

He bragged that he was smarter than the bees or ants because they had to work too hard for a living, while he, "super" fly, had friends like the spider to feed him, or he could simply collect dew from the fruits and leaves of the morning trees if he had a mind to work.

When the spider digested what the fly had said, she became very angry, her face turning red as a Red Venus Fly Trap plant.

"Get out you lazy, ungrateful fly," she screamed, "I'll feed you no more." The sly fly hit the door.

Next day, the tree fly heard the mongoose and monkey arguing about who could get the best of man in the village. The monkey was bragging about his disguise again. The mongoose claimed he spent the night in the barn feasting on plump chicken eggs.

The fly laughed. He laughed so loud and hard that the mongoose and monkey heard him. "What are you laughing at, sly fly?" queried mongoose.

"You guys are pathetic," smirked the fly. "Why, I can go into the house of man and eat from man's own table. So buzz off!"

"Mind your own business," shouted the monkey.

"I'll prove it!" said the fly. "I'll bring a morsel of food from man's table tomorrow morning."

"How will we know it's from man's table?" asked mongoose. "Besides, you should never say what you shall do tomorrow, for you yourself can do nothing. You should say, God willing."

"The man's food will be cooked," said the fly, "for fire is man's good servant, for we animals it is a bad master. If the food is cooked, it is human food!"

"You're on!" responded the monkey. "We'll be at your funeral if you fool around with man." The fly laughed, a rib-cracking contemptuous laugh.

That night, the crafty fly kissed his family goodbye and explained that he would be away overnight on a secret mission. He flew out of the Garden, down the mountain into the Valley of the Village of Man. There he spied the cottage of a wise, old man named BaBa.

BaBa was a giant of a man at seven feet tall, with white hair and a carefully sculpted coiffure of a beard. Some say he was 700 years old. He was the village historian, convener and prayer caller for as long as man could remember.

It was a Friday afternoon when BaBa climbed to the roof of his house wearing the mantle of the moon and a simple white tunic as he had done nearly 24,000 times before and issued the community call to prayer:

"G-d is the greatest,

G-d is the greatest." he repeated four times. "There is no G-d but G-d, The Creator, The Beneficent, The Kind."

Out of the houses came men, women and children pouring into the village like a faucet of rainbows from heaven. The people were adorned in colorful robes and walked with their bare feet touching the earth.

The crafty fly saw his chance and flew through the window of BaBa's house. There on the table, he saw all manner of fruit; mangoes, guava, bananas, carambola, soursop, breadfruit, peaches, papayas and passionfruit. He was in fruit fly heaven.

Suddenly, the door opened as BaBa had returned home and quickly glanced at the fruit fly on his table. "Peace be unto you, you little fly," said BaBa. "I will not harm you for you are my guest. Eat the dew of the fruit all you wish, but do not eat the flesh of my meat or the bread from my plate." With that, BaBa heated up some lamb and bread and sat down to eat at one end of the table. The fly sat at the other end.

The old man nodded off to sleep at the dinner table. The fly made his move and decided to taste the meat. It was the first meat he had ever tasted. It was good, so good that now sly fly wanted to take some for his family and for the bet he had made, for certainly the food had kissed the fire. As sly fly finished bundling up a huge package of lamb meat, the old man awakened.

"Fly," he roared, "Was I not generous with you? Did I not treat you as a guest?" The fly laughed and that made the giant very angry. BaBa shouted as he swatted at the fly with his gargantuan 12 inch hands again and again, missing each time. Every time he missed the fly, the giant broke a piece of furniture in his house. The blows were so strong and so fast that the fly might have died of pneumonia from the draft created by the giant's blows.

The fly finally escaped, but not without snatching his bundle of lamb from the table. The fly entered the garden triumphant, announcing to monkey and mongoose, "I have entered the house of man and taken food from his table. Am I not superior to you?" he exclaimed. The monkey and mongoose shook their heads and walked away in amazement.

Next, sly fly gave his family some of the meat and each was satisfied. Three days later, the old fly spied buzzard and crow arguing over the choice meat of a fallen zebra. When sly fly saw the meat, he started salivating and thinking about a way to get that meat for himself and his family. There was enough zebra meat to feed every fly in the garden.

Then the Whisperer who lurks in the garden of the heart appeared from behind the leaves and spoke to the fly. "I am a lord of the flies and a sincere advisor. Verily, a buzzard's food is a fly's meat and bread."

So as the fly approached the crow and buzzard, the seed of the Whisperer grew swiftly in his heart. It grew until it became four words on his lips. "Flee for your lives!" cried the fly, "Ice hunters are coming!" he added. "I saw them on the plain, four and twenty boat loads of men from the Land of Ice. Better fly that way," urged the fly, pointing to the East. "They are not nice. Their hearts are cold as ice, so you know." he continued.

The buzzard and the crow took to the sky, cackling four words "The hunters are coming, the hunters are coming! The ice men are coming!"

The monkey heard the cries and began swinging through the trees, sounding the alarm as only a monkey can. The giraffe and zebra fled. The elephant ran. The lion cut out. The mongoose "made tracks." The bees left the hive. The ants buried themselves alive, deep in the earth. The spider pulled up the web like a tent and got in the wind. All creatures left the garden or hid themselves. Or made themselves thin. All except the flies.

The monkey reached the village and gave the alarm to BaBa through sign language, wrapping his arms around his shoulders as if he were shivering. This gave BaBa the message that the ice men were coming. The hunters with no known compassion in their hearts had arrived. Men who put animal heads on their roofs and trampled the rights of men under the hoofs of lies.

BaBa climbed to the roof top and gave the alarm. Each villager grabbed a torch and fighting pole and formed a circle around the village, waiting for the hunters to invade from the North, South, East and West of "Snowlandia".

Meanwhile, the garden was empty except for the flies, who engaged and engorged themselves, feasting on the flesh of the fallen zebra. They even raided the meat in BaBa's house.

The village of the garden of men waited and waited and waited. The animals ran and ran and ran. Some ran until they died. No one knew that the fly had lied. The ice men, the hunters never came. Finally, everyone realized that the fly had lied. They were all, to say the least, very upset. The fly flew and fled. The fly had run and become a fugitive, "wanted dead or alive".

They searched for the fly everywhere, but he and his family had disappeared.

Flies became pariahs, a despised messiah of bad news. So anyone who saw a fly swatted at him and chased him away. In many places that still goes on today, people just shoo shoo shoo flies away.

"Shoo fly, don't bother me.

Shoo fly, don't bother me."

A song they sing and say everywhere, every night and day.

The fly's lie is at the heart of the matter. It caused the peace in the garden to shatter.

For years, the fly and his family were exiled from the land of Nod and the clean places of the earth. Chased away by cows, camels, horses, animals and man, no creature wanted a fly for a friend or to kiss his face or hands. All who associated with flies were disgraced, indeed, and banned.

Finally, one town, a suburb of Harlem called Chaos (used to be the Bronx), claimed to reach the ultimate utopian goal–a fly-less society. They even put up signs which read "Welcome to Chaos. You Heard Right We Aint Got Flies."

Soon, however, all of the animals in Chaos got sick. Sick as dogs. Excuse the expression, I am not "dog-ophobic". The animal doctor of the village was a baboon named Mabel. Mabel concluded that it was unprocessed, untreated manure from the animals (cows, horses, lions, mosquitos, manure, etc.) that had seeped into the water supply, i.e. the watering holes of Chaos. This was making all of the animals who drank out the watering hole sick.

Mabel the baboon had no cure that wasn't related to bananas and soon the disease spread all throughout the village. Then, all the animals sent a delegation to BaBa the man for advice.

"Well," said BaBa, "Mabel the baboon is right. Flies eating manure and nasty things is part of the Creator's plan. By processing manure and waste, they help to keep disease away from the land, but it is not good that flies land on our bodies and transfer filth to ourselves. So let the fly return as long as he does his duty and does not lie. Every creature of the Creator has its place on earth in its present form and we must shun the harm but welcome the benefits.

The animals sent out messengers to invite the fly and his family home. All will be forgiven if the fly repented of his lie.

But the fly had fled and was nowhere to be found. With the help of a Red Owl named Matilda, he had fled from the Land of Nod to the Land of Wake.

Matilda the Red Owl showed the fly all over the Land of Wake and brought the fly to Central Park. There, she met Max the Blue Owl and eventually Max's master – Samaria Parable the old woman.

Soon enough, the fly also met the old woman. In fact, the fly landed upon the face of the old woman all dressed in blue as she sang the blues about having plenty of nothing and nothing of plenty to do!!

"Oh fly," said the old woman, "I see that you are a fugitive-so too am I. Do not hide inside of me. They and the Truth will find you eventually."

The fly did not listen. He flew into her inner being like a bat into a cave. Then, the startled old woman swallowed a spider to catch the fly. She swallowed a bird to catch the spider. A cat to catch the bird. A dog to catch the cat. A tiger to catch all of them!

She then began to tell her story about the five husbands and the sixth companion named Grady (Greedy Deed), hoping to encourage the fly to leave her be.

"Now fly," she pleaded "you must find a writer to tell your story, or you will forever endure in the house of manure and in the heart of manure, and few will appreciate the swift gossamer wings of your potential. Repent, oh Fly." she exclaimed.

"Who will tell my story?" asked the fly from within Samaria.

"His name is John." replied the woman. "He was once the prisoner of a Nightingale, but he is out of jail. I will find him for you and me. I already sent him on a mission. He and his pen are in The Land Of Nod and already know your story."

"Really," said the fly "tell me who I am and what you think of me?"

"Flies are like the souls of men," replied the old woman "either they are majestic kings of their ordained destiny or they have chosen to be flying lies F-LIES. Which do you choose to be, my dear?"

"I choose to be a king over my own ordained destiny and a servant of The Creator/The Most High." replied the fugitive fly

"Well, come out of me, old Beelzebub and go home to repentance. There is a welcoming party and a new job waiting for you. But you must be bold and have your story told. John is already there writing it in Nod."

"Really?" replied the fly incredulously.

"Really my dear," said the old woman with great enthusiasm, "Now move along, Mr. Fly. The winds of change await you and me."

And it came to pass that out of the old woman came the fly and five creatures: the spider, the bird, the cat, the dog and the tiger. These animals ran wild and willy nilly into Central Park.

So the fly returned to the garden in The Land Of Nod and repented to all who had been affected by his lies. The Community of Being watched him carefully but at last, received him with vigilant and watchful forgiveness.

Part IV: The Enigma: The Return To Forever
And The Return of My Heart

"Are we finished now, Master!? I don't know why we had to come here." said my pen. "Can we go home now?"

"I am ready too!" I responded "But shall we return without a guide?"

"Where is your heart?" asked the pen. "If your heart is in the right place, we will go home."

"Of course, my Pen, I just want to get back to the Land of Wake."

"I?!" said the pen vigorously "you mean we...you use all of my ink and you say 'I'. You writers have no heart. No heart at all."

With that, my ink pen cried with dry eyes and fell asleep in the bedroom of imagination. I was a wreck. I knew I needed my heart to return to Wake and become my whole self.

Each day, I hobbled down to the beaches of Nod to sit, gaze at the horizon and think of a way to return to the Land of Wake. It's a daunting challenge. Nod (the subconscious and black space) is thousands of times bigger than the Land of Wake (the conscious gleaming world of light).

If only my beloved heart would appear. (No doubt I was confident that she was searching for me in over a thousand different worlds and a hundred different lifetimes).

I, John, your tour guide and writer was stranded in Nod so long that they made me a naturalized citizen. There was no way to return without my heart to guide me back from sleep to wake...Oh how I longed to see her!! Only she could make me whole.

Then one day, while glancing into the gray eyes of Nod's dawn, I saw her image in the fading night sky. The tears of the stars had almost turned into morning dew. I heard her sweet voice calling me from behind a veil.

"John, follow my voice. Behold, I am your beloved heart, your wife. Follow my voice. Do not look back or you may lose me forever....Fly, John. Fly straight up. I am carrying you with my love. You will pass seven mountains of love and seven mountains of reason. They will heave peaks of different colors. When you past the last Purple Mountain Majesty, you will be home in the Land of Wake. Wait for me and relax. I will soon join you."

I crashed in the Land of Wake like the Sputnik or Apollo Space Craft splashing in the Atlantic. My memory and body were shaken. But not frantic.

There were three things that lingered on after my experience leaving Land of Nod: the memory of the story; the recent encounter with my beloved heart and those itchy mysterious bites of Nod flies swelling slightly on my left arm.

I was back into ole Central Park, but immediately upon first seeing me, the old woman dashed back into the gnarled oak tree as if she had forgotten something...The tree swallowed her whole and when she quickly reemerged, she was carrying two large red suitcases. "Now where are my blue shoes?" she wondered out loud. "Never mind, I don't want them...Thank you, thank you...Thanks Sonny, Because of you I'm free. Yes I'm Free." She waved goodbye to me hastily and heartily and dashed to the edge of the park

"What happened to the fly?" I asked Samaria.

"What fly?" she shouted back "I haven't seen any fly!!"

She seemed terribly hurried. I was too weak and weary to respond.

"Taxi! Taxi! Taxi!" she yelled as she stuck her hand out in the air. A light blue cab descended like a beautiful butterfly in front of her. She hopped into the blue butterfly cab and it drove off up into the sky.

"Wait for me!" shouted the Blue Owl frantically as he flew into the wind. But the cab drove up furiously fast into the sky. Far too high for an owl to fly.

On the sidewalk where the light blue cab had landed sat five pieces of jewelry guarded by a black raven and a black crow, two of the fiercest defenders that I know. Two gold earrings, a gold necklace, one exquisite gold ring and a gold bracelet with an inscription which read, "Free at last! Free at last. Great God Almighty Free at Last. Give only to the poor in spirit Sonny."

In front of the oak tree sat two little blue suede shoes. Inside was a note that read, "Sonny, thanks. See you soon where heaven meets the blue shining sea!"

"Where are your shoes Mademoiselle?" asked the taxi driver as they kept ascending. Once they had reached the Blumberg Skyway (about 3,000 feet above the city skyline),

"I don't remember," replied the old woman. "I forgot to take my gingko biloba! Can you just drive, Sonny! Drive! I'm in a hurry—the 6th level of the Second heaven. Please. I've got my husband waiting for me and I'm late for dinner!"

"Your husband?" flushed the driver in a surprised voice. "All these years I've been picking you up, I did not know you had a husband."

"Well Sonny, I have common sense. I've had five husbands, one every hundred years. Lately, I've lived 6 years in that oak tree. Five Hundred years before there was a Central Park, I lived in 5 palaces. You wouldn't believe the number of rooms, Sonny. I'm tracking down the sixth husband. Now Sonny, you just haven't lived long enough." the old woman explained and exclaimed and exclaimed and explained!!

.magnificent seven.

Night descended upon the city like a brown moth. Max the Blue Owl kept guard over a vacant gnarled oak tree. Verily, this is a tale told by an idiot.

"Hey lady, you forgot your pet owl Max!" I shouted weakly and futilely into the gusting wind. But of course, Samaria was long gone!

"Forget it, Son of Night." counseled Max the Owl "She only cares about herself and wanted to avoid 'loving the highest good for herself and others'. At least I am free of her for now. You must take care of those fly bites. They are from another dimension and you need medicine from Nod. Also you must find your heart. If you find her your true heart your faith and love may heal you!"

"Thank you brother" I smiled.

"No feathers off me. Hey, I have a Red Owl to find. There is no telling what adventures we can find together!" Max the Blue Owl turned away and flew south. He reminded of my own curiosity-never satisfied…

I turned the corner of change and started walking north. For a second, the night stood still. She paused while remembering to bow her head slightly toward my beloved People's Republic of Harlemia!

I was walking in the Harlemia state of mind. Maybe tonight I would find my beloved heart. To find her I knew I must search everywhere, even within the hidden labyrinthine byzantine halls of my mind.

If she is real, then I have spent my entire life walking through a dream.

The reality of true love is something in which I strongly believe.

Love can build cities in the heart or just leave gentle glitters of stardust on your sleeve.

I John, a son of the night, was on my way!! On my way to the promised kiss of sunshine at the edge of the river of the night. I was going home!!

Then I heard a voice in the turquoise of the night- a voice like a dream.

"Follow me, I am your heart." it said.

"Where are you? I can't see you." I replied.

"Be still, mind. I will touch your hand." the voice replied.

Then she touched me. She touched my hand. I held her hand tight. I would not let her go again. As I held her hand, she turned into that beautiful woman that I had seen before in the garden in the sky. But now she was on earth with me in the Land of Wake.

"Darling," she asked, "How could you be without me? Why did you look back? Our future is ahead of us."

I answered "You are
My flame and without you I am an
Empty candle lost in the lifeless dark
What is a man who has
Only a brain but emptiness & insane
Without a heart
If man doesn't have a heart and a brain
He cannot 'make up his (complete)
mind'
Completeness he cannot find
Darling do not leave
Without you, there is no
Air to breathe
Either in the land of 'Wake' or 'NOD'
Earth without fire
Is only sod."
"What is your name, my flame?" I asked.
"I am Yasutako, your one and only love forever."
"Yasutako, I will leave you never."

We were walking through Central Park. It was spring again. The birds were on the wing again. The weeping willow shouted with happiness. The cherry blossom trees caressed the breeze.

Gladness was in the air. Children were repairing everywhere the broken benches for the elderly to sit upon. It was a new day. Max the owl came to visit us with his Red Owl friend as we sat by the magnificent fountain of Bethesda.

"Who? Who? Who?" shouted Max.

"You you you" we replied with a smile upon faces.

"You guys must have gone to day school." laughed the owl.

"And you to night school." Yasutako responded. "So, why are you out in the day?"

"I've found my red owl friend Matilda?" he answered, "and now am a day and night Owl."

"Well, we are thinking about going to the Land of Nod for vacation," I responded, "maybe write another story."

"No way," chimed in my pen, "not me, myself or I!"

"No way!!" we all laughed.

And there we were with "happy ever after" wrapped in a bow… We knew in our hearts that we would soon travel again, for Yasutako and I were the traveling type. But the People's Republic of Harlemia would be our new home. Besides, Central Park was back to her young beautiful self.

The Epilogue and Reflection
in the Fountain of Time

Sometimes it is good to flee
Especially if it's from our
Worse selves to our better selves
Some mirrors tell the Truth
And some mirrors lie
Some gates are low
And some gates are high
I travel in the Night
I walk into my dreams
Life is a flight it seems
To destinations not easily seen
I always wished that I could fly
Since I was a little short guy
Knee high

Even when I went to college
When I had but little knowledge
About the mysteries not shown
Of the heart, ear and eye
I always believed that on my own
On my own I could fly......

Back then my major was curiosity
And my minor was confusion
I found then that Thoughts and Deeds are real
What really matters is concealed
And that—gross matters itself is illusion
That hides a lesson leading to just one conclusion

DR. JOHN "SATCHMO" MANNAN

All good proceeds from a single mind
The Divine One who created heaven and earth
And put in all humans
Inherent value, dignity and worth

Now maturity enters and youth flees bye\
It takes two to tango and two to fly

With Yasutako's help we called the Blue Taxi Butterfly.
We ascended and ascended high into the darkening sky
We changed into many shapes as we went higher
We soon found ourselves beneath a spire
Sitting on an alabaster wall
of the grand palace of a king
Who was busy sponsoring
A ball of most lavish price
Just to please his lovely, beautiful wife
From the wall I saw her standing there
Taking in the garden air
I was clueless
But I noticed she was shoeless

She wore a blue dress, blue
Diamonds and an expensive blue silk shawl
She was so young
But I recognized her after all
She was the old lady
From the Bethesda Fountain place
She was Samaria Parable Jane, the same old woman
Though young now in the face
She was the very same lady
Except now we were in the palace of her

6th Husband
King Adam Smith Grady

Suddenly that lady
Recognized me and walked
Over to the wall
Where I was just a spy
On the wall
A fly on the wall
"Hello Sonny" she said "Why"
"Why did you become a fly?
And this is your lovely wife, I presume?"
"Yes to deliver a message" I resumed....
"Come back to your 5 senses Samaria
Your common sense Samaria
Greed is a society's grand malaria."
"I will not I will never" sighed the grand old lady
"I am in love with King Adam Smith Grady."
"Then so long you wretch! You will catch your fate!" shouted Yasutako
emotionally
"Husband, can we go?"

Then Yasutako and I took the Blue Taxi Butterfly back to Central
Park and resumed our normal human shapes.

In time, my heart and I became as one. I could easily "make
up my mind". Through my relationship with Yasutako, I became a
whole hearted man and she a whole hearted woman. Even my pen
found a new self regenerating ink supply.

One summer day, we were both sitting in front of Bethesda
Fountain, enjoying the rainbow colored weather. Suddenly, we saw a
dark object hurdling toward earth. We then heard a huge splash in
Bethesda Fountain.

We ran to see what it was.

Goodness!! It was the Samaria Parable, Jane!! The same old woman who had swallowed a fly; lied about his whereabouts and led my pen and me to this wild goose story. The police took her away in red handcuffs to the crazy house. Harlemia Hospital. Psych Ward.

She kept yelling "I am a citizen of Parable New York, A Phantom City...I have diplomatic immunity!" as she fought the white straight jacket.

"Parable City New York, sure lady and this is a no fly zone .... you're under arrest." laughed the police officer derisively.

Afterword 1

A man is what he thinks and loves. I have become profoundly aware of all of me and of the unity of me, myself and I with all of humanity. It is part of knowledge of the universal self. The art of knowing self is the art most forgotten in this world of dissonant distractions and dances between indecision and dissatisfaction.

If the world could only listen to its own true heart, there would a greater measure of peace-a greater level of human achievement, dignity and distinction.

Good night, my dear reader.

Next time, you must drive the A train of thought (of the travelling mind) and I shall gladly be your passenger. We will embark from the People's Republic of Harlemia. Our destination-a great land of truth and beauty.

Maybe Parable City, East of somewhere, West of Nowhere. "Be sure to pack one pair of suede blue shoes!"

Until G-d willing we write again!!

Tale From My Nightingale

Part I
The Scientific Genie and
The Girl from 136th Street

A)   Prologue

I often look upon my youth with melancholy joy
For there came a time in my life
when I had fasted
seven years from songs and poetry
The lamps in my eyes
had grown dim
My mind had become a blade
and that awe made by G-d
the gift of living,
had lost its symmetry.
As I walked down the steps of the court house
To my poetic mind
I stared into the face
Of the western sun
a bare bones veiled woman vegetating
in the corners of society with an empty bowl and an outstretched hand

Sadly I recognized her. She was Lady Liberty, The Statute of Liberty!
Homeless people sat at her feet
Reciting and chanting the poetry of hopelessness
Souls slept in the dust of the closed doorways of industry
Recession moved in. Industry the uncaring husband moved out travel-
ling East of the sun and West of the moon in pursuit of low wage eyes
And as the sun set over autumn in New York,
I found myself walking
through my beloved People's Republic of Harlem,
Harlem, with its coconut brown face searing
like the moon,
against the coverlet of a starless night.
Harlem, the turquoise kiss
Whose tulip perfume lingers lustfully in the air,
Harlem, the caring mother
who gives birth daily to a thousand eyes,
filled with dreams.
I was one of them,
a child of its nocturne
returning home.
I was on ole 125th Street and Seventh Ave this time,
(now called Adam Clayton Powell Blvd),
and in the window of
the Five and Dime store
I saw him, that bird
that would be a bane
to my heart
and a balm to my existence,
for a time
of which I have yet to reckon.
"African Nightingale for Sale"
the sign read.

His blue purple plumed regale was in bright contrast to his baleful mystic bearing. His proud beak seemed bent on tearing his way out of his bamboo cage. Yet he seemed sedated, like some pen written sage who could give life to himself by leaping from the pages of a book. He had this insidious look and demeanor, no doubt. But I had no doubt that he would be a Bel-Canto singer who could weave intricate songs, or else a scat singer who could scatter away my blues

And so six lingered nights I fought a tortured wrestling; gamely and vainly I sought to pursue illusions of my grand bargain. But that bird refused to sing. He refused with spectacular disregard for my feelings. I was angry but I will never ever say a bad word about a bird again.

"You stupid bird!" I yelled "what good are you?, you can't even sing I'm taking you back to the store in the morning" I threatened.

I heard a voice shouting three times as if coming from the walls "NEVER MORE" NEVER MORE NEVERMORE

CLOSE THE DOOR!!" it screeched.

I heard a giant gate slam inside my brain.

Suddenly I found myself stumbling into a deep immobilizing sleep. A strange anesthesia wrapped me in the ether of the night as if I were in a hospital bed awaiting some unscheduled surgery. I found myself lying in a cold naked room surrounded by four doors....I was in a room with a roof made of bamboo peelings tied to a string.

I was in some sort of cage!
I was in a cage!
I was in a cage!!
I was in a rage!
I was in a rage cage.!!!

I peered up at a space in the bamboo ceiling and there between the bamboo peelings, I saw the giant face of the nightingale that I

had just purchased and cursed peering down at me through the top
of the sprat.

I was in the cage! I was in a cage!! I was in a cage!!
I lay motionless,
pinned and rattled as if strapped down
by two indefatigable but invisible surgical assistants:
awe and terror.
And then the nightingale
said to me:
"Son of People, The freedom of your soul lies in
Four mystic tales beyond the eternal jail of your thinking
Chase no more the Green Tiger
lest he devour you.
Time is faster than the wind so fly to your pen
"O Nightingale" I pleaded
"is there no bailor for my soul
which lies pinned on this nocturnal floor?"
And my captor only replied
as he stared at me with burning eyes,
"Four"
"Four, Four, Four, and nevermore curse the bird of freedom
FOUR AND NEVERMORE"
I could learn no more
And the door to the
North of the room was ice blue,
The door to the East was graceful green
and too appealing, to be true
and the door of the south was brown
like the earthly ground
And the door to the West was red,
And it was this that turned my head.

It glowed red like a fire, a burning bush of hope far away,
Although I knew not
what lay behind its crimson face
So I opened the door to the west,
and there I saw a tunnel,
a windy tunnel styled like
the shape of a funnel,
and the wind in the tunnel
sucked me down, down, down
into a deep abyss-a deep, deep, deep abyss

Things seemed to be biting me on my hands and feet as I went hurriedly down into the windy maelstrom. Down and round I went; I tried in vain to grab the walls of the tunnel. Down, down, I saw faces and visions of faces as I floated down. Down until I landed hard on the station platform, of some sort of subway station or underground inner space railroad station. Then I saw a sign which read "Underground Railroad, Seven More Steps to Freedom",

I pinched myself drawing blood from my cheek to determine whether I was alive or dead . There was a mural over the façade of the railroad station.

It was picture of three men praying in the road, the ground seemed to be shaking and fire was coming out of their mouths. I recognized them. They were Martin Luther King, Booker T. Washington and Malcolm X politically transfigured together ! Above their heads were written some strange dates 1776 1859 1960 2060 followed by the word "Nevermore".

Near another part of the mural I saw many faces and heard a chant. Several men and women were chanting, their lips moving ceaselessly in a hum-like chant or drone. I put my ear near the mural and the chant escaped like a dancing whirlwind.
"

FREEDOM is mind
Freedom is kind
A love supreme
A love supreme
A love supreme
G-d supreme
A love supreme,
Freedom is mind
Freedom is kind

I looked more closely. I recognized some of them. A few of them were from the Sons of Liberty. Others were from the Sons of Freedom .Mounted on horseback like A Brigade or Calvary of 500:, I saw Frederick Douglass, ,Martin Luther King, Demark Vesey, Nat Turner, , Thomas Paine Marcus Garvey William Lloyd Garrison, Malcolm X, John Coltrane, Maria Grazia Giammarinaro, Harriet Tubman, Eleanor Roosevelt William Wilberforce Abizu Campos, Pedro Pietri Elijah & Clara Muhammad and their son Wallace Mohammed, Sojourner Truth, Maya Angelou, Dalip Singh Saund and many many others.

They were the vanguard of a multitude mounted on the Ridge Of Freedom. The sun and wind were at their backs Swords made of scrolls were in their hands. Swords of love. Swords of Love. Words that were swords of love.

I John saw 144,000 words of love personified and arrayed in ranks on The Ridge Of Freedom in the mural of history. They were the souls of men striving for the sweet embrace of freedom- a freedom that brings dignity and distinction with the dance of each dawn.

Among them was John Brown, who dashing with two sons and 18 others on "white horses", led the charge against Harper's Ferry to end slavery and to free the moon from an artificial night. Wearing the Declaration of Independence as breast plates over their hearts, they were riding. They were charging. They were shouting mightily: "Freedom! Slavery Nevermore! A Love Supreme! Open the Door!"

"Live or Die No more slavery in the earth or the sky(The understanding of men)

Then I thought that I heard a distant piano tinkling in the background. It was clear as a train.

Clear as a bell, as "If I were a Bell." Clear as a train. But it was not a part of the mural

I looked up. There was a train coming. It was the Harlem 'A' train coming straight at me in the tunnel. Its berth seemed wider than the width of the station. The 'A' train had taken me by surprise! The 'A' train was coming. It was right there. It was going to hit me.! And destroy the station!!

OMG, it was the Nightingale! His face carved on the front of the A train. The Nightingale, his eyes serving as light on the face of the A train that was coming straight at me! It was a blue train, a night train, a blues train, a night 'A' train going down the "Straight Note Chaser". It was a Blues train. The Nightingale was upon me.

I dove. I lay flat on the tracks. And as the train passed over me, I clung to its underbelly. as it shot out of the tunnel, winging like a bird into the midnight sky. And the train rolled across the sky of the night, making tracks in the heavens. I don't know how I hung on through the night

until the dawn. And when the morning awoke with a yawn, this tale of the Nightingale,; descended and sat upon my shoulders. Its meaning is an illumination. Its meeting is destination .

My soul had finally arrived at its inspiration place

I looked up at the dawn and I saw an unending ascending Stairway to the Stars stretched out like a scroll..

I looked down upon the day. I saw and heard the roll of a noisy wooden escalator descending far down into the valley of the city and thereafter out of sight into the pitiful black bottomless bowels of the earth.

The tale of the Nightingale sitting on my shoulder nudged me toward the rickety escalator and toward the cliffs of my own sanity.! All vanity was gone. I awakened in a strange new world of time and space.

Gingerly, I unsheathed my pen from her sparkling silver case. She wept for joy as a third eye opened wide-as wide as a bewitched bewildered night upon her sable face.!!

B) By The Tale of The Enchantment

It was 7 a.m. and morning had long drawn aside the damp dew, jeweled veil of the heavens. She gathered a robe of clouds about her shoulders as she moved brightly through an azure sky. The wind from her stirring rustled like a burning fire. The warmth of her breath had long kissed the eve of spring goodbye.

It was Harlem. Harlem where, on the streets, below Summer slipped quietly onto her throne riding the back of a crab.

A grey and white shelled crab dawdled out of Ole Majestic Fish House on 129th and Malcolm X Blvd. Weaving and bobbing like an inebriated beauty contestant on a tight rope, the crab made its way toward a heap of rubble that encrusted the sidewalk.

Vendors from sundry places like Senegal, Guinea, Bangladesh and Mississippi had already staked out their places in the sun.

The streets shouted silent Hosannas in anticipation of some yet unknown Messiah.

White covered station wagons filled with well-heeled down towners, bankers from Wall Street, socialites from the Upper East Side of Manhattan, artists from the West Village, storekeepers from Chelsea, suburbanites from Nassau and Suffolk, tourists from faraway places were camped out across 110th street and 111th street. just North of the enchanted woods of Central Park. They were waiting to stake their claim to Harlem gold. These were "the gentrification-ites" armed with real estate bulletins, down payments and dreams of cheaper rent. They were camped on the southern frontiers of Harlem waiting for people to move or be moved out of Harlem so that they could move in. Evictions make Harlem an ever changing place. But for now all eyes were upon the coronation of the crab of summer.

It was hot. It was hazy. It was a hot, hazy summer street in Harlem and the fire hydrants were turning on.

The crab began to carefully rummage through the rubble as if looking for the crown of summer, or a lost jewel, or amulet of unknown powers. Cautiously and desperately it clawed until it fell upon a discarded moldy version of Richard Wright's book "Native Son." The pages of the book fluttered open as if possessed by a breeze from an enchanted wind. And out of the dusty pages stirred a big, brown gargantuan rat with green eyes glowing like a neon traffic sign.

The eyes of the rodent, as if by signal, turned a luxuriant red. The hellish rodent, its jaws gaping, rushed at the crab. Rushed like a linebacker toward a touchdown in the land of the setting sun. The crab of summer stepped out of the way and spun into the gutter like a derailed 'A' train. The rat regrouped immediately and charged again this time knocking the warrior crab of summer on its back. This was not without cost because the rat entangled his face in the pincer movements of the crab's claws. The rat hung on, digging its switch-like nails into the belly of the crab. The crab hung on tightening her pincer like hold.

Both held on like two Suma wrestlers in a fierce lock of death. Both clung tightly frozen like music on a page. Frozen like a song never played.

Finally, the rat slipped out gouging the belly of the crab. But the crab captured the rat's paw and held on. The rat gnawed his way to freedom..

The blood of summer ran from the crab. The rat tore off leaving behind the tip of its paw in the crab's claw. Its eyes turned back to a cool green. It was summertime and the past had predicted that living would not be easy. But time after time summer had prevailed. It would no longer be a prisoner in winter's jail or for that matter a prisoner of love.

It was already 8 a.m. in the skies up above, and in the streets the streams from the fire hydrants had now given birth to full-bodied rivers. Modern Mesopotamian rivers that ran between the two gutters. Rivers longer than "The Negro Speaks of Rivers" humor, longer than a John Coltrane "My Favorite Things". Rivers muddied by the gutters of living. Hearts were in the gutters. Lives were in the gutters. Swept away by rivers. Rivers! Rivers! Running scared rivers, rivers old and desperate. Rivers, so many rivers. There were so many rivers in Harlem that could never meet the sea. That was Harlem, the neglected, the underbelly of America. Harlem, the

hopeful, talented rhythm of the summer blaring from a saxophone, riding the riffs of rappers, genius yet unborn.

Meanwhile, the covered station wagons and passengers just sat and sat and sat. On the corner of 3rdth Ave and the corner of change, a multitude of marchers led by a thin latino minister with jerry curls were marching in a circle. They shouted " Queremos Trabajos"(We want jobs!) "No Justicia No Paz"(No justice, No peace), "Queremos Trabajos No Justicia, No Paz!" We want jobs! No justice, No peace!" People were honking at them as they drove by.

Still the covered wagons were waiting. They sat.

Alia Bilquis Never Thomas (Albi for short) stirred in her room stretching, reaching for the brightness of the morning, as she had done for 15 years.

"Albi, get up!" shouted her mother, Sophia. "You'll be late for school!"

"OK Mom!" returned Albi, "but classes don't start 'til 10 o'clock. It's summer, you know."

"Well, you'll have to fix your own breakfast. I am gone and I ain't got no time for lazy little women. I left a letter from your father on the dresser, do you see it?"

"Thanks Mom," breathed Albi. Albi heard the door slam hard and then open again.

"And make sure your backside is in the house by 8 p.m. young lady!" her mother scolded.

"Alright, Mom," Albi resigned. The door slammed again.

Albi groped for her father's letter on the dresser and turned on the light. His name was Malik Never Thomas and he was her dad.

Albi, My Dearest Daughter, I love you. I am sorry that I can't be with you. I'm working on a new project. Maybe this one will give me the freedom. However, I may be in New York Wednesday. If so, I'll see yah. If not, I'll send for you in August and we'll have a good time like always, G-d willing.

Remember your prayer and to read three pages every day from the Book. Protect your five senses from corruption lest the Evil one capture you as he did our forefathers ""Uncle Thomas" and "Bigger Thomas". The fight continues. You are my hope and the hope of millions before you who fought for our freedom. Peace be on you.

Love Always, Your Dad
Malik Never Thomas (II)

A year rolled down Albi's cheek in the form of a tear as she read the letter. She realized it was almost a year since she had seen her father. Her dad was the one person she had wanted to see more of, but it never worked out like she wanted since her mother and father had become divorced.

Albi let the cold water splash over her face as she prepared for the day. Her mind flowed like a waterfall contemplating the impression that her life was making in the world, and the suffering that she could not reach. She dressed for the day and remembered the way her father had taught her to pray.

In the name of God
the Good, the Kind.
All praise is due to God
the Good, the Kind,
Sole Master of the day of judgment.
Alone, You do we worship
Alone, You do we seek for help,
Show us the straight way,
The way of those whom
You have blessed,
Not the way of those
with whom You are angry,
nor of those who go astray
Forgive us if we err or make a mistake
For Thou art Supreme in forgiveness"

Albi wept, but the waterfall stopped just as someday the hydrants on the street of summer will stop. Then the world will have become a pleasant place.

Albi's thoughts turned to school. She scanned her wardrobe and found a languid print dress, the exquisite color of African Violets. It was a beautiful but casual dress. She dabbed some perfumed oil on her wrists and ear lobes. "Nefertiti of the Nile" was its name.

She thought about Gregg, one of her schoolmates whom she liked a lot. He seemed to talk to her more when she wore Nefertiti of the Nile. She dabbed on a little more Nefertiti as a smile leaked from her lips.

She stuffed her books in her Cordovan bag and of course, Big Math Book her father asked her to read. She'd read it later-maybe on the 7th Avenue or the A train. The A train that stopped nine blocks from 136th Street. The inimitable A train that ran through the history of Harlem.

The warm winds of summer embraced Albi as she walked her way into the morning. Into the morning of streets rife with morning smells. Into the smell of bitterness mixed with hope.

"Yo girl, what's up, what's up, girl, what's up?!" squealed one of the boys standing on the corner watching all the girls go by. Watching like spiders watch a fly, hoping to capture a favorable response with sweet baited traps

Albi breezed on by avoiding the traps and sandbars in the murky 9 a.m. rivers. In the murky rivers of lives that would never meet the sea. Finally, she came to 125th Street and St Nicholas Avenue.

"Hey, Missy Me Daughter!," a voice shouted above the din of an African market of street vendors shouting their wares on 125th Street. It was a familiar voice a life guard voice who always looked out for her in the murky waters of Harlem life. It was Asha the vendor, her favorite vendor. The tall elegant African woman who had sold her "Nefertiti of the Nile." along with stern warnings to stay in school and to keep serious. Asha was almost the age of her mother but not quite that old.

"Hey, Missy, me daughter!" the voice resounded again.

"Good Morning Auntie, Asha" Albi replied as she moved closer to the voice, slipping

through the crowd on ole 125th Street. Finally, she spotted her, the Mandinka woman street vendor who always had a blue nightingale on her right shoulder.

"I got him!" yelled Asha, waving a doll over her head. "I got him!"

It was a male Mandinka doll. A dark prince of a figure dressed in magnificent African garb. A violet colored taj appearing as a crown.

A free-flowing knee length dashiki. Violet loose-fitting drawstring pants. Around the neck was an amulet or necklace of some sort with a strange inscription in Arabic and Mandinka.

"This is it auntie" exclaimed Albi.

"Yes, my daughter" smiled Asa, "Asha keep her promise, daughter I got it just for you. It comes from my country and it's very very old, older than me. I don't know how old. He is one of seven. My grandmother gave it to my sister. My sister died and so now I give it to you, you are my little American daughter. His name is Jonathan Ben Ifrit."

"Thank you Auntie Asha" smiled Albi, "and how much do I owe you?"

"Nothing, nothing," insisted Asha, "just keep reading and studying like your father and mother told you."

"Yes, I'm going to do that," insisted Albi, "Education is the number one priority. Ignorance is the throne of oppression!"

"One thing daughter" cautioned Asha(her sunshine smile abruptly receding and her voice changing into a more serious tone), "never, never, never! remove the necklace. His name is Jonathan Ben Ifrit," Ben" for short. He has great power to make you smile."

"Ok," demurred Albi, "and, err, thanks."

"Don't mention it my daughter" smiled Asha as she gave Albi a hug with huge caring amazon arms. "tell you mom and dad "Asha say Hi"

"Peace! Peace!" I will responded Albi, as she waved goodbye and melted into the summer samba that had by now captured the rhythm of 125th Street. 125th Street where Asha stood vending, the blue nightingale adorning her shoulder.

As Asha hawked her wares, "African Bracelets, 2 for $10, Earrings 2 for $5.00!" her nightingale recited a melodious Mandinka mantra which translates : "FOUR NEVERMORE"

Albi walked toward a stop imbued with history, the A train

station at 125th Street and St. Nicholas Avenue, the site of an old canal, the hunting grounds of the Algonquin Indians, the tomb of dinosaurs, the site of the Harlem riots of 1939 when the invisible people revolted against those who pretended to be their masters.

Albi peeked at the Mandinka doll and the Book in her bag as she gripped it tightly. She was approaching the subway on her way to school, Harlem's Columbia University, 116th Street and Broadway, "Project Double Discovery", "College Bound", "Talent Unbound", an equal opportunity joint.

She wanted to be a vet (a veterinarian), a doctor and a teacher. She wanted to be someone a river of whose life would finally meet the sea. Someone whose life would be as a mountain of love. Someone whose life would be a fountain of comfort for the community.

The Apollo was just ahead between Adam Clayton Powell Blvd and Frederick Douglas Bld. She heard loud voices greeting her peace as she approached the Apollo Theatre. There was a huge circle of protesters shouting and clapping.

Led by Reverend Treble Cleff Dullerton, The rotiund Pastor of The Holy Ghost Filling Station Church they were shouting and chanting: "We want jobs! We want jobs! We want jobs now?...No justice No Peace No Justice No Peace!"

Albi saw some of her neighbors there: Mr. and Mrs. Harris, Ms. Laudebelle Baker, Ms. Daisy Hicks, Ms. Brenda Jones, Mr. Joseph Bearstrong and others who were apparently not at work but marching with Rev. Dullerton.

As she approached Frederick Douglas Blvd and 125th Street, flashing red and white strobe lights seemed to be searching her face, searching her heart like a lighthouse searching the soul of the sea. It was the police. Two police cars, a fire emergency vehicle and an ambulance from Harlem's hospital. They captured the corner. Tributaries of people flowed from surrounding buildings to form a pool of great curiosity.

An extremely muscular and tall young Afro-American male, in his twenties, his face smoldering like live coals beneath a hamburger on the 4th of July, was being lifted to the streets. He had evidently come out of the subway, the 7th Avenue subway on 125th Street.

"Move back! Move back people!" the police would bark, "Go home, there's nothing to see here but reality!"

Albi swam through the crowd, attempting to reach the other side of the dead pool.

"What happened? What happened? What happened, young man?" raised a schoolmarm fifty or so year old woman, moving her hands as if treading water. She spoke to a certain young Afro-American male in a pin-striped business suit. He resembled a brown version of "Dirty Harry in the Dead Pool."

"I'll tell you ma am, I don't know," he said with a shrug of his shoulders. "They say his Walkman or ear plugs got wet in the subway and exploded in his face, leaving the earphones embedded in his skull."

"Whose they?" followed up the schoolmarm, "How come 'we' are never they?"

"Hey, that boy's got no shoes on!" volunteered an inebriated voice in the crowd. "Man O Manischewitz, they'll have to cooperate on his brain at the hospital to get that junk out of his head."

"What do you mean cooperate homey?" answered a voice from a middle-aged can and bottle collector. "Man, you mean operate! They is going to operate on his brain."

"Whose they?" insisted the schoolmarm.

"Whatever! Whatever!" answered the inebriated one. "I used to be a doctor myself. I performed heart surgery in 1966 on the soul of James Brown," he countered with a laugh. The schoolmarm lady didn't laugh. She saw the tragedy of life in face of unfulfilled destiny.

Albi continued to swim through the crowd. She was trying desperately to reach the other side of the pool, the downtown side of 125th Street Malcolm X Blvd.

As she reached the edge, a policeman held out both hands in front of him as if to stop her from exiting the pool.

"Sorry lady, don't use the subway here," the policeman warned. "There's a power failure in the Harlem subway. Where are you going anyway?" the cop inquired.

"To Columbia University, Upward Bound," Albi persisted.

"Well, walk two blocks back up where you came from, take the A train to 59th Street, then switch to the uptown 1 or 9 train. Go seven steps to heaven, I mean, errr, seven stops to Columbia University."

As Albi descended into the A train subway, a blinding darkness attacked her eyes. Was there a power failure everywhere? She knew by routine where the public waiting area was located. Strangely enough, there was no token booth clerk on duty. No baloney-faced 'everybody recognizes you' plainclothes policeman lurking in the corners. Only a foul musty odor patrolled the air, temporarily arresting any sense that all was well.

As her eyes grew accustomed to the room, Albi saw seven men, almost ancient, wiry-looking dark men, sitting on the bench in the waiting area. Seven old men wearing dark pullover shirts. Odd attire for the summer.

Seven dark emblazoned or branded with each of seven white letters.

The seven, as if weeping, sat seemingly engulfed in a ceremony of silence, as if contemplating some mystery wrapped in a puzzle, wrapped in an enigma. The letters on their chest were "RIAPSED" not "RESPECT" as you might expect on an Aretha Franklin t-shirt.

Albi wrestled with the puzzle, contorting her mind, as if wrestling with an angel of light or a rubrics cube. "RIAPSED," she thought, "Mmm…DIAPERS?. .that doesn't make sense."

Then she blurted it out. In the semi-lit darkness, in the semi-dark lightness at the top of her inner voice: "DESPAIR! DESPAIR! It's DESPAIR!!!"

Then the old men stood up and smiled, sharing their toothless grins, as if she had called each one by his name.

"Come little sister, join us!" invited one of the seven.

Albi ran away, clutching her bag, ran to the front of the platform. She peered into the tunnel, hoping to see the two eyes of the train. Yes, there it was! Thank God the train was coming, she breathed to herself. " Uncle Thomas may bow, Bigger Thomas may have fear but I am a Never-Thomas I never can Despair !" These words had been the family mantra taught by her father.

The train's seven cars pulled into the station, the doors opened wide and she was swallowed safely into the belly of the 'A' train. As securely as Jonah had ever been acquired by that whale. The seven old men banged on the window of the 'A' train, blowing kisses at her, but Albi was safe.

Albi found a seat, all seemed normal now. The train was well lit. There were people on the train, ordinary, normal New York people. People with their eyes cast down to avoid contact and their souls hidden behind newspapers, books, true romance magazines, puzzles, and wide-eyed daydreams.

Now was the time to read, Albi thought to herself, she pulled a book. She was reading. Her eyes were weary.

As the train rounded the curve, Albi slipped the Book back into her bag. The lights in the subway car went out momentarily as Albi attempted to pull back her hand. But she couldn't pull her hand back! Some unknown force was grabbing it, holding it, restraining it, preventing it from being withdrawn. Albi stared into her bag, attempting to pull back her hand with the other without success. A sense of awe and terror descended upon her, like the full eclipse descending over the face of the moon. Her brown skin became pallid and pale, her palms soaked, her arms trembled, her legs immobile like tree trunks. It was alive! It moved! The doll, it was alive! "Ifrit" was alive! Albi screamed and screamed and screamed. People began running from the subway car until they had emptied themselves from her presence.

"Calm yourself young lady," said Ifrit. "I am nothing but a lowly genie, the genie named Jonathan Ben Ifrit. I come in peace. You are now my master. Solomon was my master in the days of old. He is a master no longer. He is now with his Lord. I am the genie Ifrit mentioned in the Books. I am seeking the mercy of G-d for the mistake made by me, in rendering a service to his servant Solomon, the wise. Therefore, for an appointed term, I will show you some of the mysteries of the universe of which you inquired, by the permission of G-d, the most Glorious one who inspires…In other words, what do you want?"

Albi, in shock, was still not convinced and was trembling terribly. The genie began to take on a number of life-sized shapes. First, the image of Albi's schoolteacher, glasses and all. Then the image of her piano teacher unfolded, followed by the image of Gregg, her schoolmate, looking silly as ever, and finally, the image of her father.

"Well if you're so smart, Mr. Genie," Albi queried, "show me the letter my father wrote to me most recently," she challenged nervously.

The genie disappeared for several seconds and when he appeared again, produced the very letter Albi had read from her father earlier.

"Holy smoke! Holy smoke!" shouted Albi, "you're real," as if to convince herself that she was not dreaming. "But, you're just a doll," she insisted.

"Thank you, daughter, compliments are appreciated. Over many thousand years many have found me attractive," the genie commented.

"Can you be seen?" asked Albi.

"Only by those who can see the unseen, and yourself only," the genie replied. "However, I and most genies have the ability to appear as a vision or illusion in any form that we please. See, G-d made us out of smokeless fire, and he made you people out of mud fashioned into shape."

"How did you become a doll?" queried Albi.

"Well, after Bilquis, the Queen of Sheba (Saba), came to see Solomon, I lost my job at the temple and the palace. Solomon's evil vizier fired me, forgive the expression. Nobody wants a billion year old genie unless you know what to do with one. Other genies in my family disowned me because I work for humans. So I put myself in the service of many kings and powers, some evil, some good. Charlemagne, Richard the Lion Hearted, Kublai Khan of China, and the last of which was Ganga Musa, the great African king of the Empire of Mali whose empire boasted the great cities of Timbuktu and Jennie and great universities. Mansa Musa assigned me to be guard of his eye surgeon and to be his own bodyguard."

"I know of Mansa Musa!" exclaimed Albi, "I read about him in history class. He was the richest man that ever lived. He was worth 400 Billion dollars by today's standards. He owned a lot of gold and he gave a lot of it away."

"That's right," said the genie, "he gave me away too…I'll never forget. I'll never forget a little girl named Mulbah who warned the king that his aunt had put poison in the cassia root in some dainty meats that she had prepared for the king. As her reward, the Mansa Musa gave me to her as her slave. The little girl's mother put some type of magic necklace or collar brace on me. I was the size of a tree but suddenly, from 10 ft. tall, I shrunk to the size of a doll.

Later, I was kept in a mahogany chest for nearly 20 years after daughter became a woman. The little girl was saving me for the daughter she never meanwhile. I was buried along with this woman and her jewelry.

Some thieves robbed the grave. A dog dug me up. Then a Mandinka girl found me but after she grew up I was removed to Guinea, where I lived with seven sisters who thought of me only as a mere doll and but who were warned never to remove my neck chain by the Mufti of the town.. I had almost given up on becoming an active genie again," continued the Ben, "until you accidentally rolled off this necklace collar, or whatever you want to call it. And that's my story," he finished with a deep breath. And a sigh.

"What a long sad story, but welcome to Akirema." sympathized Albi, "You're in the greatest place on earth! Can you answer one question, since you can answer questions and see the unseen and all that stuff?"

"Why not," responded Ifrit, "what are friends for?"

"How can one people make slaves out of another without bloodshed, or use of chains? And how can enslaved people truly gain their freedom?" asked Albi.

"Wow!" said the jinn, "look and listen, but do not speak, lest you become one of the lost in the logos. You are now entering the Land of Nod, the realm of the unseen, and there will be opportunities for you to speak and seek later."

Suddenly the 'A' train car they were in lurched upward and began a steep incline up. It seemed as if the train was traipsing through the New York sky, entering the land of "Nod", a land of ideas, a land of forms where music goes before it is born and after it is played. Up it went until it came to some sort of train station platform.

"Wear this necklace and you will be invisible," insisted the genie, "and do not speak until I give you permission."

Albi nodded her head, a little frightened perhaps. She wouldn't make it to school today. The door of the train opened. They were still in the subway judging by the huge overhead ceiling. A ceiling that looked like the ceiling of the Sistine Chapel in Rome. The signs on the train platform did not read "59th Street, Columbus Circle". Instead the words said, "Welcome to the Akirema Civilization, Home of the Mental Plantation Protectorate, From 1492 Until Present and Forevermore." A smaller sign in bold red letters read:

"Despair All Ye Saggins Who Enter Here. Devlins and Sensars Are Welcome."

Albi wanted to ask the genie what a saggin was, but she couldn't speak. She just looked and listened. They began mounting stairs consisting of seven steps from the station. They alighted in the middle of a thicket of bushes and trees thick as a jungle. It was dark, except for a light, round as the moon that hung from the ceiling. They were in a jungle of plastic palm trees,

plastic cantaloupes and banana bushes, astral turfs and berry trees. They pushed their way through until they came to a clearing.

"Lie still, do not move," said the genie, "and observe."

Albi looked up and out of the bushes into a clearing in the forest, where ran a giant green tiger with black stripes, sinews stretching and muscles straining. Great monster that it was, it was running from someone or something. A man, a giant- black man, with muscles large as a mountain peaks, was chasing or pursuing the green tiger. He succeeded in grabbing the green tiger by its tail. The tiger turned and pounced on the black man, but the man held him by the throat, and the two wrestled, turning over and over on the astral turf, until surprisingly it seemed the tiger would be the one who surrendered. Suddenly a shot rang out, and the black giant of a man fell to the ground. The green tiger ran into a bush and collapsed.

A red-faced man in a white safari hunter's suit, reddish hair and beard, stood over the black man. A group of strange robotic-looking men stood posed, ready to receive the white man's order.

"Sensars, bond that saggin," yelled the safari-suited one "and take him back to the mental plantation so we can punish him in front of the others!"

"Yes, oh worshipful devlin," they replied.

The saggin suddenly jumped to his feet and kicked the devlin in his face with a spinning back-kick, knocking him out. The sensars charged him with some white antenna-like weapons which were attached to a radio-type device on their belts.

"Channel 13 Chanel 13!" yelled one of the sensars, as he began whipping the saggin's head with his antenna-type whip. "Saggin threatening Officers!" he continued.

The saggin, ignoring the blows, stuffed something like cotton in his ears. Then he began punching and kicking the sensars and smashing something in their faces that sounded like breaking glass of TV sets

Albi looked at the faces of the sensars. The sensars seemed to have miniature t.v. screens, monitors for a face. Yes, they were strange robotic-looking men who had TV. monitors for faces eyes and foreheads.

The saggin seemed to be winning against his assailants until somehow the cotton dropped out of one of his ears. Then he collapsed, cringing as he grabbed his head and ears. The devlin recovered and soon loomed over the saggin.

"Saggin, what is your name?" yelled the devlin, as he struck the helpless victim.

"Kees Epoh," replied the saggin.

"Epoh, who gave you that strange name?" the devlin smirked. "Your name is Thomas. John Henry Thomas," he insisted. "That's what's on your I.D. You belong to Master Thomas."

"You know it's against the law for saggins to own a green tiger, don't you," yelled the devlin. The saggin didn't answer. "You know it's against the law to hit a devlin, don't you?" yelled the devlin even more loudly.

"Do what you must," the saggin responded.

"Sensars!" yelled the devlin, "bind his five senses!"

The sensars held the saggin down and bolted headphones to his head which were attached to a walkman of sorts. The Walkman-like object was attached to the chain around the saggin's waist. A scream pierced from the saggin. Next the sensars put a bit in his mouth and sprayed his skin with a sense-dulling insensitivity acid.

"So saggin, you wanted a green tiger, do you?" the devlin laughed, "sensars, bring in the green tiger." The sensars disappeared into the bush and returned with the terrible green tiger on some sort of leash. The snarling green tiger immediately attacked the saggin while the sensars held him on the leash, but the saggin would not scream. This angered the safari-suited devlin so much that his face became as crimson as the Red Sea.

"Sensars, bring me water!" screamed the devlin. The saggin did not flinch. The sensars brought in water. Suddenly the devlin threw the water on the Walkman headphones. There was a sparkling explosion around the saggin's body. The saggin's head was smoking like a sausage. The saggin broke lose from his oppressors and ran, as if running would cool the fire that engulfed his head and body. He ran, running toward Albi. Albi almost screamed. She recognized him. It was the same guy she had seen that morning being brought on a stretcher out of the Harlem subway, his face smoldering and smoky. Yes, he was the same poor man with the headphones embedded in his brain. She was sure of it!

The saggin ran up the seven steps toward the train platform. The sensars were in pursuit with the green tiger on the leash, its muscles stretching and straining. The saggin made it to the 'A' train and the doors closed. Hopefully, he physically escaped, she thought, if not with his life. The headphones were embedded in his brain.

Albi was torn between wanting to see more of this artificial world and taking immediate revenge against the devlin and the sensars, or just running back home and hiding there. These confused thoughts raced back and forth in her brain, in a battle royale for control of her mind. Yet the most difficult struggle was just to keep quiet. She was smoldering inside just like the saggin, having smoldered outside. There seemed no way to cool her rage. There were no rivers anywhere. Only a desert it seemed, and a jungle of plastic cantaloupes and plastic palm trees.

Morning arrived in Akirema, with the switching on of a giant refrigerator-type light bulb which seemed to serve as the sun in this desperate world. High up in the ceiling sky, it hung like some lamp in an artificial heaven. But surely it was no heaven for the saggins.

The switching on of the giant white light bulb was accompanied by the blare of something like a ship's horn-the sound of which chased away the silence which had comforted the night. A flock of giant white metallic-looking birds flew in formation across the face of the light bulb casting their fearsome shadows over astral turf and dale. Such was the regale that greeted dawn of morning. She just wanted to speak. The genie gave the sign!

"How do I save the saggins?" inquired Albi.

"I am your servant," said the genie, "but you must come up with a plan and it must be righteous, otherwise Jonathan Ben Ifrit is out of here."

"You know that I will only seek right," replied Albi, "I am the daughter of Malik Never Thomas." She smirked.

"Without doubt," concurred the genie, "you are from righteous upbringing."

The genie spread out a huge carpet on the ground. He motioned to Albi to climb on.

"One question," asked Albi, with a mischievous smirk on her face, "why do genies make carpets fly and why do genies always use carpets? At least, that's what I've seen in the movies. What is it all about, genie?"

"What is your wish?" asked the genie.

"Carpets do not fly," said the genie "Prayers fly, dreams fly, hearts fly, minds fly. There are the 4 corners of the flying carpet. Now what is your wish? My brain cells are idling."

"To the Mental Plantation." replied Albi.

Albi closed her eyes and when she opened them they were out-side the huge black iron gate. As they approached the gate of The Mental Plantation there was a sign above which read "Welcome to the Mental Plantation Guarded By The Tree of A Thousand Eyes. Despair All Who Labor Here. Your burden shall not be lightened Nor shall our concepts be removed from your shoulders. These con-cepts cultivated here support world piece and The Order of the Now."

Outside the gate was a huge oak Tree-wide as five car lengths and as tall as the old collapsed Brooklyn Bridge in New York. The eyes of the Tree were on its leaves and they were turning North South East West in all directions like the light of a Light House searching the darkness of the sea.

The genie went into his shoulder bag and pulled out a handful of passion flower dust and held it up to wind. And the wind blew the passion flower dust into the eyes of The Tree with A Thousand Eyes and the Tree fell asleep and snored in the midst of the night.

Albi and the genie were in the plantation now. They were still invisible. As the artificial light bulb in the ceiling of this world began to turn on and the horn of the temples of dawn were

blown. There were four houses on the edge of the mental plantation. One house was called "Hire Education" or "The School Of Applied Slavery Sciences" and from it poured out saggins who ran to the field of the mental plantation in chains. Dressed in all types of uniforms, black caps gowns they were carrying heavy baskets of concepts on their heads. The heavy baskets had different signs on their sides:

1) Born with an artificial identity and color consciousness 300 lbs
2) Job only please Will never consider Self employment100 lbs
3) Utter Dependence (200 lbs)
4) Waiting for Retirement (100 lbs)
5) TGIF /Living for the Weekend (100 lbs)
6) Depending on a Promotion 100 lbs

The second house on the edge of the mental plantation was the House of Entitlement and Self Limitation Mathematics

The workers poured out of this house carrying bales to field which read:

1) Waiting for my check/Work is For Squares 100 lb
2) If I Work I will Lose My Benefits 100 lb
3) The poor enter heaven/Money is the Root of All Evil 100 lbs
4) Fear of Group Success/Rugged Individualism 100 lbs
5) No plans just one day at a time 200lbs

The third slave house on the mental plantation was called House of Dreams and from this house slaves were carrying giant Buckets of water to the field that had holes in them. The signs on the buckets read:

1) Hand to Mouth Living is Enough 100lbs
2) I waiting for my number/lotto to hit 100lbs
3) I lit my candle I know something good is going to happen 100 lbs
4) I don't have alternative plans part 2 200lbs

They ran until they were exhausted but never got enough water to reach the field of dreams to water the dreams that lay buried deep within themselves !

The Fourth House on the mental plantation was called "I've Got Plenty of Nothing". The slaves running to the fields carried huge balls filled with air. They were so big and fragile that they were constantly bouncing out of their hands, and the slaves were chasing them everywhere. The air in the balls were the empty promises of the wardens of power who made and set promises free in the night and locked them up during the morning.

The saggins from the 4 Houses of Mind guarded by Devlins and green tigers were carrying all of these burdensome and dysfunction-al ideas toward a giant white sugar type mill or melting pot called "Pursuit of Happiness".

As the saggins were pouring the contents from their heads into the " Pursuit of Happiness" mill or melting pot, the Devlins were lashing them furiously with green tipped whips. They held back green tigers in packs of seven on chains. Green tigers who were growling and biting saggins on the legs and feet if they moved too slowly for a Devlin's pleasure.

Some of the elderly saggins collapsed and died clutching their last social security checks which were stolen by Devlins from their sagging lifeless hands. Other elderly and oppressed saggins died clutching their last Lotto or laundry tickets

After depositing the contents of these burdensome ideas (grown on the mental plantation) into the mill on the Eastern side, two streams of byproducts eventually came out on the western side of the mill. From the first spigot came out pure liquid gold . This liquid was placed in small gold bar molds and carried away by a Devlin mov-ing company called "Goldmen With Sacks Inc". This liquid gold in brick mold form was guarded by fierce Green Tigers the size of pachyderms.

From the second spigot poured out a foul brown liquid which was then stored in vats labeled: " "CLAPPS BLACK GRITS" "FOOD FOR THOUGHT". A preservative and flavor enhancer were added before it was bottled in jars and sent by Underground Rail to Saggin soup centers everywhere..

"Wow" remarked Albi "thinking is either a burden or a profit .The life of the world it seems is controlled by ideas that people be-lieve in. Those who manufacturer the beliefs and sell the ideas hold true power"

"You're right" said the genie.

"Bad Ideas "the genie continued "are like seeds or concepts

deposited in the fields of human thinking and the crops evolved from these ideas enrich nourish and serve the civilization and egos of those who plant the seeds. However it depletes denigrates and destroys the dignity and integrity of those who labor under falsely planted ideas or misconceptions regarding their own inferiority and dependence . Mind planters therefore are the masters of the mental plantation. I have seen this happen for thousands of years."

"This reminds me of Plato's cave that I read in school." Albi added "The shadows on the wall seen by the cave dwellers caused by an unseen strategically set fire were the mis educators

of the cave dwellers. The cave dwellers thought the shadows caused by the fire were reality. The cave dwellers had never seen the noonday- sun and could never compete in reality or separate the real from the unreal"

"Hey genie will you help me melt these burdensome ideas. What if we expose this whole place to the sun?! The ignorance of the slave is the throne of the master, isn't that right genie?" Albi asked.

"Right Missy" demurred the Genie.

"I have a plan genie." insisted Albi. "Shatter the light bulb and open the ceiling so that the sun of common sense can enter,. When the sun of common sense enters the world, the mental plantation will disappear."

"Not Bad" exclaimed the genie " After I shatter the Artificial Light Bulb , how will you get the saggins to freedom ?"

"I, with your help, will lead them to the A train." replied Albi. The River Leading To Reality must appear once common sense lights the air or a Bridge Over Troubled Waters must emerge even if it was once submerged beneath the currents of turbulent emotions.

"Done" said the Genie. All at once the lightbulb in the ceiling shattered. An alarm went off and green tigers, sensors and devlins screamed and scrambled from their quarters in panic. The Genie shattered the ceiling with a fire ball from his pouch and the sun light began to pour in. like a hurricane. It's the first time that anyone had heard the song of light. It sounded like a mild scorching wind

In the light of the sun of common sense, the slaves of the mental plantation put down their burdens and began to run in North and East toward the sunlight. The sunlight began burning the eyes and ears of the devlins (masters) and the sensor robots their servants took over the chase trying to corral the slaves. The green tigers were also confused by the sunlight and began to mall and bite their masters. As the sunlight of common sense entered Akirema, the River of Reality began to appear from underneath the ground and soon ran on watery legs North of the plantation.

Every slave would have to cross the River of Cold Reality to Freedom.

"Quick, build a bridge genie!" yelled Albi.

"Yes missy" yelled the genie and within 30 seconds the genie had built a bridge for the saggins. The saggins ran across the bridge shouting "Freedom! Freedom!! Freedom!!!" The sensar robots with green tigers- in hot pursuit.

As the last saggin crossed, the genie destroyed the bridge. But the sensars did not give up. They ran to boats to cross the river in pursuit of their prey. The genie reached in his pouch and pulled out – a mix of zinc, ammonium nitrite and sodium chloride and set the river on fire. This stopped the boats and their sensars from following the fleeing saggins.

The saggins who crossed the River of Reality (formerly called "The Chilly and Cold River Jordan") were yet not free. They had to get past Checkpoint Montgomery. At this checkpoint, sensars disguised as saggins offered the fleeing saggins a free ride in the front of the bus of independence. Hundreds of saggins were deceived . They boarded the Montgomery buses and the sensars drove them back into the slavery of mental plantation dependence economics

Albi put on the necklace to warn the saggins not to get on the buses of return to slavery. When the saggins saw her, they listened but the sensars pointed the lasers at her. This caused the genie to throw up a blue smoke screen which caused the sensars' computers to shut down.

"Time to get out of town!" shouted the genie. "Put back on that necklace and climb on the carpet."

Albi obliged and soon she and the genie were back in Harlem, right in front of the A train station on 125th street and St. Nicholas.

C)   The Tale of the Awakening

It was late afternoon-a team of dozens of ambulances of the body mind and spirit were waiting outside of the A train station on 125th Street. Men and women whose faces seemed slightly burned poured out of the subway to waiting ambulances. All of them need-ed surgery to remove the micro chips and head phones which had been nailed into their heads like so many crowns of thorns. Harlem Hospital would be overwhelmed!

"Put my necklace on" shouted the genie "and take me to your house but you must promise to remove the necklace each night. I need to free so that I can search for my family I promise to return I am your servant."

"Consider it done G-d willing" replied Albi as she put the neck-lace around the genie's neck and returned him to the shopping bag. She was uncomfortable with anyone being her servant but having a genie in your corner was so cool !!

Albi started the long walk home. It was 7:30 p.m. The demon-strators had put down their old signs and were dancing. They were carrying new signs which read "We make jobs" "Help us

make jobs" People were signing up at the tables to help them make jobs in Harlem. It was a new Harlem. Everywhere people's senses were stirring. Ears emerged that had once been earphones.

Eyes replaced the lens of cameras. Faces replaced the screens of televisions. People were stirring. Minds were stirring. Hearts that were hid from sight and dreams that were locked up at night were free. Free at last, free at last, Great God Almighty free at last.

Sons spoke to their fathers and daughters to their mothers for the first time in years. Feelings stirred that was all for the better. She stirred in her bed as she heard her mother's voice. Her mother was on the phone in the living room.

"Gray, where's my daughter? It's 8 p.m. and she's not home," her mother asked. Silence… "Now, I know you know where she is. You young folks are getting out of hand. Where's your mother? Please put her on the phone."

Albi was in shock. She tried opening her mouth. "Mom, I'm here in the room," she managed to get out.

"Excuse me, Mrs. Manigault , I'll call you right back," explained Sophia, hanging up the phone. "Albi, when did you get home? You weren't in the house at 8 p.m. The nerve of you to come sneaking in here past the curfew…you're going to be grounded!"

"But mom," protested Albi, "I had to be here. I couldn't sneak in."

"But mom, nuts, …Don't but mom me… who broke my television and radio? Nothing's working. You've ruined this house. You had boys over here, didn't you?" Sophie menaced.

"Why no, mom," Albi respectfully answered.

"I'm no fool," her mother insisted. "I was young once."

"Get a life mom, I don't believe you. You young?" Albi kidded her with a smile.

A flash of lightning streaked across her mother's face and storm clouds gathered, beads of sweat forming on her brow forecasted eminent danger. And then just as suddenly as lightning, they both broke out in laughter, louder than a rain shower.

"I'll show you old," Sophie said as she reached for Albi, as if to grab her in a bear hug around her neck.

Albi ducked down, low and fast, and Sophie, tripping on something, went flying forward. Luckily, Albi grabbed her from the back and prevented her from falling.

"You see mom," laughed Albi, "when you're old, the hand is quicker than the eye. Mom, you're slower than molasses in January, as you used to say."

They both looked down, laughing somewhat, and there they both saw the doll. Ifrit?! Albi was in shock.

"Child, where did you get that beautiful doll," Sophie inquired, "and what a lovely necklace."

The phone rang and Albi ran to pick it up. It was her father.

"Hey dad, how are you? What's up? Where are you? Really…you got me a surprise…a secret? Really?! Wednesday? Great. I'll see you after school. I miss you too. You won't disappoint me? Promise? O.k., o.k., do you wanna talk to Mom? She's right here in the kitchen. Love you too Dad. You'll always be my dad, wherever you are."

Albi handed the phone to her mother and found a sanctuary of comfort on the soft pillow cushions that adorned the living room floor. It was painful for her to listen to her mom and dad talk since they had gotten divorced. Secretly, she had always hoped that someday they would both be in her life full-time and forever. Her mother had explained years ago when she was five that being divorced means that when your parents aren't together, but they still love you. She didn't quite understand it now. Nothing ever changes love, but love puts people through changes. Some people get knocked out of the ring, others endure the fight and get a winner's reward. But wishes never defeat the wind and quiet understanding can never quiet a storm. A storm born in the sea.

It was no surprise then, for some reason, that Albi could not contain the raindrops that welled up from the lake of her soul despite the smiling sun of hope in her eyes. She wept quietly. Sometimes it rains even when the sun is shining. Sometimes rivers long forgotten spill the guts of their souls into the oceans of eternity. Their disappearance goes unnoticed by the eyes of men. Like the beautiful rose on the side of a mountain when it dies, no one weeps for it. It weeps for itself, its own soul wondering all the time about the purpose of its existence. So, too, Albi wondered about herself-a child of love, a victim of changes that separated her parents. She knew that they both loved her, but like the sun in the day and the moon at night, they were separated by a mysterious veil.

She scattered about for her watch, trying to get a bearing on time and place. Her mother was still on the phone. She found her watch and saw that it read "Wednesday, June 24, 2024." Wednesday? What had happened to Tuesday. This was totally Kafkaesque . Had time's weed choked out a day or had the Timex watch she received for her last birthday suddenly liberated itself from the slavery of its grinding gears?

Albi looked long and hard at the doll, Ifrit, the gift she had received from Asha Its necklace gleamed mysteriously. She had remembered to put it back on the doll's neck as she had promised Ifrit.

Ifrit must have been victorious, but she knew that only the Maker of genies and men could have freed the saggins...

Albi had no doubt that her father would be proud of her. She couldn't wait to tell him of Tuesday's weird adventure. But for the moment she wondered about Ifrit. Was he alive? Or was he trapped in the body of the wooden mahogany doll? She shook the doll. It showed no signs of life. As she stared, it appeared that the doll's eye blinked or a brow flickered. She knew in her soul that Ifrit might be a prisoner for a thousand years again until it was discovered by someone that the necklace should be removed because a genie's spirit was locked inside. It wasn't fair that Ifrit should be a prisoner after all he had done. Suppose his next master was an evil one?

Just then, Albi's thoughts were interrupted by a soft persistent tapping, a rapping at her window pane, the one adjacent to her bed.

The window pane that faced the boulevard of Harlem's future...
The rapping became louder until she felt the need to investigate.
Loud enough to make her hesitate and hug caution in a desperate
embrace.

So persistent, intense and rhythmic was the tapping, it could
only have been some being or friend seeking entrance to a dream.
She heard the flapping of wings. It was a rather large blue nightingale! The same nightingale she had seen perched on Asha's' shoulder
on the 125th Street village of vendors.

She knew now the answer to her dilemma. The genie must go
free. She gently removed the necklace. The bird stopped its tapping.
She opened the window and placed the doll and the necklace on the
fire escape.

"Goodbye Ifrit," she whispered. She saw a tear glisten in the
doll's eyes. "You are free."

The blue nightingale's beak expanded like that of a pelican. It
chirped, scooped up Ifrit and winged across the eastern sky. East of
the sun it flew.

As soon as it left, a giant white raven, majestically sinister in
appearance, picked up the necklace and flew west to the lair of the
moon, the eater of nights beyond forgetting.

Albi had little time to contemplate the meaning of all this. The
street door bell rang seven times to be exact, indicating that someone
was looking for her or her mother.

"Answer the door Albi. I'm on the phone with Aunt Maydelle!"
yelled her mother.

Albi gently patted down her hair and stole a look in the mirror
as she heard footsteps crunching on the stairwell leading to her door.

"Ok, Mom," she quickly responded. She heard a knock, one she
had heard a thousand times since she was born. She unwrapped the
door with three flicks of levers.

A tall, well-built brown skinned man, with specks of gray on his sideburns, a receding hairline and a smile as large and friendly as a holiday in July melted all shadows of sadness from her face.

"Dad! Dad!" Albi exclaimed excitedly.

"Fooled you!" he said. "You didn't even know it was Wednesday." Malik Never Thomas picked Albi up and held her in his arms a long time. "How dare you try to get as tall as me," he chuckled, placing his right hand in front of his chin indicating how tall Albi had grown.

"Give me five years Dad and I'll be looking down on you," Albi smiled.

Tears of joy welled up in both of their eyes, then ran down their faces like a river or a creek. Then they both burst out laughing.

"Well, come in," said Albi.

"Where's your mother?" asked Malik.

Suddenly, Albi's mother was opening the door to her room.

"Well Malik," scolded Albi's mother, "wind mills can wait, but your daughter can't. It's been almost 6 months. It's about time!"

"Give it a rest Sarah," Malik responded. "Give it a rest for goodness sake."

"You two have a lot of catching up to do, I'm sure," Sarah said as she left the room.

"These are for you princess daughter of mine," Malik said, handing Albi a large shopping bag of gifts. "Seven books, seven principles to live by, and a $100 dollar bill in each book taped to the back to be spent only when you finish each book."

"Just like old times," Albi replied with a smile on her face.

"Like old times," her dad laughed. "And I have a surprise for you."

"Where?" wondered Albi aloud.

"On 135th Street and Malcolm X Boulevard," her father responded.

"Mom, I'm going out with Dad," Albi shouted to her mother as they headed down the stairs. After assuring and apprising her mother of where they were going, Albi and her father walked out of the house and headed toward 135th Street.

It was a midsummer night in Harlem. A midsummer night dream in the cosmos. No radios or televisions were on. No boxes blasting. No rappers ripping. No rivers flowing into futility. Just a calm cool breeze.

People were standing on stoops, talking with each other, eating ice cream or popcorn. Kids crunched Mike & Ikes, jawbreakers and other assorted sweets. People were in their homes, thinking and talking. Grandpas were telling stories about the civil rights movement and other interesting stories to anyone who would listen.

On 135th Street and Malcolm X Boulevard, a jazz band was playing on the corner in front of the Schomburg and its black history collection, A five member group were doing a rendition of Duke Ellington's "Take the A Train" and James Williams Johnson's "Harlem Nocturne."

Albi suddenly saw a vision. Duke Ellington was in the audience, along with John Coltrane, Count Basie, Charlie Parker, Miles Davis, Jimmy Hendrix, Lady Day, Ella Fitzgerald, Sarah Vaughn, Carmen McRae, Aretha Franklin and Whitney Houston. People whose music her father had introduced her to long ago . They were smiling at her.

There were young people from her school there, some newborns, some never born. The tradition would live on. People would see their roots beneath the surface. She remembered Akirema and how the saggins had suffered.

Her father suddenly ascended the stage and took the main mike in his hands.

"Ladies and gentlemen, brothers and sisters," he began. "I'm celebrating seeing my daughter again. Albi, this song is for you. I'm singing this song until all the fathers return home to their sons and daughters."

The piano began its intro and Malik's voice flew high over the roof tops of Harlem with words (which by the permission of G-d) made the afternoon clouds bend their ears and hold back the silent thunder of their joyful tears.

It seems that heaven and earth rejoices when the good in man triumphs over the obstacles of obstinance and obfuscation in his soul.

For surely the rose of the heart blooms and defeats even mighty stone and concrete to share her exquisite truth and beauty

Chorus: The day that you were born
   Gabriel blew his horn
   announcing another mystery,
   They knew I'd be your dad
   and God's love was made for you and me.
   I watched you run and play
   through the meadows of the day
   And when I was away
   your smile was all I had.
   G-d's love was made for you and me
   cause I'll always be your dad.

Bridge: Maybe I'm not cool
   my heart has played the fool,
   But when you're facing stormy weather
   remember I'll be your dad forever.
   My love's no passing fad
   I'll always be your dad,
   Through thick and thin
   There I'll always be.
   Your life is my sweet song
   and I know that life's not long,

G-d's love was made for you and me.
And when the day is through
I'll always think of you,
All the blues will melt I've ever had
I thank the Lord there's you
I am so glad to be your dad.
I thank the Lord above there's you
and I'll always be your dad. !!

The crowd roared and the clouds released their joyous thunder. A laughter of warm light rain caught all by surprise.

Albi looked to her left. Her mother was standing beside her. It was raining. She smiled. Maybe this time, the rivers, in the byways and gutters, would reach the sea of their brilliant destiny.

So this ends a tale for my nightingale.

D) The Escape

I was exhausted, but I could not sleep. I went strolling. Strolling down St. Nicholas Avenue, my heart praying that I would run into an old love that I knew yesterday. Or maybe some new other adventure. But this was only a psychic walk. I was still in my cage.

The hawk of the day is rising in the sky. He handed me a note. I tossed it out of my cage in disgust. Sleep is finally descending upon my pen, faster than the blinking of the distance between now and then.. Love to you who read. So long. I'll never say goodbye. I believe pens can write poems across the sky to be read by feature generations!

The nightingale is checking the locks on the doors of my cage

"Am I free?" I asked the nightingale. "Almost but Nevermore" it responded

"Lord G-d free me from the cage of my limited thinking !" I prayed with great sincerity.

Suddenly a huge draft from the window grabbed my cage and shook it violently like a jealous tornado. The Cage fell .like an egg.

The door blew open. I fled immediately as if from a fire. I ran straight to Harlem Hospital and locked myself in the psyche ward where no nightingale in his right mind could follow. There I chained myself to the bed at night to deter my sleep walking back into slavery.

In the next room was a blithering idiot named William Sheik Sabir loudly reciting monologues from William Shakespeare all day and night.

I escaped from my room of thought finally and ran to the A train The A train is the Freedom Train.. I would take the A train to the Bronx. Just North of another story.

As I got ready to board the A train, I saw a strange woman with a starry crown driving the train.in the engineer driver's seat. It was Lady Liberty.! "All aboard To Harbor Island of Man /Home of the Awakened Mind she cried "All Aboard All Aboard !!"

I was travelling light I threw away the old baggage that I had carried everywhere since the days of my youth. I stuffed them into a waste receptacle labeled "IGNORANCE :Do Not Recycle "

Good Lord I was on my way!!By his thinking a man builds his own cage and encages his own destiny. But I was Free and on my way to the promised land.

TO THE PROMISED LAND ./ THE PROMISED MIND A SECOND DIMENSION IN THE LAND OF NOD!!

One of seven parallel universes or heavens or skies beyond the twinkling of the mortal eye!!

A Tale For My Nightingale:
The Legend of the Stoop Sitters
On the Porch of Dreams

INTRO

They sat around in the shade,
Using the good day God made,
Eating the fruit of their words,
Sipping the milk of their deeds,
Crying the blues for their needs,
Planting the seeds of a bell,
Waiting for heaven or hell.

There were days, my daughters, when I paced the imaginary cage of life in utter confusion, thinking I would never again gain my freedom, no matter how many stories I might write or how diligently I carried out the instructions of my jailor.

I was beginning to think that my jailor was myself and that the notion of a nightingale holding me hostage was only a preposterous symptom of madness in the first degree, or else a maddening predicament that deserved my persistent meditation.

I slapped myself silly, hoping I might wake up. I hoped that I was dreaming or that I might discover that I had died and had become a vision in the mind of almighty God. Was I dead, awaiting some final judgment? Nothing would avail me an answer.

The shadow of a black nightingale pacing just outside my cage was the only clue to my reality and the four doors in my cage that led to other worlds, mysterious and unknown.

So in desperation, I opened the second door in my cage and there emerged a roaring fire. So hot was the fire, that it sounded like wild animals mating. So ambitious was the flame, that it seemed to be licking my very breath from my body and soul, as if I were its favorite flavor of Haagen-Dazs ice cream. So searing a fire it was, that I thought my eyeballs themselves would evaporate leaving me blind. My body was failing. My soul was failing. I felt myself fainting under the heat and I could not do anything about it, except unconsciously fight or surrender.

Fighting with every molecule of my will, without my body as an assistant, I struggled against surrender. I fought, like a general without an army, against a foe more formidable and unspeakable than a Mt. Everest on the march.

However, my thirst for freedom was such a spectacularly desperate desire, that my will decided I would brave even these hellish flames to gain my freedom. If only I could muster enough strength in my legs to run.

In my mind, I must have stood up. For when I did, the fire suddenly lost its lust for my soul. It lost its passion for the fight in the thirteenth round. It was as if my will for freedom intimidated the very flames themselves. Its devotion to my destruction suddenly abated. For now it seemed that the flames were sedated and my soul was restored.

I suddenly found myself behind the second door of a dream which had shut behind me. I was sitting in the middle of a roof, atop one of Harlem's pre-war brownstone tenements. The address was 266 W.131st Street. The place where I was born in the beloved Peoples Republic of Harlemia.

Miraculously, my pen and pad had survived the fiery ordeal and they seemed to be leading me into my next legend: The Legend of the Stoop Sitters on The Porch of Dreams.

I looked over the roof of the world. I heard a woman's voice in the street below, singing in the rain. It was a voice of a blues singer, a blues-gospel singer, wrenching a tune from the grasp of a rainy Sunday morning.

"Oh Lawd, look down on my people, and let them cross over into Jordan.

Oh Lawd, let not my people wander, in this wilderness.

Oh Lawd, let them not starve for the voice of thy tenderness.

Oh Lawd, it be raining, but I see your rainbow straining, straining through the clouds."

Church bells were ringing. Suddenly, I heard a chant coming from the corner of Malcolm X Blvd (old Lenox Avenue) and 116th Street.

"Allahu Akbar, Allahu Akbar, Allahu Akbar, Allahu Akbar (God is the greatest)."

The chant of the voice from the mosque, mingled with the voice of the church bell and the soulful bel canto of a blues/gospel singer opening three gates in the heaven of my brain.

The three voices joined forces. I heard rainbows roaring in the rain, winds rising from their sleep and the tolling of a distant bell.

It was a heavy rain. It was a Sunday morning rain, but it wasn't pennies from heaven. It was raining tears into the river of dreams that the western sun had kidnapped the night before. Tears from rivers that had never met the sea. Tears from the souls of a million rivers flowing into the mystic chasm of despair.

I saw my father's face before me. A 96 year old Jamaican who had long ago crossed the river and reached the other side. He said to me, "Son, tell them the story of the porch sitters, for G-d himself is sitting on the throne of judgment. He is awaiting their return, so He can tell them what they didn't do."

As I heard my father's voice from beyond, I looked again over the rooftops of the world. I heard from the streets below the voice of many waters. And I saw the people swimming in the waters till the waves of the great ocean covered their dreams. I was startled and took a deep breath full of terror and awe. So it was, I inhaled the "Legend of the Porch Sitters."

A legend born first of fire and then extinguished by the rain. For "the fire next time" had come and gone and "The revolution" had been televised and placed on the shelf of "justice deferred" by the victim's own hand.

THE LEGEND

Once in the west, beyond a shining sea, the descendants of an ancient tribe of men lived life without glee. They lived in a bastille of a brownstone house surrounded by waters.

The brownstone tenement was an island unto itself. It sat upon piles in a harbor, named for the famous statue of a lady who carried a torch in her stone heart for masses yearning to be free. The tenement was surrounded by waters, fed by 100 choked up rivers who had never met the sea.

The brownstone was called Nineveh Apartments. It was a six story walk-up with rickety winding wooden stairs. Because of the gaping hole in the roof, the tenants affectionately called it, "a stairway to the stars."

On each of the six floors, there were six windows. Three windows in the back, facing the past, and three windows in the front, facing the future. On the front of the building was a giant brownstone porch or stoop with an effaced sign which read, "No drugs, loitering or loud talking allowed".

On either side of the stone porch was a rusty brass banister.

Each banister joined the figure of a black cast iron lawn jockey, which appeared to guard each side of the stoop. Tied to each of these cast iron lawn jockeys was moored a small unseaworthy wooden sailboat that no one had used in the recent past.

The black cast iron lawn jockeys were a source of embarrassment to the tenants. According to the tenants, legend has it that many years ago, two magnificent Bengal tigers frozen in limestone adorned each side of the stoop and that these tigers used to protect the building from undesirable beings and spirits. Unfortunately, vandals had long ago destroyed these magnificent pieces of art and hence, the black cast iron lawn jockeys had replaced them.

The landlord of this floating slum building was a goliath of a man, some 6 ft. 6 inches tall. He was, however, hideously deformed with a hump on his back and blind in his right eye. The tenants called him Mr. Cyclops, Mr. Charlie or Mr. Cannibal, depending on the circumstances. He often traveled with his older son, a behemoth, whom the tenants called Little Cannibal or Cy-clock.

Both of these people had a most bizarre green tint on their skins. Some say their skins had become green from generations of feeding their souls with greed.

Well anyway, this jaded green giant of a landlord came by "once a month" to collect the rent. He was frequently dressed in a safari outfit and always carried a club or walking cane. He never made repairs. He never said hello to anyone and, if you believe the tenants, all he seemed to do was roar and hold out his hand for the rent.

If the rent was not paid on time, he seemed to be physically affected. If it was not paid for over two months, he would physically remove a member the delinquent tenant's family from the apartment. Often, these people that were removed were never heard from again. Furthermore, it was rumored among the tenants that these missing people were often eaten by the landlord's family.

But remember, dear readers, rumors, even true ones, are rarely reliable. Most times, tenants would pay their rents on time and, except in those rare instances where tenants were removed because of late payment or non-payment of rent, there were never any other vacancies created in the Nineveh Apartments. However, this green giant of a landlord kept vacant the entire top floor apartment, No. 6, for visiting tenants, mostly foreigners from across the ocean.

Every morning, the adult tenants, mainly descendants of a woman named Mama Fofama "Farewell" Manigault, descended the rickety stairs to sit on their favorite spots on the stoop. They sat there from sunrise to sunset, commiserating their fate, drinking soft drinks, some not so soft drinks, chewing tobacco, eating snack foods and swatting giant sea-born mosquitoes.

"I ain't had no hot water in my apartment in nearly 10 years," complained Big Mary, a squat-wide oversized woman with a Calico dress and size 11 flip flops for shoes. "Why don't Mr. Cyclops do something about that? I might as well jump off this porch into the harbor, then jump into my bathtub. The water's just as cold," she continued, turning to Flacca, the pencil-thin Latina lady who lived on the second floor and whose Spanish accent was still thick in all the right places. She was a fiery woman in her fifties who wore more makeup than the clown Pagliacci. Sporting a big pink camisole top and one size too small pair of blue Jordache jeans, she perceived herself as irresistible.

"Mira baby, I'm going to sue if I ever get off this stoop," whined Flacca, "and if my Jim, mi corazon, ever comes home again, I'm going to move. I ain't seen out my front window since I was born here. It's so dirty, I can only look out the back window. What Mr. Charlie gonna do?" she continued. "What he gonna do?"

"You know your Jim ain't gonna come back, not to you," said Flo, the tenant from Apt. #3. "They said the landlord ate your Jim cause you all didn't pay the rent. Wake up to reality, change your mentality. Ain't no way off this stoop except if you die and you go to the

Great Brownstone bye and bye." Flo was a tall well-built woman in her 40's. She spent a lot of time teasing her curly red-dyed hair and refreshing her makeup.

"Bruja, I can dream can't I!" shouted Flacca.

"Dream on, sista, dream on. As for myself, soon I ain't gonna have to pay rent. The landlord's son is gonna marry me just as soon as he gets old enough to go on his own," continued Flo, adding a little more rouge to her cheeks.

"In your dreams," spat Flacca.

"Hey, my little Cyclock is more of a man than your Jim," returned Flo. "Jim be a fish and bread man."

"You filthy bruja, you tobacco road, dung-eating, scraggly-headed, two by two stairwell Flossie! I have a good mind to throw you off the stoop into the harbor," shouted Flacca, grabbing Big Flo and shaking her like a Raggedy Ann doll.

"Ladies, ladies," shouted Bubba, the tenant from the fourth floor, as he rose from his chair. Bubba was a brown butterball of a man. He gingerly stepped in to pull the women apart. "We got to live and die here you know, so why don't we just get along!"

Both woman suddenly stopped. They were so angry, there were tears in their eyes.

"You know," said Bubba, "I think we should all have a talk with our landlord. He should fix up this place or lower the rent."

"You been saying that for 10 years," retorted Big Mary, "and when the green giant come around, you pee in your pants."

"Too bad you be the only so-called 'man' around here. You ain't but 3/5ths of a man no how."

Suddenly the hall door creaked, reawakening the morning. A young woman with a voluptuous figure in a tight-fitting red dress lit up the stoop. Her name was Lola, the tenant from Apt. #5.

"Got up late again, honey," crooned Bubba, "what can I do for you today?"

"Nothing at all," snapped Lola, "which is the same thing you did for me yesterday. And don't you honey me hear, cause you couldn't get next to me if you were the last man on earth and the angel Gabriel was gonna marry us himself. This is Nevarary the 14th for you," she added, turning her hips as if she were modeling a dress.

The whole stoop roared with laughter.

"Hey, you ain't my type of woman anyway!" replied Bubba. "I want a fine, submissive, corn-fed woman...a woman who, when I say 'jump', she say 'how high suh?'" he teased, trading his baritone articulation for a high falsetto rendition of the voice of his ideal woman. "She must have my meals ready on time and my bath water scented with lime!"

"Dream on scalawag!" heckled Flo. "You ain't getting nada of that!" she continued, looking at Flacca, who had burst out laughing.

"Not only that," continued Bubba, sensing he had grabbed everyone's attention, "I want that fine, corn-fed woman, after she jump up high in the air, to salute me and say 'permission to come down suh!' and then await my further instructions. Any volunteers?" Bubba belly-laughed profusely, as he demonstrated the obsequious mannerisms of this imaginary woman. Of course, he was the only one laughing.

"Don't push your luck, turkey chest," Big Mary interjected. "Ya be the only so called man around here for a reason...and remember, you're just a fish and bread man."

Now it was the women's turn to laugh.

Except Lola wasn't laughing. She hadn't cracked a smile since the crack of dawn. She had a storm in her mouth, a cloud on her brow and lightning on the tip of her tongue. Her hands were desperately astride her hips for emphasis.

"I just want to know which one of you low life, stoop-sitting neighbors of mine broke my mailbox and took my 'freedom check'. I'm going to forget who I am one of these days and somebody gonna pay me for my being born. How am I going to pay the rent? You know what happens if you can't pay." There was a deep silence for a moment. "They got to do something about this here place," Lola rambled on teary-eyed. "I'm tired of this cacka¬smelling hole in the roof and floating pieces of you know what."

"They? They? Why is it always 'They' and not 'We'?" posed Bubba.

"It's they," shouted Lola, "cause they built this place. They built this here brownstone and put us in it in the middle of the water so we couldn't escape. They send us a check in the mail and coupons once a month. They send us a boatload of food to feed your butter-ball butt. We buy everything from them. Can't you see, it's them we got to deal with? This is reality whether we like it or not."

"I'm going to sue if I ever get off this stoop," Flacca droned on miserably. "You know, things are so messed up in this brownstone that they stole my check last month too. Mr. Charlie ain't fixed nothing yet, no mailboxes, nada. That Maricon-Artist ain't gonna fix nothing either."

"You know," said Bubba, in a consoling voice, "it's them vandals, them doggone vandals coming ashore at night from the mainland. I'm sure of it. It can't be one of us."

"Sure, right!" snapped Flacca with sarcasm in her voice.

"You know," said Big Mary, "Bubba's right and it's Mr. Cannibal that's to blame. My apartment is so miserable that cockroaches are committing suicide. This morning they were jumping from the breadbox head on into the hot pot of my boiling coffee. I found some dead cockroaches in my kids' Cornflakes."

"Hey, with all them kids you got," said Flo, "I'd commit suicide myself."

"Look here, bubble lips, I ain't Flacca. When Big Mary gets roll-ing, you going into the harbor."

"Yeh," said Flo, "I'll jump into the harbor if you don't start keep-ing your apartment door shut. The smell coming out of your place,

WOE" she said turning her nose, "ain't no other way you're going to put me in the harbor."

"Give me a break," snapped Mary, "you're probably smelling your own Kit Kat bar."

Everyone roared with laughter again.

"Ladies, ladies!" shouted Bubba, as Flo started to rise from her corner.

"She ain't no lady," explained Big Mary, "and I'm just the one to beat her down too short to use the toilet."

"All you all shut up," said Lola, "just shut the heck up. Ain't nobody got a toilet that's working in this place anyway, except that Korean guy in Apt. #6."

"Where you been?" Big Mary shot back. "That Korean guy been gone. There be some Arab up there now."

"Yeh, I heard the Korean guy went to Freedom City in the mainland three months ago," Flacca joined in. "He took one of the sailboats and sent it back with the landlord's son."

"Yeh, he set up some export business over there," Bubba added.

"You mean they got an Arab upstairs now?" Lola wondered out loud.

"Yeh," said Big Mary, "them foreigners just come and go. Mr. Charlie sure can pick 'em."

"Yeh, he picks them over us," Flacca continued. "We're citizens. We was born here in this brownstone."

"You ain't no we," snapped Flo, "you ain't no real citizen."

"I'm more of a citizen than some Arabs," responded Flacca. "I passed the test."

"Humph!" sighed Flo.

"Well," continued Big Mary, "we can't expand or 'improve ourselves because Mr. Charlie keeps a vacancy open just for them foreigners, you know. They got working toilets and hot water upstairs and their roof don't leak! Yeh, he's a prejudiced man, him and his green-faced hammy-Tooling son."

"Hey, don't talk about his son like that," said Flo, pointing her finger at the rest of the stoop sitters.

"Well, well, well, if you got so much influence, why don't you ask Little Cannibal to fix the toilets," Flacca added in.

"The point is," said Bubba, steering the conversation again, "them foreigners got it better than us. We been here. We stay here all the time and we're mistreated by Mr. Cannibal. He leaves us in four walls of falling plaster, rats, roaches and long-abandoned dreams. Yet if you don't pay the rent, one member of your family may disappear."

"I'm gonna sue if I ever get off this stoop," Flacca whined again. "The food we get on that boat is porqueria. Maybe the sun does shine brighter on the other side of the harbor."

"You can say that again," the butterball man said in agreement. "We are treated like stepchildren by the powers in the towers."

"Sure enough," Big Mary agreed, "the foreigners have all the advantages. Our kids are forced to play in the basement with the rats and the roaches." The tenants all seemed to agree on this point.

Meanwhile, the sun had already reached its mid-life crisis in the sky. As it started to fall on the down side of noon, it stood still, seeming to reminisce for a while about the resplendent moments of its rising.

For it may be said that the sun is like a young boy in the morning, a warrior at noon and a philosopher when it sets. It was 1:45 p.m. in the universe. The day was not yet hoary with age.

A flotilla of boats from the mainland were beginning to sail toward the Brownstone. In the lead was a Plexiglas water craft rowed by a skeleton of a man, so gaunt one could not tell his age or guess his origin. His powerful reedy voice belied his thin ghostly appearance.

"Sandman, Sandman, Sandman, that's my name. Number Man, Number Man, Number Man!" he cried. "Win the numbers if you can! One cent brings you a dollar and excess proceeds go to 'the man' to inject lethal drugs into brigands! Number Man! Number Man! Number Man! Sandman! Sandman!"

The glass boat stopped in front of the stoop.

"Give me a '266', this house number, straight for a quarter," insisted Bubba, rifling his pocket for a miracle and finding it.

"Dame un 3 y dos (2) bolito (zeros) in the rear," added Flacca, leaning over the stoop to toss her money to the man in the boat.

"Oh, you and your bolitos," butted in Flo. "I had a dream," she continued, "that I had a fight, or I was in a fight. What number should I play?"

"Yeh?" interrupted Flacca, "was I whipping your cabeza (head) with a lead pipe?" she continued, with a fluttering laugh that even caused Flo to leak a laugh also.

"Well," said the glass bottom boat man, "let me see what 'The Lucky Cat/Sandman's Dream Book' says ... It says '266'. Play '266'."

"Ain't that nothing," cried Bubba. "I can't even have my own number. Just don't get my bet mixed up with these 'Dizzy Gillespie' girls."

"Alright, alright," the Sand Man assured him. After writing down the bets on pieces of paper, he ate them, pocketed the bets and sailed due west.

Then two more boats approached the Brownstone near the lawn jockeys. A squat Yucatan Mexican ice cream man added his "two cents" to the day's fare, stirring the afternoon with a romantic ice cream sales call.

"Helado fresco, helado fresco, helado con sonrisa! (Ice cream, ice cream, ice cream with a smile!). Coco para el loco! (Coconut for the crazy). Pina para la nina! (Pineapple for the little girl). Fruta para. Disfruta! (Fruit flavor for your pleasure). Un peso para los hombres! (One dollar for the men). Un beso para las mujeres! (A kiss for the women). His jovial manner caused the sun to think it could be young. Another boat made of black birch bark pulled up to the Brownstone.

"Prepare for your future," shouted the Captain of the boat. "Rent a coffin, rent a coffin by Hertz! Rent a coffin for your future. Be kind.

Have peace of mind. Do not leave your loved ones with a burden behind!"

Every boat imaginable arrived that day, except the mail boat. But that is another story.

Boat after boat, salesman after salesman engaged the inmates of the Brownstone. The sun was starting to get set in his ways and was waxing philosophical.

The moon was still a seed in the womb of the evening when the turquoise soul of the setting sun kissed the amber of the expectant night. The sun disappeared, swallowed whole by the jealous sea, leaving only his inspiration in the air.

The night awakened gingerly, slipping on her robe of stars. Pushing her ebonic face toward another maternity-the birth of vagabond moons, tales from near and far, sired by the lips of men, serenaded by the songs of a wren's searching for some poor poet's pen.

Meanwhile, a stupor like opera of melodramatic self-hate graced the stage of the Brownstone daily. There was dissatisfaction. But nothing changed. Nothing seemed like it would ever change.

Except that there was a love between two of the tenants' children, Omar Solomon, the son of Big Mary, and Laura Willis, Flacca's beautiful Latina daughter. The parents didn't approve, but Laura and Omar found a way to be in each other's company. They often sneaked out to the stoop each night, with nothing but the heavens and the stars as a witness.

Omar observed how the foreigners had left and never came back and he vowed that one day, he would leave Nineveh and strike out to Freedom City. He would do this for Laura, and to provide them with a better life. A life different than one of cowering from the giant and cowering from life itself.

So one night, when the moon was full and the stars forgot to shine, Omar unleashed one of the boats from the lawn jockey and set out for the mainland.

No sooner had he set out, than the water became turbulent and a rainstorm rose up from the waters, like a wall blocking his way. His dry rotten oars broke, so Omar paddled the boat with a piece of driftwood while the waves slashed through and into the boat. The storm surged, capsizing his destiny. He bailed out water with his hands and bailed fear from his heart with prayer and the love in his soul for Laura.

Omar finally arrived in the mainland, where the sun was so bright and the streets were paved with garnets. The glare from the sun and the garnets were so bright, that they blinded him for three days. For three days, he was at the mercy of strangers and the good deposited in the hearts of a few men. And especially of a woman named Dolores Dolorosa.

Dona Dolores was a grandmotherly woman who lived with her dog. She took Omar in and fed him for three months. The old woman had no sons or grandchildren, and immediately and affectionately adopted Omar.

Finally, Omar got the break that he needed. He got a job working in a fish market, cleaning fish for a man named Raymond Peters. Soon, he moved up to be a cook. Something wonderful happened. It seemed Omar's cooking brought dozens of new customers that lined up around the corner to taste what he called "Brownstone Fried Whiting."

These new customers were enamored with Omar's great cooking and pleasing personality. Raymond Peters continued to be his mentor. He'd often say to Omar, "Remember son, the customer is always right and the coin is in the fish's mouth."

Needless to say, Omar worked religiously for Raymond Peters by day. Raymond Peters, on the other hand, made quite an investment in the young man. He promoted Omar to the position of manager of Peter's Net One, Peter's Net Two and Peter's Net Three, the three seafood restaurants Raymond Peters owned in Freedom City.

In the evening, Omar began attending the University of Nirvana, School of New Resources, where he became quite enamored with philosophy and the writing of poetry. Raymond Peters contributed to his tuition. Everything in Omar's life seemed as smooth as an un-rippled pond. He almost forgot to remember Nineveh and Laura.

Then one day, Omar found himself in a most challenging situation. Her name was Ismenia Feelings. She was an intelligent, voluptuous ebony Latina woman with a warm heart, a bossan ova for hips, full moons for breasts and sunshine for a smile.

He met her quite by chance or fate or destiny, if you will. She had been hired by Raymond Peters on a rainy Monday morning. Omar was coming out of the kitchen, carrying a tray of fish from the oven, when he found this radiant glow of a woman talking with Raymond Peters. She flashed a smile that almost made Omar forget his own name. He carelessly let the swinging kitchen doors knife him in the back like a poorly-aimed guillotine.

"Omar, meet Ms. Ismenia Feelings," gestured Peters. "She's studying marketing at Freedom University. She'll be working closely with you."

Smoothing her black pleated skirt, Ismenia stood up in a respect-ful gesture to shake Omar's hand. Omar dispatched his tray, dropped his hands, dried them on his apron, all in one fluid movement, as smooth as a Moorish dervish dancer, spinning a mantra and a dream.

"Pleased to meet you, Ms. Feelings," he managed to articulate, with a quiver in his voice. His heart fluttered. His soul was hyper-ventilating as he flashed back momentarily to the face of Laura.

Soon, they were going out to dinner and long walks along the breezes of the harbor. They were becoming friends. Theirs was a beautiful friendship and they shared many laughs together.

Then one evening, Omar walked Ismenia home as he had done many times before. They had discussed the moon, the stars and the objects on Mars.

"Come in for a while," invited Ismenia. "I want to talk about YOU."

"Who, me?" wondered Omar aloud.

The night must have lasted a million hours before they kissed. A kiss that started a fiery war in Omar's soul.

"Ismenia," he sighed, as intimacy was now contemplated. "I cannot go on like this…uh, I like you as a woman and a person, but I am in love with another. I cannot live with two hearts in one breast, one that beats for love and one that beats for the sheer beauty of your womanly charms, your mind and your good cheer. Your caress, your essence, is hard for mortal man to resist on a night such as this. But when morning comes and the moon goes his way, I will regret the day I betrayed and deceived myself. This beautiful friendship would be over and we would be dissatisfied lovers, bent on destroying each other."

"Omar, how could you do this to me?" Ismenia protested. "Do you not desire me?"

"Ismenia, don't you get it?" Omar responded. "This is desire! I recognize her face. Desire is embraced by many. The offspring of desire without love is always regret, even if desire gets her way. Desire! Desire! Desire is a fire that burns itself for fuel, and when it dies out, no ashes are left as evidence that it ever even existed."

"Desire is heartbreaking illusion, Ismenia. If I burn desire with you tonight and betray my heart, there will be nothing left of our friendship. Beautiful as you are, you deserve much better than this one night of illusion that will end in confusion."

"Don't tell me this, Omar!" Ismenia whispered. "We have come too far to reverse the magic of our kiss. Too far to remove the stars in your eyes and the moon in my heart."

"The promise of the rainbow is true," Omar continued, "there is someone special for you. Ten million nights of love await you when he that was born to mate you finally appears. Oh Ismenia, don't be angry, my dear."

So Omar left that night of a million hours, kissing the cheek, lips and hand of Ismenia. Ismenia cried, but she respected the nobleness of Omar's heart. For a while, they remained friends. They agreed-just friends, lovers never.

Shortly thereafter, on a rainy Sunday morning, Omar found a letter in his locker from Ismenia. It read:

My Dearest Omar,

As much as I have cared for you and still do care, this relationship is a large source of pain for me! There is no happiness for me. There is no future for us, and I feel neglected and rejected. All I do is suffer. You only love what you love, Omar. I've tried to be a friend, but I must pass on the heartache. I couldn't stand to see you walking down the street and not be with you. I'm going to leave Freedom City. I don't know when or where I'm going. But soon, I shall disappear and forget that you ever kissed me that night. Love never dies. This is the secret of my heart. My life is nothing but stormy weather.

Yours, I.F.

Omar read the letter with a feeling of sadness in his heart, and that night he decided he would leave Raymond Peters. He loved Laura. He could not forget his mission. This way too, Ismenia wouldn't have to be the one to leave.

This time, the dream would be on him. He had the recipe for "Brownstone Whiting" and several other dishes he had not tried. He had many people who loved his cooking. To have his own restaurant was now a matter of principle and pride. His gifts he would not hide. He would save his love for Laura and by the candle of his faith abide. No matter the heartache. No matter how long it would take, he would mine his stake in Freedom City and one day return to Nineveh for Laura, the love of his youth. His heart knew all too well its own truth.

Soon, Omar opened his own seafood restaurant and called it "Omar's Dream." Within three years Omar was a very rich man. His boats were on the ocean catching fish and he had a dozen employees working for him. He also took care of the old woman who had taken him in when he first arrived at Freedom City and had no place to go.

Then one night, Omar had a strange dream. He dreamt that he was fishing in the green sea. Then a storm arose and his boat was being filled with water. The boat was full of fish, among other things. Omar went into the hull of the boat to see if he could throw some of the heavy objects away. When he saw the fish, they had the faces of his customers and of tenants from the Brownstone. Mary, Flo, Flacca, Lola, Bubba, even Laura. Omar shook with fear. What does this mean, he wondered. He went back on top of the deck and there he saw a big white fish, as large as 40 whales, steaming toward his boat. It seemed intent on ramming the boat. The fish was so large, Omar could not see the sun on the horizon.

Omar dumped the hull full of fish back into the ocean. The big fish gobbled them into his mouth, cradled them and carried them away. It disappeared into the ocean. The sun appeared on the horizon and the storm was swallowed by the sea.

Omar somehow thought he knew what the dream meant. He had come to Freedom City or "Garnet City" as he called it, and had seen some of the same foreigners that lived in Nineveh become rich men and live in palaces of teak and tinsel. Now it was time to go back and rescue his mother, Laura and maybe some of the others from a life of despair.

So on the 14th day of December, Omar set sail for Nineveh. He pulled up in a magnificent boat. It was a Saturday morning, check day, and all the adult tenants were on the stoop, making a pilgrimage around the mailboxes or what was left of them.

Soon, they were distracted by the sight of Omar's boat as it was moored to one of the six foot lawn jockeys which was still attached to the stoop.

"Hey Mary," shouted Flacca, "look what the cat dragged in."

"Mom!" shouted Omar, running up to his mother and giving her a great big kiss.

"Where you been son?" Big Mary cried. "You ain't gonna leave Momma no more, are you, son?"

"Mom, you have to come with me. Life's better on the mainland."

"One thing," said Flacca, interrupting the conversation, "stay away from Laura. You done hurt my daughter bad. Besides, her father, Jim, is coming back."

"I love Laura," said Omar, "and I want to make a future for her and all of you."

"Yeh, right," snickered Flo.

"Well Flo, ain't no giants eating or kidnaping people where I come from," insisted Omar. "There's money over there, all you can get. All you have to do is open a business."

"What's that?" said Bubba. "We don't know nothing about no business."

"The landlord's son gonna marry me," predicted Flo, who was still holding on to her fantasy.

Omar reached into his pocket and gave everybody enough money to pay for their rent.

"See," said Omar, "that's what you can do when you go for yourself-you can do for yourself."

"What about our checks?" said Lola, "Are you going to give us money every month?"

"Well, no," said Omar.

"See, this is what we know," Flacca said. "This is where we know. We can live here. Better the diablo that we know, than the diablo that we don't know."

"Yeh," said Bubba.

"Darn tootin," said Flo.

"Oh son, don't go," pleaded Big Mary. "Stay where you know it's safe."

Suddenly, Laura appeared on the stoop, looking as lovely as Omar remembered her. "Omar, is that you?" she murmured sweetly.

"Yes, my flower," said Omar. "When you bloom, the sun rises, when you fret, there's a storm in my heart. I know you'll go with me."

"I thought you had forgotten me." remarked Laura.

"Can the moon forget the night? Can heaven be right without you? I'm afraid not," responded Omar.

"But Omar!" protested Laura, "how do you know the love you left behind is still here? The flower of love dies when it is not watered. A secret seed in the heart does not blossom in the dark. I alone have watered this flower of our love with tears born in the lakes of loneliness. Waiting, watching, sitting on the throne of thorns you left me. I saw no moon, no star no sign of Omar."

"Forgive me, my love," pleaded Omar. "I could never desert you or willingly hurt you. I should have written, but I was bitten with the idea of not returning until I could afford to take you out of Nineveh." With these words, Omar gave Laura a laurel of roses garnished with precious emeralds, glimmering with hope.

"Would you let me spend my life with you? Could we begin anew?" Omar pleaded.

"You know, homey, you're full of caca," scolded Laura, as she punched him robustly in the arm and then kissed him gently. "But this time, you're mine. This time, you're not getting out of my sight. I ain't forgiving you and I ain't forgetting anything til you make things right though."

"0.k. Done," said Omar with a sigh of relief.

"Why don't you leave him alone?" insisted Flacca, who had come to her senses after daydreaming for a moment about her Jim. "He'll only destroy you and leave you lonely. Hija, I only want the best for you."

"But Mom," Laura responded, "time will destroy us all. I may live in Nineveh, but I'll die in Nirvana if I can help it. I ain't dying here.

I'm gonna squeeze my destiny 'til it grins. I'm gonna wrestle with the jinn til I win."

Omar spent three days and three nights trying to persuade the stoop sitters to move, but to no avail.

Then one night, Omar kissed his mother goodbye. He and Laura went out on the stoop. Only the heaven and stars were witnesses. They stepped into the sky boat and set sail for Freedom City. It rained all night, all the next day and the next night. It was a warm rain for his heart was full with Laura-the face in the misty night. Footsteps he had heard down the hall so often were now prepared to follow his footsteps for the rest of their lives.

It was December 19th, and dawn had drawn back the covers of the night. The stoop sitters trickled down from the "stairway to the stars" one by one to the semi-lit stoop the way they had for as long as anyone could remember. Huddled in light coats and sweaters, Bubba, Flo, Big Mary, Flacca and Lola herded round a fire in a trash can rubbing their fingers together and sipping the Java of judgment and opinions.

The morning had awakened, trembling and shaking, as if taken by a harried case of nerves or the nasty remembrance of a nocturnal dream lingering on. The haunting, unyielding dream of a beast of monstrous misfortune whose attack could not be deterred by the courageous sword of reason or the lance of enlightened philosophy lurked in the murky recesses of her subconscious.

The cold mystical winds of change blew a veil of darkness over the face of the sun, as if to blindfold another day sentenced to its destiny. The executioner, the north wind, hid behind the mystical curtain of time, chilling and sharpening the ox-like bite of his frosty breath. It was cold as fear, the coldest day so far of the year.

Then, there appeared in the morning mist the shadow of a gigantic fish, smack in the eye of the earth where the sky meets the sea. It was a whale. Some say it was so big that it was 40 days long by 40 nights wide. Some say it was so humongous that although it did ride the back of the sea, it seemed to also be part of the heavenly scheme.

A conquering creature up from a dream or else a branch of history, as if destined to create a 13th sign in the heavens. A Sign of the Whale! The frozen tale of Jonah Williams, Heaven's newest constellation!! So say the tongue waggers who were witnesses not. Nay, the signs of the times are fixed at 12 for a reason: though there be a thousand seasons that time has begot.

So as the whale sailed toward the Nineveh Apartments, the wind grew stronger and stronger. So strong that it gently lifted up the sea on its back, building tidal walls of water that could either protect or destroy Nineveh. The inmates of Nineveh screamed when the water wall blocked out their sight and made the day seem like night. The whale swam around Nineveh seven times, its tail stirring up the waters with all his might like some furious spoon stirring a cup of coffee or sifting a soup of destiny. A hungry maelstrom was created, a whirlpool whirling and whipping, gnarling and gnashing. Its sail was not easily sated by a sip of itself or sedated by the song of the north wind's unabated fury.

Nineveh's stoop rolled from side to side, tizzy, dizzy, wizzy like a ship in the grip of a hurricane, spinning up, spinning around, spinning down into the black hungry hole of a monstrous maelstrom which attempted to gulp her down whole into the throat of the ravenous earth.

Flacca, Big Mary, Bubba, Lola and Flo were screaming their souls out. It was too late. The big harbor soon swallowed their screams and the Brownstone sunk into the sea, into the darkness of the mysterious green sea. In the black hole of history, beyond forgetting.

The big white fish descended into the sea and ate the lawn jockeys, a symbol that would take it 400 years to digest.

Omar and Laura, not knowing what had happened, arrived in Freedom City. News had arrived before them. The landlord was sitting at the dock of the bay, crying giant green teardrops in the rain. His oldest son, with his wife and children, were also crying in the rain.

"I can't believe it's gone." cried the landlord, his skin greener than the greed of a green-eyed monster. "How will I feed my children?" he wept.

The blues-singing woman was walking the streets again, singing in the rain:

"Lawd, Lawd, Lawd, will you bring us to the promised land.

Lard, Lawd, Lawd, will you help us to understand.

Lawd, your voice moves on the waters and your kingdom is at hand

Lawd, Lawd, Lawd, please help us to seek your face.

No heart will you move unless it finds its place.

It was raining heavily as she sang. The church bells were ringing again. The wailing sun rose incrementally in the sky. The front windows of the Brownstone were finally clean as it sat at the bottom of the sea. A morbid human aquarium in a world of fish, a sad song in the swish of waves.

The funeral was Friday. It was, in a way, a melancholy and lovesome thing.

Folks from the town and from all walks of life gathered around. But there were no bodies down in those coffins.

They simply could not be found. Prayers from the people rose from the ground like incense from an eternal flame; like perfume heaven bound, proclaiming the sweetness of God's mercy.

The Preacher bowed his head. The Rabbi recited a prayer for the dead. The Imam calmly said (for it was his turn that day to pray):

"In the name of God, The Merciful Benefactor, the merciful redeemer. All praise is due to God, the Lord of the Worlds. Maker of men and all things in Heaven and Earth. Say not of those who die in the way of God that they are dead, they live on, but we perceive it not. We seek refuge in You, God, against anxiety and grief. We seek refuge in You, God, against lack of strength and laziness, from cowardice and stinginess, from being overpowered by debt and the oppression of men. Suffice Thou us with what is lawful. Keep us from things prohibited. Make us free from want for what is besides Thee. Forgive the sins of those departed to Thee and of those who remain behind. For Thine is the power and we submit to Thee. For Thou has prescribed mercy for Thy self in the dealings of men. Grant the departed here the paradise. Save them from the flames of regret and help the living never to forget Your tender mercy upon us."

As I looked on, peering over the rooftop of the world, I saw my father's face before me from beyond. He said, "Son, did you warn them porch sitters?"

"Yes Dad," I replied. He put on his big white Panama hat with tears in his eyes, as he turned away. But there was a rainbow in the sky and a song in the wind. A song of hope for man and jinn.

This is the tale of the stoop sitters. The porch sitters who sat around in the shade, using the good day God made, eating the fruits of their words, drinking the milk of their deeds, crying the blues for their needs.

Some say let the good times roll. But beware the bell that tolls, whether it tolls in the mountain or it tolls in the sea. It tolls not for the living or the dead, but for the loss of an opportunity. It tolls for those who sit on fences. It tolls for those who perch on porches, giving defenses for aimless Bidding, who sense not that the best part of taking is giving.

Epilogue to the Stoop Sitters

I remember going to the gravesite of my parents. The Nightingale had made the mistake of letting me out of my cage after so many years.

My soul was wrenched with withering agony. I had to find a way to escape from letting these tales be an eyewitness to tragedy. A crow and raven were sent to guard me at the gravesite (even writers under the Geneva Convent are entitled to family leave).

I knew one thing: that the cemetery was near the A train...If I could only make it to the A train, I could take it all the way back to Africa. If I could make it to the J train, I could take it to Japan. (Pick any letter or number train. I was determined to make it out of my predicament.) Times had changed, but the graveyard remains the same.

Time and Technology produced an unimaginable world. Planes were shot out of silos like rockets. A Rocket jet could cover the earth corner to corner in under 3 hours. Trains ran under the oceans faster than the speed of sound.

Using molecule displacement technology and reverse friction direction technology, the old A train could make it to Africa in just 4 hours. The J train could make it to Japan in 8 hours using current tracks in the ocean. People went to work using transporters built in their kitchens. They could be transported in seconds to their work cubicles (if the job was 50 miles or less from home.) Executives could hologram their images to meetings. And remotely supervise the work place....

At work, people were implanted with temporary chips that monitored their production, movement and even cerebral contemplation. In the case of think tank jobs, your mind belonged to company store...Others, the poor, were part of a "Dreamocracy", where you were free to pursue dollars and your dreams.

There were great changes in the land, both physical and environmental. A great change in the political landscape, and physical change in the physical landscape as well.

The migration and immigration of people flowed like unstoppable rivers. Global warming had caused a rise in the ocean tides. The shoreline of the United States Eastern Seaboard, for example, had traveled 5 miles inland. Baltimore was underwater. The Jersey Shore was no more.

Wall Street and Downtown Manhattan were like a city underwater. More like sunken Atlantis or the temple at the bottom of Lake Titicaca in Peru. No human supremacy existed. There was only swimming and dead fish supremacy on Wall Street.

People no longer frequented downtown cities on the East coast, unless they were visiting with scuba tanks and diver's masks. The Southern District of New York, which now included only Harlemia and the Bronx, was now called the People's Republic of Harlemia.

The richest people in NY lived in the heights of Harlemia, safe the from the rising sea. Brooklyn -which lost all of downtown and all of Brooklyn Heights, including the Barclay's Center, to the overflow of waters-was ruled by an iron willed despot called the Emperor of Brooklyn. He was a descendant of the ancient king of the Gypsies and, I'm told, a very cruel man.

Queens had a monarch named Elizabeth Jennings II and a parliament made up of representation from various ethnic neighborhoods along the old #7 train line—Nine

The very rich descendants, Omar and Laura, had finally conducted an underwater excavation to uncover and recover The Nineveh Building site.

After many days of diving, their archaeologists discovered the lost apartments of Ninevah at the bottom of the harbor floor. The entire building was floated to the top by deep sea diving robots and cranes. The stoop was still intact, except 2 black cast iron lawn jockeys who had been swallowed by the ancient whale.

Jars full of ancient American copper pennies were discovered in Bubba's old bedroom. That guy had money, after all that talk about being poor. Well, to make a long story short, the Ninevah Apartments refurbished became The Muckety-Muck Museum. It was called "The Nineveh Housing Site of Ancient Harlem".

My spirit was permitted to see it is as a hologram. If you're reading this epilogue, it means that I have escaped. I made it to the A train.

Alas, I have shaken the crow and the raven and the nightingale from my contemplation for years. I hope they will never find me. They will only find my blue smoke!

The Nightingale, I carry his picture in my wallet, just in case I forget to take my Gingko Biloba, thereby forgetting my pursuer.

Hey, that GB stuff really works on my memory but there are some things I would really rather forget.

One last thing, as you enter The People's Republic of Harlemia by boat and are processed at the immigration center on Randall's Island; be sure to read the sign carefully. It says: "Welcome to the People's Republic of Harlemia. No Drugs, No Gambling, No Boozing, No Stoop Sitting Allowed. Enjoy your vacation. Penalty 5,000 Dollars and 3 years jail of the nightingale."

Now please have a very good trip and a good night. I must go. I don't want the Nightingale to pick up my scent. Because I have entered the land of Nod just to tell you this tale.

The Green Nightingale
and the Golden Cage

Once upon a time in the land of Nod, in the People's Republic of Harlemia there was a lonely green nightingale whose master (His Excellency Mafish Khider) kept locked in a bare but gigantic golden cage. Now nightingales are very small birds, but she was nevertheless kept in a cage large enough to fit a giant human being. It was a cage decorated with 144 rare rubies of renowned splendor and a glaze of a thousand white dwarf pearls,

Mafish Khider was an extremely wealthy man. He was close adviser and confidante to the Shogun of Harlemia, and he also trained the palace guard who guarded his Majesty, the Emperor of New York, Jack Leroy.

He was also a man of exquisite taste and sensibilities. He had gone to great lengths to acquire the nightingale and he selected because of her extraodinary singing ability and splendid ancestry.

She was descendent of one of the Queen Nightingales in King Solomon's Jerusalem retinue- whio had been a gift from Queen Bilquis of Ethiopia. Because of this heritage, the green nightingale knew over 1,000 songs. Despite his exquisite tastes, Mafish Khider was very cruel and selfish toward human beings. To his human servants, Mafish Khider was cruelly oppressive. He hit them and humiliated them whenever he wanted and whenever he could. He made them kneel before him long hours and recite "Your Excellence, forgive me" over and over. He gave his servants inferior food and quarters.

He demanded that the Nightingale give him a private concert three times a day-morning, noon and night, as well as special occasions and holidays. He also required her to entertain his guests for hours. These arrangements and demands seemed to work for a while, until one day the Nightingale got very sick and could not perform. She lost her voice and could no longer sing.

Mafish contacted the best bird doctors from around the world-Italia, Ethiopia, the Levant, even China. None of them could find the reason that the Nightingale couldn't sing. Upon hearing about the possibility of failing to restore the nightingale's voice, the owner became very arrogant and angry. He decided to let the Nightingale go. He opened the cage. He opened the window and pushed the Nightingale out into the lonely naked streets of the city.

"You are a free bird now!" he shouted laughing derisively and shut the window-so tight that the Nightingale could never return. Mafish further ordered his guards to shoot the Nightingale with arrows if he ever tried to return. Poor, poor nightingale did not know what to do. She could no longer sing and she had nobody to sing to or bring the song of spring to.

Fortunately, it was May. In spring and summer, the Nightingale could survive eating berries and seeds. However, soon the dark days of fall would appear, knocking at the hungry door of time, whose voracious appetite swallowed all things. Time the stalker sings to his prey before he dines.

"If it gets too cold, I will surely die." the nightingale sighed. "Woe is me. I have less hope than a butterfly." she cried to herself. When the first cold day of November was born, the poor Nightingale fled deep into a cave.

"I will betake myself warm arms and bosom of Mother Earth." she thought.

There, inside the cave, she saw a fat bear who was yawning as if getting ready to go to sleep for the winter. All seemed well until, she accidently disturbed a family of red bats who summarily chased her out of the cave's mouth into the cold November midnight air.

Poor Nightingale began to pray and think what next she should do. The cold drafts of fall and storms of winter were already traveling thither aboard the train of time and the train of thought of the thinking mind had stopped a station of great concern.

The cold stare of winter brought deep rooted life to those who were prepared, and sudden death and hardship to those who had not prepared to meet her chilling song .

The Nightingale, as she prayed, came upon an ancient white haired squirrel who indeed was very kind: "O Nightingale," said the white haired squirrel, as he was stacking nuts into pyramid shaped mounds. "Please eat some of these nuts and save some for the future, or you will surely die."

The kind white haired squirrel gave the Nightingale some nuts to eat, and stored some for her later use under the cassia tree. The squirrel for sure had saved the Nightingale's life, but could not stay. He had to go bye and bye to help feed his wife, children and grandchildren.

The nuts lasted a little more than a couple days. The nuts stored beneath the cassia tree were also soon gone.

"Woe is me," sighed the Nightingale. "If the Creator does not help me help myself, I will surely die."

When she lifted her head, the nightingale saw six evil hunters to her distant right skinning and cleaning a baby deer. Seated around a camp fire, the hunters were drinking and swearing like pirates on a ghost ship to nowhere. Finally, the hunters fell asleep. They left the fire unattended and were careless, because they left a flask of rum next to the roaring fire.

When the kindling temper of the alcoholic mixture was finally reached, it burst into red flames and shot 3 fiery plumes of burning refuse into the woods.

One of the plumes hit a spruce tree, which burst into flames. Another hit the Dutch Elm tree, and the third a mighty oak tree. Three trees (part of the forest) were already on fire! The animals and men were asleep. The nightingale did not know what to do. She was frantic. Her voice was locked, or maybe permanently asleep. She flew beside the fire, trying to put it out by kicking up dirt onto the flames, but she got too close and the heat seared her feathesr slightly.

"Ouch! Ouch!" she yelled. "Ouch! Ouch!…Wow! My voice has come back!"

"Fire! Fire! Fire!" she yelled as she flew to wake up the animals. She finally reached the elephants, who knew what to do. All the animals ran and ran.

"Help put out the fire!" the Nightingale yelled.

The elephants (77 of them) were like organic fire trucks. They lined up in 11 rows of 7, filled their trunks with water from the lake and sprayed it on the flames over and over again. As the little night-ingale continued to give the alarm, she yelled "Let all of us put out the fire!"

The animals turned back and each got water from the lake and dropped it around or on the fire to contain its spread.. After all the animals fed it with water, soon the fire could eat no more and stopped eating the wood and leaves of the gentle forest.

Dawn came. The fire was gone. The eagles and all of the animals chased the hunters out of the forest all the way back to the city. The angry geese bit the hunters on the legs as they ran and ran and ran.

Before the end of the day, all of the animals came around to thank the green Nightingale for her bravery. The deer came, the fox came, the rabbits, the raccoon family, the skunk family, caterpillars, even the ants, the bees and the spider. They promised they would never see her starve or be lonely. They would teach her the ways of the forest so that she could survive. And the Nightingales promised to teach them the 1,000 songs that contain the wisdom and delight of the world if they wanted.

Still, the poor Nightingale had no family, She longed to see other Nightingales. One day, the white haired squirrel appeared with good news. He had heard of a blue Nightingale clan living deep in the western part of the forest. They too had once been captives centuries ago, but they had made their way successfully in the forest of opportunity.

After days of searching the West Forest, the green Nightingale found the Royal family of Blue Nightingales buried deep in the western woods. They invited her to stay and soon after, her voice came back as beautiful as ever. The poor little Nightingale had, at last, a community to call her home. In the Nightingale community, she could live happily ever after.

Epilogue

This is not the end of our story.

So, after a few years, it came to pass that the rich man, Mafish Khider, got very sick and soon he could no longer work at his post as assistant to the Red Shogun of Harlem, or train the Emperor's body guards. The Red Shogun then fired him and no other official in the Republic of Harlemia gave him a job because of his reputation of unkindness and cruelty to servants. Soon, the rich man lost his way and became a poor man. He could no longer pay for his maid, his butler, coachman, cook, valet, gardener or body guards. The president of the Royal Bank of Harlemia came by his home one morning with 10 strong men and took the rich man's possessions, threw them on the street and threw the rich man out of the house. The poor people came out and took away all of the rich man's possessions-even his fine silk clothing was not spared the hunger of the mob. As for the huge golden cage, it was stripped of all it's 144 rubies and 1,000 pearls. The cage itself was too heavy to transport.

The rich man was now living in the valley of the streets. After a while, it being very cold, he tried to break back into his boarded up palace.

"How will I survive the winter?" he wondered

The sheriff of Harlemia came by and arrested him for trespassing. The rich man was now poor and penniless and in trouble with the law. He was dragged before the <u>Criminal Court of the People's Republic of Harlemia</u> in irons and chains! The judge (Judge Rathbone) ordered that the rich man be jailed 90 days in county jail.

The rich man objected. He insisted that he be locked in a golden cell and be fed food (like caviar and truffles) consistent with his royal lineage and once high station in life.

Judge Rathbone became as angry as red rain, so he ordered the rich man locked in his own golden bird cage that had once been the home of the Nightingale. He was locked in the golden cage and displayed in the town square for all of the people to see. That place was called <u>Berkely Square.</u>

When the animals of the forest and the people of the town heard of the rich man's plight, they smirked and said, "He got what he deserved."

There the rich man sat, in the golden bird cage in the Berkely Square. He had sat only 30 days when a snow storm came and covered the streets of the square. He was given one loaf of rye bread per day and 1 quart of water a day. There he remained with an infamous sign affixed on the cage. "Here lies a man with a most unkind heart." the sign on the Golden Bird Cage read.

One day, the green Nightingale visited Berkely Square. He carried a bag of old white squirrel's nuts and he gave them to the rich man, who was very grateful. The Nightingale then sang 3 of the rich man's favorite songs. So beautiful was the music to hear that all the town's people came out to hear the Nightingale's song! The rich man wept. People had never seen him weep before. He asked for forgiveness from all those he had been unkind to. When his 90 day sentence ended, the rich man asked the judge that he be allowed to keep the golden cage in which he had been imprisoned, as this was his only possession left in this world, and he could use it to pay off his creditors. His application was granted, as long as his debt to the bank was satisfied. Thereafter, the rich man (now a poor man) sold the cage and paid the bank. He had some money left. With the remaining money, he had enough to rent a room for one year from Ms. Widow Spider-Black. Ms. Spider rented rooms to strangers, once occupied by her now dead husbands. Many of her tenants were flies who mysteriously disappeared.

In time, the rich, now poor, man got a job as a forest ranger in Morning Side Forest in the People's Republic of Harlemia. He learned to speak the language of the animals, and became a better man. As for the green Nightingale, her songs were adapted by people. One of them, "A Nightingale Sang in Berkely Square" was recorded a thousand years later in a Dreamocracy called America, by a singer named Nat King Cole. Google it if you dare. Travel through it on a new train of thoughts. You will hear an inner music and smile.

Afterword

Some have asked me whether all the streets of Nod are paved with stars. They also ask whether quaint dreams still run that ancient shuttle route between Jupiter and Mars at regulated times. No, not any more. Take the A Train of Thought for best results The journey is open to all !

I have discovered during my numerous sojourns between heart and mind, heaven and earth in Nod, that there are seven pairs of golden doors leading to the Land of Nod. Now there may be more, but the pairs of doors I have found are seven. I uncovered them in my search for the world of "the other" or "The other side of midnight."

Each door has two sides, each side highly esteems the other:

2. The door of deeds and the door of prayer (first pair)
3. The door of needs and the door of care (second pair)
4. The door of truth (fortitude) and the door of love (gratitude) (third pair)
5. The door of question growing from below and questions hanging from above (fourth pair)
6. The door of gladness and the door of sadness (fifth pair)
7. The door of sleepless justice and the door of vigilant mercy (sixth pair)
8. The door of patient peace and the door of kind contentment (seventh pair)

Like I said, there are other minor doors leading to these doors like many rivers that run to the seven seas. You may find these rivers under your doors, your feet or hidden under the seat where you are sitting or under your very pillow of contemplation.

Life is for service to G-d, but before service came contemplation of truth and with service came love of neighbors.

Say, count the stars in the land of Nod. They live in families called clusters. Red Dwarfs, White Dwarfs, Blue Giants, Green Milky Ways You will never ever count them in a thousand lifetimes. For there are more stars in the heavens than there are grains of sands in the deserts of the earth and in 1,000 more earths added to great mother earth..

The stars, however, are only lamps in the sky and if you see them as such, you need not count them. They were designed to host the imagination and the rational ponderings of the mind. The stars are also the words of heaven. In the pondering and in the words of heaven, you will discover patterns.

My whole book means nothing at all if it fails to provoke new and imaginative thinking. It seeks to rouse the questioning mind in each of us, including your author.

The question not asked will never enlighten a man! The good deed not done will never open the light in his soul. The stars, including the sun, are only a brightness in the physical world, but the unselfish good deed of a single unselfish man is a light seen throughout the seven heavens.

The brightness of a billion stars cannot rival the brightness of one kind unselfish human deed, or one brilliant question. So I, John, only remind you of the beautiful possibilities that attend our human existence. If we have awakened a sleeping imagination, or roused a questioning mind, we do not apologize. If we have inspired the idea of peace and reconciliation, and have endangered the security of grudges by teaching love and forgiveness, we are unashamed, unbowed and untamed.

By the token of time, men lose their way in self centeredness and often drown themselves in wells of self absorption no bigger than a teaspoon or a thimble.

Life is for those who seek Beauty, Truth, Peace and the balance between the life in this world and the life in the world to come.

Light existed before the sun and truth exists before men find it, speak it and or seek it. The crown of understanding awaits us. All praise is due to G-d to Whom all praise is due.

Keep reading the book of heaven and earth and all good books.

I John am your brother and fellow lover of "THE PEN"

The Parables, Riddles and Nursery Rhymes

Times ²
(Parable 1)

There are two tracks in the journey of this life. There are two trains that traverse those two tracks. One train runs North. It is a day train. In fact, it's called "the day train". It runs from South to North and it makes twelve local stops. One in Jan, Feb, March, April, May, June, July, Aug, Sept, Oct, November and December. There are four express stops-March spring, June summer, Sept fall and Jan winter. At these express stops, the train receives an atomic injection of energy and change.

However, at each of the twelve stops, a young soul gets on, or sometimes a group of young souls. Each soul is carrying two bags-one fully loaded carryon marked "gifts" and another empty bag marked "capacity", which must be checked in the overhead bin.

At the end of the ride, the souls go to various destinations. The first stop is one of two schools-Hire Education or Higher Education. The soul must choose. One will make him a slave, the other a free man in the city. The second pair of places most visited is "Field of Dreams" or "The Mental Plantation". The third pair of places is the Temple of Belief and the Temple of Nonbelief.

Belief is either chosen or made by one's efforts or searching, or it is handed to one by a tradition called parent teaching. Both are given to the traveler as a pair of shoes. Now, belief is a pair of shoes handed out by either a blind man or a deaf woman upon entering the train station of life. At the end of the day, there is only a night train. In fact, it is called "the Night train".

It runs from North to South. It makes 12 stops: Jan, Feb, March,

April, May, June, July, Aug, Sept, Oct, Nov, and December. At each stop, souls get on. All souls must get their train at one of these stops. Each passenger carries two bags-one marked "Good Deeds" and the other marked "Bad Deeds". Rarely are there two bags that are equal in weight, and none of these bags can be checked.

At the end of the trip, each soul must go through customs with his two bags. The bags are weighed on a mystic scale called the Heart. Then the soul is led by the conductor to see The Judge, who will determine that soul's final destination. If you're not an angel, you need a "green card". If you're not admitted, you are given a "red card" and sent out into the night. The cold dark turquoise of the night. You never again see the light. Unless the Judge grants you asylum, or new evidence of good is added to your scale. That is the light at the end of the tunnel.

Parable 2
The Three Boy Scouts Escape from Dinosaur Island

Once upon a time, Three Boy Scouts were on a summer plane trip to the island Honak Lulu- The Pearl Isle of Dreams. Their mission was to explore ancient fossils left by extinct dinosaurs. They had all won awards in science, certificates of survival, plus $10,000 each to spend as each of them liked.

Well, the plane never made it to Honak Lulu. It crashed on Dinosaur Island and all passengers died except the 3 Boy Scouts. Immediately, the Dinosaurs on the island began to descend on the plane and eat the dead and dying bodies. Each Boy Scout was able to grab a survival kit, which consisted of 5 days worth of solid nourishment (in the form of a small loaf of bread), 4 days worth of water in a bottle and a GPS, or Electronic Compass.

Each also had a survival mind kit. The first kit read Common Sense and Hope. It was taken by Alif. The second read Common Sense and Fortitude, and it was taken by the second Boy Scout Lamont, and the 3rd Boy Scout, Michael, took the kit that read Common Sense and Faith.

It was a seven mile journey out of the jungle in each direction. If anyone made it outside of the jungle, he would be rescued. Alif, an excellent survivalist, decided to eat the food sparingly and drink the water sparingly. He decided to leave a trail of bread crumbs behind in case rescuers found the plane. For there, he figured, they could trace his steps. Lamont, an excellent survivalist, decided to follow the trail out and make the Loaf of Bread and water last seven days. Michael, an excellent survivalist, decided to exercise faith in his survival skills to live off the land, and then eat one portion of bread each of the 5 days and drink a portion of water each of the 4 days after he could find nothing to eat or drink.

Alif ran out of food and water on the 5th day and was 2 days shy of meeting his rescue outside of the jungle. He fainted beneath a fig tree 3 miles from the end of the forest. Lamont got so weak because of lack of water, but was able to survive 6 days, one day before the point of extraction. He, too, fainted from lack of strength. Michael saved his bread and water and immediately began eating grubs out a fallen tree trunk. He cut open a bamboo tree, drank water from inside and then began to munch on edible berries that he recognized in the jungle. He reached the extraction point with half a loaf of bread left and a 2-day supply of water. His friends didn't die, but had to be flown to Yuck-Base hospital. Why did Michael survive?

A Parable:
The Power of a Drop

No one respects a drop
Drop a rock, Drop a sock
Drop the ball that says it all
A Drop is too small not tough
They say
A drop of justice
Is no justice at all
No way!!
Life is rough today
Nowadays everyone wants mercy
Because mercy comes in rivers
A Drop does Nothing for the heart
Nothing for the liver
It doesn't even satisfy the giver
They say
Once however drops united ruled the world
Drops united became drips
No No! No!!
Drips are not a gang!
Drips are neutral
But Drips could have a benign
Or sinister grip
On the outcome of things

Drips can have a grip
Because they are drops united

Daylighted, farsighted, unblighted
Elite "raintroopers" of power
They can fall from the sky or out of a shower
Drops in the form of drips
Can drill a hole in steel
Drops are powerful
Drips are real
As long as drops
Drip in the same place
They are a powerful focus
That can't be replaced

Once upon a time
An innocent man was
In a prison for life
Guarded by the strongest wall
There was no way out
At all

Then he saw drops
Dripping in his stall
From a place unseen
Inside the wall
In six months the stall
Gave way
And now he is still a free man
Today!
Drips rule! Drops can even go to school
Never underestimate a drop!

Once upon a time
There was a desert

On the plains
That had not lately
Seen even a drop of rain

The plants and animals did pray
They prayed for rain, all night and day
The wind blew a little lost rain drop
Dressed in blue
Who had wandered far from the family
That he knew
His family was "The Storm Family"

The little lost raindrop dressed in blue
Hit the face of the cactus right in the eye
"Rain Rain!! Rain!!!"
"I feel rain!!!" cried the cactus
"Rain, Rain!! Rain!!" shouted the scorpion.
"Rain, Rain!! Rain!!!" repeated the withered desert flower

The little lost raindrop's family
Went looking for that
Baby lost rain drop dressed in blue
His mother. His father
His brothers. His sisters
And a million aunts and uncles too.

Yes, soon enough there was a rain storm
A rain storm in the desert
The little lost rain drop had been found
And the cactus sang in his
Round barrel voice
"All praise is due to G-d!"

And for the scorpion's dance
Of praise, his choice
Was to slap his tail
On the ground, up and down
Up and down!

And the desert flower
Bloomed shouting
"All praise due to the Creator
Of all things
Who created the heavens
The sun, stars and moon
Who sent us rain
Not a drop too late
Nor a drop too soon

Lastly, there was a prince
Who loved a common woman
Of extraordinary intelligence and beauty

One day they were arguing
Over nonsense it seems
The flower he was giving her
Was crushed at the seams

They sat in a garden lush
With orchids, hibiscus and fruits a -blush
With wonderful color power
So why did he give her that crushed little flower
She wondered
"You don't care!!" she thundered.
"You don't care!!" "YOU DON"T CARE !!!

"Why should I marry a man
Who doesn't care?" she shouted and pouted.
"I do dear" he protested
And touted "You must marry me"
He insisted

"How can I marry a man
Who does not care?"
She replied and persisted.

Just then a drop of water
Rolled off a guava leaf
Fell down, from up high
And just as he was about to speak
Fell right nigh on the gentleman's cheek

Of course immediately
He wiped the drop away
But what the girl saw
Was raw emotions on display

"You do love me!
You do care!
I see that solitary tear
On your cheek.
This is what I seek
Now I believe you
And I will marry you
But not today"
She laughed and smiled in a beautiful way.

The man was overcome with joy

as tears started to roll
Oh boy! Oh boy!
Like rivers down his cheek
"Good G-d!" he could hardly speak

I say it again
My fine reading friends

Don't underestimate
The power of a drop

A drop of faith will surely grow
A drop of mercy will abundantly flow
A drop of kindness
A drop of imagination
Can defeat the last straw of hesitation

A drop can open the door of wonders
You don't need all that lightning and thunder
Begin your journey with just one drop
One drop of goodness
Can change the world
One drop of kindness
Can cure blindness
Give a drop
If that's all you've got
And watch it grow
Into a mighty river who overflows
Into the arms of the
Loving and mighty sea!
A world full of drops
Drops For you and me!\
KERPLOP!!!

The Great Meeting of the Mind
"All is mind. Mind is all."

Introduction to
"The Great Meeting of the Mind"

Western philosophy and thought is filled with conflicts that have often plunged society into a <u>State of Confusion</u>.

John Stuart Mills, a more recent Western thinker (relatively speaking), believed that evil was 'bad' because it was not useful and that good is "good" because it serves the interest of society. Therefore, what serves the interest of society is good in his eyes. This doctrine is called "Utilitarianism."

It is the current philosophy that guides the governments in most Western Societies in the 20th/21st century (and many Eastern ones for that matter).

This philosophy has led to inconsistent domestic and foreign policies. It has also led to decisions that are based, primarily either on empirical evidence or Machiavellian motives. Therefore, a certain practice may be deemed not useful to society (in maintaining the status quo or avoiding an unpleasant outcome) rather than right or wrong based upon the principles of morality.

For example, <u>Brown v. Board of Education of Topeka, Kansas</u> (1954) outlawed social discrimination in public educational institutions based not on rightness or wrongness but upon utilitarianism, and the empirical evidence presented in the "Clark Doll Test".

Moral schizophrenia is the disease of our times. In the past, Epicureans, for example, during the Classic Greek era cried, "eat, drink and be merry for tomorrow we die." This was a philosophy which justified hedonism and held no concept of accountability in the afterlife.

Plato, on the other hand, through Socrates, spoke about obtaining "The Good" and acknowledged eternal principles of Good that man should be mindful of. His teacher, Socrates, was put to death for teaching this and that human beings should be guided by natural conscience which inclines toward Good and enlightenment.

Is the discrepancy in U.S. foreign policy between North Korea and Iraq, for example, a product of "utilitarianism"?

Is its policy of opposing dictatorships consistently applied?

Is the opposition to domestic, invidious discrimination applied under a utilitarian formula?

Eastern philosophy as practiced, generally speaking, has underpinned an equally troubling version of moral schizophrenia.

The Hindu, Jainist and Buddhist philosophy of "ahimsa"-noninjury to living things-is a major credo in India. Islam, a liberating religion that teaches submission to G-d's will and the way of the balance or golden rule is a major credo for one fifth of humanity.

One will find many good, decent, religious people in these countries where these religions are practiced, as well as in the West. But there is a great divide between principle and practice when it comes to government policy, social policy, economic policy, urban policy. Policy (more often than not) is based upon the rationalization of maintaining hegemony/power for certain elites. This is an Eastern form of "utilitarianism."

This practice has led to a State of Confusion in the world, an international shadow government which has caused humanity to declare war against itself, the environment, and against the clear principles of both revealed guidance and common sense.

When society is in a State of Confusion, there must be a meeting of the mind.

People must reconcile themselves with good principles of conduct that G-d has revealed and chart the destiny of their nations either toward growth or destruction.

This book was written by a "janitor" who worked for 40 years in THE HALL OF THE MIND-a secret society (i.e., hidden from material eyes) that once met beneath the Lincoln Monument near the Potomac River when Lincoln wrote the Emancipation Proclamation-albeit on utilitarian grounds.

Gandhi convened a Meeting of Mind to overthrow British rule in India and to reconcile differences between Hindus and Muslims on the Indian subcontinent.

Adam convened it originally and as a result repented from his error.

The Society of Mind has met whenever human beings have entered The State of Confusion.

The next formal meeting is scheduled for the Isle of Man 2103, although there may be plenary sessions here and there.

This is the true account of what the "janitor" witnessed.

Judge its veracity for yourself.

Preamble

It was society "X". Generation "X". Constellation "Y".

I, "John", your brother and partner in tribulation was on the island of Manhattan.

It was a terrible time.

It was a time when children's hair was white with anxiety. Their faces were as blank as monitors or frosted TV screens. Frozen music was rapped into their ears and little was their happiness.

It was a time when women's tears fell like rain on the back of the city.

Unemployed men wandered the streets aimlessly into the ether of the night, seeking the turquoise of dignity. The bleached bones of homelessness littered the subways of society. There were wars and rumors of wars, yet the media constantly announced that all was well.

It was November 4th, *The Year of the Dragon*, and the sidewalks of the city were frozen.

It was Election Day in the State of Confusion in one Nation under Doubt. There was a Floridian stand-off and the candidates for the Presidency of human society had gathered at the August Electoral College to make their final presentations to the permanent Electors who would decide their fate, and indeed the Fate of "the Body Politic" for the next century.

I believe that century to be the 21st Century or 22nd Century, but I'm not sure. I've been afflicted by short-term memory loss.

I recall, though, that the issues that garnered the attention of the previous century had been three: the "color line," the "class line," and "colonialism." But not in that order.

Justice, for sure, had been "clothes-lined." The question of who should be privileged and who should be disenfranchised had plagued the lives of the people on all seven continents, from the Eskimo to the Bedouin, from the Swami to the Deacon, in both monarchies and so-called democracies-for over one hundred years.

Color and prejudice were the Tombstones of the 20th Century, pyramids whose capstone was white and whose base was black. These were an enduring monument to an irrational cancer.

Nevertheless, the great war of annihilation, long promised, had been averted, even though humanity had declared war against itself on at least two prior occasions. Now it was supposedly a new day.

Dear Reader, think carefully about these things to which I am a true witness. For I am a student and a teacher, a child and a man, conscious and unconscious. I am paradox, parable and oxymoron.

Dialogue

It was dawn and the nine members of the Grand Natural Electoral College (G.N.C.-sometimes called the Diet) entered the Great Hall of the Mind.

First came "The Will" (or Mr. Will), who without fanfare took the convener's Chair. He was followed by "The Reason" (Mr. Reason), a grouchy old man with a crooked cane. He didn't take a seat at first. He wandered around the hall in the tradition of Sophists and Peripatetic philosophers.

Next to enter the Hall of Mind was "The Conscience," a fairly young woman, who looked much older than her years. She spoke softly because of her frequent bouts with laryngitis and was now also hard of hearing. She took the second seat.

The Third Elector was "The Drives," a strong, robust warrior of a man who was obsessed with "All you can eat" dining, fine china, the Super-bowl, and the charms of beauty contestants, but not in that order. He took the third seat.

The Fourth Elector was "The Emotions," a damsel who wore her heart on her sleeve once too often and who was often given to fits of anger, depression, laughter, sympathy and 77 other feelings, some catalogued and others yet unnamed. She took the fourth seat.

The Fifth Elector was "The Senses," an inquisitive, lanky youth who appeared to be about the age of seven and who wore a five-pointed star tattooed in the middle of his forehead. He seemed more alert and perky than anyone else in the Diet. "The Senses" took the fifth seat.

The Sixth Elector was "The Ego." He was a meticulously groomed, 6'6" proud barrel of a man who carried a convex mirror into which he constantly gazed while combing his pate and harvesting nose hairs.

"The Ego" tried to sit in the seat of the Convener ("The Will"), but was immediately accosted, shoved away and escorted to his assigned sixth seat by the Sergeant-at-Arms.

The Seventh Seat was finally taken by "The Reasoning", Professor Harry Reasons, or Counselor Reasons, as he was affectionately called. He had wandered around the Hall, trying to straighten his crooked cane.

Counselor Reasons always wore a white doctor's coat and was considered a genius and an effective advocate by all who knew him.

He was a problem solver. He could argue on the side of any position adopted by counsel with brilliance and research.

He could find reasons for and loopholes in any wall erected by the Law.

The Eighth Seat was then occupied by "The Memory"-a short squat middle-aged woman who wore a large shady hat.

She took her seat, but unlike the others she sat facing the opposite direction, as if facing the past.

She hated the Sun, hence the hat.

She was also a very sensitive woman, given to reminiscing and day-dreaming.

She harbored a distinct hatred for Mr. Reasons and sometimes refused to cooperate with the others.

However, she was the Official Secretary of all the Council meetings and was known to take accurate, copious notes-although at times she could not always read her own handwriting.

The Ninth Seat was reserved for "The Subconscious"-He was given to falling asleep during meetings. Many thought that he suffered from acute apnea because of his loud, sonorous snoring sessions.

Even though he often slept throughout meetings, when he finally awakened (usually when everybody else was drifting off), he was fully aware of all the issues and information.

His best friend was "Ms. Memory", to whom he was engaged to be married on several occasions.

The wedding never took place, however. He sat down and nodded off in a nanosecond.

With all of the members of the Diet of the Mind having been seated, "The Will" summarily called the meeting to order after reciting a short interfaith prayer.

The Will: "Sergeant at 'Arms'," he bellowed, "let the four candidates take their seats in the dock, I mean — er — in the Speakers' Circle!"

The candidates file singly into the room and sit in the circle. Portable microphones are attached around their necks like a hangman's noose.

The four candidates were Mr. Monet Plutarch Craci (Plutarch for short); Generalissimo Dick C. Army, Mr. University and Mr. Holy-Man.

The Big Four were followed by two reporters from radio stations which the Council had allowed to tape and monitor the proceedings for the public's benefit "The Body Politic."

These reporters were a male/female duo called Mr. Information from WKIS and Miss Information from WKIL — the sister station.

These two were the expert news reporters/spin meisters of the day, and were considered excellent journalists.

Will: "Monet Plutarch, Craci you may proceed, the Chair acknowledges." Remember, under Floridian law, each candidate is allowed only three minutes."

Plutarch: "Friends, friends, friends, distinguished members of the Diet or Council of the Mind, I am greatly honored to be allowed to make my presentation — to make my case for the control of society, i.e., for the Presidency of 'Society.'"

"To begin with, I am the most popular person among the people. Everyone seeks me out. Even those who have the abundant blessing of my frequent company want to see more of me.

I own all of the real estate, the factories, the means of industry. I bought the farm and the bank.

I can buy soldiers, the best of doctors, lawyers, judges, juries, architects, Indian chiefs, etc., etc., etc.

I can even buy the people's loyalty during elections, as well as other intellectual property.

But I am one with scruples.

Everyone, and everything, in the material world has its price and value.

Electing me, dear members of the Mind, is electing reality.

I own this very building in which you are meeting, the so-called 'Hall or Body of Mind.'

I own all the seats on the stock market and lease them out to pretenders of ownership.

I own the working hours of every man and woman.

I have already bought my way into Heaven by my generous philanthropy.

Money, friends, is good for body and soul and mind.

The pursuit of money and the pursuit of happiness are synonymous.

My office shall be a government of money, by money and for money, until people perish from the planet. I will finance a glorious future for the Body Politic. No more deficits . . . !"

Will: "Thank you, Mr. Plutarch Craci. Your allotted time is up! Generalissimo Dick Army, it's your turn at bat."

Generalissimo Army: (Mighty Army for short): Greetings, distinguished males and females of the great Council of the Mind. I speak to you as one who controls 20 million men and arms and 5 million long-haired warriors or females. I control the universe's best army and weaponry.

I just listened to my brother-in-law's speech (Mr. Plutarch, that is) with great disgust.

Reality is that I am the world's only superpower. My army can take whatever it wants, whatever the people want or 'need': oil, money, territory, diamonds, presidencies, the heads of fools and kings!

If I was unscrupulous, I could take my brother-in-law's money before you get up from your seat. But we are family, and I am a superpower with scruples.

I, as President, will brook no dissent. I can establish order, enforce curfews and protect society from enemies within and without. I can do this subtly or openly.

What a society needs is security and power that all others fear-so that society can be free and enjoy the peace of the brave!

I am not one for words.

Select me and our government will have absolute power, and as the world's sole Superpower, we will take what we need. Anyone not for us is against us. Thank you, Chairman Will."

Will: "Thank you, Mighty Army General. Now we will hear from Mr. University." (whereupon Mr. University stands up in the circle.)

<u>**Mr. University**</u>": "Friends, colleagues, distinguished members of the Council of Nine, I am honored by your invitation.

Wisdom must rule. Education must lead the nation.

As you know, I hold 365 Doctorate degrees. I hold 12 postdoctoral chairs, 3 in the Sciences, 3 in Social Studies, 3 in the Humanities, and 3 in Economics.

With my wisdom, Mr. Plutarch, money would soon become my own. A fool and his money must part.

I know how to develop a productive economy, produce the best technology for industry and weaponry, war and peace.

My knowledge may prevent war and make planetary resources available to everyone.

When I am President, my knowledge of human psychology can motivate all human beings to work for the good of the Body Politic-whether these human beings are rich or poor, soldier or civilian, black or white.

Education must build and rule the nation of homo sapiens. Knowledge is power.

I appeal to those on the left: 'The Drives,' 'The Memory,' 'The Emotions,' 'The Subconscious,' and those on the right: 'The Conscience,' 'The Reasoning,' 'The Ego,' and 'The Senses' to make me your President!"

Will: "Thank you, Professor, for your help in assisting us to make up our Mind. Now let's hear from Mr. Holy Man."

Holy Man: "G-d bless this most important Council to understand my words for the good of the planet.

If a scientist climbs a mountain from the right or left, he will find the Holy Man already seated on its peak.

I am the man who interprets the nature of reality for humanity, I control what people know about the unseen, the divine-or at least they think I control it. Men are too lazy to read the Torah, Gospel or Holy Quran for themselves.

Belief is stronger than money. Belief can make soldiers in an army march in the direction that is opposite to their General's orders. For men know they will be dead longer than they are alive.

Belief can overshadow science, although there should be no conflict between them.

Everywhere, every worker believes, every soldier in the army believes, every student from this land believes that this land is the best because I have taught them the principle that 'G-d and country' are to be served without compromise. They are one and the same. To serve one's country is to serve G-d. I have always taught that successfully. And for hundreds of years it has worked.

My predecessors caused the Crusades, Holy Wars, the Pogroms. They crowned kings and excommunicated princes. I have painted the face of G-d to resemble the face of those who rule and it has worked. Although I have never seen G-d, and will do all I can to delay my appointment with Him, I say.

'Vote for me.' I will make the Body Politic believe in you. I can also make them believe against you, but I have scruples. And I believe to serve one's country is to serve G-d!"

Without warning, suddenly, the microphone died and the lights began to flicker, as if one were seating at the end of a movie.

Gunshot sounds could be heard coming from the Press Gallery. A muzzle flash streaked naked like a shooting star across the room. Mr. Information and Miss Information were shouting over the air waves: "Power to the Press, the Press United can never be defeated. . . UPI, UPI, UPI forever!"

Gunshots rang out again. But it was not bullets being fired, but bulletins-news bulletins and their shell casings were strewn all over the Hall of the Mind, giving birth to craters of scandal and terror.

The Shrapnel of Rumors were flying everywhere like missiles. But they were not missiles, they were missives.

News stories planted like landmines exploded all over the Hall of the Mind.

The Conscience ran for cover.

Reasoning could not be heard.

The Drives went into overtime, seeking a way out. Common Sense jumped out of the window. Memory fled deep into the arms of the Subconscious.

The Emotions ran wild.

The Ego was wounded.

The Presidential process was besmirched with smoke from the explosive, scandalous bulletins.

All of the candidates ran for cover, even the General who was armed but had no answer for the rapid-fire damage caused by the ubiquitously fired News Bulletins! The bulletins pierced the armor of decency, leaving mayhem in its wake.

Finally, the Military Forces responded to the call that the General made over a secret frequency!

The Meeting of the Mind was disbanded as troops arrested all of the candidates except Generalissimo Army.

Martial law was declared. The State of Confusion had just become the State of Panic.

For a while, people lost their senses and senses were everywhere looking for their parents.

All the members of the Council of the Hall of Mind were arrested except for The Will. He escaped. He ran into the countryside and moved to a different place every night, sometimes a Church, sometimes a Mosque, sometimes a Synagogue, sometimes a crypt in a cemetery where he rented a coffin from a sexton for the night.

All of the other candidates and members of the Diet were under complete arrest except Memory and The Holy Man.

The Holy Man was let out every Friday, Saturday and Sunday to give his weekly sermons, and then returned to jail while society entered its weekly activities of money-chasing and debauchery.

Memory pretended she had dementia after the Subconscious gave her up. She was allowed, however, to roam at will.

The influential Press Corps were also arrested and its members executed by the Generalissimo — all except Miss Information who became one of his consorts, and a National Security Advisor.

Epilogue Part 1

I, the Writer, "John," remember running from University to University while being chased by the Generalissimo's secret police. First, I hid at Hall of the Mind, where I was the janitor, custodian, sanitation engineer for 40 years.

There are secret tunnels under the streets on Broadway between 115th Street and 120th Street, underneath Columbia University. I hid there for nine months and gave birth to myself again.

Next, I hid at CNR on 125th Street. There is a trap door behind the bookshelves at the Rosa Parks Campus library, 5th floor. There is a Montgomery bus behind that door. I slept in back of that bus for 3 days.

Then I hid in Barnes and Noble, in plain sight/site, masking my face in successive black cups of coffee served in the deli.

It was not long before I moved on to Starbucks and then the Café at the Dead Poets Society.

It was here that I met <u>Memory</u> one day. "What happened to our Bill of Rights?" she muttered and wailed. "Freedom of Speech, Freedom of the Press, Freedom of Religion, etc., etc., etc."

I listened to her ramble on till I almost fainted from exhaustion. I retired to the basement of the Dead Poets Society. Then I heard a knock at the door. "Oh, No," I thought, "they have discovered me. There's no place to run now." Yes, it was the General's men, President for Life. I knew that my life would change forever.

They have discovered my secret name and identity. I am an African-American, originally from the tribe of Bilal. My ancestors came from Timbuktu I think.

Maybe I just made a confession. They cannot dis-encrypt the brain waves of humans can "they"? Whoever "they" are!!!

Well, "THEY" are sending me to <u>The Triple Concentration Camp</u> reserved for Freethinkers. Freethinking is a violation of the <u>Suspect Terrorist Domestic Defense Act</u> or S.T.D. section 694271.

They know that I can't be deported. I never had a country of origin that I could find. I was a slave. But my will is still free. I implore you, the student and teacher, to finish this story for me. Who must have power in a society?

Once I was just a poor janitor trying to make a living. My job was to empty society's trash, not read it, not think.

I have downloaded this story from my subconscious and smuggled it out. I am still here beneath Guantanamo Bay, along some very old Japanese-American prisoners. They are called Nisei.

Obama Clinton Bush Rumpelstiltskin!! Somebody should close this place!!

If I die here, please forward my mail to the conscience of the nation when it gets one. Also, please do not be caught thinking about or reading this work!

Epilogue Part 2

All the Nisei have died — most of them during interrogation. Strange how tyrants and predators curse their prey before they eat them.

I've been here 40 years at Guantanamo now without at trial. I've become impatiently thin and religiously robust.

I've been blessed with more luck than those confined at Alcatraz. (They really reopened that place!!)

I know that if The Will can submit to the One Lord who created all and made all men brothers, that all the other members of the Council of Mind will be free to work in harmony once again.

The result will be harmony and proper balance in the world between Spiritual Growth and Pursuit of Wealth. Human poverty will kick its diabetes and the materialistic thirst that accompanies it.

I have not read a newspaper in 40 years. No newspapers are allowed here. I receive news about the world from fresh prisoners who are added to the population from time to time.

I realize that my world had been shaped by those who pressed and suppressed the truth.

I'm nearly blind now, but I can see that social happiness is the balance between the rights of the individual and rights of society, and that before G-d, janitors and kings are equals. Superiority lies in virtue.

Unfortunately, for thinking such thoughts, I have been quarantined and placed in solitary confinement.

Before I was born, I was in solitary confinement for several months, and after I'm gone I'll be in solitary confinement again for thousands of years.

For man is born alone, needing brotherhood, and dies leaving it hopefully a better brotherhood.

Download your magnanimity now, upload humanity, Forever, Yours

John" Satchmo" Mannan

JANITOR EMERITUS

The Legend of The Tables

O nce upon a time, there was a table established in the earth. A table at which all the men and women could sit with equal dignity and worth. Some say it was a round table because all the sitters were equal beings. Some say it was in the shape of a triangle because triangles symbolize the body, mind and spirit of man. Others say the table was in the shape of a 5 pointed star that fell from heaven and man was designed on the pattern of 5.

Five as in "five alive", Five as in 5 human senses, five as in the 5 external points (head, 2 arms and 2 legs), as in the 5 pillars, 5 prayers, the 5 tastes, the 5 smooth stones of war, the 5 fingers of life and death and much more.

All of these descriptions, "food for thought" and philosophical items on the menu seem plausible, but the most important thing to remember is that the entire human family was so small that it could fit in one room and we could all sit at this one mystical magical table.

Mind you, this all happened so very long ago, before TV dinners were invented, microwave ovens were vented within themselves, before self-driving cars, self-washing dishes, self-fulfilling wishes were coded into cybernetic clouds. This was long before creative minds were solitarily confined to X Box cells and the dungeons of PS4 prisons.

Yes, this was during the eon of the first dimension. In the first dimension, men were food gatherers. The earth was lush with grapes, mangoes, peaches, berries, roots, shoots, pomegranates, figs, apples, dates and much more. It is indeed the place of verdant garden and we ate and ate from morning until eight.

One day, a stranger with a strange thinking entered this paradise and sat at the head of the mystical table. Some say he came from ourselves and others that he came from an unknown region of the mind.

He gave a beautiful speech and promised the diners possession of a beautiful kingdom that they had never seen, filled with delicious meat that had never been eaten by men. He left as mysteriously as he came, but he left all of the hearts aflame with pride and longing inside. He left hearts aflame with an arrogant dissatisfaction that had never before dwelt in the hearts of men and women.

Men soon entered the second dimension and the Table travelled with them. There, men became hunters of the animals in the land, sky and sea. Everywhere they killed, sometimes for food and sometimes for delight. They slaughtered the animals and each night the heads of families returned to the table with game, deer, antelope, bison, polar bears, boars, whales, octopus and fish of every stripe and strain.

Soon, there were wars among men over hunting and fishing territories. Men could no longer meet and eat at "The Table" in peace, and men could no longer fit in one room. But at the great council, they ate and ate and ate from morning until eight. The room that contains the Table was too small after all. It took some 5,000 strong men to move "The Table" outside in the elements of the four seasons.

During this second dimension, men began to migrate, and move about in 5 different directions. Some moved to the majestic mountains. Some moved to the humble valleys by the lake, the river or sea. Some moved to the thirsty desert. Some moved to the plains where all is plain to see. Some moved to the thick forests and jungles covered by moss and rain hungry trees. In the heat, in the frost, in the cold turquoise of night and bright diamond of the day, men did thrive. So men learned the ways of the land. They returned to the mystical "Table", their skins colored all shades of red, black, white, yellow and tan.

The stranger entered again and made a great speech. To some, he said they were better than others because of their location, and to some he whispered they were better than others because of their looks. Back then, men listened and memorized intently. They did not yet widely read books.

Soon, wars broke out among the inhabitants of "The Table". Subsequent to these hunter /tribal wars, the mankind moved to a third dimension. Men here hungered once again for the garden and learned at last how to farm. One man could grow food enough for 10 men. Ten men could grow food enough for 100 men, and 100 men could soon grow food for 100,000 people. No longer did men follow the roads that chased the animals.

Soon, men built cities, towns, and villages around farms in the mountain, desert, plains, and forest, in valleys, by the river, lake and sea and even in jungles happily. Temples followed. Men made gods of things they loved and feared, and signs which they observed in the heavens.

One day, a very observant man discovered there was One Designer, One Architect behind all of the systems of the worlds and universes.

This wise man came to the Table with pages from a book called the Mother of Books (The Mother Book). By this time, some people could read and write (most could not), nevertheless his message was clear "Message of ONE-One G-d, One Creation, One Humanity".

The stranger listened to the wise man in anger, but waited. He waited until the wise man with the pages from the Mother of Books had gone.

After the wise man left, the stranger came back and made a great speech but again in secret conversation told some men that they were better than others and that they ought to be masters of other men. The representatives of men left "the table" again after eating the fruits of harvest. They ate, ate and ate on sweet corn from morning 'til 8. They soon declared war against each other and civilization went to war against itself time after time after time!

Then mankind moved to the fourth dimension, which is the dimension of industry. Machines replaced muscles. Engines replaced horses.

In the fourth dimension of industry, the representatives of men met at the historic table of man again. This time, it took seven hundred engines to move "The Table" to a mountain overlooking the lowly earth. Men transported onto the tables replicas of tall buildings and of large sprawling factories, which made cars and clothing and guns and tanks and planes. Mankind's knowledge had risen quite high indeed! Here, they called all of their meetings "SUMMITS" because it was held in the "heights".

Before they could leave, the stranger came and addressed the representatives of men. This time, he gave an even more beautiful speech, advising men that their knowledge of science would soon give them the key to conquer the entire universe.

However, those who followed the pages of the Mother of Books confronted the stranger, grabbed him by the forelock and evicted him from the meeting. "I will be back!" shouted the stranger angrily.

The stranger had many who believed in him also, because they believed he had given them power in mountains, plains, desert, forest, valleys by sea whereby millions of cities and towns covered the earth like ants. Daily, men ate and ate and dined on diamonds and gold and copper from morning til eight.

Lastly, men moved to the 5th Dimension-A dimension of cyberspace, a dimension of information built upon a giant artificial brain, an ephemeral membrane living in an artificial cyber-cloud.

It took seven hundred computers, all working together, to transport the mystical table to a coordinate between cyberspace and the plain of philosophy.

Here, men came to "the table" via their representatives. Some

appeared by hologram. Some sent robots in their places. Some sent
E books.

No flesh was allowed. The citizens of cyberspace replaced flesh
and blood appearances usually expected of leaders. It was a world
where people were all a twitter without a context in which to consider what was real or virtual reality. It was a world in which people
forget their mortality until it was too late to save their morality.

People were everywhere, starved for the bread of human contact
and knowledge touched by human hands.

Restaurants were open for robots who ate, ate and ate salty computer chips from morning til eight. Through the robots, the whole
world was at the table once again. Each family could log on, whether
from valley, hill or plain or desert, jungle terrain.

But there entered into the room again the stranger in our
thinking, the stranger of discontent who obscured the boundaries
betwixt good and evil, and right and wrong. But in the corner of
sages was the man with sacred pages from Mother of Books talking to men, talking to robots about a Table of Life that descended
from the heavens twice. It had descended to satisfy the hunger of
man who seeks to satisfy the greatest destiny-to be a servant of the
Most High.

The stranger protested to the sage with the page, "I will not leave
for it is not time."

"We all see your scheme." said the sage with the page.

"Divide and conquer." "Divide and conquer." "Marry
Misinformation to the brain." said the sage.

"There is no superiority between black and white. There is no
superiority between rich and poor. Those with good hearts, good
conduct and good knowledge will enter the door to a supreme garden. Therein, there will be no want. Therein, there will be no need.
Therein is no greed. Therein, there will be no strife. Only a table set
with happiness and abundant life."

"Can't we enjoy these things on earth?" said a loud voice in the crowd.

"Remember and be mindful of the Creator and bring 'The Table' back to earth so all can eat." said the sage. "Advance true and useful knowledge. Eat together the breads of the world. Share the gifts within yourselves with others for the sake of The Giver and show ye mutual compassion to one to another... If you do these things, you will approach the door of satisfaction and will be knocking at the door of paradise. Perchance the Owner may answer your heart!"

Epilogue

There is a lonely Table that sits outside in the rainy storm. Thunder makes it shake and lightning adorns it like a flickering candle flame...It is the Table Of War hosted by a very strange sponsor. War (the initiation of war) leaves men with nothing to eat, dissatisfied, hungry and feeling the heat.

There is a bountiful Table that descends from the skies full of the fruits of heaven and earth, wisdom and worth. On it is a meal of great contentment. This is the Table of Heavenly Peace. Here, men feast on the fruits of peace from heaven and that grow on the side of the mountain.

Then there is a third Table descending that hovers between heaven and earth. It descends to earth every day and returns to heaven every night. The fruits of two gardens of contentment are upon it and people gather round every day to trade their experiences, ideas and exports.

The men from the dawn of mountains bring coffee; the men from the dusk of the desert bring dates. The men from the noon of the ocean bring Blue Fish and the men from the afternoon plains bring steak. They talk and share. They love and care. Each faces the two heavens with hope. Each sits at the table. Every heart knows it has a place at the Table of Balance and True Understanding.

If you are hungry, please keep in mind where will you eat?

Where will you dine? And don't forget to make your reservation!!

Prelude to "The Hole Truth:
An Ox-Tale Parable"

Once upon a night's dictation
I felt and heard a strange sensation
A voice that stabbed and stuttered
A sound which rent my heart a-flutter
at its ragged seams.

"Was this a poet's dream?" I wondered
or something I had never pondered
Not a dream it seemed nor even a ghost of Dramamine.

But a vision from the dark descending
upon my philosophic never ending
search for life and what it really means.

A bang, a fitful frantic tapping
my computer drunk, failed and flapping
on and off its face a chocolate darkened screen.

The virgin night peeled off her wrapping
stared I affixed by that frightful tapping
paralyzed and paranoid about this most
frightful frantic scene.

If I had slept, I was now awakened
My faith in peace badly shaken
by that fitful, fateful clanging
that frantic fit of banging
at my kitchen door.

DR. JOHN "SATCHMO" MANNAN

"This but a mouse trapped outside the house"
I thought opining
while looking for a silver lining
A mouse, a squirrel or nothing more.

Then in walked that bird of heaven
A Nightingale half past eleven
A baleful, beauteous bird of quaint forgotten lure.

The same baleful poet's beau
that I met 17 years ago
when I in a moment of vanity
trespassed on the edge of sanity
and wrote in a great travail
"Seven Tales of the Nightingale"

Now that baleful bird had returned
to flee, eagerly I yearned
that mysterious mystic was back indeed
but today I am just a hackneyed
hack of computer dribble
True poetry I no longer scribble

For the candle of my love had melted
melted to the very floor
to rise again "nevermore, nevermore"
that's what she said, This one from "the rising sun"
this one Ah this bamboo one

Yet I still had hope
the hope of hopeful love

always seeking heaven's hand above

But now that bird return to me
desperately I sought to flee
in vain some exit seeking
my soul and armpits reeking
of brine and fear.

Fear, Fear! Fear!! Most unworthy
to ever wear a poet's jersey
But score one for the heart team
I got up from that damning dream
and to my desk, I went crawling
pen in hand, my eyes bawling

Steady went my turquoised soul
As I slid blithely down so bold
boldly down into that nebulous midnight floor
into a hole marked "Nevermore"

And so this is it my friend
the beginning and the end of the Legend of the Hole
an "Alician" hole that
makes one wonder
what is "The Hole Truth" out yonder

In that twilight zone of imagination
of a most simple poem's,
stranger, then strange dictation!!

The Hole Truth

1) Once upon a time, seventy poets from a foreign land far away
   …far away …
Across the sea were thrown into the deepest well of history.

2) It was a well of muddy waters 400 years deep and steeped in misery.

3) Deep, deep down in the hole, into which they fell
It took a while for the poet's eyes to become accustomed to the light.

4) But no matter how hard they tried they could not access their plight.

5) The whip and lash of a World "which looked on in amused contempt and pity".

6) Yielded no concept of the dawn except that they were prisoners of some city.

7) A city which deemed them knaves.

Yea slaves of a different verse ("Version of Life")
A different word world wrapped in a coffin , ensconced in the most royal hearse of night- Nights delicately drawn by 4 wily horses of a manufactured curse.

8) A verse, a version. Rehearsed day and night.

The Ivory poetry of a curse took away their very power to unite and even though they were brothers, they soon became enemies of one another .

9) Until one day, one poet, one mind, escaped from the wicked verse of the well , the World of the spell , The spell of artificial minds woven on the loom of " made of minds"perception

10) And his mind made it to the ocean , " the ocean of the notion of true freedom ".

11) After much contemplation he made a rope from the seaweed of the "Ocean of the notion of true freedom", He determined that he would free his poet brothers.

12) He descended down, down into the well to warn his brother-poets whose minds were smothered by the ivory verse curse, the hearse of rehearsed artificiality – a World of artificial reality.

13) When he reached the middle of the well he met the guardian of the well -
a creature of frightful face whose gaze could freeze the heart in place "son of man"
asked the guardian with glee "answer these questions with truth and truly no harm will come to thee" . The guardian continued "400 years it took the 70 poets from 700 tribes to fall into this well. How many years will it take for their children to climb out – pray tell".

14) "I do not know", replied the poet.
"How many years of frozen tears frozen rhyme frozen by time must be stacked to reach heaven?"

"I do not know", replied the poet.

"How many years after the divine mind has descended to the heart will its recipient be free?"

"I do not know ", said the poet.

"Then you have failed!"

Laughed the Guardian. "and you belong to us" he cackled

'The answer to all your questions" said the poet, "is that My Lord THE LORD OF HEAVEN AND EARTH knows best!"

15) "Woe is me!

I have failed", said the Guardian "I have failed to deceive thee.

Do not despair you have ascended one rung of ladder of hope.

A ladder descended indeed from the heavens of contemplation of revelation of wondering fascination that united all poets past and poets still unborn."

"Yes you have failed", said the poet.

16) "I have often wondered how many years of deadly fights, and civil rights, and random plights, and benighted flights of fancy and marches from March to July, and reparations that sigh, and affirmative action replies from supreme courtships, with madness, mixed bout, of buffoonery and sadness must we contemplate....

How long? Too long have we waited. We were free all the time but delusions of dependency were our bonds

The sooner we unite upon our humanity and contemplate our circumstances and use the strength of good everywhere- The sooner we climb to freedom.

How fast descends the ropes of rain from heaven we will ascend into the air.

many light years removed from here."

17) Soon soon O guardian the Ocean will swell and reach the mouth

of this well and the poets once captured in bands SHALL return to the promised mind

18) "The promise land of higher contemplation that lifts, up the man of all Nations."

19) With the word, the evil guardian despaired and fell deep down, deep down into the Netherlands of hell!

The Use of Similitudes and Parables in Decoding of Nursery Rhymes

NURSERY RHYME #1

"Ba Ba Black Sheep have you any wool, yes sir, yes sir three bags full

1. One for my master
2. One for my dame
3. One for the little boy who lives down the lane"

BLACK SHEEP

Black has a positive meaning in English tradition when applied to clothing and in Christian tradition when applied to habits or uniforms worn by members of the clergy. It connotes faithfulness loyalty, serious dedication and spiritual wisdom. In business, it represents integrity.

Black means "purity in the nature of something" (WDM). In this case, we are discussing the deep struggle in the human soul for moral enlightenment/guidance. This struggle takes place at night and attracts the rain of revelation. The revelation ends at dawn when the necessity of implementing the revelation of the night in the social order becomes the mission of day activities symbolized by the color white. These day time activities of the soul are the "WHITE SHEEP" of the fairytale.

Sheep = ordinary people in the social order in their innocent passive roles and ordinary daily experiences. They can be led aright or astray by the education or miseducation of the soul (These sheep, not the leaders) If "MAN IS MIND", the sheep, particularly the White sheep, are the ordinary experiences of the good human soul in the vicissitudes of human life on earth (Without the benefit of revelation) THE BLACK sheep is that rare human soul, that human soul/mind that has undergone extraordinary searching in the cave of the night and has benefited directly from revelation, as in the case of Prophets who received it and their followers and by extension all of mankind.

Wool = Knowledge, wisdom, understanding

The author of this nursery rhyme is a very knowledgeable man. He knows ordinary knowledge (white wool) offered by society keeps the society from being naked economically, morally, etc. So he asks the black sheep what does she offer for the social order's upward development. The Black sheep answers with 3 bags. These bags are the full package that soul will need and the social soul or social order. It is applied knowledge, wisdom and understanding from the scriptures. (the Semetic language code see language Quran the Original Torah Gospel etc).

3 Bags = Three stages of knowledge to clothe the brain the heart and physical activities of man namely .The Master, The Brain And the Little boy who lives down the lane.

Master = Brain/Mind

Dame = Heart/moral compass

Little Boy = the natural appetites of physical existence/first stage of soul development

Down the Lane = Physical Level

Lower Level of man's perception his material appetites, which are symbolized by the area of the body that begins at the stomach down to the top of the knees. This is what the author means by the "little boy who lives down the lane" as opposed who are character-ized by the adults "THE MASTER AND THE DAME" the brain and the heart who live on "the steep path" or up the lane in the social body of man (mind).

As an exercise: use different substitutions for Master, Dame and Boy that demonstrate how human society balances for example in-dustry/science as "master"; the arts as "dame" and sports as the "boy down the lane". Also discuss how competing interests are balanced or harmonized in society for the benefit of all.

This helps in developing composition skills, imaginative think-ing and developing those interpretive powers necessary re. the diges-tion of the great English works of Shakespeare, Keats ,Shelley and such American authors as Melville, Poe and Hemingway that will all students to master language and get more out of reading all books that are good reading.

NURSERY RHYME 2

Sing a song of six pence a pocket full of RYE 4 and 20 black birds baked in a pie. When the pie was open the birds began to sing. Wasn't that a dainty dish to set before the king.

6 Pence = ½ dozen only = the material zone of reality or the visible/seen

If it were the complete human experience it would 12 or a dozen

24 birds = 24 hours

Pie = clock /day

Open = education

Sing = to function to higher capacity

Dish = a prepared human mind

King = the divine mind/ the entire social human order

Pocket full of rye = useless/unfermented knowledge

Birds = human soul

NEXT PHASE OF THE NURSERY RHYME IS THE MAID
IN THE GARDEN
THE QUEEN IN THE PARLOUR
One day G-d willing it may be useful!

About the Author

John "Satchmo" Mannan is the nom de plume, or nom de guerre, if you will, of Dr. Mujib Mannan. Professor of the American Experience law, literature and history at the College of New Rochelle, University of the Virgin Islands and other university venues for nearly 30 years. The author is an educator, lawyer, historian, poet, short story teller, essayist, jazz musician/vocalist and lyricist, marketing consultant, executive director of an affordable housing initiative in Harlem and a lecturer in religion and philosophy.

Born in Harlem, the author has written several books, including: Cultural Imperialism, The History of the Harlem Mosque, The Legend of Lute, Tales of the Nightingale, The Arabic Words in the English Language. etc.

His poetry is published in several anthologies, but under an earlier nom de plume John McRae, including Ghetto 68, We Be Word Sorcerers, Three Hundred Sixty Degrees of Blackness, etc. and on other venues such as the African Sun Times, Living City, The Thinker. (under the name Mujib Mannan).

His peace Haiku (poetry has been chosen for inclusion in the city of Philadelphia "Peace Project") and his Jazz C.D. "Ten O'clock Jazz" was released December 2014 by New Savoy Records.

Dr. Mannan, as a person, is interested in the entire 360 degrees of life beyond his doctorate and graduate degrees in jurisprudence, history, etc. He has written and published the within stories in the cause of awakening that aspect of the human being that ponders on the meaning of human existence, human life, the human predicament and the human potential for achieving moral, rational, and socio-economic excellence and egalitarianism.

Of all the things that Mannan does, his greatest love is philosophy. It is through "philosophy" and what he calls its nephew, religion, that the author unites his diverse interests in poetry and music into a synergistic code for pondering the gifts and vicissitudes of life.

Life, he says, "poses its ultimate truth and paradoxes in the form of questions that cause the reader to think and ultimately confess the true beauty and wonder of the creation and the human spirit".

History, philosophy and the exercise of creative and critical interaction with the natural world (in the heavens , in the earth and in ourselves) help us to formulate the questions that lead the human mind to discover the presence and mercy of the Divine Creator in all that we do and in all that we can accomplish.. This discovery and awareness of the divine will is the beginning of the individual and social man's journey toward felicity. Conformity with this awareness and with its artistic implications is the author's literary raison d'etre for the construction of a literary art hat provokes and stimulates, entertains and educates.

The author's many interests and skills have enriched his human experience and the lives of those around him.

Here he hopes to share what he has discovered and lead others to discover more than what he has discovered. Thus, Mubassa's Dream is simply one mind passing on the baton in a relay race of marathon minds who ponder the challenges and opportunities that arise in man's pursuit of winning the dignity and distinction of the excellent human life.

The author explains that each story in this book is written as narrative an allegory and either a musical composition and /or a poetic work. Each story is therefore tri-partisan in nature and is part of what the author calls "A GROWING UP BOOK" ie. a story that bestows different but consistent meanings depending on the reader's life experience and interpretation of the symbols used in the story.

Thus a person variously age 8 or 18 or 88 may discuss the same story from different perspectives and that confluence of wonder and ponder is what this author sees as success .

Author Contact: johnsatchmomannan@yahoo.com

Appendix

The Immigrant

The sun flush with sanguine dreams
rises in your blood-shot eyes
You fly, run, swim, triathlon to portly America
seeking a land of gold laid streets
fraught with green meadowed dreams of freedom
and opulent opportunity.

The city drinks your face of a thousand names
Your talents are auctioned off to the lowest bidder
Yet you survive, thrive
on bullet beans and rice, nanny porridge
and bowls of patriotic curses.

You smile and never complain as you course
through our veins wide as the mighty-mouthed Mississippi
You are the wheels of taxis
That crusher of grapes
the wine of drunk and greedy factory machines
that sing you blues in the night
You are the A student who never sleeps
You, The Mr. PC, the Master of JAVA scripted mornings

You serve the afternoon tea
In Bel Air.
You! The never late street vendor at the fair
You the wind carved on tireless feet of determination.

Night descends upon you like a brown moth
It finds you rummaging for real green cards

You wonder, Are they among those homeless,
pregnant, discarded coke cans that litter our
fruited urban plains? Or among American dreams now
made in the out-source zone of a twilight's last gleaming?

But after every moonless storm comes the dawn
Its torch like a mantle flutters in the winds of heaven
That Lady in the Harbor is expecting again
Through you, America will give birth to itself again.

They call you "THE IMMIGRANT"
Some with suspicion, others with double, dubious disdain.

But. You are our morning mirrors
You. The long-awaited California rain.

Lift up your head, O foreign one!
You are America!
You are the changing permanence
The froth of the Shining Sea
The People of "Purple Mountains' Majesty!"
You, the ever resplendent renewal
You, the unending waves of our dignity
/kissing
the face of our enduring destiny.
The faithful ancestor and the inheritor of dreams
YOU ARE THE IMMIGRANT!

For The Death of a Jazz Musician in Harlem

You went suddenly
like a cloud-burst
from the sky.

You earth master of time, rhythm
and notes that fly
high over rainbows.

You who always
wanted to die on stage
you who celebrated this rage called life
now the Composer has turned the page.

Do not fear
The song is not over.
The coffin is just a trumpet mute
Music does not die
though time may break the flute.

The people flow into Remembrance Hall
like rivers from summer/winter spring and fall
like rivers from the land of the setting dawn
and the dusking sun
There is the big one!
They gather round
to honor your last concert
in living sound.
They weep brown and blue harmonies
as they lower you into the ground.

Black fedoras flutter in the wind
white pillbox hats, purple hats, beaver skin
blue kufis and khimars, and red bandannas abound.
The streets shout hosannas.
Wide Cadillacs circle round.

Trumpet players, piano players,
saxophone sayers and singers
and other hemophiliacs of sound
coagulate for your final bow.

Soon you will know
where music goes
after it is played.

Every low note and every high note
you made
will be waiting for you.

But here on earth
children will dance
and old folks pat their feet
when they hear your sound
blowing on the street
from old jukeboxes, from new boom boxes
from Boze no Doze Radios
Everywhere where eyes tear
and babies laugh
and when time
gets weary of his wooden staff.

DR. JOHN "SATCHMO" MANNAN

You, musician, will never be forgotten
even when your terrestrial flute is rotten.
The sweetness of your life
will be music
in the all merciful ear
of the One who always heard
what your heart was playing!!!

Thoughts In An Upstairs Parlor
"Full Of Rain and Tears"
"The Sun And A Smile"

When I was a child
I wondered why rain
fell down from the sky

I also wondered why
Tears fell down from my eye
Whenever I felt upset

As I grew older
I realized that rain and tears
must fall down
to nourish the seed of the heart
so that the soul can stand up
like a flower
Likewise the only difference
between the sun and smile
are their different places of origin
but both gave light and
warmth to happiness!

The Search

My name is not important
But yours is!
I have crossed many rivers to find myself and you.

Thoughts are my parents
Words are my wives
Dreams are my daughters
Deeds are my sons

There, you've met my family
I know that there are mountains
between us.
I'm willing to climb them.
There are rivers between us.
I'm willing to ford them.

The deserts between us I'm willing to cross.
I'm ready to brave the frost
of the northern clime of my frozen mind.

I realize that the keys
to knowing you are with me
for you are the treasure
of mystery
the sophia
in philosophy

If a man changes his mind
He changes his reality
Kiss my eyes Oh Wisdom
So I can see

Notes and Reflections

The proper education
of a child
is the hope of humanity

The old see light
at the end of the tunnel
The young see light
at the beginning of the tunnel

Either I will fulfill
my dreams
or my dreams
will bury me
The proper education
of a child
is the hope of humanity

More than hunger
More than war
Ignorance is man's
greatest enemy

Notes

If Time is faster than Life
then Mind is faster than time

My mortality does not hinder me
it encourages me to be
more productive

What I say you may remember
for a lifetime
What I write may reach
one thousand lifetimes

Only the Master knows the
circumstances weight and the
dimensions of my intentions

Eye Sore
Birds soar
Lions roar
People snore
while legends lore

Service will make man king
Arrogance will
make him
a pet on the leash
of his passions.

Haiku

1. Without love no child
 Without lotus never spring
Without peace no life.

2. Night becomes not day
'til men surrender to peace
and Spring forgives winter

3 No peace rivers weep
too pregnant moons fall asleep
Spring is never born.

4 A heart kissing peace
and still making love with war
opens storm winter door

PEOPLE'S REPUBLIC OF HARLEM

ONE LOVE

© Mannan

Maiden Harlem (USA) #1

She'll snatch the stars
from the skies
with her sad, beautiful
soulful eyes

Her lips are thieves
They will steal your heart
with wonderful words
both tender and smart

You gotta believe
cause before very long
you'll be whispering her song
and dusting star dust
from your sleeve

Don't dare wake up suddenly
She may just leave, you see
and when she's gone
she'll be traveling
in the gray of the dawn

Carrying on her back
a burlap bulky sack
full of your precious dreams

She was only your
imagination it seems
If only you could find her

DR. JOHN "SATCHMO" MANNAN

you'd keep her close in mind, sir

She has all that you lack
and besides those dreams
of yours and their unopened doors
are still on her back.

Memories of Harlem
Maiden Harlem USA
Memories that the whole Day savors
Say, she gave the Big Apple
Much of its FLAVOR (flava)

She always taught what is prudent
She made both Bway and Hollywood her student
That's Maiden Harlem they say
Maiden Harlem USA

She is the most intelligent one
She has them all on the run
From Sam of Sicily
to "Down Home" Geechee Joe
They know
She's not just for show

She's no joke; she doesn't smoke
You can tell
She's rich as well
Everyday saving her good common sense
And many more hours are spent

Reading the fair book of heaven and earth

And all the knowledge of worth
in this great wide world
Oh what an outstanding girl!

Gentrification can't afford
to marry her
She can't be bought with diamonds
or bedded with furs
Never shaken
Never stirred
The force is hers

Forest brave, Tiger bold
Ain't never thought about getting old.
She's Maiden Harlem
Yes sir, and besides, she's got soul!

From The Little Mango Leaf:
A Mango Recipe For Health

In our previous story LITTLE MANGO LEAF deservedly achieves heavenly status because of his role in treating the diabetes of a renown and helpful community educator,

Studies show that *Mangifera indica (THE MANGO LEAF)* has significant hypoglycemic activity in high dose and can be successfully combined with oral hypoglycemic agents in type-2 diabetic patients whose diabetes is not controlled by these agents.

source: Clinical Investigation of Hypoglycemic Effect of Leaves of Mangifera Indica in Type II Diabetes Mellitus. by: Akbar Waheed, G.A. Miana and S.I. Ahmad. published: Pakistan Journal of Pharmacology, Vol.23, No.2, July 2006, pp.13-18

Mangiferin showed anti-diabetic as well as hypolipidemic potentials in type 2 diabetic model rats. Therefore, mangiferin possess beneficial effects in the management of type 2 diabetes with hyperlipidemia.

source: Studies on the anti-diabetic and hypolipidemic potentials of mangiferin (Xanthone Glucoside) in streptozotocin-induced Type 1 and Type 2 diabetic model rats. by: B Dineshkumar, Analava Mitra, M Manjunatha. published: International Journal of Advances in Pharmaceutical Sciences 1 (2010) 75-85

Leaves extract have powerful antioxidant activities because of high phenol and flavonoid contents. Mango leaves extract increase peripheral utilization of glucose, increase hepatic and muscle function.

Glucagons' contents, promote B cells repair and regeneration and increase c peptide level. It has antioxidant properties and protects B cells from oxidative stress. It exerts insulin like action by reducing the